Praise for *Wash*

"Amazing . . . Never has a fictionalized window into the relationship between slave and master opened onto such believable territory . . . *Wash* unfolds like a dreamy, impressionistic landscape . . . [A] luminous book."   —Gina Webb, *The Atlanta Journal Constitution*

"Wrinkle boldly tackles her heritage in this debut novel, and it's a marvel. By turns grim and lyrical, heart-wrenching and hopeful."
—Helen Rogan, *People* (four stars)

"Slavery is America's original sin. While many of us can't bear to face its legacy, brilliant writers who fearlessly explore it can bring back vital truths. Books like William Styron's *The Confessions of Nat Turner*, Toni Morrison's *Beloved*, Edward P. Jones' *The Known World*, and Russell Banks' *Cloudsplitter* form a kind of Truth and Reconciliation Commission of their own. Add Margaret Wrinkle's *Wash* to that illustrious company. . . . A lyrical story of courageous human beings transcending the cruelty and degradation of their slave-holding society . . . *Wash* tells us that vital story, a story we can never hear enough."
—Chris Tucker, *The Dallas Morning News*

"A masterly literary work . . . Wrinkle's novel does not allow us to draw easy correlations but invites us to consider the painful inheritance and implications of such a horrendous moment in American history. Rather than disapproving opprobrium and diatribes, this debut occasions celebration. Haunting, tender and superbly measured, *Wash* is both redemptive and affirming."
—Major Jackson, *New York Times Book Review*

"Boldly conceived and brilliantly written, Margaret Wrinkle's *Wash* reveals the horrible human predation of slavery and its nest of nightmares. With a truthfulness even beyond Faulkner, Wrinkle makes her novelistic debut in a monumental work of unflinching imagination."   —Sena Jeter Naslund, author of *Ahab's Wife*

"*Wash* is bold, unflinching, and when finished, certain to haunt the reader for a long, long time."
—Ron Rash, author of *Serena* and *The Cove*

"The voices of the past can't speak for themselves and must rely on the artists of the future to honor them. It's a profound responsibility and one that Margaret Wrinkle meets in her brilliant novel *Wash*. She shows not only the courage to submerge herself in the Stygian world of plantation slavery but also the grace and sensitivity to bring that world to life. . . . Narrative roles are given to Wash, fellow slaves and his succession of masters, creating a dense, hypnotic ensemble of voices similar to the effect achieved in Peter Matthiessen's momentous retelling of the life of a Florida sugar plantation owner, *Shadow Country* . . . It's from patriarchs like Wash as well as like Richardson, Ms. Wrinkle shows, that the U.S. was born."
　　　　　　　　　　　　　　—Sam Sacks, *The Wall Street Journal*

"This majestic, beautifully-written novel will both break your heart and make it wiser."　　—Charles Gaines, author of *A Family Place*

"An elegiac yet surprisingly uplifting portrait of the resilience of the human spirit. . . . *Wash* is a solemn and magnificent paean to the survival—even amid the most crushing, inhumane conditions—of the special and eternal essence within every soul. A magnificent and challenging novel of slavery, full of wisdom and the divinity of nature, that paints an ultimately uplifting portrait of the resilience of the human spirit."　　　　—Cherie Ann Parker, *Shelf Awareness*

"Wrinkle has written a remarkable first novel, one that will haunt readers with the questions it raises, and the disturbing glimpse it offers into an unfathomable world."　　　　　　　　—*Booklist*

"A significant and hugely troubling book."
　　　　　　　　—Pinckney Benedict, author of *Dogs of God*

"Wrinkle masterfully takes us on a powerful journey through the darkest past and present of this country, boldly addressing the chasm of racial divide with the scalpel of a gruesome truth. *Wash* is the epitome of courage and determination to heal the central wound of this culture."
—Malidoma Patrice Somé, author of *The Healing Wisdom of Africa*

"Wrinkle has spotlighted a crucial era in the American experience, writing with grace and intelligence."　　—*New York Journal of Books*

"*Wash* achieves something extraordinary: a full-fledged confrontation with one of the most difficult aspects of our nation's history. . . . Wrinkle has given us an honest and important expression of hope . . . a firm foothold that leads in the direction of truth and reconciliation. We would do well to take this step." —*The Post and Courier*

"[A] profound debut . . . *Wash* is a powerfully haunting tale about the captor and captive. It offers a look at both through their own narrative form expressing their true feeling."
—Esther Callens, *Birmingham Times*

"Margaret Wrinkle's *Wash* is a marvelous window into the world of nineteenth century American slavery—a powerful fusion of knowledge and imagination."
—Madison Smartt Bell, author of *All Souls' Rising*

"This exquisite novel is a gift of healing. It exposes the dark and fearsome sin that stains our history. But in the genius of the telling we are led to the tenderness at the bone, the humanity at the core, and buoyed by joy." —Beverly Swerling, author of *Bristol House*

"A unique and powerful story, *Wash* tells a chapter of our past that we would rather look away from. Margaret Wrinkle makes sure that we cannot." —Kevin Baker, author of *Strivers Row*

"Wrinkle bears witness to the inhumanity of slavery . . . A moving and heart-rending novel." —*Kirkus Reviews*

"In this deeply researched, deeply felt debut novel, documentarian Wrinkle aims a sure pen at a crucial moment following America's War of Independence. . . . The novel well evokes the tragedy not only of [its] lovers' untenable positions, but also that of their master and his fragile country." —*Publishers Weekly* (starred review)

"The complexity of the book's themes are a tangle of history and culture as well as cosmology. What the characters share, black and white, is a sense of their own stories, how they intertwine and how they are connected to the stories of those who came before. By writing in her characters' different voices, Wrinkle has put them on equal footing." —Bill Kohlhaase, *PasaTiempo*

WASH

WASH

A NOVEL

MARGARET WRINKLE

Grove Press
New York

For all those in Deads' Town
and for us, the Living.

In that land of beginnings spirits mingled with the unborn. We could assume numerous forms. Many of us were birds. We knew no boundaries. There was much feasting, playing, and sorrowing. We feasted much because of the beautiful terrors of eternity. We played much because we were free. And we sorrowed much because there were always those amongst us who had just returned from the world of the Living. They had returned inconsolable for all the love they had left behind, all the suffering they hadn't redeemed, all that they hadn't understood, and for all that they had barely begun to learn before they were drawn back to the land of origins.

There was not one amongst us who looked forward to being born. We disliked the rigours of existence, the unfulfilled longings, the enshrined injustices of the world, the labyrinths of love, the ignorance of parents, the fact of dying, and the amazing indifference of the Living in the midst of the simple beauties of the universe. We feared the heartlessness of human beings, all of whom are born blind, few of whom ever learn to see.

from *The Famished Road* by Ben Okri

Prologue

Pallas

It was one of his early trips to Miller's when I first laid eyes on Wash. Pretty soon, I learned to be gone when they brought him. Made sure to be out gathering or else seeing about folks. But that first Friday afternoon when Richardson sent Wash over here to do his business, I was home and I saw it all.

Watched him ride in on that wagon while I started my fire. Stood there stewing some goldenseal and saw Wash dip one shoulder to duck inside that small side door of Miller's barn, with Richardson's man Quinn following right behind him step for step.

Richardson's horses, one rust and one a faded gray, stayed tied to that shaded post all day. His wagon stood close by the barn while they loaded it down till it sagged. One hogshead of tobacco, high as my waist. Bolts of the same cloth they'd be wearing next year. Three casks of apple brandy. All in barter.

So I knew everything from the beginning. Can't say I didn't. But it's like Phoebe told me, everything's fine so long as you find a way to manage it. It's when you can't see what you're dealing with that you head into trouble.

Somehow it fell to me to carry Wash his supper. Everybody else stayed crossways with him but I was curious. Took him some field peas and greens with two slices of smoked ham. Miller made sure about the meat. When I got to the stall they kept him in, Quinn sat by the door on a crate. He tipped his square chin up at me as he reached out for one of the two bowls I carried. He pulled the latch back on the bottom door till it swung open and nodded for me to go in.

I bent to step under the top door he'd left bolted shut. With the late light, I couldn't see Wash too good but I felt him there. Heavy, like something fell off a shelf, and sitting real still. Then he came clear. Sitting on the floor in the deep straw, leaning his back against the far wall, resting his elbows on drawn up knees. He wasn't doing nothing but watching his fingers twirling a piece of straw.

Even from where I stood, I could see the scar snaking through the edge of his hairline. Deep enough to hold water. Right at his temple. Everybody told a different story on what happened but it should have killed him sure enough. Made me wonder who it was had managed to keep him here on this earth and what he could see out of the one good eye he had left.

At first, he seemed to me like all the rest of these men, worn out from a long day, except he wasn't sitting around with the rest of everybody. Tired feels less worn out when you got a few folks to sit with. Have a sip. Try and shake the day off.

It didn't hit me till I stood there holding his supper in my hand, watching him twirl his piece of straw. Wash was further from having folks than just about anybody I ever came across. Nobody to sit with at the end of this long day or any other day either.

I always thought I was the only one who stayed steady looking back at the world from the far end of a long rope. But watching him sit there on the floor of that stall, finally looking up at me with that one good eye and his other eye roaming the dusty wall over my shoulder, I caught myself wanting to trace that R brand fading into his cheek with my finger. I could tell he'd looked down a long rope himself and likely still did most days.

He must have took hold of my thoughts, because without ever moving, he bristled like a cat. Slammed his eyes shut right in my face, even as he stayed steady watching me. Made me feel like I'd stepped inside his yard without asking. What set me back even more was the way he looked at me after he got all bowed up. Sat way back inside himself and ran his eyes over me, just as cold as you want to be. Like he was adding up some parts.

I been looked at like that plenty and didn't need any more of it, so I edged over to set his bowl down beside him. Then I stepped away, careful not to turn my back on him. It wasn't till he reached to take the bowl and was well into eating when he stopped and looked at me again.

I don't know why I was still standing there. I turned right around and left. Ducked under that top door and bolted the bottom one behind me. Both that day and the next till Wash was good and gone.

So that's how things went between us at first, but it's a whole different story now.

Richardson

When Quinn came to me with this idea for Wash, I turned away from it. I remember thinking, surely not. But he kept after me, saying supply was drying up and we could make a killing.

We sure as hell needed to make something. My place had fallen apart after I rode off to soldier in 1812, determined to whip

England once and for all. Forever trying to make my contribution in what turned out to be a damn useless war.

It took me three years to get home and three more to drag my place back into some kind of working order. But I had set too many deals in motion at once and when the bottom fell from the market, there I sat. Dogpaddling. Trying to paper us out of the hole.

I remember even the day. It was hot as hell and dry. We had been without rain for nearly sixty days and my palms stuck to the pages of my letterbooks, leaving sweaty smears alongside my columns of numbers. Quinn came into my office with his jaw set.

No matter how short and bandy legged, Quinn was often right. That's why I'd taken him on as a partner despite his lack of capital. His father was my father's overseer but Quinn came West aiming higher. Soon as he closed the door behind him, he started in on me, relentless as a terrier. Talking incessantly about the waves of settlers moving through west Tennessee into the new territories of Arkansas and Louisiana. What they could mean for our markets.

"They're all headed for the South West, trying to get in the cotton game. All that new land going to cotton, you'd have to be blind not to see what will happen to our prices. They'll drop till there's no way for us to make any money. As for negroes, they'll go sky high. You know they will."

As I ran my eyes over my columns which so steadfastly refused to add up, I had to admit he had a point. What I couldn't get over was how easy it laid itself out before me. Stared straight at me, tugging on my sleeve. Even as I resisted Quinn's logic, I was counting the numbers in my head. How could I not, with the debts I carried?

"It's right there for the taking," Quinn told me again and again until I turned my mind to face it.

Send Wash over to my old friend Miller's on a Friday, put him with three or four per day. Even if only some take, that will mean ten new negroes, worth two hundred apiece once weaned. And with his midwife Pallas on hand to catch every single one, Miller can get the whole two hundred for each before he has to spend anything at all.

"Two thousand to him has got to mean at least two hundred for us. Even in barter, it's worth it. You know it is."

Two hundred to me for sending Wash over to Miller's on a Friday. Over to Miller's and then over to the next place and the next.

I do question what I would have done if I hadn't already been wondering how to handle Wash. With the way he kept cutting the buck and tomcatting around, I knew I had to do something or my whole house was liable to come down on me. You can't let just one get away with it. That's like having a crack in your cup. Before you know it, all your water runs out.

I saw it so clearly. My wagon taking him there and back, the money in my hand. And Wash thrashing and cussing but some-how fitting the shoe right to his foot, almost in spite of himself. Making it fit.

We all did it. It's just that some of us did it more and better. Smoother somehow. Quinn called it the Red Sea. Said the way parts for me. Says I was born to it. Not only the silver spoon but the cup and the bowl too.

I don't know about that. All I knew was I needed money and I had to do something about Wash. I remember thinking this work might even appeal to him.

Wash

Richardson had me at the top of his page. I knew it clear as day before I ever saw his damn book.

That man wrote everything down. Somebody brought a mare to put with his stud, he'd fetch his paper down to the barn. Unroll it all crackling, then tack it up on the wall where they could go over it together. Start with the name of that Eclipse racehorse written at the top, then branching down and down till his finger found his stud, with all those lines left empty for time to come. Not that I can read, but I can sure watch a man pointing to a word and saying it.

I knew where he was headed before the thought ever crossed his mind. It was me leading that gray stud into the sun. Walking him out for his neighbor Carpenter to see. Horse was past twenty but still acting bold so I looped the chain over his nose. Rested my palm on his withers to keep him calm.

I felt their eyes on me too but that was nothing new. Some folks stare at you like to eat you up. Hunting some knowing behind your eyes just as hard as they don't want to find it.

It was him seeing me with that horse. I know it sure as I'm standing here. It was Richardson watching me work his stud for Carpenter come to breed his mare that hooked the two ideas in his mind. After that, it was just a matter of time.

See, I know how they do. White folks like to stay in those books. They carry and they keep and they dig in their books, like nothing matters that don't get written in some book somewhere. Like that's the only way they can know for sure what happened.

They'll write down who they are and what they did. And their daddies and theirs too. Put it all in a book, then close it up and put it on the shelf. Just to know it's there so they can sleep at night. Like if they don't get written down somewhere and they shut their eyes for a minute, they might disappear.

But there ain't no writing this down. No book to put this in. Some of us shut our eyes at night and wake up in the morning, not written down nowhere. And still don't disappear.

Nobody who was not here will know what went on. Life looks different from the inside than the outside, but they think all they got to go on is what gets written down.

This story will come out. That's what I tell myself. Won't be till after we're dead and gone, but we won't really be gone cause it don't work like that. All these books and all these white folks, thinking the world is forever passing away. All trying to make their mark, trying to be a big man.

But ain't none of us going nowhere. We stay right here. All of us, all the time. Black and white and everything in between. All together, all the time.

Time treats me different even now. I can't stand outside my story to save my life. I keep trying to tell it without falling right in, but soon as I start to look back, I'm neck deep before I know it. Current catches me and I'm gone. Each one of those Friday afternoons when he sent me off in that damn wagon sits right here, breathing close on the back of my neck.

Part One

Sunday, August 17, 1823
Two days' ride northeast of Nashville

I

It's well past suppertime and still the heat shimmers heavy without a breeze, even high on this bluff where Richardson's broad stone house sits facing east over the river bending below. After this long dry summer, his wagon creaks cresting his last hill as late light spikes through the clouds. Quinn brings Wash back from another weekend away.

Richardson strides out to meet them, moving easily through the empty quiet of this Sunday evening. One foot in front of the next. Battered handmade boots caked with dirt. Fawn britches worn to bagginess over bony knees. At seventy, his leanness has become extreme but he still appears fit and graceful as long as he moves in the service of a clear intention. Sharp brown eyes under hooded lids and a pronounced widow's peak. He had been handsome once but disappointment and disillusion, along with two harsh stints as a prisoner of war, have long since knocked the gloss off.

Sweat has darkened the collars of all three men and horseflies torment the sticky haunches of the team. They stomp the ground where Quinn has pulled them up to wait. Wash refuses to meet Richardson's eye as he slowly unfolds to his full height, standing in the wagon bed, swaying slightly to keep his balance amidst the jerking of the horses, looking older at twenty six than most men at forty.

Richardson has owned Wash since he swam snug in Mena's belly but the young man has never once met his gaze. Even in full sun, Wash keeps his face hard to read. Holds his head a little tilted so eyes snag on the deep scar denting his temple instead. After stepping down from the wagon, Wash crosses the parched grass toward the biggest barn. Richardson, hawkish from years of vigilance, turns to watch him go then drags his attention back to

Quinn who sits high on the wagon seat, holding the reins bunched in one hand and digging in his chest pocket with the other.

A lock of steel gray hair hangs over Quinn's low forehead as he hands Richardson the thin banknote folded around a small square of thick paper listing the names. Both documents are battered and grimy from the long ride in that sweaty pocket. Richardson takes the papers and heads for the house, leaning slightly forward as if this will help him cover the necessary ground more quickly. He can already feel the liquor loosening the perennial tightness in his chest as he scans down the list written in Quinn's rough letters.

Minerva, Phyllis, CeCe, Molly, Dice, Charity, Vesta.

A big operation to have so many at childbearing age. At least he hopes they are. He has long since left the details to Quinn and it worries him some. But not enough to go himself to make sure. Not anymore. He reminds himself to have Quinn get the ages of these women who, along with Wash, have been hauling them slowly out of debt for more than five years now.

It's not only the money, although that lies forever at the heart of the matter. Richardson's interest runs deeper. He wants to know what happens and how. Which woman holds onto her child and which does not, and not just because he will need to write a refund. He wants to know, how does a child of Wash and Molly's turn out? Or one of Wash and CeCe's?

Richardson wonders whether any of them will carry Mena's face. He can still see her standing on that block down in Charleston all those years ago, so clear and somehow unbroken, with Wash already on his way. That very first time he saw her, Mena had rested her eyes on him until he felt as pulled as a fish on a hook. Her unbidden image blooms so vividly up through the years that Richardson has to shake his head to knock it loose.

As he enters his house, he calls down the hall, "Emmaline, I am unavailable." Her yessir gets lost in the thunk of his boots on the stairs. Nine long strides carry him across the echoing ballroom to the small room off the far end where men gather after dinner to smoke and drink and talk politics. His office is downstairs by the back door but this tucked away place where his books line the walls has become his refuge.

He shuts the door behind him, steps straight to the low liquor cabinet to pour himself a slug of bourbon and then stands by the window, holding his drink cupped in his palm, watching the gray wood of his big barn start to silver in the coming twilight. As he listens to the thump and rustle of his large family settling in, he knows the high window under the eaves on the far side of the hayloft is falling dark as a fist, and he knows Wash is likely sitting there in it, watching the night draw near, just like he is.

After each of these times away, Wash heads for the barn, hoping Richardson's stableman Ben has already gone back to the quarters for the night. He slips into the first stall and sinks down against the wall in the one corner that can't be seen from the door, feeling nothing but thankful when this one horse turns to stand over him, dropping its head to breathe him in. A few bits of chaff from a mouthful of hay fall on Wash's bent head as a soft nicker warms the back of his neck.

The horse returns to its hay but Wash stays tucked into that corner until well past dark. Then he stands and brushes that horse over and over, each stroke smoothing away another jagged edge of his past few days. He slips from one stall to the next, one horse to another, moving through the darkened barn as easily as a blind man.

Sometimes he runs his hands over the horses without a brush, smoothing the wide flat muscles of their necks and shoulders, down the hard straight bones of their legs, across the fluttering softness of their noses. Their slow breathing soothes him and this use of his hands retrieves them from their earlier harshness. The easy grace with which the horses receive his tenderness allows the hammered down place inside of him to open back up before too long.

Over time, these horses have become a refuge because they know nothing of the rest of his life. Usually their obliviousness eases Wash's nerves but sometimes it enrages him. That one mare, Queenie's first and last filly, was turning out needy just like her mother. Forever coming after him with that soft whinny, so insistent with her nudge nudge. Wanting some attention, some kindness Wash might not have to give right then.

Until that one bad day when he wheeled around and slapped the soft side of her nose with the flat palm of his hand, just where the pale gray shades into dark dapples. The sharp hollow thwack against the velvet give of her skin, her startled squeal sounding so loud in the quiet barn, and Wash regretting it before his blow even landed.

All that had grown between himself and this mare was gone. As steady and calm as he can manage to be with her now, his slip will haunt him. Any quick move he makes near her will be met with a flinch and that flash of panic in her eye, forever echoing his mistake back to him. Nothing for him to do but put up with it. Hope it will ease more quickly this time, even when it never does. The mare's refusal to forget angers Wash more than anything else because it is a luxury he does not have.

While he has not yet learned to check his swing, over the years he has learned to direct it elsewhere. Into stacked feed bags or folded blankets or sometimes the wall. He startles the bright bay colt named Bolivar with his sudden outbursts but he has not hit him and that's all Wash cares about. He needs to be around some creature that is not and has never been afraid of him. The solace of this is worth learning to rein himself in.

It's good and dark by the time Wash closes the last stall door and makes his way carefully up the stairs then the ladders to the highest loft where he has hidden old blankets in the hay. He does not sleep in the quarters with everyone else. He stays in the barn whether Ben likes it or not.

With this work he's been put to, enemies come easy. Wash stays three stories up with loose hay slippery near the edges and the horses to warn him. Nobody coming up here after him, no matter how mad they get. Most stay too scared of falling and breaking something with no way to set it right.

Running his eyes across the inside of this high peaked roof calms him. Each plank cut smooth then laid in flush against the next one. Each peg where it needs to be, driven with just the right number of blows. Nothing wasted, nothing crowded.

Inside those cabins, it's like a hole or a nest. Smoke coating everything and sticky with nowhere to go. He has lain in plenty of cabins and he's finished with that. Feeling the endless stream of others who have been there before him and died or lived, as clear as if he can reach out and touch them.

Wash determined early on to make his home in this loft despite Ben's constant muttering about his horses, his harnesses, his liniment and his barn. That crotchety old stableman can't come up here after him and they both knew it from the start. Richardson stays out of it because he has learned to choose his battles and Wash lets people tell the story that suits them.

That they keep him off and separate. Make him stay in the barn with the animals. As if they are punishing him when they are giving him exactly what he wants.

He tries to make it work out like that whenever he can. Makes him feel big. Big enough to take all this in and still have a part of himself where he can find room enough to stand. Makes him feel like his insides are as wide and open as the swaybacked meadows running as far along the river as he can see under a full moon.

Makes him feel bigger every time he sees that most of them don't have even a dogpatch worth of room on the inside. All that money and all that carrying on and they don't have much more than a little patch to look around and see out from. This is one of the pictures that tugs the corner of Wash's mouth into Mena's slight downward grin.

Once nightfall has swallowed the big barn with Wash inside it, Richardson turns away from the window toward the business at hand. He hides this particular book in a surprising place. A place so unlikely that he does not need a key for it.

This liquor cabinet was a gift from his godfather Thompson. Hip high and lovely, with a honeyed walnut lid rising to reveal a clutch of glass bottles, each nestled snug in its own padded compartment. The whole of it lined in midnight blue velvet scattered with stars. Old man Thompson had bought this cabinet in England with sugar money his family made down in the islands before they'd been driven out by mass uprisings. He'd bequeathed the liquor cabinet to Richardson in his will. Told him he would need it and he was right.

Everybody knows Richardson uses Wash as his traveling negro but nobody knows all the details, nor should they, is what he thinks. The squared box holding the bottles lifts enough for him to draw his secret book by its spine from this hidden compartment between the liquor above and the shelves of glasses below. Each broad page holds a span of time, covered with Richardson's careful looping track. When, where, who and how much. Page after page, lying smooth and gilt edged inside their brick red leather binding. His eldest daughter Livia had given him this blank book several Christmases ago, back when she kept urging him to keep a daybook, but Richardson has found another use for it.

He sets his glass down on Miller's unfolded banknote and lays the book open. Dips his pen into thick black ink which will fade over the years to an amber matching his liquor and writes *Sunday, August 17, 1823*. The date makes a roof over the column of names.

Minerva, Phyllis, CeCe, Molly, Dice, Charity, Vesta.

Richardson leaves room for the information to come. In nine or ten months, he will return to this page, having sent for Miller's midwife Pallas to bring him word. He will call her to this small room, shut the door behind her and wait for the details. Pallas will stand by the window, resting her gray eyes on the horizon as she trades him name for name.

Each woman, each child. Who lived, who died and when.

Richardson will mark it all down. He likes to keep track. Whenever he rides out, whether on business or just visiting, he makes it a point to pass through the quarters. Says he wants to see how they turn out. And most every time, he shakes his head, thinking, damn if they don't all carry Wash, with those wide brows like wings over crisp dark eyes and lashes so thick and curled back that they look tangled.

Clear as day to Richardson, but it often seems he's the only white man who catches the resemblance. He has never understood those who cannot tell negroes apart, especially their own. He wants to tell them, every single body possesses some distinguishing characteristic. You simply hunt for it until you find it. After that, it's obvious.

As for the negroes, they are not sure what to make of Richardson. He catches some of the tricky bits but misses plenty of the easy ones. They know all about Quinn but they hear Richardson pulls his strings like a puppet, even if the two men are supposed to be partners.

How much, is what they want to know. And which is which? How much is Richardson, how much is Quinn and how much is Wash? That is the real question lying under everything like a high water table.

∞

It is a golden day in early September and still hot as the drought drags into its third month. A trio of Richardson's neighbors have stopped by to take care of some business. Atkinson, Butler and Grange, ordering lots to be sent upriver from Richardson's store in New Orleans. A set of dining room chairs, a saddle, three crates of Madeira and two dictionaries. They are also here to get in Wash's book. Settle on some dates. The men walk together from the house to the barn to take a look even though they've used Wash before.

Richardson leads the way, half a head taller and older by thirty years than the other three but somehow the most vital of the group. The younger men turn to him continually for confirmation despite the fact that he rarely gives it. Richardson lets their chatter eddy around him as he scans his place, hunting for anything amiss.

The layout never fails to please him. The broad stone house built square on the highest point, well back from the rocky bluff over the river, with limestone-rich fields falling away from its flanks. Rows of cabins march off to the left while his garden sprawls toward the pond on the right with the biggest barn bridging the gap behind.

He had decided on stone for the house in 1792. Most of the early forts they built had been burned during Indian raids. After his brother David was ambushed and scalped by the Chickasaw, Richardson brought masons from Baltimore and had them build vertical slits into the thick stone walls on each side of the upper floors so he could lock his house up tight yet still lower a rifle barrel down through those deep narrow grooves.

He made room for two enormous underground cisterns close to the house while saving the biggest elms for shade. But he broke with custom by fitting all the necessaries inside the house itself. His initial reasoning had been for protection but he didn't like lots of little outbuildings crowded close around the house. Said it always looked to him like a hen with chicks.

So he built the kitchen inside and the smokehouse too. With a loft for Emmaline wedged between the kitchen ceiling and the floor of his drinking smoking room upstairs. Waist high is not room enough for her to sit up in, but he said she could do her sitting in the kitchen since she seems to do most of her sleeping in there anyway.

He heads now for his biggest barn. Only one of its tall double doors stands open so the four white men step into darkness, jostling one another in momentary blindness. As they walk through the dim aisle to gather in the doorway on the far side, curious horses swing their heads to look over stall doors. Wasps rise and fall, trailing a buzzing drone, and pigeons coo relentlessly no matter how many times Richardson has Wash destroy their nests.

Wash stands high in the bed of a hay wagon, breaking apart the enormous bale that Richardson ordered from Cincinnati to tide them through the drought. Wash feels the men behind him but he does not turn from his work, choosing to focus instead on the solid heft of the pitchfork in his grip. The smooth way the sharp tongs slide into the densely packed hay. His fingers wrap tighter around the worn wooden handle as he listens to the men talk about him, thinking to himself, these men like to stand around talking. Easiest thing for him to do is to stay busy. Keep his back to them.

He straightens up and takes the pitchfork in both hands, tines turned toward him so he can use it more like a shovel or a hoe, raising it high then stabbing it deep into the bale to break off chunks before tossing them onto the small square platform he will winch up to his loft to unload. He sets down the pitchfork and picks up the harpoon-shaped hay hook. Stabs it deep into the rest of the bale then draws it out to check for mold.

Just as Wash knew he would, Atkinson asks Richardson, "Don't you worry about him getting after somebody with that hay hook?"

After a long pause, Wash hears Richardson say in his dry quiet voice, "Then what, Atkinson? Where will he go then, except straight to the gallows, with parts missing after a long and bloody day?"

Wash knows without looking that Atkinson's mouth has puckered shut. Feeling the men still watching him, he stops himself from shaking his head as he thinks about Richardson. Salty old dog. Wash sets his knees and his back, takes a breath and heaves a bigger chunk from the floor of the wagon onto the adjoining platform in one fluid motion.

The men continue talking, with Richardson telling Atkinson, "You must keep an eye out. And carry that knife even when you're sure you won't need it."

Richardson's knife is thick and flat but short, riding at the back of his right hip, nestled in a sheath strung on a thin calfskin belt that too often slides down inside the waistband of his britches, soaking with sweat then drying out again until it stiffens and threatens to crack. His wife Mary used to take this belt from its hook in their wardrobe, rubbing it between her hands with oil to supple it while she watched him dress. Now that they've virtually gone their own ways, Richardson has Ben oil the belt for him, along with his boots.

Richardson continues, "Just make sure they know you have it and that you'll use it. It's a waste of time if you don't make it clear that you plan on taking one with you when you go."

As soon as the words leave his mouth, Nero comes into his mind, just as vivid as Mena did the other day. Richardson rubs the back of his neck and Butler starts nodding because he knows what Richardson is seeing. He likes the Nero story and has told it often but Atkinson and Grange look confused so Butler takes over, talking through the sudden quiet and jerking his shoulder toward Richardson as he tells it.

"You never did see that negro he bought in New Orleans? He just about carved himself a new road to China, right through the middle of that boy."

Atkinson does remember that negro. Tall, looming and fine. Except for that look in his eye.

Butler's voice rises. "That Nero'd kill you just as soon as look at you."

Atkinson and Grange shake their heads as the story comes back to them.

"How the hell you think that Nero ended up in New Orleans all the way from Virginia in the first place? That's about as far downriver as you can get sold. And likely as he was, nobody would even bid on him except for our Richardson here. Forever indulging his weakness for the fine ones, no matter what we try to tell him. Thought he'd found himself a bargain."

Grange looks over at Richardson standing quietly in the open mouth of the barn door. His hands are clasped behind him as he toes a small stone over to the doorjamb so it won't be there for any of his horses to step on. He holds his eyes on the ground, except for quick glances over at Butler.

Richardson flinches to hear Butler tell it, especially in that enthusiastic way of his. People had warned him he'd have nothing but trouble from Nero. And sure enough, within three months of bringing him home, there Richardson stood, face to face with him, Nero's hands wrapped around Richardson's throat and Richardson's knife buried in Nero's low belly up to its hilt. In the middle of the morning. Right in his own damn barnyard.

The shock of it. The feeling of his windpipe closing off. The surprise of actually being ready. How quickly his palm wrapped around the haft of his knife. The tautness of Nero's belly, his knife pushing through flat muscle to the inside of Nero's hip bone. How close they stood. The sweat beading on Nero's lip. Having to punch his knife hard to reach the softness underneath. Having to saw back and forth, pulling the hole bigger and bigger, until he felt the strength start to ebb from Nero's grip. Then the sweet rush of breath he was finally able to draw. Even now, Richardson's face twists in anger as he thinks of Nero's body sprawled out on the ground in front of him. Nero's blood all down his front, warm and slick, drying to sticky on his hands.

"Damn waste that was. Completely unnecessary," he hears himself say.

After a pause, he adds, "But if it had to happen, just as well that it happened in front of a bunch of mine. I told those that were standing there staring, I said you take this back to the quarters with you. And wherever else you might get to go too."

Butler whistles low, slapping Richardson on the back in open admiration, saying, "You keep yours headed in a straight line, don't you?"

Richardson looks at them in their weak boyish eagerness and he's disgusted. They don't see. They don't see anything at all. He never should have had to kill Nero. It was one of his more serious missteps, and he was damn lucky that in the three short months Nero was here, he'd been so disagreeable that no one had taken to him. So he had no ties, no kin, no one to take up his cause.

Richardson can still see Nero lying fallen with that great hole torn in his middle. Even then, he had such grace. Long muscled legs. Big hands with thick fingers, squared off at their ends. Honey brown eyes staring out from under broad wings of eyebrows.

He remembers the first time he saw Nero, standing off to himself, scanning the horizon rather than looking at the ground like the others. Richardson even remembers imagining what Nero's get would have been like. Magnificent. He starts to wonder whether he may have bought Nero while searching for some fine and unbroken version of Wash. Richardson steers away from this thought before it has a chance to surface and drags his mind back to the group.

"I don't think I'd ever seen a more likely negro. Bought him as a second stockman to go along with Wash here, then had to listen to Quinn complain the whole way home about what a mistake I was making."

The men chuckle because they can imagine the long ride from New Orleans with Richardson and Quinn on each other's nerves the whole way despite Nero himself being sent upriver later along with the furniture.

"The only thing wrong with Nero was, he had no regard for his own personal safety. Hell, maybe Quinn was right. Negroes like him can stir up a great deal more trouble than a hardheaded horse. And quicker too."

"End up deader too," Butler adds but Richardson cuts him off.

"I was tempting fate. Anyway, take yourselves to the house and get something to drink. I'll be right behind you."

The men file out of the barn into the late light as Richardson watches Wash send the last load of hay up to his loft with long even pulls on the winch rope. Wash has been working so steadily the visitors have forgotten about him. As Richardson turns to go, he wonders whether he's the only white man who understands that negroes hear everything, just like everybody else.

Wash feels the weight of Richardson's gaze lift off of him as soon as he's tied the winch rope tight. As he climbs up to his loft to unload the hay, he remembers Nero for himself. Never liked him much. But still, Wash was glad he didn't have to watch it happen. He'd sat up late that night just like everybody else and he'd heard all about it, whether he wanted to or not.

Talk had drifted up from the fire circle all night. The first tellings were harsh and bright, jerky and sudden, full of voices rising and falling. Cutting each other off, calling out in agreement or disagreement before settling down into a slower rhythm with less being said and maybe more being heard but who knows.

Long silences opened up as people drifted off to bed or stared into the fire. But first they went over it and over it, as if they had to tell the story till it started to quit bothering them. They were trying to make it leave them alone. What had happened that day. What Nero had done. What Richardson had done. What they would have done in his place.

That's just what you think now is what Wash wanted to say to the men still talking like they knew everything about everything. That's just what you think now. It would be a whole different story if it was you standing there.

Wash knows almost every single step on Nero's path for having taken it himself. One way or other, he has been down that road and nearly the whole way. Further than most. And all he knows is there's just no telling.

Wash

It's the storms that help me some. The ones that come in the middle of the night where I can stand outside and watch. Quiet and on my own with nobody seeing me. Wind comes roaring through, pulling the treetops in circles, trying to turn things round.

Most times, this place feels like being caught in a great big funnel, with all this water pouring through, trying to drag you with it. Nothing to grab on to will teach you to hold your breath. But when that wind comes tearing straight up the bluff, feels like it might pull his house on down.

First, it gets real still. Then I get that weight on my chest. Like God is matching my heart. Making the outside feel like the inside, pressing down on me for his own reasons, so all this other pressing ain't so noticeable.

The leaves turn and jitter, but just a little, and everything is still, like I get sometimes. There's a quiet trembling. Like everything is here from someplace else but just for a little while.

Then, when the sky peels back and tears open with thunder, that's when it feels most like me. That's when my insides match my outsides and there's no gap in between. And when the trees lash and get split by lightning, their tops torn and hurled across the yard, that's me too.

It's not till I wake up the next morning with the tall grass looking that bright bruised green and the birds busying like nothing ever happened and that big sun rising so quiet and steady that I catch on.

The world has left me behind again without even a look back. Leaving me in a storm and acting like it never went there itself. Looking at me like it never said nothing to me at all.

Richardson

My daughter Livia, my eldest girl, has a face like a horse, there's no doubt about it. But somehow she is of the most peace to me. She alone calls things as she sees them and has no barriers. As I grew my business of trade, trying to skirt what I saw as the edge, she kept after me, despite the fact that I was not asking her.

"Father, what they want to carry West with them are negroes. Negroes are what they will be wanting."

She doesn't hesitate to give me her opinion, even though I took this question to my second son, Cassius, instead.

"Look at you. You brought negroes with you, never mind it was because your brother insisted. You were glad he talked you into buying Virgil and Albert both. You know you were. Only a fool would head into raw land, having to cut and clear and build, without at least a few hands. And just think of all these settlers headed straight for Tyler's new law. They won't be able to buy negroes once they cross into the territories. They'll need to own them before they set out. And here we are. Right here. Don't make them go down the street."

And Livia would venture further, which is precisely why I don't ask her. But she answers me anyway.

"Is it because your firstborn William insisted on marrying that Celeste and setting up house with her in Memphis when he should have left her as his mistress down in New Orleans? That marriage won't bring anything but trouble, even though Celeste's cultured and mostly white anyway. William refuses to see that he cannot manage Memphis for you and be an abolitionist at the same time. But just because he's being irrational doesn't mean you should."

My Livia continually comes to my aid by refusing to protect me. Pinning me with a fierce look from under those brows I recognize as my own. No wonder she's not married.

"I know you hoped you'd have left slavery back in Baltimore by now, well hobbled by your Revolution and dying out. But that's not what's happened. The difference you're seeking is not to be found. It is simply more and more of the same. What will you do when you don't like the game? Stay out of it? That doesn't sound like you."

And she's as right as ever. I'm in it because I can't stay out of it. Plain and simple.

Strange as it may sound, it can be easier with the negroes. Some few of them, at least. My Emmaline knows better than to come to me with every little thing. I do not enjoy managing, so mine need to have sense enough to work most things out for themselves. My neighbor Miller keeps his people on such a tight rein until they check in with him about which way the sun will rise and which way it will set. If mine were like that, I'd have to replace the whole lot.

Emmaline runs the house smoothly and I leave her to it. She and my wife make quite the pair. They constitute their own army, with inventory being their strongest suit. Mary gave her the key to the smokehouse and God's eye on the sparrow is nothing to the track Emmaline keeps of those hams.

I lucked upon her soon after I came West. Took her and her boy unwillingly in payment for a piece of land, but she has proven to be a godsend. Stays close at hand instead of forever asking for a pass like the rest, especially after that husband she finally found took up with somebody else. And Mary savors the way Emmaline wears the Bible she gave her in her front apron pocket, almost like a shield.

Every now and then, I'll help Emmaline or one of hers out of a pinch but only when it's serious. She knows I'd just as soon sell than hear too much nagging. And she doesn't want me in her business any more than I want to be there. Of course, she's well into mine. When you have folks to wipe your nose and your behind both, they will know your business. All you can do is hope they won't get the chance to tell too much of it.

Far too many people refuse to accept this simple equation. Wishing things otherwise hardly makes them so. I'm not like these neighbors of mine who think their negroes don't have business of their own. That's one thing I've learned from Emmaline if from no one else. There's not a soul born on this earth that doesn't have some kind of business.

Unfortunately there are those among us, my wife and girls included, who insist on acting like children playing with dolls. I asked Mary not to involve herself so deeply in Emmaline's eldest grandson's wedding. But she worked on that damn girl's dress for months, embroidering flowers all over it, and then orchestrated what should have been a meaningless ceremony right between my garden and my pond. Almost at the house.

And just as I predicted, the many grew jealous of any advantage granted the few. It took me months to settle my place back down after that. So what can I say to my neighbors who create trouble for themselves by getting too involved? What I want to say to those dreamers is dig yourselves out of your own mess and don't expect to bring it to me. But with the way these negroes all know one another, we are bound together whether we like it or not.

You must work not to get drawn in, even as you must stay close enough to be able to see clearly and decide for yourself. Quinn started out trying to get between me and mine but I had to make him quit. Once I've made a decision, then he can carry it out, but I don't want him any closer to mine than me.

What I tell people about Wash is, most horses, you need to boss them. Bear right down on them till they buckle under. But then there are these others. You cannot make them do. They'd just as soon break their neck than take up a notion that's yours. With these few, you must study them. Figure out their natural inclination and take that as your way to go. Then find a way to let them think it was their idea.

Usually, these few are more trouble than they're worth. They'll break a leg as soon as you've put in enough time to make them worthwhile. But I can't help it. Fine is a weakness of mine. If it's a stud, he'll clean up just about any mare, no matter how rough, and if it's a mare, then God help you.

It's always best to dampen down this edge a little. Cross one like this with another thicker, duller one in order to get yourself something with clean lines but some common sense to go along. And be careful about two like this coming together. Likely as not, there won't be anybody who can ride what comes from that combination.

Not to say they've all got to be rideable. I've found plenty of use for those I could never even throw a leg over. So long as I can build my fence high enough to get them from pasture to barn and back. In and out of the breeding stall when the time comes. I will put up with a lot to see that fineness springing up in my pastures. Some would just as soon shoot a horse they can't go in a stall with, but I'm not that way. We all have our contributions to make and it is not always what we might think.

Wash is one of these few. Most wouldn't tolerate him. As hard as he tries to bury his quality, it flashes out often enough for me to see, no matter what the rest say. Anyplace else, he'd be dead in a minute and he knows it.

Maybe it's unwise of me to foster the very aspect in him that he rightly tries to hide. You'd think I'd want mine as manageable as possible. That I'd pick dull to go with dull. Dull and solid. But I just do not have it in me and God knows, there are enough like that already.

I recognized this quality in Wash, no matter how blurred, because I remember Mena having had it. She carried that same look in her eye. Remaining somehow unto herself through it all and holding her knowing close.

Much of this clarity was gone from her, and from Wash too, by the time I got them home from Thompson's place, all beat to hell and back. I could've wrung those Thompson boys' necks myself. But even now, I can still catch glimpses of Mena's fineness in Wash. Makes me wish I'd seen his father. He must have been spectacular.

I do put a good deal of thought into this. I plan it out and map it down. They know how I am about my horses but they have little idea how exacting my considerations are on this. You need a record to know where you stand.

Of course, you can never be sure that you get exactly what you planned on, short of going there or having someone witness for you. But I think Wash knows me, how I am, and that there's some sense to it. He doesn't always agree with me and I let him get away with as much as is possible. But I must draw the line somewhere. We need to remain clear about whose hands are on the reins.

I do try to leave him as much slack as I can. Like I said, he's the kind who needs to think everything is his idea. So I tell him the list, and sometimes I'll let him scotch or add a few, but we usually see eye to eye.

Wash

Wagon comes for me on a Friday, won't none of the fellas meet my eye. All they do is look right straight down at the dirt. Stand round muttering like they know something. They act like they know but I know they wonder.

Makes me grateful for times when I pass Pallas on the road. She knows her way round my mind so I need her not looking away from me. She'll stand there steady as a post, hooked in the ground like my anchor, watching me ride by in the back of this wagon.

Maybe it won't be so bad this time is what I tell myself. Plenty worse ways to get cross this field. I can hear my mamma saying that right to me, no matter how many years she's been under the ground. She says quit letting it gnaw at you like that and I do try.

Funny thing is, once I'm headed out of there, it eases off some. Depends on whether they come for me on a good day or a bad one. But things get so twisted up round here till it's hard trying to tell the difference. That'll put you right inside crazy.

And you give me any one man, I don't care how much he tells you about that one woman, there's always another one walking by, and he'd take her in a heartbeat if he knew he didn't have to answer for it.

Simple truth is, for the most part, you want it whether you want it or not. Sometimes, it's having to take it that gets me going but it's not always like that. Most times, it's not. And every single thing you do round here has some edge to it. You can cut yourself real good without even trying. I'll take this one over others I've seen and I'll handle it myself in my own way.

What gets to me is he saw it in me and he put me to it. Makes me feel nailed down in a way I want to pull up from. But it'd take too much skin so I don't.

Some days, I'll sit up to see where I'm going. But days when I already know, I'll lay back on those feed sacks lining the wagon bed, letting the trees make patterns over me. That's what my mamma never could get used to. Too many trees. Nothing open like the island or even Thompson's place.

Said it made her feel like she never could catch her breath good. That's when I used to hear her laugh a little. Saying no wonder they can't never see what's right in front of their face. There's nowhere for your eye to travel. Nothing like a straight shot nowhere.

I can see what she means, with everything growing so thick and right up on you all the time. Makes me glad for those few open places you come across sometimes. Like the trees need to stand back and get a good look at each other. A little clearing with grass growing thick and shiny. Some place for the moon to shine down on. Give you time to see somebody you come to meet walking towards you.

Course all these thick woods, that's my cover. Easier for me to get from place to place when I need to. I'm like my mamma in that my eye likes to travel but I'll always need some edges to skirt whether I like it or not.

The way Pallas first showed me the lay of the land between her place and mine made me feel like I'd never seen it before. She brought her hands together at her waist, cupping them to make a bowl and then letting them fall open. Her palms rose up, making a small flat place, showing me how the hollow after that second ridge between us shallows out towards the slough. Then she pointed with one finger to a place on her other palm, showing me where the slough narrows to a creek mouth.

She was standing off to the side of the path in that high necked dress she always wore. I remember watching her hands move and trying to hear what she was telling me. But all I could see was her stepping inside that stall at Miller's place on that very first Friday they sent me over there. Long waisted, narrow like a gourd. Wearing that same dress. And pale, with those smoky gray eyes that keep you looking even when they make you wonder which white man she got em from. Had her hair drawn back and covered for being too good.

She came in so quiet and silky, she shifted the way that place felt to me. But something about her made my palms itch that first evening. It was the skittery way she acted once I started looking at her. Made me mad at first but she was right to watch out about me. She was right.

She tilted her head to draw me back to what she was telling me. Smiled and said just wait for her near those three big sycamores at the edge of Richardson's place and she'll lead me the rest of the way. She knew I'd never find it the first time. And if I think somebody saw me turn off the road, then veer towards my right hand till I hit some deepish water, and walk up against the current a ways. Pull out on the mud flats and wait. She'll find me.

Me and Pallas, our minds see alike. Two night birds, right on each other's tail, swooping then banking. Most of the good best time we spend is at night.

Most folks is scared at night and that's fine with me. Day's got me pinned down till I can't do much without everybody knowing. But once the sun starts to slide, with everything falling into blue so you can't tell one thing from the next, that's when I start waking up. Night is when I get me to myself. Most nights at least. Now that Richardson's starting to come down to my barn later and later, I stay careful.

But most times I just want to get to Pallas. I cut straight through and she does too. I know the back way now, since she showed me. Dip down to that ribbon of boggy strip cutting through the bottom. Then the big white oak with a thick hairy

X of poison ivy vining up it. Swing wide round the stand of crab apple that draws the wild hogs, wade across the creek right by the deepest bend in case I need to hide in that cave where the bank hangs down.

Where I catch up with Pallas best is at the little pond behind the marsh. After a hot day, the night I walk through to get to her has pockets of cool scattered in the warm, just like that pond. And me and Pallas, we step straight out towards the middle of it.

Cool mud comes up between my toes, then water warm as breath and soft, rising round me so smooth the world falls away. Walk out till it licks my neck and then one last step. Can't see her but I feel her behind me while we stand there cooling off. Not much moon. Night sky curves round us like a bowl. Tip my head back, see more stars. Stand there till I get myself still and calm.

There's a spot we like on the far bank in the shadow of a big tulip poplar down in an old storm. Silvery trunk throws a shadow big enough to hold us. Hard dirt and dry grass to lay on. Sometimes we talk and sometimes we don't. It depends.

But once I wrap my hands around her middle, my thumbs touching over where she breathes in but light, my fingers nearly meeting in back but light, and her looking over my shoulder at the stars cupping down round us but light, once I get my hands on her to where I can feel her breathing in and out, opening and closing my grip but light, that's it.

Pallas

Sometimes it's not about all that. Lot of times, it's just sitting quiet, him and me. Visiting whether we're talking or not. Watching the sky turn, curled up next to our log by the pond.

We talk about now and we talk about then. Once in every long while, we'll talk about time to come, but we keep ourselves real careful about that. Most times, we stay right with where we are and where we've been. Talk about this person and that one. Both here and gone. About who did what and who said what, and sometimes it's funny and sometimes it's like walking into a wall.

He tells me about his mamma. His mamma and her bumping smack into his daddy and then never seeing him again. He's handing me pieces of his story like food and I'm holding each one real careful, memorizing the way it looks before I tuck it in my mouth. Enough times of us meeting up, I know all about his mamma's mamma and his daddy's too. I take his family for mine, like happens when you don't have much of one yourself, and I'm glad to feel them close.

As for me, he can look at me and see a lot of what happened before Phoebe found me. He feels the rest of it from the way I can turn to dead weight in his hands, with my eyes gone empty, just staring over his shoulder. He can guess most of it because the words of a story matter less than the shape and feel of it.

I tell him some about Phoebe teaching me, but mostly my story comes when I scan the woods we're walking through. I'll stop short to kneel down with a plant and he'll wait quiet, knowing I'm watching for Phoebe's hand moving through the leaves. He stands there, ready to fall back in step with me when I'm done.

He likes that I'm not scared. Go everywhere and by myself. Make my own little money too, even though they don't hardly ever call me to tend to white folks, except when it goes bad fast with no white doctor close enough to fetch. That's when they send for me, but they already waited too long and there's nothing I can do. Leads them to say they never believed in my medicine anyway. But I know how to hold myself steady and Wash does too.

Around here, you got to hunt to find what works for you. And if you got even a little sense, you learn to keep what you find to yourself. So we stay careful. We sneak and we go otherwise. He says he's not about to let anyone see his heart. Says sure as you know it, somebody will come after me just to get back at him. But I pat my knife and tell him not to worry.

∞

It is late. Dark presses against dawn as Wash makes his way home from meeting Pallas at the pond deep in the marsh. He takes the road because it's quicker. He rounds the next to last bend with his mind so full of Pallas that he forgets to pay his usual close attention. The soft dirt on the road muffles the sound of hoof beats and the wind trying to bring rain swirls in the trees, drowning out the faint jangle of bits and spurs.

Wash and the small band of tired patrollers come face to face so fast all Wash has time to think is how trouble never seems to come when you are ready for it. He calculates whether he has time to jump off to the side of the road but with this drought, the horses will hear him as soon as he steps into the dry grass. If there were less moon or if the patrollers were on foot, Wash would have a slim chance of them walking right past him.

But the horses snort to smell him better and start tossing their heads. His fingers close on the worn piece of paper in his pocket. Wash has his hand out, holding the folded pass by its corner, before the four patrollers have pulled their horses to a complete halt. They are startled too, but excited to have stumbled across some action at the end of a long quiet night.

The man closest to Wash bends from his saddle to take the pass. He shakes the paper from folded to open then hands it over to the one who can read. The other two patrollers crowd their horses closer, anxious and eager, like hounds quivering to be loosed on the scent. The one who can read holds the pass in a patch of moonlight. His voice is rough and halting even on the shorter words.

He has my permission. Leave him to himself.
                    General James Richardson.

There is both familiarity and disrespect in the way Richardson has written the pass that sets the men on edge. Somehow it feels to them that Richardson is bossing them around from way up on the bluff where they know he sits drinking and reading by the fire in his study. None of them have been inside his house but they have all heard about it.

They yank their agitated horses around while they debate about what to do with Wash even though they already know the answer. The way Richardson has worded the note means they won't be able to get any reward money from treating Wash as if he were a runaway. Still, they bicker.

Wash waits. Head up, eyes down. Working to hold on to the sweet in his mind from Pallas and ready to get home. But he knows better than to let on. Standing there waiting, Wash walks that fine line. Don't be challenging but don't call up the thunder in them by showing weakness.

The story Diamond told him the other day flashes across his mind. They had run into each other not too far from where Wash stands now. Diamond had told it so funny. Told him how he got double crossed by that crazy broken down white man of his. Said he handed the patrollers his pass like he always did, thinking it would fix things like it always did and he could get on his way. Said he was as surprised as anybody when they read it out loud. Said that crazy white man of his had written beat the tar out of this nigger, right there on what he thought was his pass.

Diamond said he knew he had gotten sideways with the old man about something or other but he thought he fixed it. Told Wash he guessed he hadn't fixed it after all. No, he hadn't. Said they tore him up but good. Said he gave that possum a run for his money, playing dead to beat the band, but said he was careful to take some fists and feet first. Can't play dead too soon or they'll catch onto you. So he had stood there and took it for a little while before he let himself fall. Lurched and tipped good before he let his knees buckle. Hit the road like a sack of potatoes.

Even with his face still swollen lopsided, Diamond had made Wash laugh telling that story. Wash had squatted there in the shade of that hot afternoon, leaning his low back against the trunk of a big maple, watching Diamond act it out for him, tipping and lurching as if to fall in the dirt. Not actually falling this time, staying standing this time, but showing Wash just how it happened so he could picture it.

Diamond says uhh to show how his breath sounded coming out of him when he hit the ground and Wash shakes his head. Rubs his palms down his thighs, smoothing his coveralls, muttering mmmm mmm and letting his mouth curve down into Mena's slight grin. It was funny watching Diamond tell it. Beat the tar out of this nigger. Then both of them laughing a little and shaking their heads in the shade.

Wash stands here now, on this same road on the night of a different day, waiting on the patrollers to let him go home. Standing so still. Waiting for his piece of paper back. Working on keeping his face solid and flat, trying not to let the corners of his mouth twitch down from thinking about Diamond. Trying to stay quiet and smooth and slick, leaving nothing else for them to read.

The men gradually accept that they can't interfere with Wash. Richardson already knows who is on patrol, where and when, or else he can find out easily.

"Like a damn hawk."

"Up on his high horse."

Wash breathes a long careful sigh, relieved that the tension has shifted away from him, but he stays on the lookout for some sign telling him he is free to go.

"Get the hell on home, goddammit."

It's the man who first took his pass. He jerks his hand in the direction of the Richardson place then goads his horse back to the center of the road. The reader drops the pass as he turns to follow. The small piece of stiff paper falls slowly, taking forever to hit the ground. Glancing first off the man's thigh and then off the horse's sweaty flank, winging down to land in the dusty road amidst all the hooves.

As soon as the horses have cleared out, Wash dips for his pass, careful not to turn his back on the men even as they ride away. He folds the paper into its worn creases, slides it deep inside his pocket and heads for home, remembering not to go too fast and not to go too slow until he rounds the bend. Once out of their sight, he gets off the road for good.

Wash follows a small stream running between the two steep ridges. Cuts past the old spring on trails he knows from running

Richardson's traplines. As he comes through that last stand of pines, the path forks. Right toward the house and left toward the barn.

Before Wash heads for the barn, he looks down the right fork at the house. Candles flicker in the upstairs window. Richardson is still awake. Still sitting in his study. Wash finds himself thankful the moon has set, making it too dark for Richardson to see him crossing the open meadow. Too late for the old man to come down to the barn and start talking at him.

Wash slips into the barn's small side door then climbs his ladders to settle into the hay with his blankets but he's too wound up to sleep. He lies there trying to calm himself after his run in with the patrollers. He has long since learned he must manage his mind. Think about Pallas. Don't think about the men on the road. Seek solace wherever he knows he'll find it. Step inside his story. As far into the past as he can fall.

It was Mena who taught Wash how to travel like this. How to use his mind's eye to keep his pictures bright and strong and close. Make himself a world to live in. It was Mena at first and then later, Rufus in his forge at Thompson's place. These two worked hand in hand to carry Wash far enough into this knowing for it to stick.

Soon as Wash can manage to call Mena and Rufus to mind, he sees them. The darker the barn the better. Mena as lean and quiet as her own grave until she finds herself deep inside a story. Then her hands flutter lightly inside her stillness. Unless somebody else walks up and then she's back to smooth as stone. Acting like she can't speak English. Rufus looks so much like her they could have been siblings except he's thicker and wider, like Wash. Gruff on top but soft underneath. Or at least he used to be.

Wash needs to take care which memories he visits and when. Some always work while others tend to turn on him. The trick lies in remembering which ones are which, remembering to choose and then talking himself into it. Steering his mind, just like he'd been taught. It was this knowing that Mena used to make it across the water with so much of herself still in one piece.

Soon as they put her on the ship, Mena dropped down into that trance of herself, trying to stay safe. But she dropped so far and stayed so gone that after several days, the women could not get her moving around like she needed to be. The captain thought she was sick. Saw her as fading too close to dying and wanted her thrown overboard before she infected the rest with whatever disease he decided she had.

That one crewman had her hanging over the edge, ready to drop her, before the situation came all the way through to her. As the pain of his beefy hands gripping her skinny shoulders made its way to her from across a great distance, she slowly became aware of the weight of her own body. She felt the space between her and the water pulling down on her and realized she'd better find some way to show herself to him or he was going to let her go.

And she did it while he was watching her. She came back from where she'd been, just like she was swimming up from deep underwater, until there she was, looking right at him from inside her own eyes. Seeing her do this unsettled him so much, he almost dropped her anyway.

It was the way she stared at him. She was barely out of her teens and slight enough to seem younger but her eyes hooked him. Not grabbing or desperate but so focused on him it was like she bound herself to him to keep him from dropping her.

He drew his hands, with her still in them, toward his chest. Just as the tops of her feet knocked against the outside edge of the ship's gunwale, it caught up to her what had almost happened. She saw it all. His hands opening. The outside of the ship rising past as she fell down through the air. Water coming up at her fast.

A shiver ran through her so strong that he did lose his grip but by the time she fell from his hands, there was no more water under her. The smooth hard deck caught her where she sprawled. She scrambled, ducked and ran, stumbling and falling, in amongst the rest of the women brought up for air, trying to look scared enough and enough like the others so that one crewman would forget what he knew he had seen.

After that day, she opened her mouth for the food and she let the women walk her around. She wasn't trying to do what some were trying to do. Holding their jaws clenched until the captain ordered enough teeth broken to force feed them. Mena was just trying to make it through in one piece.

But once she had dropped inside herself like she'd been taught, it was easy to get distracted. That deep peaceful place was so quiet and soothing that she started wanting to stay there, running her fingers across all that was familiar, forgetting about the life up on the surface she'd left behind. Until that one crewman yanked her back with the grip of his pink chapped hands.

Mena never meant to leave this life. She just lost track of time. From the very beginning, she had carried a strong sense that there was something waiting for her.

And sure enough, once she got here, there he was. She bumped against him as they were being transferred from boat to pen, or from pen to pen, she was not sure which. Each of them trapped in their own slow jerking line while being marched in opposite directions.

All hurry up and wait, with most everybody keeping their eyes down on the dirt or on the back of the neck in front of them.

It was when their two lines pressed close together at the narrow part of the alleyway that they were pushed into one another, knocking shoulders. When the whole of both lines got hung up for a minute. Just for a minute. Enough time for them to step away from each other and look up.

Her eyes move from his feet to his face. It is like she is seeing herself made into a man except bigger. After all that ripping and tearing and chaos, after this whole parade of people she does not know and has never seen before, here he is. Somebody who knows her and knows her parents too. Somebody who knows exactly where the path behind their village bends to meet the creek in the shade of that big mangrove.

They can read their stories in each other's face. She knows how he looked before he shot up, before his voice dropped and before his muscles began to lap over each other under his smooth skin. Before his family sent him inland to stay with relatives, trying to keep him safe. And he knows how she was set apart from the beginning.

And now here they are, moving past each other in long crawling lines to pour into adjoining pens with the fence between them worn rickety and loose where it meets the brick at the back corner, and nobody paying any attention at night because there's another wall circling the whole compound with broken glass jagged along the top.

Wash

My mamma was quiet but she had a pull to her. When I was little, her draw was real strong. Any gap between us was too much. She'd drag me to her till I was snugged right up against her, curled in the small of her back or the crook of her legs, and I didn't fight it neither.

But sometimes, her pull went to push and you couldn't get a grip on her no way. She had roots grown so deep, she'd be here in body but gone someplace else in spirit. Once she started dipping down in her own well, she'd get so gone till all I could reach for was where she used to be.

Guess we should have been glad she still had her inside place, but mostly what I felt was jealous and left behind. But she was right to keep it to herself. Wasn't enough to go round anyway. At least let her have her peace instead of us fighting over it, tearing it to scraps and none of us having any.

Course I didn't have any of this figured out back then. All this I've come to since.

There was no getting next to her when she got gone like that. And reaching for her just made her feel farther away. I remember sitting there, trying to hold myself steady till she came back close enough to where I could get at her. Just sitting there, rocking and telling myself everything I knew for sure.

Times like that, I felt like I was drifting with no ground under my feet. Like something might snatch me right up and I'd be gone from this world. So when she did pull me close, I'd nestle in, feeling so far from those other times I'd just about forget, till I'd hear that one little tug in the back of my mind telling me watch out. Telling me pay attention.

You see these women round here steady stitching all these little scraps together to make one big piece? That's what I'd do inside my mind whenever my mamma let me lie close against her. I'd stitch myself right tight to her.

And I remember it all. Seems strange for a grown man to keep so many bits and pieces from being small, but it's a house I'm building for myself with a roof of remembering to put over my head. Something to lie under and hear the rain falling on at night. I take what I have and I make what I can with it. Some of it is edge and some is smooth, but I take it all and I use it to make me a place big enough to get inside.

She's who taught me that. But some days, she had to work to show me. Some days I wasn't even looking, much less seeing. Especially after we got took off that island. Seemed like I could hear her better so long as we were out there on our own under old man Thompson. But once those two boys of his carried us over to his big place, there was no telling me nothing.

I started slipping away from her. Going to see about those new folks. And I didn't want her getting all fierce, hooking me to her and trying to tell me everything I'd already started to forget. Her wanting so hard scared me more than anything else but I understand it now and she knows I do.

She was African and her staying African aggravated those new folks over at Thompson's place. There was more countryborn than saltwater negroes, even back then, and most of those countryborn didn't want none of that old hoodoo. Made em uneasy.

But my mamma just stood there, wearing the distance she came across in her eyes and in her ways both. And she didn't let it die down. Rubbed most everybody sideways. Like she was dis-respecting em by hanging on to her African when this new place kept saying drop it and turn and walk away.

And most of em had. Made sense in a way. Dragging your memories along with you can wear you out, like a mule dragging a heavy load over rough ground. But then here she comes, with her hands wrapped tight round all of it and not letting go. Keeping her knowing for herself.

Made em mad enough, some would've tried to knock her loose from it if they hadn't been scared of her. Her and Rufus both. But he held his African more hidden than she did, saying there's no reason to tell everything you know.

My mamma was stronger than most, that was part of it. But at the same time, somebody had showed her how. Back before she got snatched up, those old women had taught her what they knew. Pulled her off to the side. Said they saw she had more room inside than most folks. Born with one foot in the spirit world was what they called it.

She told me she balked at first. Wanted to stay in that circle, playing with the rest of the girls. Be like everybody else. But she wasn't and she knew it. So when her mamma nodded for her to go on and go, she did. She let those women teach her till she knew how to leave when she needed and how to come back both. And how to hold on to everything while she was gone. That's how she made it over easier than most.

I didn't know much about any of this for myself back then. I just knew she was different. She was different and my being hers made me different too.

What she showed me was, you had to intend. Keep your mind in mind. Guard it and watch it and get it what it needs. Can't just go along like you sightseeing cause these sights round here will steal your mind right from you.

Best be stitching yourself to something. Almost don't matter what it is so long as it can keep you from getting swept away. Those that don't find a foothold, I keep seeing em pass right on by me. Pouring straight over the edge.

And it's not just us that's got to watch it. It's everybody. Same current pulls on white folks too. Sometimes I think maybe it's worse for them. So much more pulling on em and so much less to hold on to. What little they got must feel like reeds. After all this bending, those reeds must be getting old and tired and stripped looking, what with this storm blowing more days than not. And that edge getting closer and easier to wash over every minute no matter what you do.

Lord knows what kind of trouble I'd get myself into if I ever got ahold of where they're standing. I'm tearing things up pretty good from right here. Don't know what I'd do with the leeway they got. That kind of slack can't be no good for nobody. That's like stepping into the mouth of the devil. Walk on in and before you know it, you turn round and can't get out. You just standing there, looking out at the world through all those teeth.

And this world is full of folks already been washed over the edge but they're still here, walking round, making things hard on the rest of us. Rest of us feels real few sometimes.

Richardson

All my father ever told me was to make something of myself. He was forever reminding me that we lived in a new world where a man would have to be blind not to be able to get ahead.

It was 1781 by the time my brother David and I made it home for Christmas. We had just retired from the Continental Army, Independence from England secured at last after seven long years. Our mother made her usual teary fuss but he was all business. We'd barely sat down at the table when he started in on me.

"You and your brother were lucky to make it through this damn war in one piece. This water is not going to run clean for a while, if ever. You best bite into this world and chew. If you want to go West, fine. But don't go empty handed.

"Gather as many land grants as you can get your hands on, go as far as you can and get there first. Once you secure a toehold, you can always parlay it into a town."

"Look at me," he was fond of saying. "I came here owing seven years and now everybody owes me."

I couldn't even picture him an indentured servant. A ragged and hungry fourteen year old, stepping down into some dank hold, headed for this unknown place. It seemed impossible. But here he was, rich, fat and full of advice.

"Take up land. Get it under cultivation. Patent it to put it in your name. Then resurvey as soon as you can to add all the adjoining vacant land to your parcel without having to pay for it. That's how you do it. Then you keep on doing it because without property, few men are thought much of. How do you think I turned fifty acres into one thousand and a town to boot?"

He'd ask us this favorite question time and again. Just like that, he'd remind us, snapping his fingers then peering at us as if he'd made a joke. And there it was, his land stretching out all around us. His town thriving on the road out of Baltimore. He was insistent about the road. Said that was the key.

"Without a road, a town can never prosper. You must have a good road and the county seat both."

He said this last part over and over. He still tells me now, in almost every letter he writes, asking about what he hopes is my empire and saying he needs to come see it for himself soon since he's nearly ninety.

I'm working to make my Memphis out at Chickasaw Bluffs but it's a hard place. Roughneck boatmen from up and down the Mississippi, along with a muddy mix of frontier settlers and come-to-trade Indians. All of them rowdy with alcohol and difficult. I chose the name Memphis because it means enduring and beautiful and I need it to be both.

Buying the Bluffs was an enormous investment but it should pay off. People warm to my William immediately. I take great pride in this quality of his since I lack it myself. Pretty as he is, he can talk to anybody. Perhaps due to his profound democracy, he is welcoming without seeming weak and this strikes a crucial balance on the frontier.

William knows full well that I sent him out to the Bluffs as much to protect my negroes from his incessant leniency as to give him a good start but he doesn't let it bother him. He is handy with managing my second store and his eye for reading counterfeit money serves us in good stead.

I still believe the troubles we are having out there stem more from the place itself and its history than from anything William has done wrong thus far. But we're dug in pretty deep so this venture needs to succeed.

Debt has always been my father's worst fear. He loves to tell detailed stories of great men, even celebrated ones, who find themselves falling into debt then watch everything they've built get dismantled brick by brick. Brick by sodding brick, he'd start repeating whenever he'd had one drink too many.

I remember being determined not to let debt happen to me. I made sure I was the main surveyor measuring every tract before I started buying and selling land myself. My father lobbied hard to secure me the federal commission to draw the Indian boundary line so I could steer it where we wanted it to go, keeping Memphis on our side instead of theirs. Then I had myself appointed tax collector and I still list myself short whenever possible.

I hear my father saying no need to tell everything you know and I see Wash's book tucked in my liquor cabinet upstairs. I do record some income from it because everyone knows he's my traveling negro, but no one else knows the true numbers except for Wash. I tuck most of that money straight into my pocket. My farm does not begin to pay my debts and nothing is cheap with ten children and six of them girls.

My wife Mary anchors the far end of my dinner table. She is an appropriate woman. Appropriate and capable. But my eyes don't catch on her in a room full of people and I have never once gotten that drifting feeling I remember so well from Susannah. That feeling of falling. But Susannah is dead and buried. Now I work to remind myself that expecting love in marriage is a young man's folly.

Mary gazes at me through luminous blue eyes set wide in her serene face, choosing all the while what she will notice and what she won't. She's the kind of person who can walk up to an overlook and not see a thing. By the time she's near enough to the edge to attain the vista, her mind has already turned back to the picnic she has brought and how best to arrange the spread.

I can see now that, like many people to whom something truly severe has happened, Mary has always refused life at some level. It was late spring when she stood up from working in the field outside her family fort just in time to watch three Cherokee tomahawk her only brother and her father. She ran and hid until I went looking.

She was sixteen to my forty when I took her in and determined to become my wife. I was surprised to find myself drawn to anyone after the deadening that had settled on me in my twenties after the shocking loss of Susannah and our son. But it seemed wherever I turned that fall, there Mary was, eyes shining. Before long, she was pregnant and it was settled.

William and Livia were born before we ever got around to marrying. Back then, thank God, preachers were still scarce. Created a legitimacy problem but I was able to sort it out during one of my legislative terms. Wrote my first two children into law, changing their name from hers to mine.

As luminous as Mary was at sixteen, I can see now that she has always been oddly hard, closed somehow. I attributed this tendency to her trauma and thought it would melt away in the course of our life together, but it has gained ascendancy instead. She chooses not to look too deeply at whatever she feels she can do nothing about. It makes me want to shake her sometimes. Turn her face to the storm.

Especially since she has brought the Bible into all our days, leaning ever harder on it. I fail to see how people can hold that book between themselves and life as if to stave it off. That book with all its horror and lust and bloodshed. But I've decided this is not for me to understand. So while I have been Mary's husband for more than thirty years and have no real complaints, I would not say I've had much company.

And yes, I have made family again and again with a woman I neither recognize nor understand anymore. Once the candle is out and I can no longer see that flat look in her eye, I lie down beside her and draw up some kind of wanting. It is during these times that I feel we are not completely apart. And there's no room for the Bible between us either. There's no room for the Bible when I feel her palms clutching my back and pulling me to her, when I can feel her wanting something beyond order and the smooth functioning of our household.

But by and large, I feel more connected to the horses I've raised, the negroes I've owned, and the accounts I've tended than to my wife and most of my children. I build a world and they live in it, knowing nothing of its geology. Protected and innocent while I do the work of turning the crank, finding the necessary momentum wherever and however I can. They don't want to know the details, only the results.

I first laid eyes on Mena in late March of 1796. I remember the year because that's when Thompson told me his big news. He was doing some final buying for his boys and we'd planned our visits to overlap as usual.

Charleston was in full bloom. You could smell the jasmine even in Auction Square. I had been at the market all morning and was about to leave to meet the old man for lunch when I saw Mena standing in a line along the brick wall that ran down the far side of the yard. She was in a raggedy group from a rogue ship so the prices were low.

Thompson had always warned me to stay away from direct imports, insisting that countryborn were much more manageable than saltwater. And these few did look pretty poorly, scuffling amongst themselves and keeping their backs to us. Mena was the only one facing forward. She stood perfectly still. Tall and thin with her hair cropped close.

Idle curiosity really because I was shopping for men. But then I saw the flat net of muscles across the top of her back and the smooth curve at the shoulder. And she stood evenly on both feet without cocking a hip like so many do.

Then she turned to look at me. You would have thought she felt my eyes on her. She didn't glance at me and then away like most of them. Mena gazed at me even and steady until I began to wonder what it was she saw.

As the line moved forward towards the block, she took only as many steps as needed to keep her place, trailing her fingers along the wall, coming to a stop when the rest did. All without ever taking her eyes off me. After long enough of that, I had to look away.

I was relieved when I bumped into Edgar, a friend of my brother David, even though he stood there talking at me for a full five minutes without realizing that the smoke from his cigar was drifting into my face and I was not actually listening. I acted as if I saw someone I knew so I could walk away from him.

As soon as there were enough men between us so Edgar could no longer see me, I turned back to the block. Mena was the next one to go and still watching me. She did not quit even after they got her up there. The whole situation gained momentum as the men around me began to comment.

Even the auctioneer noticed and he started in with a familiarity that made my skin crawl. I must have lifted my hand just to put a stop to the whole thing. I don't know what made me do it and I regretted it instantly. But to say I had not meant to buy Mena makes me seem as if I did not know my own mind.

Edgar stood there, glancing back and forth from her to me, smiling as if he'd discovered some secret.

"I thought you said you came down here to buy a few men. Only men. Must be something else you're hunting," he said, letting his voice trail off as one corner of his mouth lifted.

Without even thinking, I told him I planned to lease her out. As soon as I said it, I knew it was a good idea.

After signing for Mena, I went straight to meet Thompson for lunch. He had one restaurant he preferred. Said he wanted gumbo stewed from a roux as dark as the men who cooked and served it.

I was late and he hadn't been able to wait. He sat in the sun by the window, staring down into an enormous bowl, and didn't lift his head until I pulled back my chair and sat. He smiled at me through the rising steam, holding a great hunk of torn buttered bread in one hand and his glass of golden ale in the other. I'd never seen him looking so well.

He dipped his bread into the thick brown stew brimming with chunks of pale shining crabmeat. As he lifted that bite to his mouth, he nodded for a waiter to bring me more of the same. We made a point of eating heartily whenever we met, still trying to ease our shared hunger from twenty years ago.

We'd spent most of 1777 chained together on a fetid prison ship anchored in New York Harbor, after being captured early on by the British in yet another sloppy retreat. Thompson was full of stories, and our long confinement on that floating hellhole gave him plenty of time to tell them to me. He said he had to talk to keep his mind off the stench making his eyes sting. I said at least his stories drowned out the sound of our bellies gnawing on nothing.

He loved to tell me how he'd carried his family up from the sugar islands after his father stroked during that last mass poisoning in 1757. One uprising too many, his father had said. These damn Africans will soon gain the upper hand. Too many of them, too few of us.

The stroke had garbled his father's speech but Thompson said he could understand "get us the hell out of here" whether his father spoke it clear or not. North Carolina had offered them good terms and low prices so they brought the whole family and what few negroes had not been infected by insurrection fever. Sold off the rest to buy fresh.

Sitting there chained to Thompson, listening to him describe how best to manage negroes when we should have been out fighting our Revolution, weighed harder on me than on him. I was still a hothead in my twenties while he seemed old to me at forty.

I listened to him but I was determined to steer clear of slavery whether our Revolution managed to kill it off or not. After growing up around it, I'd already decided negroes were not the way to go. Nothing but complications and there's no end to it. My plan was to head West. Take hold of this far edge and build towns like my father did. If we lived. If we ever made it off that prison ship.

But Thompson became a kind of father to me during those months and we stayed in touch after our release, visiting every chance we could find. And it turned out his advice has served me well since I've ended up far deeper in this business than I ever imagined.

So the news he delivered to me over our bowls of gumbo on that fine spring day in Charleston came as an enormous surprise. He listened intently as I told him about buying Mena almost by accident and not quite knowing what to do with her. Then he set down his empty glass and said maybe he'd take her for long term hire in exchange for a healthy cash loan. His eyebrows jumped as he sat back in his chair.

Thompson told me he was washing his hands of his whole place. All nine hundred acres and two hundred negroes. It was his sixtieth birthday and he was getting out. He was sick to death of running what he called that damn empire patched together with mud from an endless swamp. Sick to death of all those negroes waiting for him to slip up or look away. Said it was those damn Ibos that first showed him he'd never have enough eyes to settle his place down for sure but he'd soldiered on for years before finding his way clear.

When I said would that we all could, he raised his glass. Told me he'd finally made enough money that his children should be able to take over. Campbell was into his twenties and Abigail had wisely married the family banker. Eli would find his way soon enough.

Thompson's enthusiasm was almost contagious. He'd found a ramshackle house on a nearby island called Nags Head and he was moving out there. All he needed was a brand new negro to take with him. One with no ties yet to anyone or anything. He said Mena sounded perfect. Of course, neither of us knew at the time that she was pregnant with Wash or that it would take me nineteen years to get them back.

Thompson

All I wanted was to be left alone and Mena looked like she knew how to do that. I had my boys carry us to this island the following week. Showed them the house I'd bought for nickels. They were horrified. Called it a rickety shack and stood around in my sandy yard fussing about my living out here by myself.

They took so strongly after my wife's mother, there was not a trace of me in either of them. Both of them so blond and clean featured, they looked almost girlish. Campbell leaning tall and thin and hesitant towards his younger brother Eli who took the lead in everything whether he knew how to manage it or not.

I worked hard to give those boys and their sister a good life but I never expected they'd always want more. More money coming in so they could buy fancier things, trying to act like they're not living in the middle of godforsaken nowhere. I wanted to tell them we're not in England, for God's sake. We're in the New World. Why would you want to go back to all that old rigamarole?

But I guess it's whatever you don't know and haven't had that pulls on you. I'd walked the halls of Parliament and known all those people. Same warts and gas underneath those fancy clothes, and even the powerful are weak to someone. To be fair, I'd spent my time chasing those same things but I was finished with it while my boys were just getting started.

As I walked them down to my crooked little dock, I remember wishing I could find a way to like them more. Never suspected I'd be so glad to see those two climb back in my boat and go. Said I didn't want to see them or anyone else from my place except for every three months to drop off my staples and send my man Paymore when they couldn't make it.

This house had just what I needed. Two rooms, each one backed up to the big central fireplace. Good broad windows with shutters that closed tight. A porch looking out over the sound in the distance, a kitchen attached to the side, and a loft upstairs for Mena. Plenty of room up there and it stayed warm next to the chimney. Row of small windows ran under the eaves and two at each end swung open for a cross breeze and some light.

The whole house was sheltered even as it had a long view. It sat in a dip at the top of a small hill. High enough to dodge rising water but squat enough to duck the wind. Wind coming off that water could tear the hair right from your head.

Thickets of wax myrtles growing close kept us pretty well hidden. A wide meadow full of rusty gold grass fell away towards the sound shimmering behind a row of pines. Huckleberries roped with vines made another dense thicket all the way to the road which was deep sand and slow going. Bad road, tangled woods, and two big dogs made sure no one snuck up on us.

Good people out here but kind of woolly. No real pirates left but it was a pretty rough crew. We came from all walks of life and we pretty much left each other be. My boys tried to turn up their noses, but to me it was a relief. I've always liked all kinds and my wife did too. A bit of an adventurer she was. Could talk to a post. She would have enjoyed this place. Should have come here sooner. Brought her with me. Might have saved her from the fever.

The land and the weather out here made good levelers. Didn't matter what you came in with. All that mattered was what you could do with what you had. There was some filching going on, drawing the ships onto the rocks to gut them for whatever they carried. But I kept my back turned. Did not get involved.

They were roughnecks but they had some ethics. Watched me nod just as normal as anything when we rode past each other and pretty soon, their scrawny wives started bringing me pails of blueberries. I nodded to thank them and sent Mena over there every now and then with a bird slung over her shoulder.

I taught her the island but soon found she knew more than me. She was good about melting into the woods. Got so she could scare me half to death, stepping out only when I rode right up on her. My horse shied every time.

I taught her how to speak enough English to be useful and how to use my gun in case anything happened to me. My boys would've dragged me home and locked me up for sure if they'd known. But Mena wasn't going anywhere. She kept her eyes on the water, but I could tell she knew that pulling something with me wouldn't carry her back as far as she wanted to go.

She had it all right with me. Some work cooking and cleaning but not too much. I tended to wear my clothes until they stood up on their own and I was a threat to cook a little myself and check on the garden too. She was spared the heavy chores since I had our staples dropped off every few months. Candles, preserves, soap and jars of smoked meat. She had wood to gather but the storms did most of it for her and gathering gave her a reason to go to the beach. Not bad. Not bad at all.

I had Mena on a task system and she kept her own clock as soon as she had her chores done. She rose in the dark so she could make it to the ocean and back before breakfast. But I started waking earlier and earlier myself as the days lengthened. I sometimes made a dawn ride. One loop around our end of the island and through the dunes. My old gelding seemed to like the change of pace and it sure beat lying in bed, staring at the ceiling. Aging angered me to the point that I was drawn into an endless fight against it. Trick was to keep moving so I added a swim whenever I could manage.

On my early rides, I sometimes came across Mena hovering at the water's edge with her eyes locked on the horizon and her long dark dress growing darker from where she kept stepping into the surf. She looked to me almost like a setter on point, pulled towards whatever it was she saw out there.

That first time I saw her in the water, I watched to make sure she was staying in the shallows, then I rode on. But when I came to the house after putting my horse away and found her fixing my breakfast with her dress wet up to her waist, I started to worry she would drown. I tried forbidding the ocean but soon found I had no leverage I was willing to use so I just fretted.

Then one day I was up first. It was a hot calm morning with no waves. One big sheet of water glowing glassy pink and so still that I stepped right in. Softest water I ever felt. I must have lost track of time because Mena was coming through the dunes, headed for the water just as I was stepping out of it. Made me glad I had kept my drawers on. Gladder still that I was finally finished with all that business.

But something about that morning made me realize I was tired of worrying Mena might drown. I decided to teach her to swim, just like I'd taught Eli and Campbell. First, how to float so she wouldn't panic from sinking. I stood facing her then lay back in the water, lifting my eyes to the sky, breathing shallowly and letting water fill my ears. Then I stood up and gestured for her to do the same.

It took her a minute. She kept kneeling in the water instead of lying back and I kept telling her no. Stay stiff like a plank. Then she'd nod and do the same thing. I turned her facing out to sea, laid one palm on the small of her back and used the other on her forehead, telling her to lean back but lie flat.

"Don't crouch and quit kneeling, dammit."

Soon as she did like I'd told her, I saw why she'd been working so hard not to. Soon as she lay back, soon as her dark billowy dress lay drenched against her front, I saw her belly for the first time. It reared up so round, I couldn't believe I hadn't seen it before. She was good and pregnant. Five months by my best guess. My mouth dropped open as she lay there floating in my palm but she kept her eyes on the clouds. Wouldn't look at me but she started breathing shallow just like I'd showed her. When I took my hand away, she floated on her own.

As I stood beside her, watching that soft pink water lapping close around her swelling belly, all I could think was time is strange and there's no escaping it ever. I felt that door I work so hard to keep bolted shut swing wide open and I was furious all over again at Sissy for refusing to let me teach our boy to swim.

After I lost my wife, it took me five years to go to the quarters when it should have taken me forever. Sissy somehow managed to make it seem like she was choosing me when nothing was further from the truth. But her husband was already dead and she needed gold pieces as much as anyone. Soon enough there was a son. And from his very beginning, my third boy looked and acted so much like me that my chest caved in to lay eyes on him.

But I tried to leave him to Sissy. Thought it would be easier on everybody. The only thing I insisted on was that he learn to swim. That big lake wrapped so close around my place seemed to be asking for trouble. But Sissy said she didn't want that water touching even his feet and she pitched such a fit when I sent for him that I let it go.

So when this third boy of mine, the only one who actually resembled me, when he ventured too far afield on the day he turned fifteen, and when those hooligans from the next county over called him a runaway and chased him with dogs into deep water on the far side of my lake, when he went in over his head rather than let them catch him, it did not take him long to drown. The biggest dog kept after him so he was still kicking and thrashing as the water came warm and maybe even welcome into his lungs.

Those damn crackers dropped him at the back of my barn like they were throwing something away. I stood over his body laid out in my last stall for the longest time. Everything about him was me. Back when I was young and strong and thought I knew. All of it covered in a golden cast.

There was not much else of Sissy to be found in his face, no matter how hard she'd worked to keep him from me. And it was his resemblance to me that did him in. It was his looking like me, talking like me and acting like me that had set my neighbors so firmly against him.

When I knelt next to his body, I had to grab fistfuls of yellow straw to keep myself from running my fingers along all the echoes. Brows and jawline, shoulders and elbows, even forearms and hands. Somehow I knew Sissy would not want me touching our boy. Not even now.

I tried to wrap his body so she would never know about that last dog but I was too late. She'd caught word and pounded on the stall door, saying let me see, he is mine, let me see, over and over until she was screaming and the horses were with her in her panic. I lifted the latch before too much of a crowd could gather.

I could not bear to watch her running her fingers over our boy's face then trying to mend the gashes in his forearm so I turned and left. Made sure she had what she needed for the funeral and worked to put it out of my mind. I buried my third son deep and then hunted a rock heavy enough to hold him down.

One morning, I had myself convinced Mena had run because I could not find her anywhere. Rode up and down the beach until I saw her folded dress nestled under some sea oats. After I reined in my gelding to look, I found her face breaking the wide smooth sweep of the water's surface. She floated right outside the waves, rising and falling on the incoming swells, drifting along the shoreline with the current. I had to watch for a while to make sure it was her and not a piece of driftwood. Every now and then, she'd break her float, twisting to burrow down into the water like it was a blanket.

My horse shifted his weight and snorted. Chewed the bit and tossed his head, trying to jerk his mouth free, so I loosed the reins and let him walk on out. I'd have stayed awhile longer but the morning was too soft to fight him. He veered away from the beach and headed back through the dunes towards the house.

Mena was always where I needed her to be so I let her have the water. The fact that I could deny her wasn't enough for me to do it. I did tell her later to be careful about who saw her out there. That some folks might think she was a witch to be so easy with it. She looked at me nodding then went her own way just like always.

Her belly swelled all summer while she swam and worked and swam. She kept going in even as the water started to cool because Wash was big inside her. There was a long late summer that year and the water coming up around her belly seemed to be the only thing that gave her relief. So Wash knew the movement of water before he was ever born. That and the rip and crash of the waves too.

I thought about having Paymore carry our midwife Lucy out here to bring Wash into the world. After all, Wash and Mena were my money to Richardson and I could not afford to lose either of them. But Mena shook her head no. Said she didn't want strangers close while she was down. Besides, it's not like I had one foot in the grave. I was still a good enough shot and if I couldn't pour hot water over some meal then God help me.

Wash kept us waiting well into November. He was late being born, as if he didn't want to come. Or maybe he was storing up. I watched Mena good but she slipped through my fingers. Shut her loft door right in my face and didn't open it till well after I heard him yelling. By the time I climbed the stairs, she had him settled in her lap, sitting close to the warm chimney. She tipped one shoulder back so I could see him good. He was fat and healthy with big eyes shining bright in his dark square face. Sized me up as solemn as a judge before turning back to her.

I left them to it and we stayed lucky that winter. Wash was a good baby and quiet but he'd look right through you from day one. Made you want to hear what he had to say well before he had any words. Sissy would say he's been here before and I'd believe her.

He didn't start to really fret till late spring but he sure made up for lost time. Enough of his coughing wail and I'd jerk my head towards the beach, telling Mena to take him and she did.

Soon as the water started warming, she went right in. Kept him tied tight to her, either facing her chest or else looking out over her shoulder from his place on her back. Often water was the only thing to soothe him. Seemed like no time at all before she was taking him deeper into the waves. Cupping her hand over his face and ducking into the curl but always bringing him up before he had a chance to panic.

I watched her lay those memories into that boy. Pale green light arching around him, a roaring going down into his bones and water pouring. He was quiet like her but I saw that slow smile break across his face as those white patterns of foam slid down his skinny sides. Pretty soon, he could swim on his own and hold his breath for a long time too. Worrying her and me both until he'd pop back up with a small round stone in his hand, beaming.

Wash

My mamma kept pulling me into deeper water, telling me it was safer there, but it was a long time before I'd believe her. Used to be, I'd stay right at the edge thinking I knew best. But that shorebreak knocked me round till I learned to take her word for it.

She'd watch me come staggering out and tilt her head, with one side of her mouth crooking down, trying not to smile. She was saying you can let me tell you or you can find out for yourself, either way. I'd lie down beside her till the sky stopped spinning. Enough of that and I'd head straight for the deep where she liked to stay.

We'd bob out there, watching the backs of the waves rise up as they rolled away from us to crash on the sand. She showed me the foam pulling into new shapes. Said that's what happens in ceremony. All that swirling, that's what spirit feels like when it gets to moving. Even in this quiet water out here, it's rising and falling like breathing. You feel it tugging on you? That's how spirit moves, once you learn to listen. And you can drown on dry land just as easy as you can drown in this ocean, so pay attention.

She made altars all over that island. The first one I barely remember. It was in a real hidden place where palmetto leaves brushed my face when I stepped through and saw two mud people, all worn down. Ancestors. They was us and we'll be them was what she said as she sprinkled water and some ash then knelt there talking to em for a long time.

I was still small when we went one day and found em broke in half, kicked in the dust. She wrapped the broken pieces in a white cloth and took em to the water. Held em under till they melted, then rinsed the cloth out good. Looked out over the waves like she was saying go on home. Maybe it's safer there.

After that, she always made her altars look like an accident. Just some junk so nobody else saw it for what it was. She made one in our loft but she left it real makeshift in case Thompson ever climbed up there. Just a small pile of stones laying on a bed of pine straw in the far corner.

And she made offerings too. Long curved seedpods for the life they carried. A faded turtle shell for patience laid inside the pale curved rib of a fox. A few scattered shark teeth sharp enough to cut. Wild pink roses from the bush beside the front porch steps just because she liked the smell.

She'd take each treasure and breathe on it, or else rub it against her throat or inside her elbow, then lay it down on the pine straw. Whenever it started to feel crowded, she'd nod at me to pick a few to take and bury at the foot of our favorite trees. Sometimes she'd take a pocketful of petals down to the beach and wade in the water to scatter em till they drifted in a bigger and bigger circle.

She'd talk about it some but told me watch out for words, no matter what tongue. Said she didn't get time to learn everything for sure so she just tried to see with her heart.

Make some place to kneel and leave your offerings. It keeps you thankful. Take your journeys in the spirit world first. Be sure you go all the way there and back in spirit before you even step out your own door. It's easier for God to keep an eye on you, knowing what you have in mind. And make your piece. Keep that talisman strong and wear it till it's done. Then lay it somewhere safe but not till after you make your next one.

She made my pieces for me when I was little, chewing a small patch of leather till it was soft enough while she gathered what she knew I needed, then stitching everything up tight inside.

She'd wear it awhile before she strung it round my neck or else my waist. She never even told me what was in there.

Then one day it was time for me to make my own. She sent me to find my treasures. Told me bring back only what I needed the most, but I was about to turn seven so I came back with a shirttail full. Laid everything out, all proud. Then I looked up to see her holding my next piece of leather so small in her palm. I had so much too much, it hurt my throat.

She just folded her hand closed and sat there, tipping her head and waiting on me to do like she said and choose. That was the day when I learned how a shark tooth, a tiny piece of hair from those dark spidery tree roots and some pebbles worn almost back down to sand can be enough.

Thompson

The one time I caught Mena at her mojo, I was riding over the dune just as she was laying some animal bones in a shallow grave and covering them with sand. I pointed from her hands fluttering over the hole to my own chest and back, raising my eyebrows to ask if that was some version of me she was burying.

She shook her head no with some force. All I cared about was that it wasn't me. Beyond that, I knew to stay out of it. I kicked my gelding on along, telling myself I'd best beef up my own prayers.

When she talked to Wash, Mena's ribbony murmur sounded like a small creek running over stones. I remember wondering what stories she could possibly be telling him that went on and on like that. But I was glad she was bothering to teach him, glad to have enough slack to grant her some and more than glad that I knew enough by then to leave her well alone. Every time I heard them, I rode on past.

What Mena caught on to right at the beginning and never did let go of was the sun setting over the sound. She'd get everything done and ready for my supper, then she'd stand there, so still she was almost trembling, with her eyes fixed on me till I'd nod and then she'd be off. Drawn down there like a magnet, every day as urgent as the last, for as long as the light held. With that boy trailing right behind her, steady as a hound and taller every day.

It took me years of watching to see what she was doing, but even before I understood it, I let her go. She seemed centered on it somehow and she always had her work done. My supper laid out and everything else put away. I hate having someone hovering over me while I eat anyway. If I can't ladle my own food, I might as well climb on into my bed, fold my hands across my chest and get ready to meet my maker.

It was not until I went riding after an early dinner one summer night and came across her showing Wash the sun setting over the sound that I understood the whole story. I watched her hands flutter in the air, making what looked like mountains running down to the water. Then she made a circle of sun with one hand and drew it down behind the flat floating line of ocean she made by holding her other palm out parallel to the ground, letting it rise and fall a little to show the waves.

That's when I saw it. She'd found a sun that set over the water the way it must have done at home. The way it must have been doing when they stole her. What her hands did next, going around her own neck and making to drag her off, that's when I knew how it had happened.

She'd gone down to watch the sunset like she always did, even though the trouble had long since started and her family told her not to go. I could tell when she wagged her finger at her boy, saying no, don't you dare, she was being her parents talking to her younger self. She had nodded and smiled but kept going to the water. And that was when they caught her.

But here she is, and she's found the sun setting into the water instead of rising from it, with Wash growing up straight and strong and not getting hit.

Wash

It was in the quiet of the sound where my mamma told me stories. Soon as we stepped into the trees, the roar of the waves fell away. Like the woods was one big mouth closing up with us inside it. Old pines leaning against each other with vines tangled between em and a bed of sea grass grown long like hair, all matted round their trunks.

Might have been spooky if we hadn't known it so well. We knew to cross the swampy part close by the double sycamore instead of higher where the water stayed murky, full of jelly lilies. We knew the black snake with brown marks lived in that one log hollowed out from rot. We knew how to stick to the deep sandy paths and stay away from the wide hardpacked trails that other folks used. And we knew how to disappear whenever we heard somebody coming.

Horse might smell us and spook or snort a little, but most folks would kick him on past without looking too close. Said the place was haunted. Those thick woods gave them the willies so they either went round or else hurried on through. But most times, that bogey man was us. Just us.

We'd work our way through the woods, picking chinquapin nuts for the winter. Get to the sound by midmorning. So quiet with still water stretching as far as I could see. One big mirror making two of everything and shallow enough for me to walk way across that smooth floor of pure white sand, giving under each step I took and drifting like sugar behind me.

At the near end, there was a tiny curved beach between these two trees so old their wet black roots fanned in the air from the sand washed out underneath. Just like sitting in a circle of great big spiders, my mamma said as she settled us in. Made me think of how old man Thompson used to shake his head over her, muttering about how she wasn't afraid of much.

But truth was, she had a whole different set of things to be scared of. Said it wasn't so much the thing itself as being surprised by it. That's why she told me everything. Said she wanted me to be ready, come what may. Wanted me to know whatever I needed to know, and since she had no idea what all that might be, she told me everything she could think of. Started this telling long before I ever understood her and there wasn't nothing she didn't tell me she thought I could use.

Sometimes all I got was the rhythm and the shape of the story, the rise and fall of her voice and the shapes she made in the air with her hands. Sometimes what happened in one of her stories didn't come clear to me till much later. I'd find myself in the middle of some trouble, then I'd see her hands moving in my mind's eye, the look on her face all those years ago. Then I'd say to myself, oh. Here it is. This right here is what she meant.

She never knew how much time she had with me out on that island under old man Thompson. We knew he'd die one day, and his boys stayed itching to get their hands on us, so she made sure I had hold of all my people and my places. She told it to me over and over like she was drawing pictures in wet sand. Feeding them feeds us was what she said. That's how we watch over each other.

But I had to wait on her to get ready. And I knew not to ask questions. Best sit still and watch her hands move. Seemed like the telling was as much for her as for me. She was homesick and wanted to keep her people strong and bright in her mind's eye.

Her mamma, round and sweet. Grabbing you close, making a game out of giving you some sugar. And her daddy, so serious he was scary. I know just how he was from watching her tell me about him. I'd seen her get just like that, drawing up inside herself and giving you that look. Made you think twice before bothering her.

She knew my daddy's people too. My daddy's daddy was soft and kind of nosy in a way, but most folks didn't mind. When you went to him with trouble, he helped you if he could. And my daddy's mamma was kind of standoffish, or maybe she just seemed that way next to her husband staying in everybody's business. And my mamma's brothers and sisters, all older than her, with children of their own. Her nieces and nephews. My cousins. She told me about every single cousin I had. How they were like and not like me.

I loved it when she talked about me. How I had my uncle's eyes set so square in my face. Said I had my daddy's wide hands and her narrow feet. Where these bony shoulders like bird wings came from she had no idea. She'd lean into my side, rubbing my back, making me smile.

Said she knew it might make it harder on me, having such a strong clear picture of how our life was before. But she was not about to have a child of hers walk through this world, no matter for how long, not knowing who he was and who his people were, both the living and the dead. Harder or easier, she was not going to have it.

Enough of my mamma's stories and I could feel our people all round me, the littlest ones jostling and playing so close and the older ones darting through the clearing. I'd turn my head real quick, thinking I saw somebody at the edge of the woods, but I never could catch em with my eyes. I had to settle for their breath on the back of my neck and their hands steadying mine. I mighta been spooked by it but my mamma treated it so regular. Pointed to my goose bumps, then smiling and rubbing my back so calm, saying there they go, trying to get next to you.

It was luck, she said, finding the sound. A place where the sun fell down in the water like it did at home. She never thought she'd see that again ever. Day falling into night didn't feel right to her here. Said the ocean looked like it felt left behind at dusk.

She never did get used to facing east. Made her uneasy. So she gave thanks every night for the sound, for the sun sliding down into the water, letting it shine that gold back to the sky, and sending the rest of the world falling into pink and gray and shadows. That was how it should be, she always said. That was right.

∞

It's those times I think about when I get up on em. When Richardson sends me someplace and I have to get up on em, I think about all those hearts of mine, crowding so close beside that quiet sound. I keep my mind turned towards how I'm handing all my people some new bodies to live inside.

All those spirits hovering round me as real and hollow as shadows, I want em right here by me. I want mine right here in this world where I can get at em. I want to grab em with my own two hands and feel em wriggling and squirming to get away from me. Running to their mammas, asking who is that scary man.

I want these little ones of mine crawling all over everything. Some will make it and some won't but they will all be mine. They'll be up under white folks and they'll get messed with and beat down and broken, but they will be mine whether they ever know it or not. And some will make it and they belong to us and us to them. My mamma and my daddy and theirs, running in the blood of these children I keep dragging into this world.

They will look in some scrap of mirror and they will see us. Showing up in the shape of their eyebrow or the feel of their tongue sitting inside their mouth. They will see us out of the corner of their eye and feel us breathing close, laying our hands on their hands, whether they ever know it for sure or not, we'll be gathered close. All the time.

So that's what I do. I get up on em, one after the next, and I keep my heart full with all those spirits of mine. I'm pulling my people back into this world so they can be here with me. Right here in this world, cause I know this world won't last. These here will die off and mine will breathe in new air and it will be a new day.

So bring em on, those that's messing with me and laughing. It's all right. I know who gets the last laugh. Go head, bring em right on.

So I got me a setup and I try to leave most of the rest of it alone. Sit in the sun on cool days and move to the shade of the willow on hot ones. Not like the rest of these folks round here, always trying to get lighter and stay lighter. To hell with that. The darker I am, the less will show.

And I keep most everybody looking out for the back of my hand. Most of these little ones stay on the jump from me. I know what folks think of me and sometimes I let the way they see me rise up in me till I'm cutting the buck real good. Fighting just to feel my hand coming down, till I can read my scars like words on a page.

Life comes over me in waves, with the bad and the good twined tight together, making me take all of it or none. And what I do know is I can't stay here without nothing at all. That's like a plant stuck in his little patch of dirt, with rain just too uncertain.

They can take me however they like. I ain't got a thing I can do for em. Too many of em sitting on ready, wanting to run and trying to plan, but I can't fall for it anymore. I been through that door enough times to see it don't lead nowhere. Can't none of us see far enough, even in our mind's eye, how far we'd have to make it before we'd be out of these woods. I'd rather be here, with my hearts and my having everything worked into some kind of manageable than having to start over some place else, with this same mess and folks I don't even know.

And I'm a Washington for Richardson too but he may be getting more than he bargained for. My face and my ways starting to crop up on most places round here. Some favor me more and some favor me less but it's me everywhere all the same. He laid that big man's name on me and I'm making my own country, then weaving back and forth across it, going to see Pallas.

It's hard on her just like it's hard on me, but life is hard in all kind a ways and this is just one of em. We can't have each other to ourselves but her knowing and mine go together some kind a way. Day or night, she's pulling most all mine into this world and naming plenty of em too. Hers is the first face they see, so we got less but at the same time, we got more.

Parts of your heart will jump up trying to catch onto life, and you can't do nothing but slap em back down, so we stay real careful. We meet out and away and secret. We find our time together and it's sweet enough to last us these long stretches in between. Drives me clean out sometimes but Pallas sees more to me than anybody and I can't make do with less.

But it sure did gall me to have this be what Richardson ended up wanting from me. Working you to death is one thing but this here was something else.

I saw from the beginning this work would set me apart from the rest. Sooner or later, they'd put me with somebody's somebody. And that was just the start. I saw trouble stacking right up.

But I wasn't in the field and I wasn't driving and having to give folks the lash. And I was getting enough to eat. More than enough. As for set apart, growing up the way I did, with a mamma like mine, I was already set apart anyhow.

Besides, I was still young and Richardson was careful to sneak it up on me. He started me out slow and kept me to the fine ones I'd already been eyeing. Like Nelle. Right from the first, he made sure he let me think it was me choosing. Like I didn't do nothing but fall in a tub of butter.

And it didn't take much. Get my hands on her good, feel her snug round me and let it come over me. Running up my spine and cresting over my shoulders in a wave, keeping me curling into her. Ain't no way it ever feels bad.

And I looked away from the rest. Looked away from em watching me. Back then, they still bothered to hide it. Wasn't till later when they stood in the open.

But pretty soon it added up and added up, stories started to go round, and I got riled. Set to work on not letting em take nothing from me. They'd bring her to me in that barn and I'd think about all kind a things, trying to keep myself to myself. They'd nod at her to take her shirt off and she'd stand there unbuttoning, one slow hand after the next, till her cloth fell open and she glowed whether she wanted to or not, so I'd call a picture to my mind.

Bright pink skin of a possum, just been yanked inside out, all crisscrossed with blue veins and deep red ropes of blood ringing the holes where the skin tore from the head, paws and tail. I'd fill my mind's eye with the inside of that possum skin till no matter what she looked like, I'd just lay there, heavy and soft between my thighs.

It worked but only for a minute. Quinn told me I could find a way to hook up with my business or I could sit and wait for a whipping. Watch everything get taken away from me bit by bit till I was right back in that far field, shackled with the rest of the troublemakers and bringing up the rear.

I saw us all chained together, trying to hoe that last row with some cracker riding close on us all day, dark to dark, straight through all those goddamn songs. I'd already got put in the far field once, back at Thompson's place, and I'd already decided I wasn't going back.

This way, I didn't have to be tied to nobody. Didn't have to ask nobody for nothing. Besides, it had already made me mad, Richardson messing with the only thing I'd ever known for sure. This one thing was mine from beginning to end, and here he comes, trying to put his foot right in the middle of me.

I wasn't gonna let it happen like that. One way or other, I wasn't gonna lose feeling good. Not in this lifetime. It got so I didn't care how they messed with me. Right or wrong, I went with it more than against it. And that's how I made it all the way to now.

So I take it all. And the perks and the treats too. Sit in the shade of the willow and pocket that extra bacon. Go see Pallas when I can so long as I keep coming back. Even that damn Quinn, watching me through the stall door with a hand on himself.

At least Richardson keeps him off the girls. Says he doesn't want no mixing. Not when he has gone to this trouble to start some fine lines with me. Says he's building something and the last thing he wants is some trashy snaggletooth strain seeping into his plans and draining the African right out. He tells me he has a reputation to look after. That people come to him for his negroes.

He tells me all about it, like I need to hear whatever words he wants to wrap round this work. Then he says I need to keep a very old truth in the front of my mind. There's always some evil to balance every good.

Richardson

I have learned over time to carry Wash to other places. Let him do most of his work away from home and let mine have their own families. You must give them a reason to do right. Thompson was certainly on the money about that.

It's best to keep everything as separate as possible. I decided to stick to my own rules after one exception I made nearly bit me right back. I'd received Delph without wanting or needing her. Accepted her in repayment of an old debt and planned to sell her on my next trip downriver since money's always much more useful to me. She was midway through her twenties so far as she knew and surly but light skinned and lean, with those Chinese eyes so many seem to favor. She wouldn't be on my place long, and pregnancy would increase her value, so I put her with Wash.

Didn't take her but a day or two to go after him and she went after him good, never mind the dullness of that oyster knife she'd found. And she near about got him too.

I had him in the barn showing him to Pendleton and Ames to see if they wanted me to write them in his book. They were all standing close. Pendleton had his hand on Wash's shoulder and Ames was looking hard into his good eye, making sure he believed me about the wandering eye being from an old blow.

I thought I heard something before I nodded to Wash to drop his britches and turn around for them to check him, but I was as surprised as anyone when Delph came hurtling from that pile of hay, heading straight for his crotch and screaming to wake the dead.

Thank God Ames had a quick way about him and grabbed her knife hand. All I could see was over Wash's shoulder with his wide back to me and his britches down around his ankles. Then the back side of Ames with that crazy gal's free arm flailing like a pinwheel, her legs kicking at him in a frenzy and that knife glinting in her other hand. I was damn lucky she didn't nick Ames, not to mention carrying off Wash's grab bag to the great beyond.

I have learned to be careful about just exactly which ones I put Wash on, and where, because these incidents echo out like rings spreading across a lake from a thrown stone. And it was not enough to get Delph off my place immediately. I sent her to be sold that very afternoon but still the story traveled. There's a pair of eyes to see every single thing and word gets out regardless.

Even with Delph long gone, the picture she made busting out of my hay pile with that knife in her hand, coming after all of us in a way, although what she was after was Wash's in particular, that picture lasted much longer. That picture loomed large in every single mind on my place, whether they'd seen it or not.

I heard mine telling that story over and over, the way they do every single thing that happens around here. I can't always make out that muttering, murmuring way they have of talking amongst themselves, but I knew damn well when they were telling that one. A steady flow of story, torn here and there by rising chuckling.

So you must be careful what you buy, what you keep and, most of all, what you put together. If she is quite fine, then maybe I will run some risks, but you must be careful.

Quinn has changed his mind about my using Wash as our traveling negro. Now that he knows him better, he says I'm a damn fool to breed for sense, and works as hard as he can to keep Wash's get from around here.

"You are digging your own grave," he told me. "All our graves for that matter. Thinking is not what we want. Working is what we want. Work and picking and grubbing and yessir and nosir and being damn grateful. We need them so thick they have to work to wipe their own ass.

"I don't understand how you of all people, with your damn books, can fail to see this. Let your horses be fine, but for God's sake, keep your niggers muddy. Can't you see? Each of these smart ones adds another log to the fire they've been trying to build all along. We've only just now gotten a handle on these murderous savages and here you are refusing to look logic in the face with the negroes."

Quinn frets constantly about impossible uprisings and fantastical conjurings. Especially since Denmark Vesey staged his doomed rebellion in Charleston last summer. I keep trying to calm him down.

"Vesey only started a rebellion, he didn't come close to finishing it. They never do. And anyway, he's dead. That negro is dead, along with plenty of other perfectly good hands that likely had nothing to do with it. Lost to hysteria."

I tell Quinn it won't come to that. Not all the way out here. One of them will always turn before it amounts to anything. You can be sure of it. But Quinn just stands there, breathing so hard I can hear him clear across the room.

I think it must stem from the time he spent tending those boatloads of white refugees that landed in Baltimore back in 1794, fleeing the slave revolt down in that island hellhole they now call Haiti.

Quinn loves to tell me about it as if I didn't know already. How Toussaint and Boukman drove out the last of the whites with fire covering the northern plain. Told them they could come back and then killed them all. I can almost predict the moment when Quinn will tell me again how that island is proof that these negroes will do anything.

Every time, I try to remind him of the facts. It was the only successful negro slave revolt in history. The only one. On a small sugar island already torn to shreds by the English and the French fighting over it. Doesn't take much initiative to seize the advantage there. That kind of thing could never happen here, no matter how many newspapers keep us up nights worrying.

"Try to have a little more faith. There are ways to manage negroes if you will only learn them. And Wash's get are not our problem. They are springing up in pastures other than ours. And Quinn, they are children."

"Well, they aren't going to stay children! Before you know it, they'll be crossing into our fields, torches in hand, along with the rest, freed by all these old men trying to clean their slate before they meet their maker. It will happen, that much I'm sure of."

He starts in on his favorite stories about witchcraft and slaughter, about bayonets and infants cut from women's bellies, but for some reason, on this one particular day, he stops short.

"Or maybe you aren't worried about it, pushing past seventy the way you are. Maybe this isn't yours to worry about it, is it?"

"No," I say, smiling and shaking my head. "No, Quinn, it is not. You got that right."

Quinn is not always the blind fussing mole that he seems. Sometimes, he can see a little way down the road and a minute into me.

"Yes, I do want to leave everybody with something to do and dammit why shouldn't I? I came into this world fighting. Always fighting so these children of mine would even have pastures to worry about. I made this place from nothing and then rescued it from the dismal straits you let it fall into while I was off trying to win my last war. And I will leave it to my sons. If they can't figure out how to hold on to it, then they don't deserve it. A man who has not had to work and grab and claw usually does not amount to much and sometimes not even then.

"Quinn, you worry too much. Besides what the hell else could I do with Wash at this point? It would be throwing money away to pull him off it now."

"I say sell him down the river and get another one in here more like a plank. And nothing like that damn Nero either. I told you and told you about him but you wouldn't listen."

I cut him off because now he has made me angry.

"Dammit, Quinn, it was you who pushed me into this in the first place, with all your complaining about how we needed cash because the trade on our boats from New Orleans was not going as well as you'd hoped. And it was me who was arrested in Philadelphia for unpaid bills, for Christ's sake. And then had to sit through that mockery of a trial before you could see your way to sending me some of my own money.

"Let's not forget, it's my money sunk into these boats, my place carved out of nothing, my head working all this out instead of being split open by some tomahawk. I've made it this far, dammit, without having to take every idea you try to shove down my throat.

"Now I am well aware that as one man I cannot know and see everything. And I am of a generation that's being left behind as the world moves on, so I try to remain open to your suggestions. You do have a good idea every now and then, Quinn, and I take it.

"I didn't want any part of this whole scheme when you first brought it to me. And look at me now, counting and recounting the money we're making off your good idea. But what you don't seem to understand is that people pay for quality. You could get a dullard in here, but I guarantee you, you will spend more time and trouble covering more folks for less income, and many more chances for things to go wrong.

"You want to do something differently, you are free to do as you see fit. Go get yourself your own stockman and start your own line. Do whatever you want so long as you keep your man and your mess away from my place and my clients because I have my hands full."

∞

It is mid-September of 1823 and getting brittle with still no rain. Richardson rides through the gate into his yard at dusk. His gray gelding Omega stops right where his stableman Ben stands waiting.

Each time he dismounts after this long ride home from judging, the hard shock of his feet hitting the ground jars him more.

Omega stands close to him, large and hot, sweat having turned most of his light coat the color of his dark skin underneath, especially on his chest, belly and throat. He's still catching his breath from cresting that last hill. This rangy honest gelding has been by far the best of Gamma's get but Richardson wonders how many more miles he has in him.

He rests his hand on the worn smoothness of his saddle seat and the stirrups swing empty. The gelding chews his bit with a jangle and thunk, foam covering his lips. He tries leaning into Richardson, wanting to rub his face, itchy with drying sweat, up against something. Anything. Richardson digs the butt end of his crop into Omega's shoulder to keep him back and the horse snorts in frustration.

Richardson runs his eyes across the broad stone face of his house then past the cabins to the big barn behind. As always, Chatty has seen him coming and opened the big gate for him, and here's Ben reaching to take the reins.

But Richardson can't get the day off him. It had been his turn as magistrate when a negro woman a few towns over decided to carry herself out of this world, taking as many white folks with her as she could. The neighbors had panicked, calling hers an insurrection when they should have known it was more of a quick run to freedom. That's what his people called it whenever somebody went off like that. Real insurrections were much quieter and slower to build. More deliberate and more impossible.

Judging didn't used to get to Richardson but for some reason, this case kept running through his mind all the way home. That quiet slender woman sitting so still in his courtroom. Her slitting the husband's and wife's throats with a pastry cutter she had sharpened. The two of them dead in their bed. How her low keening had woken the couple's three small children who had come into the room in the middle of the night to find their parents lying in pools of moonlight and how they had automatically turned to her for comfort.

Her standing there with the blade still in her hand, her dropping it to grab those white children to her, and her holding them tight with blood all over her dress. How the neighbor had found them piled together up in her room in the attic. In her bed. She was holding the sleeping children in her arms, looking out over their heads through the window, watching the sky lighten.

All of it keeps coming back to Richardson, bright jagged images flashing into his mind. The way she sat so still and so straight, staring at the wall behind him, not even bothering to defend herself. The feel of his hand bringing the gavel down, the sound of the gavel landing on smooth wood and the rope hanging from the gallows.

Then writing a check from the state to reimburse the dead couple's estate for the loss of the woman. Richardson guessed the money would be held in trust for the children because they were still so young. He was trying to hurry and get it handled before too much of a crowd had a chance to gather and watch and then wreak havoc on their way home. He was trying to keep other people's negroes safer that way.

Riding back home through the dark falling in the woods, he could not stop wondering what had been the thing that tipped her over the edge. What had crossed her mind as her hand wrapped around that pastry cutter, having sat up half the night sharpening its blade against the stone of that big kitchen fireplace where the sound was muffled by the fire popping and crackling? What had it felt like standing over those people's beds, before and after?

And now, standing in his own yard next to his sweaty horse, turning to hand Omega off to Ben, he wonders whether Ben knows already. But Ben won't look at him, not even when Richardson pauses, hanging on to the reins a moment too long before laying them, smooth and worn shiny, across Ben's waiting upfacing palm.

"Did you know her?"

He and Ben stand there in the curve of Omega's neck, the horse's warm breath surrounding them. Ben keeps his eyes on the ground, closing his fingers around the soft leather of the reins and nods yes, he knows her. He thinks to himself about Charlotte being Heddy's wildest girl and here she has finally hit the wall that has been waiting for her all along.

Both men stand there thinking about her people long since come to cut her down and take her home until Omega dips his big gray head to nudge Ben's shoulder hard, knocking him off balance. Ben leads the gelding past the cabins to the barn where he'll strip off his tack, walk him cool, rub him down with a twist of straw to loosen the drying sweat and then feed him.

Richardson turns toward the house. He'll have to tell them about it. He can already hear their questions, fueled to a fever pitch by fear of an insurrection, stoked by that small quiet woman. A part of him wishes he was ignorant enough to believe an insurrection was even a possibility out here. He envies his family their obliviousness.

The smooth leather of his knife sheath lies warm against his hip under his clothes and all he can think about is his hands closing around a drink. He hears Thomas Jefferson saying we're holding a wolf by the ear but cannot afford to let go and he finally begins to understand why old man Thompson went off to that island to get shut of it all.

Richardson manages to slip up to his study uninterrupted. He shuts the door softly behind him and goes to stand by the window, leaving his candle unlit so he can look down through the trees instead of seeing himself reflected. And so no one will know where he is, for a few minutes at least. A pale harvest moon rises huge and fast, dwarfing his whole place and casting its improbable brightness across the broad floorboards.

Richardson, like Thompson, had carried in his mind the picture that had prevailed just after Independence. There had always been slaves but there had also been plenty of free. There had been free negroes Richardson had respected. Done business with and argued with both.

The Revolution had opened a window and he, like many of his fellow soldiers, had hoped slavery would slip right out of it. It wasn't only a new country they'd wanted, it was a new world. But that window had closed and slavery had strengthened instead, doubling its grip on all of them.

The liquor has loosened his chest some but there's still not room to draw a deep breath. And he can't hide in his study. He must go down to dinner. His family has already gathered and sits waiting. They fall silent when they hear his boots on the stairs. Eager to hear the story he doesn't want to tell.

The smooth golden brown wood of the long table glows in the candlelight amidst the clatter of serving spoons against platters full of food. Roast chicken marinated in a sweet brown sauce and slow cooked until it falls off the bone, legs splayed out as if drunk and coming off with one tug. Wine glows deep red in its glasses. Family silver from Baltimore lies heavy on creamy linen napkins. Late lilies from his garden stand in clusters, pale and fragrant. Everything is beautiful and orderly but Richardson cannot find the pleasure he usually takes in it.

He looks down the table at his much younger wife anchoring the far end. The flatness in Mary's eyes grows flatter still when something like this happens and tonight his gaze slides right off hers. She's already decided what she thinks about the double murder and the hanging without having heard a word from him. An unfortunate matter well handled and over with. No need to discuss it.

Most of their children sit gathered between them, eager to hear more. Livia and Lucius sit opposite each other on his left and right hand. They are his undeniable favorites, along with William. Livia is well past grown while Lucius remains runty at twelve, but they mirror one another, each carrying their father's long narrow face, pale against dark brows and hair. Sharp brown eyes that don't miss much. They even flush the same pink, high on each cheek whenever their tempers flare, just like he does.

Diana, Caroline and Cassius bunch together in their late teens and early twenties. They all carry their mother's rounder features with her chestnut hair that Cassius has started to lose as he works relentlessly to usurp William's favored position.

Only William, Adele and Augusta carry a real mixture of both parents but William has been posted to manage Memphis, Adele has been married off to a merchant named Singleton to establish the Richardson store in New Orleans, and Augusta rarely comes to the table anymore. She always claims to be reading in her room but she can never come up with any titles when Richardson asks. Little James cannot reach the table yet and Mary Patton won't ever be able to manage it so Emmaline feeds them in the kitchen.

Richardson's father's gaze bears down on his from the portrait on the wall. The force of his father's ambition has poured over him for as long as he can remember and it has carved him into this particular shape. This drive to acquire and expand will gain momentum as it barrels through the family for generations but the first bull's eye it found was Richardson.

He has done everything that was expected of him, but as he looks down the long table, feeding his large family from his own land, nothing feels like he thought it would. Here is the life he has worked so hard to provide, and they are taking hold of it just as he had intended, but he worries they do not know what they need to know. His children look at him so brightly he finds himself wanting to pull one or the other aside to make sure they understand fully. All the considerations that must be weighed. The ramifications of this course of action or that one.

Trouble is, he doesn't know. Not anymore. Not for sure. He feels their unasked questions lurking and finds himself grateful for his wife's focus on the surface of things. Scenes from the day keep flashing through his mind. He feels a yearning pulling inside him but he does not know what it is for. All he knows is he feels most alone when surrounded by his family.

He drinks to fill the empty space around him and then speaks harshly, trying to take the edge off it. He pours himself drink after drink and watches the level drop in the decanter as the bourbon gradually gives him room to breathe. At the same time that it warms him and allows him to feel his feet on the ground, the liquor distances him from those around the table. Or maybe it magnifies the distance that already exists. He sits there listening to them talk but none of it touches him.

He watches his family from this faraway place like he's seeing them through a pane of glass. He wants to tell his story but he does not know how or to whom. Maybe Thompson could have heard him but he's been dead for years. Richardson's not even sure what his story is, just the dim sense that it may be through the telling that he can drag his life back onto the course he set for it long ago.

One last thoughtless comment about the murder and he has had enough. When Caroline asks whether Emmaline has a pastry cutter and whether she should be allowed to keep it, he pushes back his chair with a rough creak and stalks out of the dining room with his wife's quavering objections fluttering in his wake.

Richardson takes one of his long rambling walks to get away from his house full of people and no one to talk to. He heads for the barn and finds himself talking to Wash. Drinking and telling Wash all the things he cannot say as they sit together with the night falling between them. Mesmerized by the sound of his own voice rising up out of him, Richardson pours his rivers of words into the dim quiet stillness of that big barn for Wash to take or leave behind. It is as free as he has ever felt.

Wash

It was the day he rode home from stringing up Charlotte. That was the first night Richardson came down here well past dark.

Used to be, he'd come to the barn at the end of the day, like he had to tell me something for tomorrow, like it wouldn't get done right less he made sure. Then he'd stay through nightfall, acting like it was an accident, like he never intended it.

And used to be, I was all right so long as he had company come to stay. Made him have to leave my barn by dinnertime. Go sit at the head of his table so they can eat.

I always thought he didn't have it in him to come see me after full dark fell. But that day he strung up Charlotte was when he started coming later and later, talking at me into the damn middle of the night, always sitting a little too close and forever holding that flask. Telling me all his insides whether he meant to or not.

At first, it made me feel big because it gave me something on him. Like he was giving me a stick to jab him with. But as time went on, I saw it wasn't a stick for jabbing him or hitting him neither. It was bigger. More like a heavy wooden beam. A beam I couldn't hardly lift. All his telling did was pull me too close to hit him good.

His wife likely thinks he's out tomcatting, but he's down here trying to get his story straight. But he's not talking to me. He's talking to night. Talking to whatever will hear him and not talk back. And he's not even standing next to any kind of truth yet, so I go between listening to him and watching the shape of the story he's telling himself. I work to find parts I like so I won't get caught so hard in hating him. Come daylight, he's not the same man. I can't hook the two together.

He tells me how he grabbed and he took all his life because everybody knows a man is made of what he has. Makes me have to stare hard at the step he's sitting on, with his talk pouring round me steady as a stream. Makes me wonder about moving back to the quarters. He's not about to come in there after me. But I know I can't stand that, so I see can I stand this.

I sit sideways so he can't see in my face whether he's lit another lantern or not. Rest my eyes on the stone footings across the aisle, picture the river they came from with that greeny water pouring. Run my eyes up the walls, looking for spiderwebs and swallows' nests. Count the hatchet marks on those beams and wonder who made each cut.

Sometimes it's new, what he's telling me, but once he starts coming down here later and staying longer, that's when he starts circling back round. Makes me wonder whether I might do more than nod. Maybe he's telling me his stories over and over till he sees me latch onto em. Put em in my mouth and chew.

He never does tell me what I want to know. Some word on those laws he keeps writing, reining us in tighter and tighter. But he loves to talk about what they set out to do. Him and his brother. All that clearing and those forts they built.

Didn't seem to do em no good since he keeps telling who got killed and when. How those Indians were quiet as the devil and every goddamn where. How they'd sneak up behind a man, knock him to his belly, then kneel on his back to grab that forelock. Pull it tight and lay their blade across right at the hairline. And your friend looks out at you from under that blade, hoping it's sharp enough so he won't feel the cut till he's already bled to death. Cherokee did just exactly that to his brother David but he ain't come close to telling that day yet and I doubt he ever will.

I like hearing those wild Indian stories better than all the mess round here. Who voted him postmaster and who didn't. Who blocked him from getting the county seat in that first town he made. All about this new Memphis he's working to build out on that muddy riverbank. Who's hell bent on stopping em and how. Who knows best and who can't see the big picture.

I'm thinking it must wear a man out, knowing better than everybody else all the time.

When he starts in on me, I try to call up what my mamma told me about how to think about things. She already told me about Richardson naming me and boy, does he like to go on about that. How he gave my mamma the name Washington to put on me. How I was the first negro born to him and he wanted a name with some weight to it, so he wrote to old man Thompson, telling him mark it down.

It's mighty strange to hear him talk about Thompson being like a father to him. He says they came close to starving and stayed close ever since. Hard to believe those two sat chained together for nearly a year. For a free man, he sure has spent some time behind bars and it shows. Weathered as hell and still looks hunted.

My mamma had already told me about that night when Thompson read her that part from Richardson's letter out loud. She was building him a fire with me strapped tight to her when she heard him say mark it down. Told me she didn't mind much. She had her own name for me and didn't want it in any other mouth anyway. Some pieces you don't share. She said we needed a name for em to use and this one was fine. Wash. Every time she said it, she heard waves and saw water sheeting off me. Sweeping me clean.

And just like he can hear me thinking about her, that's when Richardson starts in on seeing my mamma at the sale. Telling all over again about seeing her standing on that block, staring at him till he raised his hand for her. Said it felt like she saw something in him. Felt like she lifted his hand right from his side. Made him bid on her.

You'd think I'd want to hear about my mamma but her name in his mouth makes me feel cornered. He thinks he's talking about her on my account, but all I want is for him to keep his mouth off her. That's when I start needing to put my hand on him. Make him leave her alone. Stay the hell away from her.

She always said Richardson was just like his daddy. From what she'd heard, that man's got something to say about everything and never did learn to say it to himself. She said every man grows up to be like his daddy, one way or other. I ask her do I and she nods yes with that smile crooking down.

Soon as I see her nodding yes in my mind's eye, I'm gone from that damn barn. Away from Richardson talking at me. That's what I do when life gets drawn tight. I drop down inside my story, just like she showed me. Let my mind carry me back to some ease out on that island.

What my mamma did was, she took me down to the water and she painted my life out for me to where I could see it good. There were some parts I'd ask her to tell me over and over and she did.

"Tell me about seeing my daddy. Tell me about that."

And she'd smile and drift and I could tell she was seeing my daddy, as clear as that first time she laid eyes on him. How she was still looking down, even after she'd stepped one foot in front of the next along the gangplank, coming off that boat. Knowing something else was coming and not knowing what it was.

She told me how she held her eyes on her own two feet. Trying to keep track of herself. Looking away from the light flashing too bright off the water and away from all those eyes. Sometimes she'd add in a piece she left out before. How they stopped at the edge of Charleston Harbor. Threw buckets of salt water on em. Cut their hair and greased their faces.

I listened to every story she told me but mostly I wanted to hear about my daddy. Her seeing him for the first time. Her watching her own feet and bumping smack into him before she ever looked up. She always grinned telling this part, her top lip catching a little on that crossed over tooth she had.

I made her go slow, all the way from my daddy's feet to his face. His one foot a little pigeon toed and the other one with that scar from running not looking where he was going. When she saw that shiny old scar wrapped round his ankle, she remembered the bright red blood dripping down on that day when they were playing tag and he stepped too close to the sharp point of an old staub.

How his family sent him away to keep him safe while he was still scrawny, puny she said, so she had to take him in real slow before she saw that long ago boy was this same somebody standing in front of her right now. How he was himself and somebody new at the same time. How she could tell from the way he was looking at her, she was herself and somebody new to him too. How all the pieces came together, all at the same time.

How they did not get to say one word before the lines started moving again and people bumped between em. How it was not until later that night when they found each other in the moonlight falling on the two open pens, side by side, with a gap at the back of the fence where he could slip through.

How it was better that way, with nobody knowing what they were to each other. How they sat up that night and the next. Leaning braced against the wall, trying to stop the swaying from being on the water so long. She said turning her head to look over at him made everything tip and spin at first, so she sat watching the ground and feeling the sound of their words falling on her skin like rain on a dry place. They talked and talked but low. Then they sat still, looking at their legs stretched out side by side.

And the next night, how he laid his big hand down careful in the warm dust between em. Then he lifted it, leaving his palm print just as clear as a track. How she laid her own palm down in the print he made, and then they sat looking at her littler hand laying inside his bigger one. How she lifted her hand out of his print and laid it on his flat low belly in the sticky heat. How she lifted her hand, leaving her pale dusty print floating there, and how it kept saying mine. Mine.

How he left his prints all over her but light. How she looked up at him with that big moon rising over his shoulder and she knew they were making me. Come what may, they were making me.

She told me every single story she had. I didn't always know how to make sense of what she told me, with some running through my fingers and some sticking with me. But she told me her stories so many times and in so many ways, said she was laying her staples inside the pantry of my spirit. I might not see the shape of each one right away but I'd find it when the time came.

She even told me about waking up that day when they had her hanging over the side. How she looked down at all that heaving blue and came right on back, lickety split. Said she knew she had things to do and I was one of em. And no, she didn't know what happened to my daddy after those first two nights but every time she looks in my face, she knows he's with us both.

Soon as she was taken to a new pen, she had to turn her mind to finding the right buyer. Told me she saw right away she had to take hold of this new life or it would sure enough take hold of her. So she hunted till she found her eye drawn to one tall skinny white man who stood calm and quiet. Looked kind of hawkish but greeted by most everybody. Not a big talker, just small nods.

But when he did speak, the other men leaned close to make sure they weren't missing something.

Somebody decent was what she kept saying. Steady enough so we might be safe.

Hard to believe that tall skinny white man she told me about turned into this one, sitting here like he can't get close enough, drinking till I can smell the sweet coming off his skin and telling me everything I don't want to know.

Part Two

Friday, August 7, 1812
Nags Head, Outer Banks, North Carolina

Old man Thompson was lucky in that he got exactly the death he'd hoped for. Fell asleep with the sea breeze coming in over him one day and didn't have to wake up the next. Wash will soon turn sixteen, the Thompson brothers have been itching to crack down for years and Richardson is nowhere to be found. In his last letter to Thompson, he said he was riding off to his final war, determined to whip England for good this time.

Mena and Wash take care with where they put Thompson's body, even though it's just for the time being. No telling how long it will take for his boys to get word and it's still full summer. They dig the old man a grave in the dip between two dunes where the sun hardly hits and the sand stays cool but does not seep wet.

As they step back to look at their work, Mena points to the crest of the biggest dune with its waving crown of sea grass and says it looks just like a camel. Wash isn't sure he believes her but she looks at him like she's not teasing then kneels to draw one in the wet sand with a stick.

After they line the hole with broad palmetto leaves, Mena heads back to the house to prepare the body. She makes Wash help her no matter how he tries to squirm away. Tells him she needs him to get ready for life to start closing in on him. When he balks, she steps toward him and he knows she means it.

Thompson had left his favorite pants hanging over the back of the chair next to his bed. After they get him washed and dressed, they stand together beside the old man. Wash stares at his face, mesmerized by death, while Mena looks out the window trying to picture what comes next. All she sees is a bright tangle of green.

A shaft of sunlight falls onto the earring Thompson kept in a clamshell on his bedside table. Silver with small pearly bluish stones dangling. Stones that disappeared into his wife's thick dark hair or lay against her neck when she tipped her head to the side to tease him. He had told Mena about his wife and she had listened.

Mena puts this earring deep inside one of his pockets and the few small shells he had collected in the other. She sets aside both his gold watch that has not worked for years and the chalky white dolphin vertebra he loved to draw. She figures his boys will be hunting the watch and she can hide the bone in some tall grass near wherever they decide to bury him for good.

Then she has Wash help her wrap the old man in that red blanket he favored. Once the blanket is wrapped good and tight, she and Wash turn him from one side to the next so they can slide a sheet under him to carry him by. He's still heavy, despite the weight he lost at the end, so they have to drag the sheet by its corners over the smooth places in the path and stop several times to rest before they make it down to the dunes.

After they sit for a while beside the grave with him and let the setting sun slide across his face one more time, Mena pins that last flap closed. They lower him into the hole. She sets more palmetto leaves crisscrossed on top of him and tells Wash to be careful when he shovels the sand back in. They use four big rocks to weigh down several old boards from under the cabin but she worries this will not be enough protection from being dug up by something, so she and Wash sleep beside him that night and the next until they can feel the old man sitting with them by their fire and glad to be gone, both at the same time.

His two boys arrive three days later. The morning flashes out with a hard glint, coming as a surprise after a calm succession of cloudy days. It's already hot by midmorning when Paymore edges

Thompson's boat up to the dock. The light falls so sharp onto the bright water that his paddle breaks it into shards.

Mena had guessed the boys would arrive early on the third day after she'd sent word and the gulls had confirmed it by wheeling and calling. She and Wash stand together just beyond the far edge of the crooked dock. Each an echo of the other without realizing it. Tall and slender in their wrapped cloth, forearms crossed, hands cupping opposite elbows. Right on time. Waiting. Watching the shards of light off the water flash brightness into the faces of the old man's sons.

Eli's blond prettiness has hardened while Campbell's remains soft and open despite his being the eldest. Each brother steps across the small rocking gap between the boat and the dock without looking at the water, the younger in the lead as always. Their heels ring hard against the planks then fall quiet as they step into the sand, heading for the house.

Mena and Wash woke early and have been busy. They have the house ready to close up with all the goods packed in two crates. They even brushed most of the sand off Thompson's blanket before they laid his body out on the kitchen table. His rifle lies beside him, cradled on top of his few changes of clothes. His three books. Rousseau, *Robinson Crusoe* and a Bible. His watch and his spectacles hold down two small stacks of papers. The first stack is ink drawings. Mostly scenes of the island. Rocks clustered in a tumble at the point. The rise and fall of the dunes. The view from the porch across the meadow toward the sound with tall pines marking a jagged border.

The brothers march into the front room only to circle aimlessly around the table, sneaking glances at their father with his face fallen in. Eli pays no attention to the drawings but Campbell, holding this last drawing in his hand, looks out the open door at the same view of the sound shimmering behind the pines.

"This one's nice, don't you think?"

Eli's eyes skitter over the drawing and out the door as he moves on to the second stack of papers. A few unsent letters. One to each of them and one to their sister. And, as always, one to his wife, no matter how long she had been dead. Thompson had also started a letter to his third son but the words taper out quickly, turning into a series of ink drawings. Mostly different views of the dolphin vertebra Mena has already hidden in her pack.

Eli crumples this last letter in his fist. Campbell pivots at the sound and stands staring until Eli hands it over. He bends to smooth the paper flat on the table but seems disappointed to find only last week's date and the words *my dear boy* hovering over a scattering of small sketches. Campbell sets this last letter beside his father's body and follows his brother out to the porch where Wash and Mena wait.

Wash is already a head taller than his mother and filling out. Eli steps close to him and takes hold of his chin, turning his face to the sun then lifting his top lip with one thumb to look at his teeth. Wash spins away from him shocked but Eli grabs his collar to jerk him back around. Mena steps close behind Wash, her fingers closing around his wrist before he can lift his arm to strike. He wrestles against her grip but only for a minute because he feels the iron in it.

It's all different now, she tells him over and over in her old tongue. I told you. I told you and you promised me.

Wash holds himself still until Eli lets go. Paymore steps onto the porch to help the brothers carry their father's body to the boat. Eli follows him inside and starts directing everybody which corner to take, how to distribute the weight properly and who should go through the door first.

Once they've disappeared down the path, Mena leads Wash back into the house, still holding him by the wrist like he's a child. She looks at him hard until he nods that she can let go. She smooths the crumpled last letter full of drawings and slides it into her pack then pulls the shutters closed. Stands in the doorway, taking one last slow look around, then turns her back on it so sharp and quick it's as if she's daring the house to try calling out after her.

By the time they reach the dock, Thompson's body lies longways in the belly of his boat. Mena can see Wash still has it in his mind to run. He's thinking he can hide despite her swearing to him those Thompson boys would hunt him down and these roughnecks out here would turn him in for gold. Even if she had not seen it in a dream, she already knew by the way Eli had looked at Wash every time he came to visit his father.

Mena levels her eyes at Wash, herding him onto the boat by force of will. She gives the key to Campbell then puts her hand on Wash's shoulder to steady herself as she climbs into the rocking boat to sit pressed close against him. His eyes keep jumping to the shore but she doesn't care so long as he stays on that bench beside her. His breathing does not settle until the pines lining the path to the sound are out of sight.

Mad as Wash is at being manhandled by Eli on the porch and lost as he feels at being wrenched off the island, he is soon overwhelmed by the big Thompson place. Nine hundred acres wrapped around a lake stretching to the horizon, quarters full to bursting with nearly two hundred people and more girls than he has ever seen.

Some boys are still boys at fifteen but some are already young men like Wash, as physically graceful as he is shy, nodding yes or shaking his head no, with rivers of words damming up behind his lips as he walks in step with his mother through the quarters to the farthest cabin. Raising his eyes here and there, trying to make some sense of this place so as to better map his course.

He knows how to read the sky for storms. He knows how to hunt and track and trap, how to ride and cook and sew and swim and catch and bend to fit. But when he goes looking for answers inside himself about this place, they aren't there. He misses the quiet of the island but he feels the pull of all this newness, even though it knocks him off balance.

And the girls turn his head till he's flustered. All the longing that's rising in those girls, they send it straight for Wash. The rest of these boys, the girls have grown up with them. Seen their mammas snatch them back when they made trouble and watched them squall like babies. But all they've seen Wash do is walk tall and dark and beautiful behind his mother. Holding himself to himself, with his voice and his lip darkening into smoky shadows even as he still carries the sweetness of a child.

Mena knows how it will be. It will be some girlwoman, a little bit older than the rest. She will dowse for Wash like water and she will find him. Draw him off to the side then draw him up into himself. Make him into a man. Her man. It's hard on Mena, thinking about Wash no longer being hers alone, but she'd rather it happen with this girlwoman who knows how to look after herself than with one of these young girls so flighty they can't stand still.

It's nice when one of you is older and can take the other by the hand. She had put herself in Wash's father's hands like she knew he wasn't going to drop her and he didn't. But the women had been telling her all her life how it would be so she was prepared. They had told her how his fingers drumming on her skin would be his calling God up inside her, just like her feet drumming on the skin of the ground had always been her way of calling God up inside her.

She knew this to be true because she had felt it for herself through her whole childhood, with her bare feet drumming their small perfect patterns into the soft dust until she felt God start coming right up from underneath the hard dry ground to move through her and through all of them. So on that second night, when Wash's father's fingers first touched her skin, when she became the drum, and when she heard feelings like sounds being called up through the hollow middle of her, this new thing did not seem like a new thing at all. It was instead the one thing she knew for sure in this brand new, upside down world.

The women had told her how this would be, but the pieces don't fall in place until they fall in place inside of you. Some people, this learning happens too early and some it happens too late but Mena was lucky in that it happened to her right on time. She only wants something close to the same for Wash.

He starts out trying to learn this new life by turning to his mother but the others tease him for it. Their calling him a mamma's boy burns in him even though he's unsure what they mean. Pot calling the kettle black is all Mena will say about it, but pretty soon Wash starts slipping away from her, sliding around the corner of their cabin even as she's calling him, acting like he can't hear her.

She has known best for so long and she has always been right. But now she does not seem so right to him anymore. He's itching to know things on his own. And he has heard the others start to talk about her and it worries him. That she's too serious and too dark too. Thinks she's better than the rest. Might even be some kind of witch, with all that African.

Mena knows she's being standoffish but she also knows there's plenty of time to make herself indispensable. She's using the time before they're hooked in tight to see this new place clear so she will know how to survive it. She hasn't stitched the two of them to anybody yet because she's still deciding whom to choose.

But she can't get too mad with Wash. She sees how it is for him to have real people right next to him instead of misty clouds of spirits chasing him across that windswept island, so she lets him run and play and fool around but she tries to watch sharp too.

What she's given Wash seems so little compared to what she wanted him to have coming into this world. She wanted a group of men who could take him off to initiate him like they did the boys at home. She had loved watching those boys straggle away, looking so pitiful, only to come walking back into the village weeks later, no taller but somehow bigger, carrying such a knowing in their eyes. Now she wishes she had paid more attention to what little the boys would tell her.

Mena thinks back to her father and grandfather and brothers and uncles. How they had acted, what they had said, and the meaning that lay behind those words. All she knows is that death must draw close. It must make sure you die to childhood before you can call yourself grown because everybody knows you can never become an ancestor without having gone through some kind of initiation. But how close must death come? And how do you meet it so it will pass on by?

Her mother had told her that a girl's coming of age heads straight for her. When it comes time for that first baby to make his way from belly to out, that's when she will stand on the brink between the worlds and be able to see across. She will be her own threshhold. And Mena had found that truth for herself. When she brought Wash into this world, she'd been carried to that place in the veil where it goes thin. But what about him?

She wishes she had looked more closely at every bit of her world when she was growing up so she could give more of it to Wash but it had been wrapped so close around her, she had no idea she would ever be without it. The women had started teaching her but they did not have time to finish, so she knows the shape and feel of ceremony but not how to recreate it all by herself. She tried to show Wash the rituals she remembered but they felt hollow and small out on that island with no drumming or dancing except what the two of them did. It was when she tried to show him these patterns that she felt most alone.

It was harder to call God up on her own than it had been with everybody moving together at home, so Mena was in a way relieved to come over to the big Thompson place, with all these new people sitting in a circle around the fire on Saturday night. People talking, telling stories and making music, letting the music swell amongst them like a live thing and then having to move.

She waits a few weeks before deciding to let Wash go to the fire. The night is soft and even a little cool. As they draw close to that glowing warmth, the near side of the circle falls quiet. The dancing stops. A fierce woman named Agnes leans into the gathering, brandishing her worn Bible and complaining about what she calls carrying on with the devil.

"You all had best watch out for carrying on like this and acting all niggerish when what we need is the Lord."

Sissy turns from her slow circle stomp and stares the woman down.

"That's not the devil, that's God. I'm not putting up with this mess all day and most nights and give up on God moving in me too."

Mena's heart blooms open and she feels a loosening in the middle of her chest. As she draws a suddenly deeper breath, she knows this place might be worse than the island in plenty of ways but it will be better in others. She looks over and sees Wash standing just within the rim of firelight, watching the music start up again. Paymore's long fingers slap the smooth side of a cut off piece of hollow log and Core makes drumming sounds with his hands, alternating between the side of his cheek and his open mouth. The sounds the men make start to move through the women and the girls, like the music is trapped inside them and dancing its way out.

Wash looks and looks. He doesn't realize his mouth is hanging a little bit open until his lips have gone dry. Mena sneaks peeks at him and she can see him saying to himself, this is it. This is what she's been trying to tell me.

Wash looks over at her and she nods as if to say, see? And he nods to say yes he does see, with his eyes shining.

Wash

We landed at Thompson's just as the man was coming up in me and those girls circled so close I couldn't hardly see straight. I wasn't used to so many folks at one time. Not right there with me, living and breathing. I'd stick round as long as I could stand it, then I'd slip away to the barn or the woods, saying I had work to do. But trying to keep my mind on my task was like trying to hold my hand on something hot and all I wanted was to run towards those girls.

I remember feeling that connection rising in me, liked to turn me inside out. A little like running with the island ponies, grabbing some mane and swinging up, feeling their muscles moving under my legs wrapped round so tight, with their backs rising and falling in waves, all of us pouring through the salty flats, kicking water everywhere. This new feeling was like that but bigger and more in the middle of me.

I'd play chase with the girls and wrestle with the boys and all of it made me feel funny inside. I'd be running after one girl, panting with laughing, and I'm grabbing her skinny arm she's flailing behind her. I'm pulling her to me and when I'm pulling, I'm feeling that feeling. I want to pull and pull but there's nowhere closer to pull her. She's already up against me and then I guess I'm squeezing her too tight till her screaming giggling turns to more like screaming. And she's twisting and yanking her wrist out of my grip, drawing it to her chest and rubbing it while she backs away. Looking at me like she's scared of me. The rest of the girls fan out, leaving us boys with nothing to do but jump on each other.

One time, I was standing there looking at the ground, still puzzling over a girl pulling away from me, and that's right when Friday jumped on me from behind. My head snapped back so hard I heard my teeth slam together. I had an eyeful of clouds and I was stumbling forward trying not to fall. He was the biggest of the boys before I got there and his arm was hooked hard round my neck.

I don't know what led me to it, but he was on my back and I felt his face real close over my shoulder, so I curled in a running somersault, trying to land him on his head while I ducked and rolled out of the way. Worked like I thought it might. There I was, bouncing back to standing, and there was Friday, laying spreadeagle on the ground, just blinking.

I stepped round to where I could look in his eyes and asked him was he all right. When I put my hand out to help him up, I felt the rest of everybody thinking something new about me. All I'm thinking is how I just got lucky, but something stopped me from saying it. Something in me liked all those new folks looking up to me.

That was the beginning, I guess. Then it kept happening like that wherever I went. At the very first, it felt good. I spent my whole life to fifteen without nobody round, then there's folks swarming me like bees. Sizing me up. Either trying to take me down a notch or else trying to get next to me. And I wasn't doing nothing to make it happen except being myself. Felt like a nice surprise back then. I wasn't looking for it or asking for it neither. It just came, like to visit me, and it turned my head for a long while.

Then I got greedy. Started trying to make it happen instead of letting it happen. Wasn't till later when I started trying to stop it from happening. Tried to take it apart. Let all those scared and broken parts show so folks would quit heaping their hopes on me.

But way back when I was first chasing those girls and wrestling those boys at Thompson's place, back then it was still easy. So smooth it made me feel like all roads led to me.

One Sunday after we'd been there awhile, I was fixing the rope swing on the sideways branch of the old sycamore down in the bottom for the little ones like Sissy told me to. And then there was Minerva, sneaking between me and the speckled trunk of that tree, looking at me, all full of I don't know what. She was leaning back against that trunk and watching me. Reaching out every now and then to tickle my sides while I had my arms up, trying to set that ladder.

I'm telling her wait but she won't and she's laughing. She's almost as dark as me. Her eyes shine bright in her smooth face and they tip up at their outside corners, making her look like she's carrying a secret. She's tall for a girl but bony. Skinny still with her raggedy dress tight under her arms.

Something inside me wants to move in on Minerva, press her against that trunk and hold her tight between me and the stillness of that tree. Feels like somebody new moving inside me, trying to make himself at home. But I don't know what to do with him yet so I'm just standing there, like I'm caught in a trance. I can't move. Not even my hands. I'm still holding that ladder.

But Minerva didn't know what she was hunting. She just wanted to put her front up in my front and then turn and run so she did. I chased her but she was fast and she wanted to get away. Before I'm even close to catching her, we're running up into the edges of Sissy's fire circle in the quarters, out of breath and laughing.

Sissy took one look at me tearing after Minerva like that and sent me after some dove eggs. Told me she needed em to stretch some soup she was fixing. I saw a couple of the women cutting their eyes at each other and leaning close when I left but I didn't think too much about why till later.

So there I go, loping round the corner of the barn to the far shed where she told me to climb quiet as a mouse up that ladder to sneak her some eggs from where that dove was nesting inside the eaves. I lift the hanging door at the top of the ladder and it's just big enough for me to stick my whole top half inside.

I'm feeling round on the ledge along the back wall with my hand, hunting for the nest like she told me to, and my eyes are getting used to the inside being darker than the outside. Quiet as I am, I hear it straight away but I have no idea what it is. I'm hearing something moving before I'm seeing anything and I get goosebumps.

Then I start to see through the dim and it's Rufus and Cleo all wrapped up in each other down on the floor. Rufus is the biggest saltwater man on the place and then some. He's the blacksmith with his own forge and Cleo runs the hospital those Thompsons built to keep us on the job. Everybody stays kinda scared of em both, but here they are, all wrapped up in each other on a blanket they laid on the straw.

And here I am, looking right at em. They don't see me yet but I see them. I'm standing there, half in and half out, leaning my hips against the ledge with the swinging door resting on the back of my shoulders. I'm feeling round in the shadows for the prickly straw curve of the nest and those smooth warm eggs. Trying to pick em up real careful and slip em in this pouch hanging from round my neck without dropping em, and remembering to leave one like Sissy told me.

But really all I'm doing is watching Rufus and Cleo moving into each other so smooth and slidy slow, like that big king snake I found in the grain one time. She's laying on her back, facing up under him, and he's laying on his belly, facing down over her. I can see her hands running up and down his back, slow and smooth like breathing, and I can see him moving into her and into her, like he's going somewhere important. Her legs wrap round his hips and her calves shine where they press flat against him from how tight she's holding on. All I can do is look and watch and see, saying to myself, oh.

Just then Rufus sets one hand in the straw to lift up a little so he can lay more alongside Cleo. And then I see all of her, laying full out in the straw, and she's running her own hands up and down her own self, like she's her own candy. He bends his head down and puts his mouth on her. Sucking like a baby, with his leg snaking over her, and she's arching back like she's stretching.

And that's when she sees me. She's looking at me and looking at me and I can't move. I'm thinking she's going to jump up yelling but she don't. I had one egg put in my pouch but I'm still holding the second one in my hand. So much going on, I know if I move a muscle, I'm going to drop that egg, but I can't stay there. I don't know what to do so I just watch her watch me watching her.

Then she taps his shoulder, smiling a little and saying look here. Cat got somebody's tongue. I can see the muscles in Rufus's back working when he turns his head to look over his shoulder. He locks in on me and I feel twice as still as I was before.

My mind is yelling move, run, go, now. But my body won't budge. I'm thinking, this is just how that chipmunk feels once he's caught in the cat's eye. He knows he needs to run, but he don't. Like he can't tear his eyes off that cat's face, and you can see his heart beating hard right there behind his little front leg. There I am, holding on to the ledge with one hand and holding the egg in the other, with that swinging door resting on my back, and I can't move to save my life. I can't even turn my head away or drop my eyes.

I can't stop from staring at her laying in the straw even though I know I'm gonna get my behind torn up worse than it has ever been.

I'm looking and looking like I'm seeing it all for the first time and I am. I mean I seen naked before but not like this. Running my eyes over her feels like an itch being scratched and my insides flip over.

She nestles back under him and I'm thinking I'm in some trouble now. Then I catch on they're more tickled than mad and he's probably not going to skin me alive when he sees me next. I slip that second egg in my pouch real careful and light so it won't crack against the first. Reach with my other hand to lift the swinging door so I can get myself out of that shed without falling. Grab the sides of the ladder with both hands before I take my foot off that high rung. I hear Rufus and Cleo talking low and laughing soft. My knees just about stop shaking by the time I make it to the ground and I feel so big inside I don't know how to make room for all of me inside myself.

When I get back to that fire circle, those women sitting round shelling peas and fixing supper take one look at my face and they bust out laughing and falling on each other, all of em shaking from giggling.

Sissy's voice cuts clear as a knife through all that carrying on, saying what happened to you boy? You look like you seen a ghost. You think you might make it?

All I can say is yes ma'am, I think I might make it and no ma'am, I did not see no ghost. And then that one littlest old lady says now come on y'all, leave him alone. And I'm looking over at her, saying without saying, thank you, thank you, thank you.

Good thing was, Rufus wasn't too mad about it and neither was Cleo. All she did whenever she saw me was smile a little to herself and shake her head. And Rufus started acting like we was family, even more than he did before.

Soon as I saw him, I knew he came from the same world my mamma had. I could tell by how much he looked like me. He saw it too and he stayed good to me from the first. Even before that day in the shed but especially afterwards. He never made a fuss but he'd nod as he was headed out. Tip his head towards where he was going. That was his way of saying come on and help me take care of some business.

He had his own forge and after watching me awhile, he picked me to work under him. Stepped onto that Thompson porch to ask for me. Told those boys he'd make sure I learned to do right. Told me he had a hunch I might be just the one.

Rufus stayed busy, him and Cleo both. He got himself hired out all over the county, so he'd been places and seen the world, on top of him being saltwater even longer than my mamma. But he was different from her too. He showed his African when it worked and hid it when it didn't and, on account of that, he made her mad at first. But Rufus looked past that and straight into her face. Said she looked too much like his auntie for them to stay crossways with each other.

She'd sit by his fire while he waited for Cleo to get home and they'd trade words. One by one, pointing first at something close by and then farther away. Pebble, crate, cookpot. Wind in the leaves. She'd give up her word for it and then he'd give up his, both of em pleased when their two words echoed each other. They spent hours that way and it softened em both. I'd sit there listening, following em as far as I could go. I'd see my mamma make a shape with her hands and I'd try to call the word up in my own mind, then I'd hold it real careful till Rufus gave up his.

It felt good to reach down through the new sounds of this place to find my childhood still laying there underneath. My mamma worked all my life to build a world inside my mind and then here came Rufus. Proof the world she'd built inside me was a boat and might even float.

Once Rufus took me into his forge, I was good and hooked. So much to learn, felt like I wouldn't never touch the bottom and all of it linked together. He had all his jobs lined up on the wall where he could see em hanging there. That wall of his held everything from brands to gates, hinges and latches for all sizes, chains and shackles and padlocks. Andirons and pails of nails. Stacks of blunt, squared off rods sat waiting for him next to a bucket of horseshoes.

That overseer Pickens was forever sticking his head in the door of our shop, hollering about what he needed and did Rufus have it ready yet. Rufus would just step closer to his forge and work his hammer faster, sending bright bits of metal flying in a bigger and bigger arc till they landed on Pickens's sweaty pants leg or shirtsleeve, biting him hot and harder than a horsefly. He'd lean his face towards Pickens, squinching it up like he was trying hard to hear over the roar of the fire and the ringing of the hammer and the sizzle of me dunking cooling metal deep in the quench bucket. Then Rufus would shake his head like it was too bad he couldn't stop to hear what Pickens was trying to say because he was in the middle of a big job.

But I couldn't stay out of trouble whether I tried to or not. Folks were always trying to put me up on top of the heap or else push me off it. And those Thompson boys kept after me, coming down hard, saying they needed to knock me into shape. They was testing me. See was I tough and quick enough for em to fight me. They'd meet their buddies out in the woods, setting their best boys against each other for bets. Lots of drinking and big talk but the stakes stayed real high out there and I didn't want any part of it.

Rufus didn't mind when I started coming to his shop nights too. He knew I was trying to stay out of the way. He'd be sitting there with a candle and a cup, forging pieces that didn't make no sense to me. Not till one evening, when that saltwater man from a couple of places down the road walked over to visit his wife. Man barely set foot inside before his eyes fell on the piece Rufus was making and he lit up, talking a mile a minute, never mind we couldn't catch a word of it. And stayed in the doorway like he didn't want to come too far inside.

Rufus just watched the man awhile. Then nodded at him, tipping the unfinished piece towards him so he could see it close before turning back to stoke the fire. It was one of those birds sitting at the top of a long staff. Those saltwater negroes loved those birds, even though they acted scared to touch em. Before Rufus got through making one, they knew what it was and they'd stare so hard, looking hungry to run their fingers along its wings.

I knew there was a story there but I knew just as well not to ask. But something about that man in his shop that night made Rufus decide to show me. He held the staff by its base, tipping that bird on top towards my temple and raising his eyebrows to ask can you see it?

The man knew exactly what Rufus was trying to show me and he stood there smiling with his arms wrapped round himself. Rufus stayed calm but the man twitched with wanting me to guess. Seemed like we stood there forever till Rufus started talking.

"This bird is your head. Your mind's eye. Sit on top and see from on high. Both this world and the next. When life gets tight, remember this bird and you know how to go."

Rufus straightened the staff, looking at me, asking do you see? And I'm nodding.

I thought about what Rufus was telling me. I knew about having my heart tied to another world. My mamma holding all her people in her mind's eye so strong till I saw em too. She had taught me how to move between that world and this one, no matter how hard I'd tried to leave that hoodoo behind when we first landed at Thompson's place, back when all I wanted was to be like everybody else.

Rufus called me back into myself and just in time. Reminding me I could leave this new place whenever I needed. Whenever things started to heat up, I could just go. Like that bird. I could lie in the tall grass and let the island ponies graze closer and closer. I could float outside the waves and I could feel my mamma's eyes warm on me. Old man Thompson's too. Felt good and doing it saved me more than once.

Whenever those Thompson boys honed in on me, I'd make my mind into that bird carrying me to the ocean with its roar steady and mounting. Took the edge off whatever mess they had for me that day, reminding me of a bigger world. I got so good at not letting em get to me, I stumbled into a whole different batch of trouble. They needed me beat down and scared looking, not all peaceful and full of ocean inside. Rufus spoke real sharp to me about that.

"Show em only what you want em to see. No more, no less."

He told me God gives every single one of us this bird, but some folks don't pay no attention to theirs. He said using your mind's eye to keep track of what you've had and lost is what makes it good and strong. Lets you see farther.

Made perfect sense to me because my mamma worked it like that. But not everybody was that way. Most folks round here called that old stuff conjure. Just some crazy saltwater African mess and stay away from it. For most of em, that other world was too far away. Never close enough to see it clear but always close enough to stay spooked by it.

Those that was scared of my mamma and Rufus, they grabbed up that Bible like it was going to save em. Save em from themselves is all it's going to save em from and not much else is what my mamma said. Said only thing to save any of us is remembering this world here is not the one you came from and keeping your own pictures strong and fresh.

Besides, she knew how it went. Said those folks will wave that Bible and quote you your sinfulness, but when that baby gets sick enough to die or when that mind starts to go in a young person, then here come those Christians, hunting them an African, asking can she fix it.

So I knew that faraway gone look Rufus got whenever he was seeing some place in his mind's eye, and I stayed real quiet whenever it came over him. I knew he was headed for a story. Sometimes just shifting in my seat was all it took to call Rufus back from where he'd gone and then he'd shut right up, acting like he was giving away some inside part of himself he never meant to show.

One night, he's picking out the pieces we'll use the next day, telling me about each one. Saying metal comes all kind of different ways. Each piece holds good and bad inside, both at the same time, and it can go either way. Just like us. Saying each piece holds a record of every single blow. Just like us.

I looked round that nighttime shop and every piece looked the same to me. All of it dirty and dusty and I remember starting to wonder. Maybe deep down underneath, Rufus is crazy. Then he leans to dig in the scrap heap and turns to me, holding two pieces of a broken file, one in each hand.

"Look here at what happens to hard."

I finger the jagged teeth of the file, then its broken edge.

"Plenty hard when you use it right. But breaks easy. You see?"

And I'm nodding while he's rummaging for a different piece of metal.

"Now, this piece. Wrought iron. You can knock it to hell and back before it breaks."

In the time it takes for Rufus to say those words, he's hammered the piece into an L shape over the edge of his anvil with only three blows.

"So soft it's weak. Shows every stroke but gives and gives before breaking. And lasts."

Rufus stops to look at me and sees me working to remember what he's telling me.

"Look at people and watch how they do. You know old Juba, wandering round, crazy and jabbering with nothing to eat but what we give him?"

I nod.

"Juba's like this file. He came in too hard and he let this place break him in two. Now he's wandering the scrap heap. Juba's how you know hard ain't enough. When you start to find yourself getting bowed up, and I know you will, I want you to think about this file."

He's leaning forward, holding a piece of the broken file in each hand, waving them a little, bringing the two broken ends almost to touching. I'm sitting there on the bench and I can't take my eyes off those two jagged edges of that broken file, looking like they're trying to kiss across the space between em.

He's asking me do I see? And I'm nodding, yes I do, till he says good and tips his cup up.

∞

Most of the rest of the people on the Thompson place steer clear of Rufus, even though they are not exactly sure why. All the little ones hear are warnings. You best be careful about that smith. But when the children ask be careful how, nobody will say.

Most people remember only what their parents tell them, not the whole of things. And if their parents don't know, or don't remember, then there's nothing to tell. Sometimes even knowing and remembering won't help with the telling because so many of the words are gone. All the stories they need to tell well up in their throats, choking them. And they are so tired and there's no way to explain it. Africa was another world and it hurts to try stretching their own minds around it any more, much less the minds of their children, so they say just stay away from him.

These countryborn children cannot see their own saltwater fathers when they were young, poised on the cusp between child and man, standing naked and awed into silence before the head smith during initiation, feeling the rumbling sweep of his incantation swirling around them, his careful hand on them and then his more careful blade. Death draws close during circumcision and it is the smith, with his sacred chants and his cut made with the knife he has forged, who makes this boy a man on this day. It is the smith who has his hand on the latch of the gate between this world and the next, because everybody knows this boy can never become an ancestor unless he has first died to childhood and been reborn a man at the hand of the smith.

As these saltwater fathers look helplessly into the uncomprehending eyes of their countryborn sons, it feels like too much to explain. Too much to have lost. So these fathers can only watch Rufus, so strong and steady as to seem arrogant, with his assured place, his shop and his cabin and his wife, and resent him. They cannot see his lineage or its source so they cannot surrender to it. Then these fathers tell their own never-to-be-initiated sons to stay away from that blacksmith because he's a damn conjure man.

So Rufus is a priest with no church and no followers. He has little of his leverage left and he uses it carefully. He knows it's best not to need anything from anybody and he isn't too good at hiding his opinion on that.

When Wash came along, Rufus started to wonder whether he could put all he knew inside this boy's head. What Rufus will come to see is that Wash carries inside of him a bowl into which all manner of things can be poured because this is how he has been raised. Even before Wash started to turn away from Mena, she saw it would be Rufus who picked up where she left off. She could have been jealous but instead she gave thanks for him.

Rufus turns to teenage Wash sitting next to him on that bench in his nighttime shop. Takes hold of the lanky boy's face by the jaw and turns it toward him. Looks into Wash's eyes hard, hunting to see what kind of man will this boy make. Wash does not flinch and Rufus feels his heart open.

Soon enough, it's Wash's second winter on the Thompson place. One of those clear cold days when the world falls so quiet it feels empty. Wash has gone for a load of charcoal when the Thompson boys come to the door of Rufus's shop, saying they need an R brand.

Eli's in the lead as always, talking before he steps across the threshold. Telling Rufus to drop whatever else he's doing so they can help their neighbors get a handle on this latest spate of runaways. Saying how they might even make themselves some money. Talking about how an R brand leaves no doubt. Eli steps close.

"You see a negro you don't already know, and he's wearing that R brand on his cheek, then you know for sure he's run off. You can collar him right that minute and you'll get some reward money for sure."

Rufus knows it's the excitement as much as the promise of cash that has Eli agitated. Bounty hunting other people's negroes is something Thompson never would have stood for, but this is the next best thing. Eli tells Rufus to make them an R.

"Do it like the other brands but make it nice. Put a leaf on the stem."

Takes Rufus a minute of standing there thinking about it before he says anything.

"Can't make it like the rest. Need a short stem so I can choke up on it good."

He feels their hesitation and turns away to lift their own stock brand off the wall before turning back to them, letting the heavy tip of the big brand drop toward Eli until it hovers close to his face, T for Thompson just to the right of his nose.

"Long stem on a heavy brand gives you shaky aim. Not much room on a face."

Rufus can see Eli watching the muscles in his arm working to hold the heavy brand steady, then looking over at Campbell. Then both brothers nod at Rufus, mainly to cut that long moment short, with Campbell saying whatever you think as they leave. There's not much they can do about it when Rufus is right and he usually is. They can, however, take credit for his good ideas and they usually do.

Eli pauses on the way out, stepping back across the threshold of the shop, saying let me write you an R and looking for some chalk. But Rufus steps in his path before Eli can get too far, making it seem like all he's doing is reaching for another stock brand he has just finished for Everett Roberts. He lifts it off the wall and lets the head of the brand drop close past Eli's ear to make a print of the letters in the soft dirt floor. The three men stand there together looking at the E and the R written side by side in the dirt and all Eli can say is all right.

As the boys head back to the house, Rufus sees Wash coming in with a full load of charcoal. He shoves two rods into his died down fire and starts to map out the brand in his mind, muttering to himself what he knows better than to say to those boys.

"I'm making it but I'm damned if I put a leaf on it."

Wash walks through the door asking him, what? Rufus tells him to get the bellows going. Wash dumps the charcoal in the bin all at once, making a great clatter and a cloud of soot. Rufus frowns at him but Wash keeps at it, asking what's next? Rufus stays quiet.

As Wash stokes the fire with the bellows, Rufus uses the chalk from his pocket to draw an R on his anvil. Then he measures his line to see how much iron he'll need to make the letter and where he'll have room to weld the stem on. His chalk R glows white on the shiny dark anvil but Rufus lays a hammer down over it before Wash has a chance to see.

Sends him for more charcoal just to get him out of there, saying never mind the bin is already full, do what he said do. Wash doesn't want to leave so he lingers until Rufus gets mad enough to straighten up.

"Tell you what, why don't you take the week? Go work for Pompey on the old tobacco barn. See can he teach you to mind."

Wash knows better than to slam the door behind him but he mutters to himself as he stomps off to find Pompey. Rufus watches him go before turning back to his work.

This R brand calls out Rufus's name just like everything else he makes. There's a liquid grace to the shapes he coaxes from his iron. Everybody's work looks a little different. Some is taste and choosing but most is in the rise and fall of one man's hammer, as individual as a fingerprint. No matter whether he's making workaday hooks and hinges or fancier specialty items like fire screens or candlesticks, the way Rufus works his metal makes his pieces look like water moving and the boys can charge more for his work than any of the rest of them can charge for theirs.

Even this R is a river, hooking around to loop back on itself. And the leg of this R kicks up at its tip, looking like nothing so much as the foot on a leg running. Rufus does this part on purpose. That foot kicking up is his way of saying good luck, safe passage and God be with you.

Those who get Rufus's R laid on their face can finger the scar and when they reach that foot at the end of their R, they'll think about the next time. They'll feel their own legs running hard through brush and swamp, carrying them right on out of there. The whole way.

Eli rides through the yard, calling for Rufus as he passes by his door. Asking has he got it done yet. Saying hurry up, we're headed out.

Rufus walks out of his shop carrying his file in one hand and the new brand in the other. The letter is still cooling from orange so he holds the brand halfway down its shaft with a thick gritty rag so he won't burn himself.

"Ain't cleaned up good yet."

"Don't need to be perfect so long as we can read it. We got three to do over at Henderson's. Said he might shoot the one who started it so we'll do a trial run on him. See how it turns out."

Rufus has already told them he has too much work to ride with them, even though it's usually him who does the branding. He has a reputation for being quick and careful. But he's staying here today so he carries the new brand over to where Eli sits on his horse, waiting for his brother. Rufus likes that the brand's still hot as he hands it up to Eli, who has forgotten his gloves in his rush.

Eli yanks his horse around and spurs him forward, furious with Rufus for once again doing exactly what he told him to. No more, no less. His burned hand stings as he canters down the drive, carrying the brand like a crop.

Rufus does not want to think about the men soon to be branded, so he steps closer to his forge because it radiates the same kind of hot dry heat he remembers from home. He feels the yellowgold sun of his childhood pressing in on him, lying on his skin with a weight like touch.

At home, there was always some air to breathe. No matter how hot and hard and bright the sky pressed down, there was some shade to step inside. But here, it feels like the air has turned into a thick piece of meat you have to bite into to get some for yourself. As blazing as it got at home, as blindingly bright, Rufus never once wondered where his next breath was coming from. In this new world, that worry stays with him every single day of August and sometimes July.

And when it rains, the mud here is never soft and tender like skin. As a child, Rufus had loved the coming of the rainy season as much for a break in the long tension of brittle dryness as for the silky shiny mud, rising ticklish and slick between his toes, and the awakening of long buried frogs, salamanders and lilies.

Here, the wet sticky hot is all the time and not a relief from anything so Rufus moves closer to his forge. And when that dry heat starts to bake him, he falls right back into his past.

∞

A red dirt path curves down out of the mountains, widening into a road as it heads toward a string of villages. There is an altercation on this road. A woman standing there with her two boys. One a small eight and the other a tall twelve. She pulls both sons close against her belly, begging the catchermen, no not these. Please.

She tells them there's a much bigger stronger man alone in the forest right now. She tells them about Rufus who was not called that then. She describes the sacred clearing where he works alone preparing for tomorrow's iron smelt. Making offerings and saying prayers so the process will be fruitful. She describes him out there alone and vulnerable, delirious with the heat and the spirit. The men don't understand and move closer.

She points to their guns and their knives, lifting and dropping her hand as if she is hammering the knife blade flat, then pats her chest as if it is she who made them. As soon as she does this, the men look at each other, running down the list of special orders in their minds. They know there is at least one for a blacksmith. Taken whole and unharmed for an old man named Thompson in North Carolina. For his boys.

As they turn away from her, she feels her heart hammer in her chest. She tells herself there are other smiths. Maybe she figures Rufus can be spared. And she has heard the missionaries talking about how smiths are sorcerers and sorcery is the work of the devil. With the way everything in her world has been turned upside down by these raids, maybe she has begun to think these men of God are right.

At least Rufus is much older and stronger than her boys. He has a better chance of surviving. This is what she tells herself as she hurries her boys home and inside.

The road is hot and sunny but deeper in the mountains there are pockets of cool where the trees have grown so large the ground under them never gets direct sun. These places stay green long into the dry season. Rufus likes to be with these old trees, feel them towering over him. As he prepares his offerings, bending to sweep the ground at the mouth of the furnace's tall clay chimney, laying out braided grasses and vessels of palm wine, he has the sense something is watching him and it does not feel right. He keeps stopping to listen but does not hear anything.

When he gets to the point where he has to put his whole mind into his prayers, he calls up his spirits and they come to him. Swirling up through his feet and legs, running up his spine to spread across his shoulders like a mantle, shimmering warm at the crown of his head before pouring down his arms and out through his hands. He is in the middle of it all when the catchermen get so spooked by the sucking swirling feeling that they stand from their hiding places, circling him with guns aimed.

He is stunned. Secret sacred chants hang from his mouth like ribbons. No one is supposed to see or hear any of this. He feels betrayed. Why haven't the spirits let him know? He knew it had been harder to call them up on this day but he had persisted. He had bent them to the strength of his will and they had come. They had come but they had come blind and deaf and they are useless to him now.

He pulls in a deep breath, as if he is trying to suck back inside himself all that these hiding men have just heard, even as he can tell by looking that they don't speak his language. His chest expands with the effort and the air burns his lungs. Time is passing but Rufus cannot take hold of his mind to steer it. One slow step at a time, the circle closes in on him. It is as if he has become one of his beloved trees with roots branching down into the earth from the soles of his feet.

He and his friends had sat around the fire discussing this exact moment again and again. What they would do and how. They sat around their fire, shrouded in the blindness of their youth, determined that such a thing could never happen to them.

The men step closer. He knows if he runs, they might not shoot him in the hopes they can catch him unharmed later. He knows the woods better than they do. He still has time. He sees himself breaking and running, sliding like oil between the outstretched hands of the men. He even sees them turn to look after him empty handed and forlorn.

It is just as he watches himself slipping out of their sight when he feels their hands close on him. They are jubilant, yelling as they grab his arms, jerking his hands behind his back to tie them together. Rufus does not struggle. Something holds him still. They are as surprised as he is, manhandling him to the ground as if he were fighting, until the truth of his stillness seeps through their hands and arms to their heads.

They tell themselves that he must be as dense as he is big, nodding to one another while jerking him with the tying of their knots. But that picture of Rufus standing tall and strong, chanting in front of the furnace, swims in their minds, raising the hair on their arms even as he's tied on the ground.

They pull him to standing and walk him in the direction of the coast. He can turn his head just enough to see the clearing behind him for the first few steps. Because Rufus is looking over his shoulder and walking downhill while he is being pushed and pulled, the tall clay chimney tilts at a crazy angle, falling down over and over again in great jerky flashes with each step.

How had they found the secret place? Why had he not run? Why had he let himself be marched down the mountain, past the compound of the woman with her two boys, past the edge of his own village? It's shut up tight as an armadillo during this raid but still full of people hiding as if dead behind smooth clay walls, with the smallest children stuffed inside grain pots or buried underneath mounds of dried corn.

And even though they are hidden, these villagers turn their faces away as Rufus is led past them. They shut their eyes to him, thinking they are escaping, thinking maybe it will be all right because there are other blacksmiths to make their tools, circumcise their boys and do their magic. They hold tight to his family, insisting it would be madness to rush the raiders' guns, saying it would only lose them many more.

Some soothe themselves by deciding maybe Rufus had been too strong after all. Too young to have so much confidence, too hardheaded to surrender fully to a life of working with the spirits. The ease with which Rufus went through his initiation had troubled some of the elders. They had wondered what would bring Rufus to his knees, give him the humility needed for a long and fruitful life.

His grandfather's thin keening wail rises fluid and graceful into the hard white sky until someone finds him in the dark of his hiding place and claps a hand over his frail old mouth. The men marching Rufus hesitate but only for a moment, then they spend the next hour debating which animal kept calling like that, as if it were midnight in the middle of the day.

By dusk, his sacred bead has been cut from his neck to lie buried under the waves as he's loaded onto the huge ship with others from all along the coast. The rumor that Rufus is a blacksmith has become just one story among many.

The captain stands short, thick and watchful. He's almost as rough with his crew as with his cargo. They are white but they are poor and from nowhere with nothing and nobody. They work like the devil and die like flies. When Rufus sees the captain take some skin off the back of one crewman for hesitating, he knows to keep his head down.

He doesn't know the word the crewmen keep using for him but he figures it out soon enough because they use it every time they catch him fingering metalwork, whether it's the fittings on the boat or the chains holding him. He runs his fingers over the hammered metal, picturing which blow where, in what order and how many. Partly to distract himself and partly to feed the picture of himself he's trying to hold on to in his mind. That picture of himself as a strong useful man with a life and a calling, plenty of chickens, tobacco and pumpkins brought to him in payment for his work.

He is careful to stop his mind before it gets to his wife and the new baby boy who finally came after years of waiting and prayers, before it gets to those catchermen rising up in the midst of his chants. He stops because his neck is still torn up from his last struggle. He was not trying to hurt himself or break free. Nothing is that clear. All he knows is that letting those particular pictures into his mind makes him feel like he's dreaming a nightmare where the ground keeps disappearing from under him until he's falling backwards toward some sort of unknown jaggedness and can't keep himself from thrashing.

They set him apart from the others but he has no idea why. All he knows is he has never let himself be used by anybody except for the spirits and he won't start now that he's lost everything else. He clamps his mouth shut. His belly growls and his mouth waters but he refuses food. He does not know where his ancestors are or why they have forsaken him, but he will not let it be said that he turned his back on them by continuing to live even as he is being dragged away from them.

His grandfather always told him this world we live in is merely the marketplace we visit, while the other world where the ancestors live is home. This life we can touch with our fingertips is only the smallest part of the whole. Rufus feels himself small and pulled onto his grandfather's bony lap. There is much more, the old man would say with longing and excitement in his clouded eyes.

During his own initiation, Rufus learned how right his grandfather had been. It was during those weeks of ritual when Rufus saw for himself how thin the skin is that divides this world from the next, and how easy it can be to move between the two. When he traveled to and through the spirit world, he saw, in strands of glowing light, his connections to all those living in this world, to all those not yet born and to all those dead but not gone. He saw each of us, along with every creature and tree, every stone and river, strung like beads throughout a web both delicate and durable, vast beyond imagining, stretching backward to the beginning of time and forward to its end.

This knowing has always freed Rufus from fear. Until now. He tries to tell himself this ship is only the smallest part of that bigger whole but the farther he is taken from what he knows, the less sure he becomes. It is not that he wants to die. It is not that simple. It is more that he wants to step back through the skin between the worlds before it's too late.

After several weeks, Rufus's bones rise beneath the surface of his no longer shiny skin, pulling its ashy grayness taut in the dim light. The captain orders Rufus brought to his cabin. Fifteen hundred dollars is a great deal of money and he is counting on it. Rufus appears in the narrow doorway, pushed from behind until he stumbles and almost falls. Deep shadows fill the hollows of his cheeks and collarbones. His thick muscles have thinned to wiry cords which cross his bony chest like ropes. The expression on his broad face is so inward as to seem blank. The biggest of the crewmen stands behind Rufus holding a chisel and a hammer.

"Can't get his mouth open."

"I don't want you breaking any teeth. This one is my ticket."

The captain surprises himself by dismissing the burly crewman without having him chain Rufus to the hook in the wall of his cabin. As he ushers the crewman out and shuts the door behind him, he mutters you're starting to look like a shipwreck yourself as he pulls back a chair for Rufus across the table from his own.

Rufus stares at the smooth golden seat of the wooden chair then back at the captain. There is a chain running down his back from the collar around his neck. It circles his waist where his shackled hands are clipped to it then continues to the shackles at his ankles.

This chain rattles against the buttery wood as Rufus sits, shifting to the side to avoid resting on the chain. He holds himself erect as he scans the cabin then locks his eyes onto a jagged scratch on the wooden floor, determined to block out what he has just seen.

The cabin is small and dark but the flickering light licks the treasures brightly enough for Rufus to recognize them. Iron staffs topped by sacred ritual objects. Forged by smiths for use in ceremony. Then sold or bartered, or worse, given to this white man. In appreciation for his business.

Rufus saw the two birds before he managed to look away and they hover in his peripheral vision still. Flanking him. The undersides of their outstretched wings catch the light of the captain's gas lanterns and Rufus feels the man watching him. He wonders how those birds can possibly help him now.

The captain tugs on a rope hanging from the wall. Soon there's a knock at the door. Cook hurries in to set a steaming plate in front of the captain. He pulls a knife, fork and glass from pockets in his apron, setting them one by one on the far edge of the table from Rufus, refusing to look at him sitting there, naked and filthy despite the bucket of cold salt water the crewmen had thrown over him before bringing him here. Cook pours a slug of golden rum into the glass from a bottle on the captain's shelf and leaves without asking if that is everything.

The meal is not fancy but the steam rising from it fills the small cabin with the warm round smell of potatoes and the salty bite of bacon fat. The candlelight catches the golden liquid in the glass, which tilts a little with the roll of the boat, and Rufus feels his mouth water.

The captain says nothing. He nods at Rufus and digs into his dinner. As he chews, he runs his eyes over nautical charts on the table next to his plate, stopping every now and then to lift the glass to his mouth. Rufus can feel the warm tongue of liquor unfurling down his own throat. He clamps his lips together, thinking of his father and uncles gathering to talk. How they spill that first sip as a libation for the ancestors, then watch the dry ground soak up the spirits before anybody says a word.

After the captain has pushed the last of his dinner onto his fork with his knife, after he has run the heel of his bread around the smooth circle of his plate for the last of the gravy, then topped it off with the last sip of his drink, he reaches to pull the rope again. When Cook comes back to clear, the captain tilts his head toward Rufus, saying call Pinson to get him settled for the night.

After a few days of this, the captain pushes his plate across the table until it sits right in front of Rufus who stares at the far edge of the floor so he won't see the birds. He steadies his mind by running his fingers across a link in his chain, feeling for hammer marks. The plate cools untouched and shadows fall deeper into the hollows between his bones. The captain takes the plate back, eats his dinner cold and feels Rufus slipping through his fingers.

The next night, the captain rises and comes around the table. He sets his plate down in front of Rufus and raises one finger to signal he will unshackle one hand for him to eat with. Pointing first to the left and then to the right. Which will it be?

Rufus looks at him for a long time. Fans out the fingers of his right hand as if he's just stretching them. The captain nods and bends to unlock that one shackle. He picks up a thin piece of balsa wood from his desk, no wider than two fingers and no longer than his hand. He sets this harmless utensil next to his plate on Rufus's side of the table and then sits back down in his chair to wait.

Rufus resists the urge to rotate his freed wrist because he does not want the captain to see how good it feels. He lets his fingers close lightly on the balsa wood, trying not to grab it so hard that it breaks but unsure of his muscles after so long. The steam and smell of the food rise into his face, his mouth waters and his stomach curls inside him like a fist.

They sit across from one another for what feels like a long time until the captain reaches into a shelf under his desk for a second glass then leans across the table to set it in front of Rufus. He reaches forward to pour a slug of golden rum into it. Then he lifts his own glass and tilts it toward Rufus, looking dead at him.

With that salute, something inside Rufus gives. The wall he has built between himself and the fact of those birds tilts and falls as he turns his mind to face whatever new life might be coming toward him. He scoops a bite of mashed potatoes onto the tip of the balsa wood, the gravy having cut a brown delta through the pale. Lifts it to his mouth. As his lips close around that soft savory bite, the captain smiles.

Once Rufus begins to eat, always with the captain, always with that slug of rum in his own cup, he starts looking like a man breathing in and filling up instead of a man sighing out and collapsing. Their shared ritual is their mutual secret. Both crew and cargo would be enraged. Too many lines being crossed. Cook stays quiet on account of all the captain has on him. He knows if he opens his mouth, he'll be stepping off right then and there. The strength of the captain's reputation for breaking Africans, for cracking even the toughest nuts, depends on secrecy.

All the captain will say when he tells this story later is that he scanned Rufus until he found the one kindness that hooked him, then granted him that one kindness over and over. Used that soft spot to drag Rufus back to the surface of this strange new world. The captain believes it is this one carefully chosen kindness, the lift and tilt of a shared glass held in the one freed hand, burning like a star in the midst of the degradation, that finally brings Rufus to heel.

And the captain is partly right. But the birds came first. It was seeing those sacred birds atop their ceremonial staffs, leaning toward the corner of this captain's cabin, that knocked Rufus loose from the only world he knew. Once he stood separate and alone, the toast tipped him the rest of the way. Served as some kind of witness. And these evenings with the captain do suggest to Rufus that all is not lost, that there might be some way to navigate this new life. Even as he wonders whether he can use this special treatment to unseat the captain, he knows his lot is well in with the man by now.

What Rufus does not realize is that the captain reads each of these thoughts as they cross his mind, no matter how closed he keeps his expression. The captain knows exactly how seeing the birds will affect Rufus. That's why he has them on his wall. He has years of experience trading with the kings along this coast before their power started to fade. Negotiations had stretched out over days, forging relationships as well as understandings, teaching him to appreciate the complexity of his opponents.

So the captain has been reading Rufus rather than those nautical charts all along. He recognizes the calm arrogance of superiority Rufus can never quite hide and decides to grant him that rather than try to beat it out of him. He will say Rufus has royal blood because this will raise the price. Only a fool tries to buy royalty, but since they are fools, they won't see the trouble there. Africa remains a mystery to those men crowding the markets in

Charleston, Savannah and New Orleans. Since that fact works to his advantage, the captain plans to keep it that way.

He will tell these buyers whatever he feels like telling them and they'll be glad to hear it, cherishing those nuggets of information, correct or not, because everybody wants life to come wrapped in a story. Most people prefer a good story over one that's accurate so he plans to oblige.

The captain has learned a few phrases from various kings which he enjoys trying out on Rufus. His favorite expression happens to be in a language close enough for Rufus to grasp its meaning. When he has to sit and listen to this captain tell him that it comes down to knowing how much you can afford, Rufus finds himself starting to agree.

∞

Wash

Rufus was West African, like my mamma and me, but not from the same stretch of coast. From what I heard people say, they doublecrossed him. He was sold by his own. And he acted up pretty bad coming across so he got seasoned hard.

What he told me was, once he decided to live, it was just one thing after the next. And he's got sense enough to know a sweet spot when he finds it. Said he hadn't been on the Thompson place more than a day when he first saw Cleo and that was that.

And he knew those boys were pushing them over the broom for the children they'd have but he didn't let that ruin it. Said he'd find some kind of way. Might even buy em both with the money he made from forging at night.

Rufus and my mamma and me, we all looked alike, but that don't mean we got treated the same. So far as Rufus was concerned, he was quality and they needed to show they knew how to handle him. His coming to those boys as a special order from their daddy, his being the last present they ever got from the old man, gave Rufus some leverage. He said they had to learn to treat him right so they could show him off good.

But I was a whole different story. The way their daddy treated my mamma and me out on that island for all those years burned those boys right up. Running buck wild was what they called it. Said I was nothing but green broke and spoiled.

What Rufus said about it was if you can't ride a green horse and you need to beat it to make it do right, that's you being a man. But if you can't ride a well broke horse without having to beat it, that's just you being worthless.

They stayed back off Rufus. Seemed like he turned them a hair timid, so Rufus took that slack and he ran with it till folks started calling him Prince, with that shop his castle. He'd been there a year before we got there and had the place pretty well sorted. He knew folks talked about him but said he learned a long time ago to let sleeping dogs lie.

I remember stepping onto the big house porch, fetching those boys some more drink and hearing em talk to their company about Rufus and Cleo. How much they were making on his metalwork. Then watching Cleo walk by and calling her their insurance on Rufus. Saying I sure would stay around for some of that. Egging each other on, saying I know you would. Then all of em laughing till one started coughing, making his drink splash on the porch.

Made me mad but Cleo walked through that talk like it wasn't even there. Seemed like she shut everything out till all she saw in her life was what she wanted. Her cabin with Rufus over by his forge, set off from the quarters some. Closer to Pickens than I'd like, but they had what they needed.

Then one day, I remember everybody dressed up for a corn-shucking. Strolling, meeting and greeting like everything is fine. And for that minute, it is. Those Thompson boys acting proud of themselves, like they was saying see, we can do this. We can let these fine nigger women deck out and have themselves a good man without jumping all over em.

They stood on their porch, calling out good evening Cleo, good evening Rufus, you two sure do cut a lovely figure tonight. And I watched those two just smiling and dipping their heads, saying thank you, like none of that nasty talk from before ever happened. Cleo told me they was having too good a time to get tangled up with those boys and their mess. But it made me mad, watching them shucking and grinning like everything was fine when it wasn't.

Course I didn't see this for what it was at the time. I mean I saw it, but took me till later to understand it like I do now. Back then, I was mostly confused. I was confused and I was headed right into those two boys' worst nightmare, just as sure as the devil. All I needed was time.

Eli

Something about Rufus always took me right back to that first and last batch of saltwater Africans my daddy ever bought. Same stance, same peppery smell. Even that copper bracelet he wore.

I was seven and peeping through the cattails, watching my daddy ride in the lead with his overseer Grove bringing up the rear and a line of ten new negroes walking chained together between them, headed for the lake. But those Ibos didn't look like the others. They looked like they came out of some picture book. Sea monsters drawn in the blank spaces on my daddy's maps, rearing up from the water next to the boats.

I caught a few glimpses, then they were gone. I never heard a word about it that day. Then a ruckus just before dinner the next night. My mother had fretted all day till my daddy rode into the yard. I heard them in the hallway as I was coming down the stairs. Low talking ran tight like a wire till I stepped around the corner. My daddy wheeled to look and I saw him scared for the first time. He looked skinnier and his hair stood up from him running his fingers through it too much.

My mother tried to calm him down. Saying that's a good idea, go do it now, then calling me to her with her hands, pulling my head against her belly because she knew I liked that. I never guessed she was doing it to cover my ears so she could finish what she was saying. I felt her voice humming inside her. My daddy listened and nodded and turned on his heel like he was back in charge.

"Right, I'll start now. Go ahead with dinner. I'll be back."

Me and Campbell and my sister Abigail sat clustered together at my mother's end of the table. All while we ate, she asked us for stories about our day like we always wanted her to do. And she leaned in like she was listening, but I could tell she was with my daddy in her mind. Her face was flushed too pink because she was already sick. We got sent straight to bed afterwards.

It wasn't till after lunch the next day when I could sneak away to see for myself. It was hot and the bugs were loud. I headed out through the far corner of the front yard, past the smooth cut grass into the tall reeds where the ground starts to get soft and sinky closer to the water. I knew I wasn't supposed to go down that far, but those Ibos were working there and I wanted to see. I heard the tearing grunts of their shovels biting into the mud sounding like snuffling dragons. Just a little farther. If anybody caught me, I'd say I was hunting the eddy where the tadpoles swim thickest. I'd say the ones I'd already found died before turning into frogs.

One more step and I fall through the reeds where the bank drops off. I land in a pile of dirt and mud so slick I can't stand. I'm looking up at one of those new men, much closer than before. I'm right at his feet. He looks down at me from inside a cage made of cut saplings standing in rows for bars, sunk deep in the ground. And there are more laid across the top, making a ceiling for this cage that's big enough to hold all those Ibos where they dig my daddy's canal.

The grass is trampled and the ground torn up. Nobody sees me yet but him. Sitting in that slick mud, staring up in his face, I know it's this man, these men, that had my parents so upset last night. This muddy bank is where my father was while we sat with my mother eating dinner. He was down here with Grove and Grove's boys, building this cage.

What I look for first is the door. I don't know whether I'm looking for a door so they can get out, or so I can get in, or just because every cage in every story I ever heard has a door and a lock and a key. Maybe I want to see it for myself so I can know this man is locked in there good and won't get out that night or the next to hide under my bed. I run my eyes over the whole thing twice before I let myself be sure. There is no door. These men do not go in or out. Ever. They sleep here on the banks and then wake to dig some more. My daddy built this cage with these men already inside it.

This one man looks at me so hard, I keep expecting him to try to reach through the bars and grab me. Then I see he can't. His hand might fit between the bars if he turned it sideways but not his muscly arm. I see where he tried. I see where the skin is worn flat and shiny into an almost perfect ring halfway up his forearm. That is as far as it will fit.

He squats and we are face to face. He's got scars. Three lines coming down his cheeks from under each eye, like the lines I draw coming out from the sun. I'm still looking at those scars, wondering who put them there and did it hurt, when I feel his grip tight on my calves. Both legs.

I didn't know I was so close but now he's got me and he's pulling. Trying to drag me inside with him even though I won't fit through the bars. I fall on my back, scrabbling for something to grab but it's all mud. I twist around to see the bank rising behind me. There's a root running down, thick enough but buried deep in the bank.

I get one foot braced on a sapling, but he's pulling and my foot is muddy and sliding. I'm scratching at the bank, trying to wrap my fingers around that root. Just as my braced foot slides off that edge, I get a good grip. He's still pulling, but now I'm pulling too and I'm strong.

I look over my shoulder at him and he raises his eyebrows like he's surprised. I start kicking at him and he starts looking around. My daddy is standing farther down the bank with his back to us. All I have to do is yell but I don't have any breath. All my daddy has to do is turn around. By the time he does, I'm standing knee deep and covered in mud and the man has gone back to shoveling, acting like nothing ever happened.

I'm standing there shaking, watching my daddy run towards me. When he starts yelling at me for getting so dirty and for coming down there in the first place, I can see he's still scared. That was the day when I first saw him trying to act like he knew. Mud topping his boots and he didn't have a handle on any of it.

All I could think was, things won't be like that for me.

Thompson

What my seven year old Eli didn't know was that two of those Ibos I bought had already run. Their very first night here and two were already gone. The first without a trace except for a chicken he'd snatched on his way, snapping its neck to silence the cackle. Then the next one, just as gone, but not before tracking his muddy footprints right up onto my overseer's porch. Right up to the window of his bedroom. The window Grove had left open so he could better hear his dogs.

The windowsill where this second Ibo had left a scattering of small smooth stones not from around here and a bone. A pale, flattened out, T shaped bone that would fit in the palm of your hand. Chipped out from inside a turtle shell. Bottom of that T tapered into a point sharp enough to prick yourself. And this second Ibo had done just that, leaving a few drops of blood to turn dark brown along the windowsill and across those stones, letting the night breeze blow in quiet and soft across all of it, carrying his mojo into the room where Grove was sleeping.

I left so early the next morning that those first two runaways had not turned up missing yet. But I made it home just before dinner to learn I'd lost a good eleven hundred dollars and stood to lose more if I didn't fix it right quick.

My wife was furious. Not to mention the hell I would catch from my neighbors, trying to explain how it was that two fresh unseasoned Africans were now wandering loose. And everybody knew Ibos were the worst. All the old men had warned me to steer clear of them, but I thought I could save some money.

We all start out thinking we know. I was certain I could handle saltwater Africans. All my knowing did for me was to bury me knee deep in the muck of my canal I'd bought them to dig. After those first two vanished, I had to make the rest stop digging long enough to build a cage around themselves right there where they stood. Cut saplings, hammered them deep, then braided the whole cage from pillar to post with chain. Had to rebuild my cage further down the bank after each day's work just to be sure those damn Ibos would be there in the morning.

And you bet they slept there. Nighttime was the trouble. I had Grove's oldest son sit up all night with a fire and a gun, hoping he wouldn't have to shoot. Then I stood there all that next day with mud cresting the top of my boots, watching those swags of chain running from neck to neck, rising slick and wet up out of the water, stretched tight by their bending to dig. I had em so pinned down they could hardly finish a good stroke. My precautions doubled the days it took, but what was I to do?

It was my young Eli watching me that burned like salt in the wound. He came down to my canal even when he knew he shouldn't, played in that dirt pile until he was covered in mud, and then stood beside my cage, thinking he knew better than me at seven years old. I was torn. I wanted to watch him find out otherwise even as I wanted to protect him from the rip and tear of it.

Eli

That was the first time I walked away from my daddy while he was talking to me and I liked it. I did. I used my dug out root like a step to climb that bank, then I slipped through that wall of reeds and walked until I couldn't hear him anymore. I left him behind and it felt good. He never should have yelled at me.

I went straight to our swing. I swung by myself at first, feeling the mud dry tight on my skin, then Pompey and Smart came from the quarters. They wanted to climb up and stand with me like we always did. The three of us could get that swing to go pretty high by leaning way back and then way forward, using our weight. So that's what we did.

They kept asking me how'd I get so dirty but I wanted to go higher. Everything felt different and I couldn't get high enough. I looked at Pompey's dark brown hand holding the rope right next to mine and seeing that made me want to let go. I told them to stop but they wouldn't, so I leaned way back and used my foot to push Pompey off the swing. I said I mean it and I left a muddy footprint on his back. He landed on his feet but he looked at me funny and took Smart back to the quarters with him. I called after them, saying fine with me, that's just fine with me. And it was.

When I lay in my bed that night, that ring mark was all I could think about. It wasn't the man's grip on my legs or me scrabbling in the mud. It was that ring mark worn shiny against the dull gleam of the rest of his arm. Worn shiny from reaching through the bars and reaching through the bars and getting stuck at the same place every time.

Even while I was lying in my own bed, I wondered was that man out there right then, sticking his arm between the bars till it got stuck then twisting it some more? Like my sister twirls her finger in her hair and twirls it till it's good and snarled, then my mother works at the knot, asking her what is she so worried about and can't she see she's ruining her hair, until my sister wails I don't know, I don't know, and my mother yanks to untangle it.

That worn shiny ring mark looked so naked compared to the rest of that man's arm, looked to me like that one Ibo had finally taken off a bracelet he'd been wearing his whole life, and I started to wonder what his neck looked like under that collar. It was a slippery feeling, as slidy as when that man was pulling on me, and I didn't like it one bit.

My daddy sold those Ibos after they dug that canal but we lived forever on the edge of something worse happening without ever knowing whether it would or when. We never talked about any of it but I guess I was mad at my daddy for never knowing enough and always acting like he did. And for never being able to make that slipslidy feeling go away. I swore to myself I would get rid of it for good.

Wash

That day came just like my mamma worried it might. A road leading right straight to me on a late winter day, after we'd been at Thompson's big place almost two full years. Don't know how I dodged it that long. And I was doing exactly like they told me to, but they started messing with me anyway.

Rufus had put me out of his shop for asking too many questions. Told me not to come back till I learned to mind. Sent me to help Pompey and the fellas shore up the old tobacco barn. Made me mad at first but by midmorning of the second day, we got a real rhythm going. Joking and laughing but getting it done.

Then everybody falls quiet. Here comes Mr. Eli needing to see for himself and everybody's supposed to stop and speak. Somebody told him making his people look him in the eye and greet him might make us mind better. He's always hunting him some improvements, but most times, all they do is slow us down.

So here we are, standing round stopped, with the day moving along and every single one of us with something we want to do once we get through with this job. I can see he wanted to step inside our circle while it was still a living breathing thing but now it's gone. He's heating up cause he can't quite get us to bend to him and he can't see why. And here comes Campbell headed cross the field but it looks like he'll be late like always.

I stepped up in Mr. Eli's face on the wrong day is what I did. I should've known better. I did know better but I went on ahead anyway.

I was picking up on everything. On the little man trying to be big, trying to be a peacock swaggering but didn't have no tail, and all us standing there looking at the ground, waiting for him to go back to the house, until he starts needing to make somebody mind. Wants to make sure he still can and wants to make sure we see him do it.

And who was the one fool blind enough to get caught looking right at him? Who was the one fool dumb enough to try moving things along by turning back to work, raising my hammer over my shoulder and bringing it down with a great big whonk over and over and loud?

I hear him step behind me and say well would you look at Wash lifting that hammer like he thinks he's a big man with his mamma still his shadow. I know he's about to start in on me good. I've seen him do some of the other fellas this way, and I seen the fellas just let it rain right down on em. Looking at their feet like they ain't never seen em before. Standing real still, trying to wait for it to quit.

Seemed to me all that humble pie and yessir and nosir made those two Thompson boys feel bigger and bigger, especially the little one, till he had to tan him some hide to let the steam off. But I wasn't gonna give him that. No sir.

I caught myself pointing this out to him using that careful way his own daddy taught me, sitting on the porch of his rickety old house through those long quiet days on that island. I should have known better than to talk about his daddy but there I was. Me. Tugging at my cap and telling him how it was.

Saying here we go, trying to get the side of this barn shored up so it won't fall in on nobody, saying it shoulda been done right the first time and you'd think they'd see the sense in letting us get on with our business. It was the gospel according to me and it was feeling good. Being right was feeling good moving all through me and looking him in the eye felt good too and seeing his mouth fall open.

Somebody ran to get my mamma but she was nowhere near enough to help me. I was too far gone already. The quiet grew and stretched till it was a live thing between us, moving and breathing, and into that quiet went all the staring and the muttering of the rest of everybody, standing round watching.

Most dangerous thing you can do is make a man feel weak but I didn't know that then. He had to do something. He couldn't let it go. My hammer getting snatched out of my hand and coming down out of that big blue sky up against my temple taught me that, and I been looking at the ground ever since.

I don't remember it from happening but I've been told it enough times till I can see it for real. That hammer coming down, not the claw or the head, but the side. I was somebody else's nigger after all.

Lucky for me I had that cap on. Kept it from digging a hole right into my head, but didn't keep it from making this dent. Fool that I am, I turned my head and looked straight at him while my knees buckled. Not that I was seeing him. I was probably seeing bare willow branches crisscrossing blue sky.

It was quiet with a breeze that day. Nobody moved. I went down like a rag doll, they said. Landed on my belly, cheek to the ground, hit side up. My dark cap turning darker. Catching the blood seeping and I'm staring across rough winter grass with one eye swelling shut.

I lay there and he stood over me with my hammer hanging from his hand. Everybody else was watching their feet, waiting for those two Thompsons to move off so they could see about me.

Only blessing was, my mamma didn't make it to me till after they were already gone back to the house, saying they needed to send for somebody from Richardson's place to come carry these troublesome negroes home. Too bad he was still locked up in Canada but he needed to send somebody to fetch us. Wrap us back up in cotton the way their daddy had, or else let them go ahead and beat us into useful. Said the last thing they needed was to owe Richardson a bunch of money for two dead negroes.

I was in a trance was what I heard. Laying there with my cheek flat to the ground. My bottom eye was open, staring and blinking, but slow. The top one was swelling shut by the time my mamma made her way to me. She was breathing hard from running fast. They stood up from round me and let her come inside their tight circle. First thing she did struck em odd. She laid down on the ground, right alongside me, facing me. Said she had to see could she look into my one eye.

They said she talked to me in that old tongue of hers, running up and down but smooth. Talked to me steady and low before she ever touched me. Somebody said it sounded like she was washing me with her voice, dipping it in cool water and laying it on me to bring the swelling down. All before she ever touched me.

She said I looked like I was seeing her while she was talking over me and I must a been. I do remember bare willow branches moving cross the sky when she finally let em roll me onto a tarp so they could carry me inside. But she made em wait till she was through talking to me, through talking to me and laying hands on me both, and that took a while.

They told me how she laid there, down on the ground with me. Face to face. Laying her palm on my cheek so light, her fingertips touching the edge of my cap. Then she took her hand from off my face and laid it in my palm. The hand that was trapped under me when I fell. How she turned her other hand so she could slide it palm up under my free hand where it lay out in front of me, palm down on the grass. And she stayed steady talking like water pouring.

Before she was finished, she reached down to lay her two palms on the soles of my feet, talking to my mind and my spirit, telling em to stay with my body, telling em not to leave me. Then she cupped one hand over the top of my head but not touching it, just talking to that space in between, while she ran her hand real close along my back. All the way to my tailbone and then back up. All without touching me. I don't know how close I was to leaving but I do know, after everything she did, I was in this world to stay.

They rolled me onto the tarp and carried me way inside the back of the barn where those two boys don't hardly ever go. She took my face in her hands to look in my eyes. Said open em wide as you can now, then you can close em. That's when she saw my good one was trained right on her but this other one was looking over her shoulder.

Keeping an eye on things she called it, grinning at me a little while she doctored me. She said she wasn't worried, but she was talking too fast and shiny bright. Everything still worked, fingers and toes, and she said I'd always carried too much in my eyes anyway. Maybe it'd be easier for everybody now that I could only use one.

I think she was hoping to herself this wandering eye of mine might finally look after me.

Eli

All I was trying to do was make everybody do right. Knock my house back into plumb. But when I lifted that hammer up over my shoulder into the quiet of nobody seeing me yet, time slowed down to molasses, and I heard myself wondering why won't folks just do right.

Then I heard my daddy forever telling me, remember now, every time you lose your temper, you lose your money. That right there was when I saw I didn't give a damn about the money because I had plenty of it and what I was hunting was my temper.

But once I looked down at Wash lying on that cold ground with his temple stove in, once all those men I'd played with as a child stepped back from me forever without even moving, I hated my daddy more than ever for being right right right all along.

∞

Wash

That was the first time death drew close. Taught me a lot and then kept on teaching me. It's still teaching me, even now, after all this time.

My mamma told me how it would be. Said we'd hover close just like our people did. But it takes time to let this knowing catch up with you. Lots of time.

And by now, I've had plenty. Drifting out here, watching you all. Trying to tell you what happened and how. Trying to see can I get back inside my life, find me some kind of handle on it. Telling it helps me make my mind big enough to hold it all.

It's always the dead who got to stretch out to the living. You get so you can read a living man's mind. See straight into his heart. But what you got to tell him ain't always what he wants to hear, and the living can be some kind of hardheaded, acting blind to us even when we could save em some real time and trouble. But some things stay slow to learn and I know it can seem easier to slog on the hard way. I remember making that exact same choice myself.

It was hard being a living boy turning into a living man and keep my heart open to the knowing my mamma laid into me. Soon as we landed at Thompson's place that summer before I turned sixteen, I started having trouble living in two worlds at once. I got tired of our folks dead and gone but still trailing after me.

Used to be, I liked feeling em gathered round me. Used to be, they stayed one step ahead of me, not behind me, and they showed me where to put my foot next.

But once I started growing up, once we got yanked off that island and put with all those new folks who saw things so different, it got harder to live in this world with my heart tied to another one. I decided I didn't have so much room inside me anymore. I wanted that whole spirit world to fall away so this new world could stand before me, stripped clean and mine to walk through.

It hurt my mamma to see me dropping the knowing she gave me by the wayside. She saw I'd be needing it but she let me alone. She knew how I felt. She even told me so. One of the few times she could get me to listen to her.

Said she'd felt the same way at first when those women kept pulling her aside. Told me how she didn't want to go, how she wanted to stay in that circle, playing with the rest of those girls, all of em growing up that one big trellis together, vining and twining together like everybody else did.

But she had more room inside and she got pulled out of that circle so those women could give her more knowing to hold on to. And it didn't matter that the rest of the girls never knew the half of it. Those women told her she best learn to hold on to her own self, all by herself. Build her own trellis. Told her how everybody growing up one trellis all together like that ain't always good. Said it can make you weak to where you can't stand on your own anymore. Can't see clear. Said every village needs some few who can make their own.

My mamma tried to make sure I built mine. One that fit me just right. But back then, what I wanted was to vine up that one big trellis at Thompson's place, woven together with everybody else. You shoulda seen me. I knew it all. Yessir and nosir and I can figure this better than y'all. Still thinking there was a way to win at this game.

I turned my back on my mamma and on all those spirits she'd cloaked me with back at the sound. I felt em follow us from the island, but I walked on down the road, trying to get away from em. When they kept on following me, I yelled at em like you yell at stray dogs. Told em go home. When they stayed steady after me, I started throwing handfuls of pebbles. Then rocks.

I thought if I could just slip away from this cloud of spirits, then maybe I had a chance to make it through. The way they stayed crowding round me made it harder for me to fit through small spaces, and seemed like small spaces was all we had over at the Thompson place, so I slapped em down. I turned my back and I walked away.

But time made me lucky. I didn't get too far along that road before God gathered em right back round me with that white boy's hand bringing my hammer down on the side of my head.

That's what my mamma was doing when she laid her hands on me. She was wrapping my knowing right back round me, all my spirits and all my stories, everything I'd pushed away. I lay there on that winter grass and I felt em crowding round me again. It felt good and that's when I started to see.

When you have your people hovering close and flanking you, it's not simple like it can be without em. But going on without em wrapped round you, it stays too cool and too tender. That's when I saw I wanted my people gathered close round me every chance I got.

But I was lucky. I came to my knowing early. Some folks never do figure it out.

After Eli knocked me in the head, it took a long while for me to get back on my feet. My mamma worked double time on the smocking Sissy passed on to her and those Thompson boys started getting some good coin for my mamma's stitching. They sold her christening dresses as far as Baltimore and New York. Talking about how dark she was and how they liked seeing the pale of fine cotton finally shining some light up into her face.

My mamma kept her mouth shut, humming her growing up songs to herself and pulling her needle and thread through that cotton. With me courting trouble, Richardson locked up in that prisoner of war camp in Canada and those boys not about to spare somebody to carry us all the way out to Tennessee, life was getting tight.

It was her trying to find out about Richardson that riled them. It was her looking at the ground like she didn't have a thought in her head when they talked to her, but then hovering close to each and every visitor, all quick and slick, trying to get some kind of word. That's what got under their skin. They saw she was aiming to get us gone from there. Before I led em straight to killing me was what she told me. Trying to keep me alive. At all costs was what she said. At all costs.

It killed em to be feeding me while I was down so my mamma split her cornmeal and fatback with me but it wasn't enough for her to begin with. If Rufus hadn't carried us those strips of squirrel and possum and coon he snared then snuck smoked while he made his charcoal out in the woods, I doubt I'd ever gotten back at myself.

Soon as I did, I went right on back to his shop ready to pick up where I had left off. Trouble was, I couldn't really see straight anymore. I could see a thing plenty well. Even two things at the same time. And none of it was blurry. But I couldn't always tell how close something was. Or how far away.

Wasn't too much of a problem. I'd stretch my hand out towards an edge and stay ready to grab ahold of it whenever I got to it, acting like I knew what I was doing, so nobody caught on to what I was seeing and what I wasn't. But in that shop, you got to set a piece just right then send your hammer down on that one right place at just the right angle, telling the metal which way you want it to go. You need to be able to see your edges clear.

Started out fine that first morning back. Felt good to be back in there with Rufus. All the jobs lined up on the wall. The sound of the fire. No talking till nearly lunchtime.

"Trying to keep you out of trouble."

"Trouble came to me, didn't it?"

He nodded and that eyebrow went up, "Right straight for you."

I knew Rufus was worried about my seeing from the way he acted. He tried to start me out slow and easy but I wasn't having none of it. I went right at it because I needed to know too. Started in on that ax blade he'd been saving for me to finish. But soon as I missed my first strike, Rufus was quick to stop me and put me on a different job. I knew he'd been watching me out of the corner of his eye the whole time, ready to jump in before I had too much chance to see what the trouble was.

I'm standing there holding my ax blade with my tongs, looking at it laying there on my anvil, watching it cool. I'm looking at that first wrong dent I made with my first wrong blow on my first morning back when Rufus turns and wraps one hand round my tongs right below where I'm holding em. Then he holds out his other palm for me to give him my hammer. He steps between me and the anvil, saying why don't you find that other blade I finished yesterday and see does it need oiling.

I stood there looking at that big old back, watching his hand lifting my hammer up and letting it drop, watching him finish off my piece. Smoothing out my blade. After a minute of me standing there behind him, Rufus stopped, like he could feel my stillness. Then he threw a look over his shoulder, saying well if you don't want to oil that blade then go carry me in another load of charcoal.

When I looked at the charcoal bin and saw it was already full to overflowing, that was when the mad rose up in me like fire roaring from the bellows. I knew better than to grab his shoulder and turn him to me so I stepped round from behind. I stood facing him across that anvil where he had laid my ax blade cooling. I was mad with him for treating me like I didn't know nothing, like he could keep anything from me, like I wasn't even grown.

"What the hell do you think I don't know? What you think I can't see?"

Rufus tried to turn away but I followed him, circling round, trying to stay in his face. But he kept turning, making me bark up at him like a hound that's got something treed.

"What you gonna tell me about how to do now? Huh? Huh?"

I'm good and yelling now and Rufus stopped turning away from me. He laid my hammer down then he let go the tongs and my cold ax blade fell to the floor, jangling and clanging. He turned towards me, slapped me across my face and told me to shut my mouth. I knew how close he was by how his shape filled my eye but then he went blurry from tears welling up. I don't know how long went by before anything happened.

All I know is after a while, I heard my teeth chattering together, loud as bones being played inside my head. I remember trying to stop the sound by clamping my jaws shut, but soon as I'd draw another big breath, they'd start up again. I couldn't clamp down hard enough to keep my teeth from chattering and still breathe at the same time.

Next thing I know, Rufus has me pulled close. One arm wrapped round my back real tight with the other elbow resting on my shoulder, making a fist that's falling real light, over and over against the good side of my head.

Rufus had pulled me to him once or twice before when I was littler and he was proud of something I did or tickled by something I said. But this was different. Those other times had been easy and relaxed. He'd grab me and then turn me loose right quick, moving on to the next thing.

This time was different. Rufus stood so still he felt like a block of wood. His arm wrapped tight round my back felt like a board trapping me and I started to panic. I'd never wanted to get away from him before and my head didn't fit under his chin anymore. My ear was right next to his cheek and I heard him say something sounding like I'm sorry, but so soft I'm still not sure whether it was just him breathing. I looked over his shoulder at his shop wrapped warm round us, knowing there was no place in it for me and wondering what the hell was I gonna do now.

I just waited for him to drop his arm so I could go. Soon as Rufus loosed his grip, I turned and headed for the door. That's when I saw I had to duck to get through it. Tall as Rufus all the sudden. Guess I'd been laying there growing all that spring while my mamma was healing my head.

Found out later, those Thompson boys called Rufus up to the house that same night Eli hit me. Told him to pick out some other boy for his shop. Said I was coming up too much trouble. Said only a born fool would keep putting me in that shop with him and all those locks and shackles and keys. They'd send me so far out in the fields I wouldn't hardly remember Rufus or Cleo or none of em.

He'd stood there on the porch nodding, saying lemme sleep on it. Telling em he'd pick somebody in the morning. Trying to buy himself some time till Cleo could hand him the name of some boy she knew wouldn't get on his nerves too bad.

Wasn't till later when Rufus told me how he stood there saying to those boys, mmmhmmm and yessirrrrssssss, all slurred like that, letting em think he was drunk and hearing em laugh at him when he stepped off the porch. Said he even felt drunk and dizzy too from trying to smother being mad at em for taking me and ruining me so easy. Said he was so mad, he barely had enough juice left over to make his mouth and his face do what he needed em to do till he could walk away from that house.

Said all he knew was he wasn't seeing things too clear himself anymore and he needed all the help he could get. Wasn't too long after that when Cleo got sold and Rufus started going downhill.

∞

There is no particular thing that leads Cleo by the hand toward poisoning those Thompson boys that summer after Eli hit Wash. Life has started to get better instead of worse after some of old man Thompson's friends pay a few calls, telling those boys they need to stop having these troublesome incidents with their negroes. Reminding them that Eli still needs a wife and make no mistake, people talk.

But every time that overseer Pickens steps over the line, one or another young man comes to Cleo in her hospital, asking for poison, talking about what he's going to do to that overseer man. How he wants to stand up there in the doorway of Pickens's house, watching him lying on his floor jerking and drooling, pulling his furniture down around him. Cleo just shakes her head.

"No you ain't. Not in a million years. That won't fix nothing. Knock him down and it'll be somebody new. Use your head now, use your head."

Those are the things Cleo says and she means them. But there's always a deeper layer, running underneath all the reasoning and the making sense. It is this deep down layer that leads Cleo's mind through thinking about poisoning those Thompson brothers. About them dying and being gone. Stopping them from talking about her the way they do.

Her everyday mind knows it doesn't make any sense. Knows she can usually find a way to make things all right. Knows she wants to keep seeing Rufus coming through their cabin door, earning enough money to buy them both before too long. Knows there's some other white man who would come in even if she did somehow kill all these here. She knows this and she tells it to herself over and over but that underneath part is not listening.

It isn't anything specific. Just a rise in the river. Given a certain amount of rain within a certain time, a river will jump its banks and there's nothing anybody can do.

As Cleo goes about her work in that little hospital, she sees how to do it. She watches herself in her mind's eye, grinding those medicines into some kind of poison with her mortar and pestle. The cool of the stone bowl warmed by her hand cupping it. She feels the give and crunch of the medicine as she grinds it down. Even turns her head to the side so as not to breathe any of its dust.

Rufus always tells her she best be careful where she lets her mind go because it remembers and holds the tracks of every step. And he's right. All that running her mind over it she does just to get herself through the day starts adding up and spilling over. Like Rufus says, even when your mind wanders, it's going someplace, and all that traveling adds up. Builds momentum until you got to go somewhere and do something. Cleo just stops stopping herself, that's all. Once she lets herself grind up the poison, it's already done.

All it takes is one pass through the kitchen where Hannah has left the fire untended to carry a dish into the dining room. When Cleo looks down into that cookpot and sees those chunks of good meat in it, she goes ahead because she knows none of hers will get any. Pours her powder into their stew with a couple of stirs and walks back out the door. All of it as smooth and easy as a dream.

It isn't until later that night when it hits her. Sitting with Rufus on their bench, leaning against the far side of their cabin, she hears herself telling him what she has done. The words drop from her mouth like marbles in a steady clinking rush to fall still in the dust at their feet. She says it so casual, mixed in with other things about her day, that Rufus does not hear it right at first.

"Maylene had her baby and we named him Early because he was. Justice finally broke his fever and recognized me. I poisoned those Thompsons that was at the table tonight."

Rufus sits there, warm and easy next to her. Relaxed. Thinking about going fishing with Wash. Digging for worms. The rock of the boat. But now there is something nagging at him, like a bug in his face he needs to swat but his hands are busy.

It takes him a long while to turn and look into her face and in that time, Cleo sees she has taken her life and broken it with her own two hands. Then Rufus is on his knees on the ground in front of her with his arms wrapped around her hips and his head and shoulders in her lap. She looks down onto the back of his close cropped head and she watches it tilt back and forth, feeling him saying to her no. No. All without making a sound.

She cups his head in her hands, asking God to please wake her from this dream, but God is nowhere to be found. She lets her hands be soft and heavy on Rufus's head, smoothing his brow toward his scalp. Waiting for lights to start coming on in the big house. Seeing now there is no way every one of them got enough poison to kill them all.

Rufus lifts his head to look at her as he rolls back off his knees onto his haunches, not even asking her what will they do now, knowing she does not know. He moves onto the bench to sit next to her again, letting what she has told him come in on him anew. Feeling himself cut open on a blade so sharp that he does not yet feel pain. Only a sudden breeze, cool on the wetness of laid open skin.

He lets his head fall back and rolls it side to side against the rough wall of the cabin. He is holding her hand. He feels the edge of the cornering strip on the window and he raises his head off the wall only to let it fall harder and harder against the edge of that strip until he can feel something besides the echoing empty space of Cleo not being right here by him and with him.

"You got to go. They'll tell."

"Nothing to tell."

"Road leads straight to you."

Cleo nods.

A few lights come on through the dark. Both of them can hear a horse galloping down the long drive.

Rufus draws her hand into his lap.

Cleo waits.

"Where I'm gonna go they can't find me? Everybody know me. How far I'm gonna get, running and tripping and falling all the way? Dogs'll catch me by tomorrow sundown."

Rufus looks at their bare feet side by side in the dirt.

"Can't see just how it will go, but I don't want it like that."

They sit together. After a while, Rufus stands up slow as an old man, still holding her hand, drawing her with him down toward the old dock that's overgrown and forgotten by now. Behind the low wooden wall gone silvery, with the lake water lapping underneath.

It isn't until early that next morning that they come back. What almost saves Cleo is the way she comes walking up from the old dock, hand in hand with Rufus and love hanging off of her like moss in the trees. Nobody can believe, in the face of everything that's about to happen to her, that a woman would be trying to find her some sugar.

Once they reach the quarters, Cleo looks quietly into Sissy's face until the older woman stops yelling. Then she opens her fingers. Rufus's warm palm slips from between them and Cleo feels the cool morning air take its place. She turns away from both of them and heads to the house to see if she can make herself the only casualty.

Sixteen people are sold that day. There is no telling anybody the facts. Eli wants the entire kitchen and hospital staff off the place immediately. Sold before word gets out. That is how his grandfather always said to handle it and he knew about poisonings. They do not beat Cleo because they want as much money for her as they can get and because Eli does not trust himself not to kill her.

Besides, he says, no one died. Just a whole lot of cramping, throwing up and bloody diarrhea. Once things calm down, Eli decides it makes a good story. He tells it for years.

∞

Wash

Soon as those Thompson boys found out I couldn't see straight, they put me in the field. Like they'd been waiting on the chance. Said they wanted me at the far end of the last row. Told that damn Pickens to run me into the ground.

They were caught between wanting to whip me trying to make me do right and not wanting to send me home torn up. I'd a thought the feel of that hammer coming down and sinking hard into the side of my head woulda lasted em a while but I guess not.

I heard em figuring how they'd tell Richardson about my scar. They decided they'd tell him that boom swung round and nailed me before I saw it coming. Even though they'd been yelling at me, I hadn't looked in time. They'd tell him I was plenty strong but not too good at listening.

Once they had their story straight, they told Pickens to watch for leaving any more marks on me, but said he had some leeway seeing as I was so dark. Said he'd have to whack me pretty good to make it show. That's like trying to find your way on a moonless night is what they said.

And Pickens sure did like to mess with me. He knew the hardest thing was for me to see other folks knocked round and can't do nothing about it. At first, I spent my time trying to watch where he was headed and then trying to get there first. The bigger boys were on their own but I didn't like seeing the mammas falling in the dirt. I stayed so busy trying to stop his hand from coming down, or else trying to make it come down on me instead, it's a wonder I got any cotton in my sack at all.

Pickens got so he'd do it just past my reach. All I could do was make sure he saw me looking at him good. Then he got so he'd be sure to do it just on account of my watching. I was bringing him down harder on us and everybody started cussing me. Said put your damn nose in your cotton sack and keep it there.

It took me a while to learn not to look. That was where I tripped and fell over my growing up. That right there was where old man Thompson was wrong to leave me to myself for so long. Out on that island, full of storms and roughnecks, folks could see folks. Not all the time, but more times than just a few. Storm coming and you need some help battening down your house, they helped you. Somebody got a gun, you get out the way, no matter who it is or isn't.

It didn't matter that my mamma was somebody's negro. When those chickenlegged wild boys from up island heard the old man died and came snooping through the woods to mess with us, she stood on that porch with his gun pointed right at em and she was ready to use it. They backed off sure as you know it.

This place was a new world and old habits die hard. But I finally learned to mind my own business. Pickens couldn't whip me but that didn't mean he couldn't knock me round good then stake me out in the hot sun by the canal where the marsh grew thick and the mosquitoes covered you like a blanket. So I let it go piece by piece, my picture I'd put together out there on that island about how the world worked and how people are. Only some people, I started telling myself. Only some people.

Rufus had kept me out of trouble until that hammer. After that, I was in the field but good. I tried fighting and I tried running, but everything I tried came right back round on my mamma. At first, those boys did it real direct. Made sure I knew each day I ran off and stayed gone in the swamp was one more day my mamma didn't get her rations.

But I knew they wouldn't take it all the way since they needed her to make those christening dresses to sell. My mamma knew it too. She sat there, wadding that pale cotton, shaking it in her fist at me, saying go!

At first, she tried to hold me back. She worried for me out in the woods but with the way things were going, she saw I'd likely be safer there. She didn't think they'd kill me just to get me home. She hoped they'd leave me alone. Glad to be rid of me.

Folks did that a lot. Ran up in the woods and stayed for three or four days. They weren't going nowhere. Just needed a break. Trying to clear their head before they did something stupid. All she wanted was a way to get word to me when time came for us to leave.

I made my way pretty far up in the swamp on the far side of the lake. Slipped out and back as often as I could. Then I started staying longer and longer. Weeks at a time and it burned those boys up. I stayed careful but there was folks tucked everywhere. Even in deserted looking places. People all round and somebody always ready to make that dollar.

Those times when I was on the place, I'd go by the shop sometimes after leaving the fields. Take Rufus some toddy. He practically lived there now Cleo was gone.

When I wanted some quiet, I'd go sit with him. It stayed close and hot inside but it felt good to me. I'd pick up a rag so gritty with soot and scale, it was heavy in my hand. Just holding that dirty rag made me bite down with missing working in his shop.

I'd sit there for a long time, sipping and looking round the walls lined with hooks full of jobs done. Running my eyes across all the brands for horses and cattle hanging on the wall. Then Rufus has one of em in his hand. A real small one and he's digging in the dirt floor with the tip of the staff. He's bent forward so the letter on the other end waves near his shoulder, up by his ear, and I'm laughing a little.

"You'd think they'd get sick of seeing their own damn name everywhere."

"They stay so blind. Can't see a thing if it don't have that name written on it."

"What's the one you got? Lemme see."

Rufus holds the smallest brand by the middle of its short staff. He twirls it end over end from his shoulder till the letter points straight down, hovering over the dirt floor. But I still can't see it. He leans forward, lowering the letter real careful and slow, laying it onto a smooth soft spot in the dirt floor where it'll take, then grinding it some before he lifts it. I'm looking at the pattern in the dirt but I don't recognize it.

"What's that one?"

"That's a R for runaway. I was working on it that day I put you out. Sent you over to Pompey, but you had to show off how you know best. Trying to be a big man. All you got was knocked in the head. Coulda killed you myself."

It was more than I'd ever heard Rufus say at one time. And I'm quiet, remembering driving my mamma crazy with my Rufus says this and Rufus says that. And I remember getting stronger and taller. The feel of the morning sun on me that day when I told those Thompson boys what I thought. That hammer coming right out of that bright blue sky down on the side of my head. The long darkness after that and then being sent to the field.

All of it felt like it happened to somebody else. Like that old me was somebody else. Different from who I was now. Rufus felt me drifting and he pulled me back to him.

"You left me. You up and left me with that squirrelly fool Cicero. Can't shut his mouth to save his life."

I'm shaking my head, smiling. I can see Cicero down here in this shop, standing on Rufus's last nerve.

"Bet you keeping your mouth shut for the both of you."

"Mmm hmmm."

Seemed funny to me. Rufus and me sitting there talking like two men, when it wasn't too long ago I was a boy and only way I could see Rufus was looking up at him.

"What's the rush, little man? They make a man outta you soon enough. Few good whippings, they knock the boy right from you, am I wrong?"

I'm shaking my head no.

"I'd a made you a man but you didn't have time to give me the chance, did you?"

And I'm shaking my head, no, I guess I didn't.

"You got too busy."

"Mmm hmmm."

"And look at you. You a man now and all you got is time."

"Pretty much. That's pretty much it."

We sat there, drinking and watching the candlelight falling across those Rs Rufus kept making all over the floor at our feet.

"Now you hearing me, hear this."

I lifted my eyes to look in his face.

"If that day ever comes when I need to lay this R on you, you best know this my name I'm laying on you. You belong to me and always will. Even when you too hardheaded to see it. You mine. You hear me?"

"Yessir."

We sat together for another long while after our drink was gone. Then Rufus stood up and I followed. He knocked the brand lightly against the workbench to get the dust off, then twirled it back end over end so he could hang it with the rest. Took the candle and opened the door, nodding for me to go ahead.

Once we both stood outside, he turned to lock the shop up, asking me over his shoulder, when we going fishing? I headed off my way, calling back to him, Sunday evening. And he headed off his way, saying see you then.

That hammer set me back some but I was still too big for my britches. Still starting mess and hearing my mamma less and less. Pretty soon, she stopped jerking me back from life and started getting that faraway look more and more. Seemed like I heard Rufus better for awhile, but I started losing him too. It wasn't his drinking, it was what he was trying to tell me.

Used to be, Rufus calling me down was the only thing could make me do right. Used to be, Rufus saw straight inside me and the things he told me about the world made sense. But the more beat up I got, the more grown I thought I was, and the less I heard him.

I kept running into the swamp and started staying longer. Making sure Pickens knew I wasn't going to let him jerk me round. I'd come back and get more work done in one week than most did in two, so they put up with me. But even then, seemed like trouble kept coming right for me. Like I was calling it. Like it was saying to me, you will not leave me.

Rufus kept telling me, play dead whenever those boys try to mess with you. Play dead, like a piece of hide those dogs fight over, and sooner or later they'll leave you alone. He tried telling me it was my thrashing and jerking, trying to get away, that brought out the mean in em, but I wasn't having none of it. Big tall Rufus telling me play dead like a possum. Telling me bend down when I ain't never seen him bend down. Didn't seem right.

He kept trying to tell me how life don't work how I think it do. And the very first thing I need to let go of is how things oughtta happen instead of how they do happen. Told me I was hogtying my own self, but I wasn't having it. One day, I looked into his face and told him, I'm getting tired of hearing you tell me what you need to do is.

That was the day when he saw I wasn't hearing him no more. And that was the day he got through with me. He folded right back inside himself, nodding at me to say all right, you go head on then.

After that, I felt him loosing his grip on me and all of us. He drank more and more but he never got sloppy. He just got gone. I went down there to sit with him every now and then but he sat stiller and stiller. Didn't make his own pieces in the evenings anymore. Told those saltwater negroes to go back to wherever they came from. Said he didn't have nothing for em.

He got so he'd talk when he never did talk much before. Used to be, he'd hold it all inside his head. Used to be, Rufus was like he had a whole world inside him, stocked with whatever he needed and enough to go round for everybody. But once he started to go downhill, all that started to change.

Now that I look, I can see there were signs. But back then, I wasn't reading em. Not yet. Just seemed to me like one day, Rufus stopped living in his mind like it was a place. He started talking out of nowhere, telling me every thought he had, like telling it was the only way he knew how to make it real.

That's when I saw what had always drawn me to him. Up until that day, he had always carried himself. He didn't make you do it. That's why he was easy to be with. Well, not anymore. Pretty soon, he was talking more to feel himself breathing and he was long past hearing anything I had to say.

And he talked and talked. Talked about Cleo and not knowing if she was alive or dead. Talked about how he ain't got the same give in him. Said he'd been took too hot too often till no amount of temper can set him right.

When he made me look at what he had forged that week, seemed like it wasn't nothing but chains and shackles and padlocks and I knew he was done helping me.

∞

It is early spring of his third year on the Thompson place by the time those boys drag Wash home from his hideout in the swamp. He's been gone nearly a month this last time. The trees haven't leafed out yet but his hunger made him careless. Somebody saw his smoke and turned him in for a dollar.

Campbell steps down off the porch to hand a coin to the skinny white man who brings the news while Eli goes to get the wagon. Neither brother knows this is the same man who had chased their father's third son to drowning in the lake years before. Thanks to him, they have Wash back by midafternoon, lying tied in the back of the wagon, still unconscious from that last kick.

Eli tells Rufus what needs doing, saying be sure to call us when you get ready.

Mena has spent the morning filing the edges of Rufus's R brand. She tells him to press hard but quick. Says she wants it to go clear through the skin. Cut it like a knife so she can stitch it closed. There's no way to hide a burn so she wants him to make a cut. A quick hard kiss and then let up is what she keeps telling him. She has ruined his R brand by filing it down like this and he'll have hell to pay if they look too close before he has time to make another one.

Rufus sits on a stump by the fire, balancing the stem of his brand across the toe of his boot. He lifts the stem end to send the letter down into the heart of the fire then pushes it down to lift the letter from the flames. Seeing if it's hot enough yet and not too hot. Takes longer to heat in the open fire pit in front of his shop but there isn't room enough inside to lay Wash out.

He and Mena have mapped it out ahead of time. Soon as they lifted Wash from the wagon and laid him beside the fire pit, they figured exactly where to put it. Together, they held the cool brand to Wash's cheek. They saw that bringing the R in too close to the side of his nose would make the top of the letter nick his bottom eyelid and the base of it spill onto his mouth. They decided to pull it out to the side. Let the circle of the R loop around the point of Wash's cheekbone and let the leg of the R run onto the broad flat side of his cheek, toward his ear.

Wash will only be able to hide it some by keeping his face turned to that side a little but there is no other way. Even the boys will see the rationale in it. They'll have to anyway. And now here they are, back down from the house. Muttering urgently to Rufus as Wash starts to stir.

"Put that R front and center so people will see it and know to fetch this running away young nigger back home."

There's something about Rufus right then, either his being bigger than them, or older and more competent, or maybe it's the way he holds his brand lightly by its stem in his left hand, but when he says slowly and quietly, staring at nothing but the brand, I ain't putting his other eye out, the Thompson boys fall as silent as everyone else.

After what seems like a long time, Rufus stands. Takes one glance out of the corner of his eye at Mena straddling Wash with her hands closed around his face tight as a vise. Holding him still for Rufus and telling him to look at the sky. Then she's looking at Rufus, saying without saying come on, I got him, and she does.

The R glows orange as it leaves the fire. Too hot now.

Rufus takes a long breath in and holds it, waiting for the breeze to carry just enough heat off the letter. He wants it cooling down as he lays it onto Wash's cheek. Has to be just right. Rufus has run this whole thing through his mind. Seeing how to slow time and steady his hand. How to use enough force and not too much.

All you can hear is the fire. Rufus draws another long breath then lets it out real slow so he can hold himself still. He swings the brand up, holding it by the end of its stem with his left hand, then he chokes up on it good with his right hand as he bends down over Wash. All in one smooth motion. Aiming sure and steady for the small plane of cheek framed by Mena's splayed fingers, holding her boy's head tight.

Careful to make sure the brand meets Wash's face level with it, not at an angle, which would make the top or the bottom of the letter cut deeper, Rufus lays the light hot weight onto Wash's left cheek. Then he adds a quick jabbing push. Just to cut through the skin and no more. One quick kiss.

He feels the give as hot metal slices through skin. Then he dunks the head of the brand into the quench bucket so fast the sizzle lands on top of the murmuring. Wash passes out again, his recoil torquing his whole body except for his head because Mena holds it tight.

Everybody stands quiet, all eyes glued to the dark S his body makes on the pale dirt. The smell of his having soiled himself rises in the heat of the fire, mixing with the smell of burnt skin, until finally the two Thompson brothers break from this shared trance, twisting sideways to look at the faces ringing the circle, shrugging their shoulders as if to slough the smell off themselves. They cough into their handkerchiefs then hold them over their mouths and noses, muttering all right then.

But still they linger, as if they hope staying another few minutes will transform their triumph over Wash into one that actually feels like victory. Nobody meets their eyes. The silence begs them to hold forth but something stops them. When they can't take it anymore, they turn to head back up to the house with Eli calling over his shoulder.

"All right. Get him cleaned up and back inside. It's done, it's over and it's dinnertime."

Wash

All I remember is everybody standing ringed round me in a quiet circle. And my mamma muttering over me in that old tongue about how she was not going to have me losing my other eye or my mouth, nosir she wasn't. Said I had plenty else things to see before I'd be anywhere near done with this life.

Then there I was, back on a pallet in the darkest corner of our cabin, with her fighting to keep me here and me pulling to go. Neither of us believing what they did, with those boys going on about how I'd given them no choice. How they weren't going to have to worry no more about me running off with this R written on my face. Said I was not their nigger after all and they owed it to Richardson to try and keep track of me. Too many places to run around here, but this R will bring you back home right quick was what they said.

Once my mamma got me back inside, she had some fellas bring a big table and lay me out on it. She poured that liquor down my throat. Then she wrapped my fingers round the edge of the table so I had a grip on something. She made sure somebody held me down hard. I think it was Rufus. She quick mixed something up and I could hear it slapping against the side of the bowl.

She poured her medicine on me and let it burn. The liquor made me so I could toss the burning from one side of my mind to the other, catching my breath in between. She told Sissy to hold my face tight, squeeze the edges of that burn close together and make sure they meet all along the cut.

Then she bent over me and sewed those edges shut as much from the inside as she could. I heard her thanking God for that little hooked needle she had from her smocking. I felt my skin tugging but the burning and the liquor and Rufus held me hard and the needle was as sharp as the thread was thin.

She took her time, laying those edges in just right, smooth outside edge flat against smooth outside edge, curling the soft inside back down where it belonged instead of letting it bloom bright red like it wanted to. And she muttered over me, talking to herself while she worked.

She kept my face wrapped with poultices to draw the heat from the burn and she slapped some more on there right quick whenever the boys wanted to come look so they wouldn't see how well she was smoothing their writing off my face. She kept a welt on me. A welt made out of chewed root stuck to my face with shiny sap glistening. Said she was trying to keep the road clear for me, come what may.

"You never know when leaving may be the right thing and you don't need that call made for you."

I fell into a deep dark place and they let me stay there. Let my mamma tend to me so long as she kept on with her christening dresses. They did try to bring a doctor in there to see about me, but that old white man took one look at my mamma standing in the doorway of our cabin and he turned right round and left, saying boys, I am not your man.

I'm not sure how long went by, but I know by the time I got back outside, everything was green hot and buzzing.

Part Three

Early summer, 1815
Two days' ride northeast of Nashville

When Wash and Mena finally make their way to Richardson's place, it is midmorning on a beautiful early summer day in 1815, soon after Richardson has made it home from his last war, beaten down and close to broke at sixty two.

He'd been captured by the British and locked up, just like before. Except this time, he had his oldest son William with him and he thought they might die there. Prisoners of war in a camp outside Quebec called Beauport. Most of his fellow officers had negotiated early releases and were making successes of themselves as politicians but not one of them could get him back to the battlefield any sooner. He was paroled so late there was barely time to rejoin the fight before the war was over.

He's been home for a month and a half but he's still a good thirty pounds underweight. Lean as he started out, he looks truly hawkish now. His long narrow face has become a place of edges catching light with hollows falling into shadow.

When he looks down from his upstairs window, he wonders whose wagon is pulling up under his big elm. He has no idea that this hunched figure sitting in that wagon is the same luminous young woman he had bought without intending to down in Charleston during the spring of 1796. Or that the hobbled lump she sits watching over is that boy of hers he had heard so much about in Thompson's long letters through the years.

Fine stock, the old man had written. Growing up straight and tall. As careful a hunter as you would ever want and looks right at you solemn as a judge. Quiet and graceful as a cat.

So what is this sorry broken down pair doing in his side yard?

He stands up quick and mad but as he comes down the wide stairway, he feels how much time has passed. Each step brings a new ache and pain from sleeping on cold stone for too long. Nineteen years since he last saw Mena and he's never seen Wash even once. But his own children seem like strangers to him, so why should these two be any different?

He pauses inside the door with his hand on the latch, trying to brace himself before he swings the door open and steps out, but he's nowhere near prepared. He stands right next to Mena for what feels like forever but he has to bang on the side of the wagon to make her turn toward him. Looking into her face is like looking down a tunnel.

He reaches to draw back the burlap covering Wash but Mena's grip closes tight around his wrist before he ever sees her hand move and her eyes nail his mouth shut. Once she feels the tension leave his arm, she lets it go. As he pulls his hand back, he lets it fall loosely onto the edge of the wagon. She sees he wants to at least look so she lifts the edge of the burlap.

A tall young man lying on his side curled up like a baby. Long clean lines clouded by caked mud. One knee swollen yet nevertheless bent, with his ankles shackled to his hands for the whole ride. Goddamn those Thompson boys.

This is before Richardson's eyes reach Wash's face. Before they come to rest on the shiny globules healing into a bright R on his cheek. Even with the potions Mena has caked on it, Richardson can still make it out. He looks at her and she looks right back, as if to say I know.

She'd given Wash something to make him sleep throughout this last leg of the trip so when she pulls his shoulder into her lap to show Richardson the rest, Wash rolls slack against her and his face turns to meet the sky. Even with Wash's eyes closed, Richardson takes one look at that dent in his temple and knows his right eye will not be right at all.

When he asks Mena if Wash can see out of it, she nods carefully and speaks in a faraway voice.

"He don't like to be surprised from that side."

"Goddammit!"

Richardson slaps the side of the wagon with such a sharp crack that even Wash stirs a little.

"I can fix him. Give me time."

Mena is worn out but she draws up tall inside herself, knowing Richardson needs to catch at least a glimmer of what she had been on that very first day he saw her. It takes all her strength. When he sighs and nods at last, she nearly collapses from the strain but manages to hold herself still. Richardson turns to the driver who hands him a letter. He stands there reading it without realizing he has started muttering aloud.

"Those goddamn Thompson boys. Of course they won't tell me why they had to lose their temper like children and tear up another man's property. Their father would have to reach out from the far beyond and knock those boys of his across the back of the head before they would do right and probably not even then."

Mena seems to be holding her breath so Richardson tells the driver to take them to that last little shed past the others. He turns to call Emmaline and almost bumps into her standing behind him.

"Dammit, a person could trip over everybody forever underfoot. Gather up some quilts and blankets, a lantern and a bucket with some water. Get them well settled out there till she heals him up, then I'll put them in with the rest."

Richardson

When I look back on it, I remember being furious about the brand but I didn't have much time to see about Wash and Mena because I had bigger troubles. I'd partnered with Quinn before leaving so he could help Mary manage, but she couldn't bring herself to hand him the reins, so my place lay in a shambles when I got home, with those two bickering.

I had plenty of work to do but I couldn't seem to get to it. Somehow clearing my name from charges of misconduct seemed more urgent than my debts. I'd ridden off to my last war gunning for glory only to ride home with mud all over me. And I couldn't get clean no matter how hard I tried.

There was a part of me that would have just as soon left it alone, no matter how wronged I felt, but people kept asking me about it. Or not asking me, which was worse. There was a hollow ring to those dinners they held in my honor that first summer home, with so many questions still floating around, even though my closest associates would not permit themselves to ask me anything directly.

I could hardly blame them. The reports were that I had been rash and precipitous, disobeyed orders, and that the entire blame for the massacre should be laid at my door. It was even said that I'd turned tail and run, only to be savaged by Wilton's Indians. Dragged from my horse, scalped, and disemboweled, right there on the battlefield!

Mary looked at me with those wide blue eyes and told me I should be glad that I was home in one piece. But I wasn't. I wasn't in one piece at all. And it felt like the only thing that would put me back together was to set the record straight. McKee's history of that war was shot full of holes, so I hired a writer named Kendrick to write it right. I'd publish my own book. Get the word out.

All that damn Kendrick did was drink my liquor and chase my daughters around my table, but that was just more of what I didn't know at the time.

Everybody has a different version of what happened but I never could get the thing untangled, no matter how hard I tried. It was not me who lost those men, it was Montrose who sent me ahead then made sure our supplies never got there. It was Montrose who turned my men against me from the very beginning, but people will believe what they want to believe and there are no exceptions.

When our continuing troubles with England came to a head in the spring of 1812, I was determined to rescue our Revolution from the politicians despite the fact that I was already nearly sixty. To hell with Montrose's suggestion that the veterans of '76 should guard the home front. Perhaps I was too impatient and maybe I should have waited longer for word from Montrose before taking over our combined forces and marching them towards the fighting. But I'd already waited nearly two months at the recruitment center for him and I felt sure he'd be glad I took the initiative.

I moved slowly and cautiously upriver towards a fallen Detroit, struggling to gain and maintain firm control over two thousand men, with winter coming on and British-allied Indians everywhere. When I finally arrived at Fort Defiance with my men tired, hungry and verging on insubordination, the last thing I expected was to find myself rescued by Montrose himself, arriving triumphant with the news that he was back in command of our joint army.

He gave me only the left wing, which was mostly his Kentucky men, then delivered a rousing speech in which he fired them with mission and purpose. My frustration was so extreme that I was tempted to resign altogether but I remained faithful to my responsibilities. Things went downhill from there.

I waited all that fall at Fort Defiance for orders from Montrose that never came. All through October, November and December, struggling with mutinous men, poor supplies, constant raids from various Indian nations and always the increasingly crushing cold. Morale is difficult enough to maintain, but when you are spending the winter mostly outdoors and nearly naked with nothing to do, it's next to impossible.

Then sickness struck. There were often three hundred sick at a time and I was losing three or four men per day, with the whole regiment wondering why they had come so far from Kentucky if not to fight. All I could do was drill them, which was beginning to seem absurd. After realizing my men could starve closer to the action just as well as farther from it, I issued my controversial order to advance to Frenchtown. I was determined to strike a decent blow against the British and our prospects looked good after we drove them from the town in our first skirmish.

It wasn't until I received Dixon's letter warning me that Montrose had been conspiring against me all along that my bad luck began to make an awful kind of sense. Dixon wrote that had Montrose not managed to wrest his command back from me, he was planning to withhold supplies until his men became boisterous enough to mutiny so that he could then rescue me himself. But even as I held the evidence in my hand, I refused to believe it. This willed blindness has been one of my continual weaknesses.

I remember it all. The heavy shudderings of the first cannon fire. It was still almost full dark. In the disorientation of waking, I wondered what the deep cracking booms were. I'd been expecting a British counterattack led by Wilton, but I thought I had more time. Time to get my weakened men fed back up to snuff, time to get good defenses built and time for Montrose's long promised help to arrive so we could finally strike an adequate blow against the British.

And yes, I should have sent sentries up each of the two roads leading into town that night, but my William had said I was being unduly harsh with the men, unreasonable with all my drilling and protocol, especially after our successful taking of the town just a few days before. That night I had allowed myself the thought that maybe William was right, maybe I was being too strict, so I sent only two scouts up the one road.

I was still asleep when the attack came. I did not even have time to dress properly, just stepped into my breeches and pulled my jacket on over my nightshirt before rushing out into the graying dawn.

The British were shooting hard from the front with Indians flanking either side. My men were under withering attack in an exposed field where they too had been woken by gunfire. I tried to form them into a line but it was no use.

In moments like that, time slows down without giving you any more of itself. I do believe I will continue to see for the rest of my life my men pouring past me with the Indians right behind them. I even put my pistol on one of my own, trying to get him turned around, but he just shouldered by.

When I saw that there was no reversing the situation, I retreated with them in order to try to set up a second stand in the woods on the south side of the river, but the Indians soon swarmed us there as well because Wilton was paying top dollar for scalps.

William and I were captured together by one chief who wanted my jacket for himself. When he escorted us to the rear of British lines, we saw we were vastly outnumbered and agreed it would be suicide for our small group to hold out, no matter how staunch. By this time, I had become convinced that Montrose was not only not coming with reinforcements, but that he was probably well on his way back to Fort Wayne, having cast our fortunes to the winds.

When Wilton insisted on our immediate surrender, I tried to secure the proper guarantees for protection of my wounded men. But even as we stood there discussing it, Wilton's Indians approached the bodies of our dead to plunder them, then moved towards some who were only wounded. Those wounded were guarded over by friends, brothers or cousins, but the Indians kept coming until one of my men shot an Indian right where he crouched.

I never will forget the expression on my William's face, looking first to me, then to Wilton, then to that last fallen Indian, then back to me. I could tell all these various pieces had not yet fallen into place in his mind and I wondered if they ever would since I was having difficulty with them myself.

The terms of our surrender were hammered out before midmorning. I should have paid more careful attention but I was still stunned. In shock, I guess, and I remained that way throughout our forced march to prison at Beauport where William and I were herded into an open pen to stand huddled together with my men in the driving rain. Along the way, we passed the bodies of my two scouts, their scalped skulls gleaming against the dirtied snow.

I spent most of the next morning writing our secretary of war, trying to counterbalance what I knew would be the gist of Montrose's letter saying the defeat had been my fault. Even as I wrote that letter of account to my government, the Indians were on a rampage of their own. I should have known what would happen but when Doctor Simms told me the details later that week, I was so sickened by the story that I heard it only in part.

It is only occasionally, shielded by years of retrospect, that I am able to take my mind back to the truth of what Simms told me. That the Indians had retreated the afternoon of the battle for feasting and an all night celebration. That it was not yet midmorning on the next day when they rode back into town two hundred strong, with faces painted red and black, to make short work of my wounded men who had been left there, supposedly under British protection.

They tomahawked the more wounded so as not to have to manage them, then they took the less wounded captive, binding them onto their horses and parading them through town in an attempt to gain ransom. My sergeant Lipscomb asked that they lead him to one house where he was known, but when the couple proved too frightened to come to the door, the Indian leading the horse shot Lipscomb in the head and left him on their doorstep.

When Simms told me that the bodies of the men under my command lay there for several days until they were half eaten by hogs, I shut my mind to it. Of course, it is always the things we try to forget that we remember and it was no different for me.

I lost all perspective. I kept thinking if I could only retrieve the small trunk of papers captured from me during the battle, I could mount an adequate defense. That trunk held signed papers from Montrose proving that I had done exactly what he'd ordered of me. Without those papers, it was his word against mine. And once he killed Tecumseh, butter wouldn't melt in his mouth. Still, I fought to clear my name until debt threatened to swallow me right up. Debt and drought together.

∞

It is a hot sunny Sunday afternoon, late in Richardson's first summer at home. The whole place has sunk into a quiet haze by the time he finally steps out of his study. No more letters to newspaper editors today. He's given up on the impossible task of rescuing his reputation, at least for the rest of this afternoon.

He's heading for his garden, drawn by the heavy sweet smell of his tuberoses, when he sees one of his negroes limp to the fence of Gamma's paddock off the back of the barn, hook his elbows over the top rail and stand there watching Gamma's new smoke gray foal.

Richardson notices this silhouette standing by the fence then realizes he has seen him there before. Standing in that same position at other quiet times, watching the horses while everyone else is busy with supper. Richardson had assumed it was Ben but today he pauses to look a minute longer.

It is Wash. Up and about. And tall.

Richardson goes the long way around so Wash won't see him. He walks through the cooling dim of the barn aisle and into Gamma's stall, which opens out to her paddock where the old mare stands dozing in the sun as her foal wanders nearby, still tentative and wobbly, not yet venturing far.

Richardson stays well back in the stall's deep shadow so he can get a good look at Wash without being seen. Gamma catches Richardson's scent but chews her hay unconcerned. She knows him. He has been there for most of her foals and she has carried him over nearly every trail, both in daylight and dark. When she tangled with a bear who clawed her rump before she broke its arm with one good kick, Richardson had tended to her himself, talking softly through the medicine's sting. With him standing in her stall, she does not worry about Wash as long as he stays on the far side of the fence.

Richardson watches Wash put his hand through the rails palm down so as not to scare the foal then wiggle his fingers to lure him closer. When Wash grins, Richardson notices he has fine even teeth. Then the healing scar on Wash's cheek buckles from the tension of his grin. Richardson feels a fresh wave of anger surge through him.

He can see Wash wants to climb the fence to get closer to the foal. He puts both hands on the top rail, bending his bad knee to set one foot on the bottom rail. But he's not moving around well enough yet. He's still clumsy and he knows his clambering over, maybe even falling, will scare the foal and the mare too. His quick scan of the barnyard also tells Richardson that Wash knows he's not supposed to go in there.

Richardson understands the urge Wash has to run his fingers through that new foal's shiny coat, still silky soft from his long swim inside his mother's body. To feel that small muzzle explore his palm. To scratch the foal's narrow chest until he wiggles his upper lip and grunts with pleasure. To do this often enough that the colt will walk straight to him as soon as he hears him or smells him. Unafraid. Richardson knows all of this precisely. The solace that animals offer.

Wash drops into a squat, wincing at the pain that shoots through his healing leg. Richardson nods in approval without realizing it. Wash knows horses. And sure enough, now that he's at eye level, the foal heads toward him, checking back for mamma every few steps. Wash lets the colt make all the moves. Lets him think it's his idea.

Richardson stands in the dark stall, watching Wash talk the foal toward him through the brightness. Before long, Wash has the foal butting against the fence and pawing at him, impatient with wanting Wash to come in and play. Wash shakes his head and laughs softly with the foal so he does not see Richardson step from the deep shadow of the stall into the open paddock.

The first he knows of it is when the foal wheels around, spooking so hard on his still unsteady legs that he almost falls over, desperate to put his mother between himself and this new man who stands inside his paddock. Wash feels caught out as he hauls himself back to standing, holding his face flat so as not to wince from the pain in his knee. The foal stands at the far edge of his mother's shadow, tossing his head in an aggravation of confusion and fear.

"Fine piece of something, isn't he?"

Wash nods.

"Carrying his mamma's head and his daddy's legs."

Wash nods again.

"Guess I got lucky. What do you think?"

"Yessir."

Wash looks at the ground, waiting to be dismissed and hoping Richardson will not hold him there by trying to talk to him.

"How you doing?"

"Better."

"Yes, I can see that."

Richardson walks across the paddock toward Wash, running his hand along Gamma's swayed back as he passes by her. Once he's facing Wash, with the fence running between them, he reaches to take hold of Wash's chin so he can lift his bowed head to look into his face.

As he turns Wash's face into the full sun, all Wash can see is the jagged light bouncing off the water in shards on that day when the Thompson boys came for their father's body and for them. As Wash struggles to keep his breath even, he feels Mena's grip on his wrist, telling him everything's different now. He hears her saying I told you and you promised me. He lets Richardson look.

The scar from the hammer runs several inches through Wash's hairline at his right temple. Like a slim hipped river has run through there long enough to wear down into the earth of Wash's temple until it lies thin and shiny at the bottom between smooth banks rising on either side. Almost deep enough for Richardson to lay his first finger inside it, if not for the bend of it.

The tail of that scar fades out before crossing Wash's forehead but it leads Richardson's eye diagonally down across the bridge of Wash's nose to the top inside corner of the R for runaway written across his left cheek, with the leg of the R kicking back toward his ear.

"Damn. Anything on you they didn't get?"

Richardson doesn't expect an answer and Wash doesn't give one. He keeps hold of Wash's chin, turning his face first to the sun then away, tilting it back and forth to watch the R show up in raking light then disappear in shadow. Saying nothing but mmmh mmmh. Each mmmh coming out of the deep of his chest hard and bitten off.

Wash looks over Richardson's shoulder and tries to force himself to breathe. His right arm tingles with wanting to knock Richardson's grip off his chin.

"Your mamma did a good job with that R."

Wash fights to hold his arm down by his side for just one more second then another.

"Wish she could have done something about that dent."

Richardson lets go.

"I don't intend for you to need to run off from me."

Wash drops his eyes to the round top of the fence post, counting his breaths. Working to keep them steady.

"That R gives free rein to any fool hunting reward money. You're liable to get picked up and taken in just running errands for me. Word will get to me but you need to try to stay in one piece until I can send somebody to fetch you home. Best if you stay close by until this fades some and people come to know you as mine."

Wash keeps silent.

"You hear me?"

"Yessir."

"You want to help with the horses?"

"Yessir."

"All right then, tomorrow."

Wash

You'd think I'd have settled down some. But seemed like I healed up from that brand just as hardheaded as ever. Most folks, you can beat their knowing right out of em. But some of us, each lick lays our knowing in deeper.

I didn't know exactly what it was I knew, but I wasn't going to be shaken loose from it. I'd felt my knowing start to rise up in me back at Thompson's place, before my troubles started. And even though it felt mostly broken and gone, I still held tight to it.

I was a raggedy old yard by the time we landed at Richardson's. Hardpacked and weedy. But still, I snarled at any threat to my little patch. Somehow, I musta known my blooming out self was tucked away inside me, curled up tight and laying way down deep, along with Rufus and Cleo and Minerva and all my people my mamma had laid in me so careful before that. All of it, laying in there, just waiting on me to pick it back up.

But I didn't know I knew this yet, so I limped round Richardson's place with everything new to me all over again. I kept to myself but there wasn't a thing I could do about the talk. My scars made sure I was a story and no matter how beaten down people get, they stay hungry for a story. They took mine and they passed it back and forth. Talked all round me before they ever said one word to me.

At first, I was too busy being mad and hurting to want their attention on me. I wanted to stay in that far off shed but by the end of that summer, Richardson put us in the quarters with everybody else. Said we needed to get back to work, just like he did.

My mamma started in on her stitching, but I took one look at that crowded cabin and went straight up to that highest loft of the big barn, no matter what that crotchety old stableman Ben had to say about it. I stayed holed up, hating everything and Richardson the most, until it started to dawn on me, stoking my own fire might not be enough.

My mamma kept telling me I'd get hungry for more, like it was a warning on something that had already happened.

And sure enough, soon as I started feeling better, started coming down from the hayloft, there they all were. Sitting at the fire circle in the quarters, talking and cooking and carrying on. Just like at Thompson's place but with a whole new set. And before too long, this new batch grew round me like a vine. Wasn't even three months yet and there I was, listening for the hook in one of Albert's stories or shaking my head at Virgil's lies, whether I meant to or not.

Life goes on, my mamma kept telling me, life goes on, and I felt my inside soften to her words just like it does when that one horse breathes close and warm on the back of my neck.

I visited her cabin plenty but she knew I couldn't stay there. I was still too mad. Quick to take offense and quicker still to fight about it, so I needed to stay off to myself. But I did feel myself starting to turn more towards life than away from it. I was still a young man, waking up again, and I couldn't help from wanting to go and see and do and taste everything.

The only real sting about my healing up was how much it seemed to please old Richardson. He kept coming after me. Said I had a gift with the horses. Made me his pet, sure as any new colt. Said he was trying to pull me back into the world of the living. Made me want to say I may be broke but it ain't for you to fix.

With the way Richardson stayed after me, it was better to be out of his barn than in it, so I rode with Ben all over this county and the next those first few years, taking our yearlings round to those folks that had bought em and bringing their mares back to our stud for next year's batch.

It was riding with Ben that gave me a chance to see the world. That's how I met Nelle over at Bennett's place and started talking to her. That's how I met most of the rest of em too. I liked Nelle the best but she wasn't the only one. The girls loved me. Always had. All through my troubles and maybe more because of em. My mamma grinned about it when she wasn't worrying over it.

It was people from neighboring places whose eyes snagged on me the most. Who's that and what happened to him, with the story always sounding better than the truth. All those girls growing into women, they came right straight for me, wanting a story of their own. And there I was, ready to take em up on it.

Each one was new and different and better than the last. Each one was a new world I wanted to walk through till it sunk into me.

Richardson had no way of knowing what those girls were to me. He didn't see how each of those girls was the only way I had to empty my mind from that hammer and everything since. He didn't know my moving soft and slow and sure with Nelle or with Beck was as close as I came to swimming in that ocean I remembered from before, floating outside the breakers, rising and falling, with everything feeling as new and shiny as when I started out. He just thought I was a hound dog.

So maybe it was more than him being broke and watching me work that Eclipse stud for Carpenter come to breed his mare that led him to put me to stud. Maybe it was all those girls sneaking out of this barn. Maybe he figured if I was forever getting after it anyway, what was the harm in making me be his money? And once he gave up on his good name, I guess putting me to this work wasn't no big step. But it sure took me a minute to catch onto the switch.

Bennett came for the weekend. Brought two of his mares to be bred, said he wanted one last crop before that fancy horse got too old. And he brought Nelle to look after him. She made sure she was the one he picked so she could see me again. Two whole nights and she spent both of em up in my loft with me.

There I was, being real careful and thinking I'm so smart, with Nelle good and on her way home before I step to the doorway of the barn after finishing my chores. I'm standing there watching their wagon about to pull out. That's when I hear Richardson talking to Bennett. Thought it was about the mares but it was about me. He's telling Bennett all about me.

How he bought my mamma and put us out on that island with old man Thompson. How I ran into some trouble with those brothers but now I'm coming along nice. Real nice. Too nice maybe. Then they laugh, talking about how the girls stay after me.

Then I see Richardson stepping closer and Bennett bending down from his high seat with his hand on Richardson's shoulder and his mouth next to Richardson's ear. I see the man's hand snake out with a wad of bills and I see Richardson tuck the money into his waist pocket, asking Bennett what was the name again?

And I hear Bennett say Nelle, that would be Nelle. And Richardson says good, I'll mark it down, as he turns away saying thank you, pleasure doing business with you as always. See you at the dance. Bring whoever you want.

I stand there, hearing this and feeling my belly drop. Watching Nelle leaning over the far side of the wagon, saying goodbye to some friends she made here. I see her brimming with sugar, knowing she's thinking about me, and meanwhile, that damn Richardson's taking me and her both and putting us right in his pocket.

He bet on me. He bet Bennett I'd get with Nelle. He bet I'd do just exactly what I did before I ever did it. Then he took that money and put it in his pocket.

I stand there like I'm rooted. I don't even nod at Nelle waving goodbye to me. All I can feel is the big barn door sucking me back inside and before I know it I'm trying to break whatever's laying right there by me. It's a rasp and it won't break, no matter how hard I swing. So I stab the tip into the center post and start in on the closest horse.

Queenie is standing there tied in the aisle. I grab her by her lead rope, jerking her till she panics, scrambling to get away from me, her squeals and whinnies echoing through the barn, and I'm yanking her towards me, muttering run away, you want to? You can't run away from me, can't run away from me now, and she's pulling back, but I'm pulling her closer so I can slap her.

I guess Richardson heard the ruckus from out in the yard cause I hear him yelling. Then he's standing in the doorway. By then, I'd let go of the mare. I turn to face him with Queenie behind me, backed against the end of her rope and blowing loud rattling snorts.

"What the hell?"

I look right at him and I say, nothing. It wasn't nothing. Bucket fell off the shelf and she spooked is all.

He looks at me. He runs his eyes over everything till they catch on the rasp hanging from the center post.

"What's this?"

I just look at him.

He reaches out, wrenches the rasp loose with one hand and sets it down on the trunk where it was lying before. Never takes his eyes off me.

"Everything all right in here?"

I'm nodding yessir, with the calming down horses stamping and snorting all through the barn. He looks at me a minute longer but I guess he don't see nothing cause he turns to go back up to the house, shaking his head.

Richardson

I'd set Wash to working the horses in the beginning because he seemed to have a gift, but I had to pull him out of the barn after the first few years. That temper of his snaked out one time too many and Ben was finished with him.

"Half the horses in this barn head shy from the way that boy gets after em."

"It only takes once," Ben kept saying, as if I didn't know that already. "It only takes once to wipe away years of work, just as sure as a wet rag."

Ben wanted Wash out of the barn and I couldn't blame him, especially after Queenie spooked on account of being manhandled, we both knew by Wash. I'd sent for Hobbs's man Homer to come trim her feet right, but it only took her five minutes to shy away from him then rear up and fall over backwards, breaking her neck after having given us only the one foal. All that careful time we spent bringing that mare into this world and all those fine foals yet to come from her, all of it gone.

I watched Ben backing our big draft gelding through the barn door so he could hitch him to Queenie's body and drag it out to be buried.

"Question is, what the hell do I do with him now, Ben?"

And Ben shook his head, saying I don't know and I don't care but I want him out of this barn today.

I set Wash to work in the field but by day two, he'd sent the pickax into his own instep then worked until dusk in the mud so the foot festered. Almost had to come off. Seemed like Wash was determined to pull himself under, if for no other reason than the satisfaction of taking money from my pocket.

Every single thing I put him to backfired. Finally, in a fit of anger, I carried him off to sell. But nobody bid. Atkinson was fond of reminding me that most people stay too busy to put up with such a troublesome negro. They had heard about Wash and knew better than to spend their money on him.

I had to bring him straight back home with me. And he looked
pleased about it the whole way. Burned me right up. Like he was
spitting in my face. Seeing how much he could cost me. Breaking my tools and fighting other people's negroes just to make me
pay the fine, digging his heels in and making a damn show out
of every time he refused to do right.

He even made me give him the stripes, knowing I pride myself
on not having to. He knew how each lashing, even when well
earned, unsettles everybody on my place. Raises old buried grudges
like hackles on a dog's back.

But Wash's favorite way of messing with me used to be his
whoring around, especially once he saw how much trouble he
could make for me with all the mammas coming to me to complain. Even after I sent him to the fields. Maybe more so.

At my wit's end, I went to Mena to ask for some help. But
my time for going to her was long gone and she looked right
through me. Even as I was asking her, I could see her thinking
you should have known better. You should have known better
all along.

I could see her deciding I am done with helping white folks.
Time to let whatever will happen here go ahead and happen.
Then she looks at me through my talking at her and says, "I am
through. You hear me? Through with it."

I should have paid more attention to Wash. To him and to everything else. But I remained obsessed with chasing my good name
through a past that wouldn't stand still while we sank ever deeper
into the hole. We'd just lost our second cotton crop in a row and
the drought was running into its third month while prices for
negroes rose steadily.

When Quinn came to me, wanting to get us into the breeding business, I already knew Wash was an unlikely choice. But he was like catnip to the girls and that R brand made sure he couldn't run off easily. I needed to make him do something and I'd tried everything else.

Bennett said he heard about a man back East who was doing it but he didn't see why. Too many negroes there already and the land was depleted. The market was out here with us. Some had started walking theirs west to sell but the journey wore them down.

And Bennett had a girl named Nelle. Good worker and sturdy but kept too much to herself. Wouldn't settle down and start breeding. Wouldn't let any of his men near her. I bet him that Wash would be able to get near her. Nearer than near. And he did. So it was a gamble at first and it went from there.

Wash

I used to go to the girls cause I liked em and I liked liking em. But after I saw Richardson tucking Bennett's money into his waistband, saying Nelle, good, I will mark it down, that's when I started to slide. It wasn't about me and the girls anymore. It was about me and Richardson. Seemed like everything everywhere was about me and Richardson.

Sometimes, I thought I could hear Rufus trying to tell me something. Show me some way through. But it was dim like an echo and fading. Whatever he was trying to tell me was good and true but it was not here and now. All I could do was shake my head on my new wide shoulders and charge at things, breaking as much as I could.

And you bet I made Richardson give me the stripes. I wanted to make sure he'd have trouble selling me and he did. Most he could do with me was loan me out and he did that before I was ever even born.

But he couldn't never break his bond with me. That bond with me was one he made with my mamma on that day he raised his hand for her. And I knew he saw her in me and it meant he couldn't turn his back on me. Couldn't walk away, even if he wanted to.

She always said you can tell a lot about a person by watching the way they act. She studied those men milling round during the sale, those men thinking they were the ones doing the shopping. She looked and she watched till she found her eye drawn to the one man she was hunting. A man whose manner went several layers deep and not just a coating.

She picked Richardson like she picked my daddy. My mamma picked and chose as careful and sure as walking a fence pole. And she let him know she had. Said it's a rare person who can walk away from somebody seeing some good in you and counting on it.

That's what she did to him. She counted on the good in him. She said without saying, I see you seeing me. And sure enough, he looked at her and he saw her and he raised his hand for her. And he kept her. Hired her out instead of selling us. For all those years. And sent for us soon as he got home.

She told me she knew all along, just like he'd had to buy her, he'd hang on to me. Said she could tell he knew his own kind well enough to know right away, soon as he saw me, what I'd bring out in em. He knew I'd make em knock me back over and over till I didn't get up anymore cause I can't learn to look away.

∞

Richardson walks through the speckled light falling under the trees onto the thick short grass. The old man moves in a way that makes everybody else seem like they are standing still. A sleek hull cutting through water. Looking, seeing, sizing up. And always carrying that list in his mind, parceling out tasks and chores to just the right people with just the right amount of detail. This way of his is what has kept most of his people on the job. His seeing what skill they have. Seeing it, calling on it, expecting it. Somehow his seeing them like that feels like respect, even though all he's telling them is how to put more money in his pocket.

It can be hard to catch his attention as he stalks through the day. He's impatient because he wants everything sorted out well in advance of any situation that might arise. His mind feels clean to him, like a scythe. Even if it falls too quickly at times, often before the request has been fully voiced.

What Richardson has worked to learn, both from his father and from Thompson, as well as from his years of experience, is to discern the rule lying buried within the situation. Sort the exceptions from the rule, keeping these to a minimum. Weigh the costs of making the exception against its benefits and then decide. This is painstaking work and thankless, requiring what feels to Richardson like eternal vigilance. Throughout most of his life, he has had no doubt that he was earning his privileges through the carrying out of his responsibilities.

Wash watches Richardson from where he sits seething in the shadow of an overhang. Stewing over what happened with Nelle. All that sweetness and sugar turned to money in Richardson's pocket. Wash can't find one way of being himself without Richardson managing to turn it to his advantage. Whenever Wash takes hold of life like his mamma keeps telling him to, seems like Richardson finds some way to snatch it right from his hands.

Feels to Wash like it's time for him to start taking. And he has. He misses that mare Queenie, even as he savors having taken something from Richardson for once. And he knows what he wants to take hold of next. He wants to take that hawkish face in his hands and squeeze all the lean life from it. Everything Wash is and knows keeps shrinking down into that one thirsty pull.

Even as he remembers Rufus telling him don't let your mind slip into that smooth groove, it feels too good. He thinks of Cleo gone and Rufus without her but still, he lets his mind trace his want like a scent. Wondering when that day will come to pass. Seems like he won't even have to make it happen. It's just going to come his way, float right downriver until there it is, just in front of him, well within reach. Somehow. Sometime.

He moves up and down the rows of cotton and tobacco, or else he sits under an overhang in the quarters, just far back enough to stay in shadow, and he lets his mind go wherever it wants. He hears Mena trying to draw him close but he keeps his back to her.

And through the blur of each day tumbling past him full of work and worry, Richardson senses the catch and pull of Wash studying him without really knowing what it is. Just a vague distant underwater sort of tugging. At first, Richardson assumes it's some task needing doing that keeps slipping his mind.

But soon enough, he realizes it's Wash watching him. Richardson knows this is what happens when you give a man a life he cannot hook himself into. Cut off from anything to want or anything to have, all the man has the time or inclination to do is watch you. His watching you day in and day out is enough to drive you clean out of your mind. Nor is it safe.

Richardson decides to override Ben's wishes by putting Wash back with the horses. He wants to see whether Wash and the new chestnut stud bought as a bargain last week can find a way to knock some sense into each other. He senses Wash spoiling for a fight and decides it better be with that horse instead of with him.

Most everybody else on the place had shrugged their shoulders when he sought recruits to work with the new horse, shaking their heads to say no thank you and sweeping the barn aisle thoroughly so Richardson would see they were being good workers despite their refusing his request. He saw they were afraid and he did not blame them. They had heard the squeal and seen the head toss that broke Ben's shoulder on the first day. Heard Ben's body hitting the wall and seen him come scrambling over it. They may have found a way to smile about that story by now but they're none too eager to step into that stall themselves.

When Richardson goes to the quarters to tell Wash what he has decided, Wash maneuvers Richardson into the sun while he stands in the shade. As usual, Richardson can't quite read Wash's face. The older man pauses before he turns to go, holding the dollar in such a way that Wash ends up reaching to take it without its ever being fully offered. Nodding yes, he'll give it a whirl as he watches Richardson walk back to the house.

The next morning, Richardson and Wash stand outside the second stall of the stud barn. Both doors shut. Top and bottom. Richardson has kept the chestnut stud the whole week without food and a full two days without water. Says it's the only way he'll let somebody close enough.

Richardson holds a loop of thick rope weighted with heavy hooks at both ends. Wash holds a bucket of water with a bucket of grain sitting there waiting. There's a long thin slot in the wall of the stall, just above two more buckets tied inside, close to the corner.

Soon as Wash pours the water through the slot into one bucket, he's supposed to pour the grain into the other bucket. His doing this should give Richardson just enough time to step inside the stall and hook the rope to the wall, with a loop around the horse's middle so he can't break his neck from pulling back. The trick will be Richardson stepping out in time.

A small group of stable hands has gathered to watch but Richardson ignores them. Wash stands next to him, feeling the weight of the water bucket pulling on his arm and wondering how this will go. Whenever Richardson moves close, time slows down.

Wash wonders whether he will pour the water and the grain like he is supposed to but then bolt the door behind Richardson so he can't get back out of the stall. Even tied to the wall, the stud can likely do some damage. But then Wash feels those eyes on him, watching him standing there next to Richardson. Wash can see those same stable hands, none of whom like him very much anyway, sitting in the courtroom telling the judge everything that happened and then walking home to get that dollar. He decides no for now.

Richardson puts his hand on the latch and nods over at Wash. As Wash pours the water and then the grain through the slot, Richardson steps inside the stall. Two beats and he's out again, bolting both latches as the horse erupts behind the wall. Richardson looks at Wash and then at the wall as squeals and thuds echo through the stud barn.

The small group of spectators falls away murmuring and Richardson runs his fingers through his hair, rubbing his scalp hard to make that tingling feeling go away. He opens the top door, telling Wash to watch the horse till he wears himself out and he'll be back to check on them by dinnertime.

Wash

That damn fool stud started striking at the wall soon as he found out he couldn't pull away from it. He headed right at it like it was a living thing. Cut his knees up from striking. Screaming then snaking his head down hard. And the whomp of his teeth hitting wood with splinters flying until chips and dents circled out from that hook in the wall like stars in the sky.

He broke a front tooth from striking at the hook and that tooth stuck straight out till his top lip kept catching on it. Seemed like the weight of his top lip pressing on that broken tooth bothered him more than those bigger cuts on his legs or the one over his eye.

I don't know how long it went on. All I know is I went through hungry and back several times while he sweat new wet through layers of dry caked salt.

Every now and then, he'd stop for a minute. Stand there trembling. Leaning against the rope. Breathing hard, flashing bright pink inside his nose, with his top lip jumping to keep from pushing on that broken tooth. Blood dripping on the straw. A minute of quiet before it would start again.

In the end, it was tiredness that stopped his pulling. Wasn't till then when he finally saw what we'd been trying to show him all along. Soon as he let up on the rope, the rope let up on him. Once he let that rope fall just a hair slack, it quit grabbing at him. He drew one long shuddering breath and let his head drop to the straw.

I stood there watching with my elbows hooked over the stall door. That horse carried every blow he ever took right along with him. He stayed mad at the ones he already took and madder still at the ones to come. The fine in him was pretty much buried by the time he got to Richardson's, but still it flashed out some from the clean way he was put together and how he moved.

I remembered feeling that very same fine rising inside me back on the big, spread out Thompson place. Working with Rufus and feeling my knowing coming together inside me. All the girls clustering close and the boys looking up to me.

Then that one day when I decided I'd had enough. I heard the sound of my own voice telling those brothers what I knew for sure and I saw that hammer coming down on me, dark and blocking out the light. I felt the ground pressing up against me, with my mamma hovering over me and one brother saying to the other, damn, Eli, what you trying to do? Kill him?

And I felt myself struggling there by the fire in front of Rufus's shop after my long peace of living in the woods. My mamma's grip was hard round my head and I saw Rufus bringing the orange hot brand down to meet my cheek. And then getting dragged here, holing up in this barn, hating everything and Richardson the most. Finding my way back into life all over again, only to end up back in the field. Till finally I was headed right straight for him, hungry to wrap my fingers round his neck.

I saw myself rearing against the rope wrapped round my middle. I saw myself striking at that wall stretching out forever in front of me, till I finally saw the only thing giving was me, over and over, till finally it was plain old tiredness that rescued me. Taut turning to slack, and then my breath coming long and slow, carrying the trembling away and washing me clean while I stood in the quiet of Richardson's barn.

At the end of that long day, I unlatched the door and went in. All that was left was a flicker in his eye so I moved closer, talking to him, letting my voice rise and fall, smooth as my hands running over his thick coat crunchy with dried sweat, saying well I'll be damned, Mr. Big Man, what you think about all this now, hmm, what you think about this now?

I didn't throw more grain in the bucket for a treat. Not yet. We'd have to deal with that tooth first. But my hands went for the places I knew felt the best. I stood at his shoulder, running my hand down his broad chest to scratch between his front legs then running my other hand up to his mane, crabbing my fingers together along the thick crest of his neck. Once he felt me scratching him, he started to relax.

I'm saying that's better, hmm, this is better, it's better from here on out. I'm leaning my forehead into his neck, tasting salt on my tongue and laughing to myself and to him, saying well I'll be damned. I'll be good goddamned.

I stood there for I don't know how long, rubbing and feeling his muscles give under my fingers. It was much later when I started feeling him lean back into me. Just a little but he was doing it.

"All right now, Mr. Man, all right now, we'll see."

I turned to leave the stall, bringing my hand up from his chest to run it along the crest of his neck and then real light along his back where the saddle would sit if we ever got that lucky. My hand was rising across his rump and starting to drop to the top of his tail as I headed on past him for the door. Good thing my feet was moving slower than my hand and I was still standing at that horse's midsection when his near hind foot sliced through the air right in front of my face.

All right, all right, we'll see about that is what I told him and I steered clear on out of there.

Took me a while to learn. Young man I was didn't know nothing and stayed trying to keep it that way. Looking back from here, I still don't see how I didn't get myself killed.

I couldn't let nobody tell me nothing. But it eased off, that need to do like I say and nobody else. Ran smack up against my wanting to be here. Somehow, somewhere, and not just from my mamma, I always had the real strong feeling I came into this world to happen to something and I had to see how.

Turns out there's a way to give in without losing. You got to find some slack in you. Just this side of your breaking point. Each of us got a different breaking point, according to who you are and the life you get born inside.

And if somebody shows you how, you might can move that breaking point from where it started out to where you need it to be. But sometimes, you can't. Who you are and the life you get given won't never fit together and you leave this world as quick as you came in.

A real hothead like I was won't last long. And I wouldn't have neither if my mamma hadn't stayed steady working on me. Rufus had a pretty good go at saving me too. Not that I was much help to either of em. Soon as they got my breaking point buried deep, I'd drag it right back to front and center. They kept telling me hate cost too much but I didn't want to hear em. I liked feeling my heart sharp as a blade cutting through the world. Itching for a fight. Problem was, there weren't too many fights I got to have, much less win.

It's a wonder I made it but I did. It was on that day, watching that horse, when I found my way to a place inside me where I could stand. I looked out at everything and it dawned on me just like morning. I wanted to be here, stick round for it, whatever it was. I wanted to see it come.

That was the day when I took over from my mamma working on me. That was the day I took hold of my own insides, moving everything where I needed it to be to stay safe.

Richardson was back by dinnertime to see about that horse. Telling me about him like I didn't already know. Settling in on that fourth step, leaning his back against the side wall and smoothing that flask to shiny with his palm.

Seemed like he couldn't hear himself think unless he was talking at me. Started out with the horse but then went on and on. That night and the next few. Enough of that flask and he'd get good and snagged on his last war, hashing and rehashing, no matter how many times he said he was through with it. He went over and over it. What he set out to do, what went wrong and all the ways it went wrong. How he tried and tried to straighten it out but now he's starting to see some things never do get straightened out.

Watching him go round and round with his story, I remembered seeing that one red pullet behind Ben's cabin, gone addled. Circled round and round, pecking after one spot. Going after grain that wasn't there till her beak was bloody from hitting the ground. Then the rest of em got after her and that was the end of it.

Richardson kept saying Montrose doublecrossed him all the way from here to Sunday. Pushed him and his men right up against starving. And they were Montrose's men to start out with, making it worse. Said that same damn bunch of Kentucky men had almost mutinied on him from wanting their old boss back.

Said he looked at them, gone pale to blue and knee deep in the snow, pulling their own sleds upriver after they already ate the horses, and thought about asking em did they want their old boss back now?

Said he never ceases to be amazed by what men will do when you push em hard enough, and sometimes even when you don't. Guess we all got our blind spots.

He went on about how Montrose screwed him and kept on screwing him until he ended up behind bars all over again. Just like his first war, gunning for glory then locked up again, sitting on cold stone for years. Except this time, he was outside Detroit. Called it godforsaken Canada. Said he thought he'd die there.

I already knew this part of the story for myself. His being locked up so long was what left me with those Thompson boys and I thought I'd die there too.

How is it some things come so easy and others come so hard, Richardson always wanted to know. But he never did wait on an answer. Just kept on telling me how he hired that man Kendrick to write it right. If the government won't give him his inquiry, then Kendrick's book will set the record straight.

I held my mouth shut to keep from telling Richardson that man won't set nothing straight. I saw it just by watching him walk across the yard and that was before he got in the liquor good. But Richardson didn't come down here for my opinion. That much I knew for sure.

Folks will take hold of whatever story suits em best and nothing you can do. Don't matter if it is your story, once they start in on it, you can't never get it out of their mouth. No matter how hard you try. All you can do is find a way to hang on to knowing you know better.

But what I started to see was the more times he came down to that barn talking at me, the more I meant to him, whether he knew it or not. My mamma told me and she told me, but it wasn't till this point when I looked and saw how right she was.

She always told me, even beat up and crippled like I was when they carried us into Richardson's yard on that very first day, she said you're worth something to him and don't you let him forget it. Said it was her being his had sent her out to that island with old man Thompson, and it was my being his had kept those brothers from killing me.

If I meant something to him just by being in this world, then my being smart and strong and hardheaded raised my count. And all his talking at me did too.

Find you a way to be his money was what she kept telling me. Make yourself worth something to him and be sure to stay that way.

Everybody goes through being deaf to his mamma, no matter how much sense she's making, but what she stayed steady telling me started to sink in. After watching that chestnut stud, I started hearing her better. More clear.

Used to be, I was my whole world. All I knew to steer by was this great big ocean inside me with all kinds of storms moving across it. Used to be I'd head right into a squall. But Rufus was right. Throwing yourself round just makes em feel more the man. Gives em the excuse they been hunting.

I finally started looking at the whole of it instead of just the storms inside me. Trying to get my bearings. It was taking hold of the big picture that helped me wrap my mind round Richardson putting me to this work.

It was just like Rufus always said but I didn't see it till now. He was always telling me, doing this lets you have that. I couldn't see what he was saying back then, but soon as that knowing clicked inside me, there was no stopping me. If this work was what gave me a steady pass, if this work was what let me go where I needed to go right when I needed to go there, then bring me the next one.

It was just as I was hitting full swing when my mamma was starting to fade and all she said about it was how some things turn out to be just a shadow of themselves and I needed to hang on. I jerked back from her at first, when she clutched me tight to her and sounded so fierce, talking about how all these little ones of mine gonna tear his house down in the end, but I did right like she taught me.

When Richardson sent me someplace, I did what I could to go easy on em, and I looked for my own coming up over there the next time. On all these places round here. Somebody didn't like his list, they came to me and I'd see what I could do. They knew, just like I knew, won't be much. I always said, if you don't want eyes on her, then keep her dirty and skinny and out of the way.

And just like she was waiting on me, hanging on till I stepped up and took hold of myself, my mamma died with peace on her. She knew she was leaving me safe and going home. Told me I had everything I needed and I'd be fine.

I do wonder if she saw all I had coming down the road to me. Every single one of these little ones comes carrying some shade of her. Maybe that's why I kept at it. Maybe I was doing some good, keeping her with me long after she was gone.

∞

Mena told Wash two things before she left. He had to learn to rest and he had to find himself some joy. No matter what and no matter how. He had listened to her without realizing how much of his joy was wrapped up in her. But after she died, he started to see how he was truly off to himself and alone.

Everybody else can get together, eat and drink and talk or even fight, just to blow off some steam. But let Wash walk into that pocket of open space between those cabins where everybody gathers late Saturdays into Sundays and he can see them all draw back a little and tighten up. He knows they don't like having to look at him because of the pictures he pulls up in their minds. Makes dinner turn dusty in their mouths.

And it doesn't help to head over to some other place where people don't know him so well because he has already been sent to most of them. The rest have heard all about him and think they know something.

He sneaks out to Mena's grave whenever he can manage and it helps some. Richardson had wanted to bury her in the family plot up by the house but Wash was glad Mary wasn't having that. And he didn't want her in the cemetery Richardson kept for his negroes either. Mena always said it stayed too cluttered in there for her to see where she was headed.

Wash was relieved when Richardson let him have this one thing. Permission to bury her somewhere secret. He found a good spot, high on a sloping spit of land jutting out into the river where it runs wide and deep around the bend, right at the far edge of Richardson's place. Under a group of sweet gum trees where she can see the sun shine gold on the water as it sets.

He hadn't had time to take her there to show her because she went quickly. As soon as her clear burning spirit started to flicker, it only took a day. Once she knew she could take her eyes off Wash, all she wanted to do was look where she was going. Said she wanted to make sure she got there.

Wash finds some good rest with an old woman over at Pleasanton. A little bitty scrawny woman who had known his mother, Binah rides herd on the smallest children while everybody else is in the field. After Wash is done for the day, he goes to visit with her. Sits on the stump next to hers while she sucks on her pipe whether it's empty or full. She pats at Wash sitting there next to her, nodding and patting his leg like he's not a grown man.

Together they watch the children. When one boy toddles over to the fence and manages to clamber up to the first rung, Binah calls to him. He turns his head to look then wobbles hard and starts to cry. Wash goes to the boy, takes him around his middle to pull him off the fence and carry him back to Binah. When he sets him down in front of her, the boy steadies himself with one hand on each of Binah's knees but stares up at Wash and keeps on staring long after Wash has sat down on his stump.

Wash smiles back at first then has to look away. He gets snappish with Binah and rough with the boy. Stands up and paces, kicking at sticks and looking for the horizon. He does and doesn't want to know whether the boy is his. He can't yet see himself in that small square face with its steady gaze. Wash doesn't know what he himself looked like as a toddler but he hears old man Thompson telling him about how he came into the world.

"Solemn as a judge. Looked right through me from day one."

It won't be until later that Wash starts seeing flashes of himself and of all his people Mena had told him about shining from the faces of his growing up children. By that time, he will have stopped sitting with Binah. It's too much and too close. Easier to come and go and then stay gone.

After a little while, Binah tips her head to call Wash back to her and he comes. She looks around sharp then digs in her pocket for her talisman. Gnarled worn leather stitched with red and soaked in spirit. She holds it out to Wash and he takes it even though Mena always told him never touch somebody else's piece. With Binah, he knows it's all right. Just holding her piece makes him feel calmer.

When he sits back down, she turns to him and takes one of his big hands in her two bent feathery ones. Opens his fingers out and lays his palm flat against her throat just over that hollow dip. Presses it tight. His fingers reach almost around to the back of her neck.

She sits there staring at him with her chin dipped so she's looking up at him hard. The loose skin of her throat slides under the weight of his hand and the force of her grip. And they just sit there like that until he starts to feel her pulse. Until her pulse grows and grows under the flat of his palm, throbbing all the way through his hand and up his arm then crowning warm across the top of his head.

He catches his breath and cuts his eyes over at her but she stares right at him with her face falling open in the light of the spirit, telling him as clear as if she is saying it out loud, you feel that? You hear that? You ain't got nothing to worry about, boy.

After that day, he sits there next to Binah, in amongst those children playing in the dirt at his feet, some of the littlest ones his, and he leans back against the wall of the shed, dozing in the shade and feeling almost peaceful.

But not all these children want him around. Especially the boys getting almost old enough to leave Binah behind as they head for the fields. They can't see why he sits with Binah while the rest of the grown folks have to work, and there's something strange in the way their parents act toward Wash, so they keep sassing him, no matter how many times Binah tries to knock it out of them. Makes him glad to disappear into the woods running traplines even if it is for Richardson.

What surprises Wash is that he finds himself glad to have Richardson's favorite son wanting to tag along behind. Even as a slight and tender ten year old, Lucius looks just like his father. Sharp brown eyes under dark brows with that same widow's peak. He stays forever after Wash who finds some peace with Richardson's boy. Remembering what Mena had told him, Wash lets himself have it. But he doesn't let Lucius know he's anything but tolerated and he never takes him to Mena's grave.

It is months of following Wash along Richardson's traplines before Lucius dares to ask him anything. That is the bargain. Lucius can tag along but he has to keep his mouth shut. Wash can hear the questions he wants to ask burning inside him anyway.

What happened to your head? Why don't you have to go to the fields with the rest? Where do you keep going off to in that wagon? How come you know what your daddy looks like if you've never seen him?

But Lucius knows better than to ask those questions and soon enough, they give way to other questions because there are still plenty of things that need knowing.

"How do you know the deer came through here?"

"How do you tell your direction when it's noon?"

"Why did that dog bury her puppies in the leaf compost?"

"Did she mean for them to die?"

Wash lets the questions pour over him like sweat running down. He keeps on doing whatever he's doing, bending to check or set a trap then rising to walk on, pausing only to pull back a low branch to reveal the double crescent moons of deer tracks in the damp earth or to shake his head no, the bitch had not meant for her puppies to die.

Wash only speaks after they've been quiet for a long while, dropping an answer into the stillness as sudden as a fish jumping and then gone. Lucius will wonder whether he heard it at all.

"She was trying to keep em warm."

Lucius stows Wash's few comments away, wrapping them up in soft cloth to take out later and study over.

Wash starts out putting up with Lucius as just one more thing, thinking God sure has been thorough with him this time. But he feels forever alone these days and Lucius is new like a pup and playful. Sometimes Wash has to hold his hand back from knocking that innocence right out of the boy but most times he manages to let it please him. And Wash hears Mena talking to him as they walk through the woods.

"Little enough to take pleasure in and a body gets stuck in the mud not letting God touch you at all, anytime, just because life won't go the way you want."

And Wash likes the way the boy hangs on his words. The attention feels good. Almost makes him want to say more but then he hears Emmaline muttering, don't never trust a white child over the age of twelve and most don't even make it that far.

Wash keeps his stories to himself but he teaches Lucius the trees and the birds, the tracks and the nests. He pauses, listening to the red fox call until he sees the boy hear it too. He makes sure Lucius knows how to keep an eye on the sun and how to listen for the river to find his way home.

It feels good to give over some of the knowing that Mena and Rufus had filled him with but Wash makes sure to stop before Lucius has had enough. Always keep them wanting more. Never let them see the bottom.

Lucius stays careful. Careful to keep his mouth shut and careful to sneak up to Wash's nook in the high loft only when he knows Wash is gone. Long after he has watched him head off down the road in the back of his father's wagon. Lucius tries not to leave any sign of the hours he spends up there but Wash can usually tell. He shakes his head, both annoyed and somehow pleased the boy needs him that badly.

It is almost a full year of Lucius walking in Wash's shadow before Nero wraps his hands around Richardson's neck on that cold bright morning in the barnyard and ends up lying flat on his back with that great hole torn in his middle.

It is the next to last Monday in December. The shortest day of the year. Wash and Lucius make it home well past dark after running Richardson's northern line of traps. They move toward the lights of the place, feeling the almost snow as a wet mist on their faces. Wash navigates through the last of the bare trees by memory while Lucius stretches his stride, still trying to step inside Wash's tracks across the sodden ground long after he can't see them anymore. The cluster of small bloodied bodies knocks against first one leg then the other as he switches his burden from hand to hand.

Something has happened on the place today. Wash senses it before they are within a hundred yards. It makes him feel old to realize he doesn't even want to know what it is. All he wants to do is wrap his numb fingers around a warm cup of something and put his feet to the fire.

Without a word, Wash stops and turns to hand his catch to Lucius, holding back a possum as he looks down at the boy sharply reminding him not to tell. Lucius tucks his chin in a nod as he takes the additional weight then struggles for a minute to balance his load. Their single track forks into two as Wash heads for the barn and Lucius turns toward the house.

Wash knows it's most likely Nero. He saw early on how that whole story was going to go and decided to steer clear. There are as many ways to hold out as to give in and some of them can get you killed. Sure enough, the fire circle in the quarters is abuzz and there's a dark brown stain on the hardpacked dirt beside the big barn door. And just inside that door, a pair of long boards laid across two sawhorses. Blood there too. Wash walks right past those sawhorses and climbs up to his loft. He knows he will hear the details from there.

Lucius slips into the kitchen just before dinner. He hands Emmaline their catch and asks her what happened. She tightens her mouth and shakes her head as she pulls a pail between her knees and starts skinning a squirrel. Lucius leans against her thigh, looking over her shoulder, and asks again, what?

She cannot bear the thought of answering his endless questions. Even hearing them will be hard for her tonight so she tells him it's dinnertime and he needs to go sit at the table with everybody else. But first wash those grubby hands. When he comes back to stand beside her instead of going into the dining room like she told him to, she wipes the shine of grease from the corner of his mouth with her thumb, asking him whether he likes squirrel or possum better. He raises his shoulders along with his eyebrows like he can't really say, dragging out the moment in the hopes that she will relent and tell him the story that everyone else already knows.

He leans against her as she turns back to her task and she lets him. Despite all her warnings to Wash, she's been breaking her own rules with Lucius. It's not that she loves him. It's just that there's a dent in her heart that fits his shape because he has been pushed right up against it for so long. Him and nobody else.

Richardson put her son and her husband out in the quarters, saying surely that was close enough, but it wasn't. Her grandsons are scared to come in the house and she can't leave the kitchen, so she lets herself enjoy the fact that Lucius comes to her first, before his own mother and father. It gives her a little something to have so she keeps it. But she's not telling him this story. Not tonight.

Lucius finds his sister Livia in the passageway and asks her what happened. She sets down the ladle she came for and bends to put her face close to his, placing one warm hand on each of his narrow shoulders. She tells him in a low steady voice that everything is fine, his father is fine, they are all fine, but one of the new negroes is dead because he started a fight. She says it's been taken care of now and everything is fine as she turns him toward the dining room and tells him to go on in and sit down.

He slips into his chair at the dinner table just as his mother starts to say the prayer. While they have their heads bowed, he studies them. After a day spent following Wash through the woods, his own family looks so strange to him. Like people in paintings come down off the wall. Walking and talking, saying please pass the salt and yes you may be excused. He is right there with them but he feels like if he reaches for any one of them, none will be close enough to touch. Not even Livia.

The prayer ends and the conversation starts back up, bouncing harsh and jerky as it veers both toward and away from the one thing no one is supposed to mention. Lucius looks into his father's eyes as he is asked about his Latin lesson and all he can feel is the impossibility of conveying to him the wide sweep of the horizon from that high rocky bluff overlooking the river, the smoothness of the small furred bodies he and Wash collect from the traps, the steady quiet rhythm of Wash's hands building a fire then skinning a squirrel. Humming over it as it cooks. The tenderness of those small juicy chunks of meat, crisp to burnt at the edges. Lucius holds worlds within him that his family does not share and he must wait for all that life to subside before he trusts himself to speak. He watches his father growing impatient with him but he can't find any words the old man wants to hear.

"Did Nero get in a fight with you?"

Richardson looks down the table at his gathered family. He feels the rest of their unasked questions hovering close, full of that exact mix of eagerness dancing over fear that he hears in his hounds' voices when they have cornered a bear. As Lucius starts to break the silence with a second question, Richardson tackles the thing directly only to get it over with sooner.

He tells them that they are not to worry. There will be an inquiry which will settle the case for good since he has plenty of eyewitnesses. Most of his people. Too many of them in fact. He tells his family with a harsh bark of a laugh that he might even get his money back since Nero hadn't been here three months.

Lucius remains puzzled, his perpetually raised eyebrows hovering high under his dark widow's peak, but as soon as he opens his mouth, Richardson snaps at him to close it. Hurt rises in the boy's eyes but his father doesn't care. As long as it keeps that mouth of his shut for tonight. Richardson stows the whole story away and drags the conversation back into safer waters, grateful to his wife for leading their children through planning Mary Patton's upcoming birthday party.

All he can feel is the smooth sturdiness of the wall he has already built between himself and the incident. He does not turn toward it again until everyone has gone to bed and he is finally alone in his study, drink in hand, diary open. Time to make sense of the day.

He can feel himself slowing as he draws closer to Nero but he takes great comfort in the detailed texture of his list of small things accomplished. *Filled yesterday's orders, sent two wagonloads of nails down to the dock, placed orders for seven harnesses and extra bits to replace those sold last week.*

He writes his way toward Nero but he feels himself pull up short. When he gets to the point where nothing else happened before Nero stepped up in his face and wrapped his hands around his neck, when he gets to the part where everything grew unbearably bright, blowing out to white before darkness started to seep in due to lack of oxygen, when he gets to the part about the feel of his knife setting its shoulder to the wall of Nero's low belly until it finally broke through, bringing with it a weakening of Nero's grip, then the darkness rolling back as he sucked in a deep breath and the world returned from blown out white to its usual vibrancy, when he gets to Nero's sudden gracelessness, falling slack and dull at his feet, when he gets to all that, he wonders how to tell it.

The weight of the glass in his palm is all that anchors him as feelings surge inside him, raising the hair on his forearms. He cannot avoid knowing that a part of him finds what happened this morning thrilling, the exhilaration of feeling his own strength, saving his own life. As he waits for these feelings to settle into some kind of clarity, all they do is flutter inside his chest. He downs more bourbon trying to still them but it doesn't work.

He looks at the quill pen in his hand and his fingers smeared with ink. Pulls aside the blotter sheet he uses under his writing hand so as not to smear the neatness of his record. The last line reads *settlers keep buying bits at double the price. Remind Cassius to bring more back with him from Singleton in New Orleans.* After that last line, the golden straw color of the page spills open into blankness.

Richardson wants to tell these days. Lay his life across those empty pages. Record this event like he records everything else. He knows readers will come along later, wondering. But he knows just as surely that his answers will never add up. They'll be stretched taut as a tanning hide over the vast confusion of this time he's living through. No matter what words he finds for what's happening to him, he knows his truth will never reach these readers. Not without Nero's hands around their necks. But he wants to write it down, whether it creates any clarity or not, if only so he can leave it here. Close it up in this book and then walk out into some new day clearer and more manageable than this one.

He dips his pen in the ink and brings it to the page but he pauses there for so long the ink beads up and rolls off the nib to land in a tiny juicy globe. Dark rich brown hovering against the pale expanse. Richardson curses as he tries to blot it but in his haste, he makes a deep spreading stain which fills the space of all the words he could have used.

In the end he writes *Sent the new negro Nero away for burial.*

He reminds himself to put someone his people trust in charge of the burial so they won't get wound up from worrying about him selling the body to the new medical school over in Knoxville. Since stories get passed from hand to mouth until they are forged into something stronger and more alluring than facts, whatever few facts there are can act like kerosene on a hay fire.

The sky outside the window pales from black to deep purple and the birds start to stir. There is too much to keep track of and no rest for the weary, Richardson thinks, as he pushes back his chair and heads down to the kitchen for some of Emmaline's coffee before everyone else is up.

Richardson

I'm not sure what I thought about Nero. I'm not sure what I thought about any of it. What I know is that I took one step and then the next. Each step I took ruled out the one I did not take. Wiped it clean off the slate and there was no going back.

But I also know I never could see clearly from where I was standing. It was all a mist and I kept stepping forward into it, trying to see through to the other side. Then that became the road I went down.

I'm not certain about choosing. There are so many parts I would not have chosen. Most in fact. It seems a waste of time and breath to lay out the ones I very much regret, separate and distinct from the ones I only partially regret. What good will that do?

We knew what was happening from the very beginning. We saw the snag, fighting to free ourselves from slavery to England while continually hitching negroes to our wagons. I was young and flush with my own power but I caught glimpses even then, thanks to Virgil and Albert. Those first two men I hadn't wanted to buy showed me everything I didn't want to see.

You can't work alongside a man all day, raising the roof of your house, and not know what he's made of. Certainly, there were some whose eyes were dull and flat as fish, too beaten down or confused or plain simpleminded to lay claim to much of anything. But there were always those few who looked at you in such a way that you knew you were seeing another human soul in those eyes. Those few rendered knowing inescapable.

I'd bought Virgil and Albert for that look in their eye, and Nero and Mena too for that matter, whether I should have or not, and they were full of thoughts of their own. There were plenty of moments when the veil between us thinned and I could see right through it. It was these moments you tried to shake loose from your mind and forget about, because it could confuse you when you looked in there and saw somebody.

Didn't happen very often. Most of them learned to close their faces right up. It took them a while, and some growing up, but they'd get to where they'd do it before you had a chance to see much.

It was the little ones who had not yet learned how to make themselves unavailable. They'd stare right at you, open as a flower. And I have to say, it felt good, even if it was unsettling, looking into a pair of negro eyes that weren't slammed shut like a good strong door.

I always had the sense some few other men out here felt as I did. Not that anyone had articulated it or ever would. Just that there were times, near the end of a gathering, when this room full of men standing around smoking and drinking would fall silent. So quiet and still, with the blue of our smoke muscling through the lamplight as slow and sure as a big king snake. And whenever the fire crackled unexpectedly and quite loud, not one of us even flinched.

It was as if we felt, at some very basic level, beyond calamity. Those of us who were honest surely knew that our work and our lives had carried us far beyond the bosom of any family, and we knew just as surely that there was nothing for it. We built a dam and spent our days watching for seep. Forever writing laws designed to patch things up. But there are laws and there are people and between them there will always lie a gap.

I often thought the only thing that gave us strength was the simple fact that there was no other way to be. I never did understand those who tried to soften the blow. What was the point of that?

We all knew the arrangement and we were each set on our respective course. The die was cast. Emmaline knew the truth of this as well as I did, whether she would ever admit it or not.

Part Four

High summer, 1819

Pallas

Just from them telling me about Wash, I knew what the problem was right away. All that putting him on other folks' people, he's bound to pick up something and this one was bad.

Thick set, bandy legged man named Quinn stops by Miller's place, looking for me. He steps right inside my cabin and starts talking. Telling me what the man's privates look like and how he won't heal. How he and Richardson need this trouble sorted out because they've got dates booked. Commitments to meet. Says they are losing money every day this thing drags on.

I'm looking at the floor to keep anything from showing on my face. I'm thinking of that first time I saw Wash. How he was sitting in that stall where they kept him. How he ran his eyes over me like all I was was parts, just his road to get somewhere, and no me there anywhere.

I was tempted to leave him to wallow in it or else give him something I knew wouldn't work. But Phoebe always warned me be careful. Told me doing like that would come back around and slap me in the face, even with white folks. She kept telling me let God decide. Said God takes care of most things. If not now, then later. Take this medicine just as far as you feel guided and don't go no further. No matter what.

Once Quinn started in again, I heard Phoebe saying we got to look out for each other because Lord knows, nobody else will. I started to collect my things and told the man to go on home, I'd be there by late afternoon. That would have to be soon enough because I had some gathering to do.

Soon as he left, I went down by the creek and pulled bunches of prickly ash. Boil the bark for a tea with some left over for Wash to chew. Give him a new stinging to take his mind off that other burning. I had some bloodroot from when I last collected with Phoebe. I can still see her showing me how that thick veined leaf wraps right around its flower standing so straight, like a woman wearing a cape.

As I came back around the side of the hill, there was a patch of goldenseal growing knee high. Same kind of root with a strong dye but yellow. I always kept some of both those roots with me. Ever since Phoebe used that same red and yellow on me when she was bringing me back into this world, they stayed two of my steadies.

I figured I'd have a fever to break so I found some pale pink rocket flowers growing tall by the roadside on my way home. Grabbed hold down low and took the whole thing since greens can't do nothing but help.

I made it to Richardson's right at suppertime, handing the reins to Ben, knowing he'd get my horse cooled down good before letting him eat anything. They took me to the cabin where they had put Wash. I paused with my hand on the latch to pull myself together before I swung the door open.

Once I got inside, I couldn't see how I'd been thinking of not bringing him some relief. He was sunk way down into the middle of himself, like he was trying to curl his spirit around him, even though he was laying flat out on his back. Wouldn't look at me.

It was hot and he was hotter and smelled. Sweating. With flies moving over him, adding stinging bites to the deep burning I knew he was already feeling. That fever ran high, trying to kill the sickness, and the two heats fought each other, sapping his strength.

There were a few folks in there with him but they weren't doing much. Hovering just like the flies, seemed to me. I pointed towards the door with my eyes. Watching them filing out, I kissed Phoebe in heaven for giving me this medicine that made people listen to me.

Told Wash first thing we do is break that fever. I had two boys
tote his pallet into the shade behind the springhouse. They jostled
him hard and liked seeing him weak. They were just coming into
manhood and I could tell what they thought of Wash. How they
thought they would be so different from this. Lord help em is
all I could think.

They set him down rough and I got them gone soon as I could.
Told em to bring me one of those water troughs from where I saw
it laying empty behind the barn. Clean it out good and bring it
as full as you can carry it. It came back teetering but more than
halfway full.

I used those same two boys to help me get Wash off the pallet
and into the trough. I knew he didn't like them touching him,
but once he was laying inside that trough of cool water, with his
arms hanging over the sides, his hands splayed on the grass and
his head resting back, he felt better. Looked like Moses in the
rushes but bigger.

I sent those two boys away and called over two others. One
small and one bigger. Both nice and quiet. I gave my bucket to
the little one and walked them around to the front of the springhouse. It was cool and dark inside. I lifted the containers of butter
and milk and set them on the thin flat stones laid in real smooth
around where the springwater wells up.

The little one's eyes near about popped and I knew I'd cursed
him by letting him see all that butter and cream. He'd be dreaming about it for a long time. I just hoped he wasn't going to try to
sneak some on his own and get his behind torn up. Sure enough,
Emmaline sent Chatty to sit by the springhouse door making
sure nothing snuck off while I was in and out of there. Fine, just
leave me be.

I showed those boys how to dip the cool water. Tote it to the trough and pour it in real careful. Don't let the lip of the bucket touch the water Wash was laying in. Pretty soon, I had cool spring-house water rising around him, hot water boiling for his tea and him chewing those rocket flowers. He heated that water faster than the boys could cool it, so I'd just pull the plug to drain it and start over. Each time we drained the trough, I could see some of his heat going with it. He was feeling better just being out of that cabin and having the flies off him.

My hands on him was helping too. Always seemed to. My hands felt good on a body. They stayed cool, no matter how warm I got. Sometimes I'd lay one on the small of my back and one on my belly. Calmed me right down.

After a long while, we stood Wash up and draped him across our shoulders to get him back in the cabin. He was real glad to be laying flat again. But I could tell it was hard on him being in the quarters. Looked like it hurt him to have folks so close, with him not able to get away. Sick as he was, he was always straining towards the door. And he wouldn't look at me with his eyes open or slammed shut, either way. Acting just like a baby child does, thinking if they don't look at you then you can't see them. His eyes stayed hard on the ceiling, like he was waiting on it to do something.

Wash

Maybe I did like being a big man. I know I did. At first, I went after it like I was going to break through to some other side. And they did fall away. Most times, all those women fell away. Like they were veils between this world and the next and I stayed steady trying to break through. I knew where the hell I was headed and I kept trying to push past em. Never did get there though. Caught some glimpses, but I never did get there.

Each time I went after it, I felt it coming nearer and nearer to me, opening up and opening out, and I'd think I might make it across. But then that feeling good way down in my low belly would always bloom and there I'd be, like a fish flopping in my coming, with that whole other world I kept trying to reach fading away from me, drifting like leftover storm clouds.

It was only when I didn't push and didn't get out ahead of myself that I ever got anywhere. Pallas was the one who showed me. I guess I thought she was so thin and almost see through, maybe she'd be the one where I could finally make my way over to that other side. Even laying there sick as a dog with my parts on fire, I still thought about getting up on her. Like that was the only way I could see a woman.

But Pallas came and she sat by my bed. Laid that cool hand on my forehead, gave me some bitter tea to drink. Laid another hand on my belly, telling me I was getting better, even though all I felt was burning from my chest down to my legs with roots running up the small of my back.

But even then, even when I couldn't picture getting up on her without it feeling like a heavy weight was falling on my bare foot, I wanted to grab her. Even then, I saw myself leaving marks on that pale thin arm from taking too tight a hold and her trying to pull away.

But I didn't. Something about the way she looked at me told me I could reach right through her and she'd still be standing there staring at me. She wasn't just some place to walk through to get from one side to another. She was a whole new place and her knowing mocked me.

Looked like she was telling me, fine, go ahead and grab at that if you think you need to, but you won't never reach it. And meanwhile, there's a whole world over here, passing you right by. But go on ahead, running after whatever you think it is you need and don't worry about it none. Most people never see what's right under their nose anyhow.

And smiling. Watching me wanting to reach right through her and then laughing at me. That's when I thought maybe she has some knowing I don't. By this time, I'm laying there looking at her, and she knows I'm seeing the way she's reading me.

All I said was, maybe you might show me something sometime. And she just looked at me. Didn't say yes, didn't say no, so I knew she was at least considering it.

Pallas

I had to stay over at Richardson's for a couple of days, seeing about Wash, which was fine by me. I liked staying with the old women and having children around me.

While I was over there, Richardson had me clear up all the other ailments. Some coughs and colds and worms but nothing too bad. It's usually the little ones and I want to say give em more than that shirt to wear and they won't stay so sick. Spend your money on clothes and shoes and you won't have to spend it on me.

At least Richardson saw this. He kept his people fed and clothed so there wasn't too much else for me to do at his place except some odds and ends. But he always wanted to know what I was doing and why. Lord that man could lurk. He'd step so quiet and stand in the doorway while I was seeing about somebody, but I felt his eyes on me from the beginning.

Sometimes he'd just stand there. Other times, he'd come real close and peer over my shoulder. Whenever I was at his place, I had to remember to close my satchel and keep it between my feet or else he'd be poking into it. Reaching in, picking up my medicine, looking at it, smelling it. Asking me what was this root and that one. Most times I'd make up a word, except for the real easy to find plants. Call me selfish, but I didn't feel like giving him my every little thing.

I stayed at Richardson's for several days, pulling Wash into the clear. I hoped Elsie's baby might come while I was there and save me a trip back but she kept swelling with that baby not even thinking about coming.

But it was just as well since I needed to do some collecting. Wash turned out to be a bigger man than I remembered and thick. The dose Phoebe had said to use on somebody his size didn't do nothing. I kept having to add more and more till I'd used most of my stores.

I was glad to get out of those quarters and I hoped their woods might have some medicine that was hard for me to find at home. Went to ask some of the women where was a south facing hill sloping to some water and most of them looked at me with their eyes wide like they were scared to go off the place. I kissed Phoebe in my mind's eye again for making sure I didn't end up like that. Afraid to go anywhere or even be alone.

I went in to see what Wash knew about plants and where to find them. I sat by him and laid my hand on his forehead. Lifted his cover to look and laid it back down. His fever had broken with his sores drying to crusty. Told him most times, the worse it looks, the better it's getting.

We hadn't talked much except for me telling him, I'm laying this on you now. Letting him know where to expect a touch and

what kind. Hot or cold, sharp or smooth. I figured a surprise was
not what he needed. He never said anything but he had started
looking at me. Once he took his eyes off the ceiling, he'd watch
my hands first, then he'd watch my face.

Sometimes when I'd be sitting by him, staring out the window, waiting for him to wake up, I'd feel something on me and
I'd realize he wasn't asleep after all. He'd been watching me. But
it was hard to catch him looking at you even when you felt it.

And there he was, even as sick as he was, still looking at me like
I was a piece of something. Right from when I walked through
the door. Almost made me glad to see him baking in that fever.

But I'd learned to keep myself wrapped clear around myself,
just like those bloodroot leaves wrap around that flower standing
so straight. And I remember doing just like that, standing way
back inside myself, watching him trying to look at me.

And sure enough, after a while, he started to shift and soften,
just as sure as if he was cooking. Pot gone to bubbling on the
stove, and he's sinking down into that boiling water, softening
like a big bunch of stiff squeaky greens. Not all at once but in
bits and snatches.

I'd catch him looking at me and I'd hold his eyes with mine till
I felt the air between us buckle and waver and I felt him starting
to see me. And maybe I did know something after all. Made me
smile. That big man staying so sure he was all alone in the world
and ain't nobody ever thought his thoughts. And then there I was.
I think I drew him up short for once. I did.

And Wash knew where to find the roots I needed. Seemed like
he found some relief in thinking there was something he could tell
me I didn't already know. Told me exactly where I'd find a good
big patch of goldenseal under some sweet gum trees, high on a

southwest facing slope where the river bends. He never said that same patch of goldenseal was growing right up from his mamma's grave. Took him till much later to tell me that.

I said thank you very much and was there anything else he needed. He asked me could I check on that new foal. Make sure he's coming along all right. Said the bay mare was maiden and she had shut her first baby out, whirling to kick whenever the little man tried to nurse. Wash had been going to the barn every day and holding that skittery mare against the wall where the foal could get at her. But then he fell sick and didn't know whether Ben was handling it or not. He asked me to see if she'd taken her foal on good and was he getting enough milk.

I walked through the barn on my way to the river and I found the mare soon enough. Young and fine, bright blood bay going to black on her dish face. No white anywhere. My eye was drawn right to her because she was so jittery, bobbing and weaving in her stall, pacing around then sticking her head out over the door and ducking it in again. Like she was waiting on something but didn't know what. I figured with all that pacing she was doing, there was no new foal laying on the floor asleep the way he should have been. I walked to her stall door and looked in. All I saw was straw.

I went on out knowing I wasn't going to tell him. Got what I needed and came back. I tried to leave my news about the foal outside the cabin. Tried to keep it from him till he was better and could sit with the mare to ease her.

I came in and kept my back to him, acting like I thought he was asleep while I went to fixing the root for him, but he knew before I told him and I felt him tearing down the middle. When I turned to check, he looked straight at me but it was like he was looking into a well. All I could do was pull the rocker close and sit by him, laying my hand on his heart while he tried to stretch himself out to make room for this new loss. So I did. Kept my hand on his chest and just sat there.

After a long time of his heart burning right along with the end of his fever, I felt him start to burn clearer, his spirit opening a little, laying itself out under my hand. I wasn't taking on his hurt but I wasn't shirking it neither. I just let it drift off through me somehow.

Wasn't until I lifted my palm a long while later when he turned and looked at me. I drew my hand into my lap and we sat there looking at each other. Not pushing, not pulling, not doing anything. Just looking.

Next thing I know, I'm lifting my head up off the back of that rocker. Late afternoon light coming cross the room and I'm waking from another dream about flying low and close over some wide shimmery water. Except this time, the water was his dark brown chest stretching as far as I can see and the light kept moving on it so pretty.

I looked over at him and I could tell he was dreaming real sleep dreams instead of those tossing around fever dreams that hold you trapped between asleep and awake. I knew he was through the worst of it and I started gathering my things together. I left some root for him to chew and I walked past the barn asking Ben please get my horse ready as I headed up to the house for that banknote to carry to Miller. I got home right along with full dark.

Wash

I woke up in the pitch dark with Pallas long gone. I lay there knowing whatever I needed to do to get me some more of her, then so be it. I knew my needing to see Pallas gave Richardson the kind of leverage he ain't never had over me, but right in that same minute, I knew this was a rope I wasn't about to cut.

∞

Richardson

I'd heard about Pallas soon after somebody left her on Phoebe's doorstep over at Miller's place. Saw Miller at a party that next night and he told me about her. Same old story. Baby left in a basket with no note. Somebody white lay down where he shouldn't have, then sent his troubles packing.

Even as we wondered who the father was, we knew there was no telling. Not yet anyway. Miller said he'd decided to leave it alone. Said he'd have chosen his Phoebe to raise her anyway and there was nothing wrong with free money. We drank some more and worked on what he should name her. I was the one who came up with Pallas Athena, which turned out to be perfect.

I didn't hear much about her for a long time. Miller did say she grew up so lovely he'd had to send her over to Drummond's for a while just to keep his own boys off of her. Said he was trying to follow my example. Draw some kind of line in the sand, no matter how shifting.

But on that day when I sent for Pallas to see about Wash and she came, I saw immediately why she'd ended up on Phoebe's doorstep in her basket. Now that I got a good look at her, I could see she'd sprung right from her father's high forehead. She had him written all over her face. Especially those eyes. I'd met that striver from South Carolina during the war. He'd wanted to be governor but he couldn't stay out of his own quarters and it had started to matter.

Pallas would have been the last straw, so he must have sent her as far from his wife and his critics as possible. And that's how she'd landed at Miller's place. But things seemed to have worked out all right for her. She was all grown up and carried her spear and her armor well. Gray eyed goddess indeed.

Still, I'd love to know how it had happened. Somebody must have known somebody. But that's almost four hundred miles. Lots of links in a long chain.

Quinn fretted continually about what he called their network, insisting that the negroes had woven a web of trade among themselves which spread across the entire South East. And not just cowrie shells and mojo. He claimed they were stockpiling knives and guns as well. He couldn't ever produce any proof but he'd worry that bone whenever I'd listen so I stopped.

But it was seeing Pallas grown up into the spitting image of her father that made me start to believe in Quinn's network. How else could she have come such a long way?

Wash

Everybody round here had some kind of story. I decided early on to try leaving Pallas alone about hers. Even before we started talking, I decided to let her tell me any old thing she wanted about who she was and where she came from. And I'd just stand there with her, not pulling on her, and see how it felt. I knew she'd like it, with the way she kept slipping from folks' grasp everywhere she went.

She tried to hide her shape under lots of cloth but it stayed giving her away. Seems like it was calling out to me and if it was calling out to me, Lord knows who else had already heard it. Sure enough showed in her eyes. She didn't get to say this is not yours, this is mine, to those boys over at that Drummond place, but she sure as hell wasn't gonna let none of us get up on her without asking.

God help the man who reached out to take hold of that skirt, trying to pull her round the corner of a cabin with him, thinking she just needs a little persuading. I've seen em start to try and I've seen that look in her eye. She carried her satchel to draw poison out of people, I bet she could put some in without missing a beat. Made my hands fall open thinking about it.

What surprised me was she had heard about my mamma. At first, all Pallas wanted to do was listen to me talk about her and for once, it was all right with me.

Some folks are better to talk to than others cause they give you a chance to tell things to yourself. Talking to em can bring you new words. Some folks feel like a deep pool and you can drop anything in there and you aint got to worry about it coming back at you some kind a way. Pallas was like that. Once I started telling her my stories, then she was carrying me with her, and it mattered to me what happened to her.

I didn't know much about her in the beginning but I knew enough to watch my step. She was like a colt been slapped too often. Can't settle down unless people stay good and away, so I did.

Made me think of one time back at Thompson's place when we opened a crate of glass those boys ordered all the way from Baltimore for windows on the big house. By the time that crate made it out there and we got it open, it was full of shards and flakes. Some big enough to cut yourself on but most too small to even pick up. All scattered and shining like frost, driven into the dark nap of that velvet they came wrapped up in. Bigger pieces sliced holes right through the cloth. I can still hear those boys cussing and kicking that crate once they saw inside it. Made that glass break some more and fall, crackling then thumping.

With Pallas, I had to see whether we should try putting the big pieces back together till we had enough to see through, or should we just go on and crunch em down to small enough pieces so we could lie on em without getting cut up too bad.

Course Pallas knew better than I did, she wasn't the only one broke enough to need fixing.

Pallas

I didn't have a story. Or if I did, I didn't know what it was. There's different parts I'd heard from different people and there's some I made up to fill the gaps. All I know is they found me and that's what I've had to do too.

Phoebe kept telling me stories about animals bringing me here and I do remember believing her at first. I know none of the women round here was my mamma, and nobody talked about my daddy except to shake their heads.

"Wonder which white man it is she looks too much like?"

"Somebody told somebody the baby died and they buried her real quick before anybody could see."

"Buried her right here on Phoebe's doorstep is where they buried her."

And Phoebe laid her palm all warm and soft on my head, saying yes ma'am, right here on my porch step where we found her screaming her head off is where they buried her. And look at her now, coming up so nice.

I was a child who died and was reborn. I do know I remember most all of everything I've ever seen, even from real early. I'm bundled up and moving moving moving. Looking down and seeing way down, looking over somebody's arm from up so high, like riding on a horse, with the ground slipping past and tree branches spidering overhead.

I knew these pictures were from my beginning but I learned not to talk much about them. Folks got spooked. But my memories stayed good to me, even the bad ones. They gave me some room to walk around inside my life. Somewhere for my mind to go.

That's what I had. No story. Just my memories and how I felt about things.

I got feelings about things as clear as somebody telling me something. That and I kept waking up staring at people. Seemed like whenever I laid my eyes on somebody, they could feel it and trace that line of sight right back to me. They'd stomp off mad or else knock me out of my haze, yelling damn, quit staring at me girl. Put your hands to work or I will for sure.

I wasn't trying to do nothing but pass the time and you can't sleepwalk through your whole day. But I started to learn. Turned my eyes down and let em run across the ground, from the soft pearly cool dust at my feet to the hardpacked dirt of the barnyard to the blue green grass growing so thick between the cabins and the springhouse.

I was wanting to move and go and see and do from as far back as I can remember. When I was a baby, walking drunk and weaving and slow, I'd reach for something and get jerked back. Even after I was old enough to run through the patterns of bright sun falling through trees, old enough to run giggling in circles until I fell down in the grass panting, everybody kept telling me just be still.

Said they stayed too busy to see about me, so they started tying me up to keep me from wandering off. Told me they had to after all the crazy things I did and kept on doing. Found me one day inside the bull pen. I was standing right in front of him. One hand resting on his knee and the other reaching up, patting his soft dewlap moving as he chewed, his breath warm on me.

Another time, I had headed across the creek. Far side branches was shaking from a hawk trying to rob that jay's nest. I started picking my way cross the rocks to go see. They called after me but that high spring water was too loud. Next thing I know, some big man snatched me right off that rock, carried me back squeezed too tight under his arm, and all of them yelling at me about how I need to quit heading out like that. Don't I know I can't go nowhere?

I just wanted to get a good look at those birds. But they said they can't spend the whole day watching after me so they tied me to the corner of Phoebe's porch. Said they'd have to tie me good till I could learn to do right and stay close to home.

I still slipped away sometimes but those times got fewer and fewer until, by the time I got to be a bigger girl and could likely untie my own self, all I could think about was getting jerked back. So I learned to sit and wait and watch. Feast on what was close and let the rest of it go on by.

I'd count the rings of the trees in the cut end of the planks edging the porch. And I'd snuggle close with the hounds in the cool dust underneath, laying so still most folks forgot I was there. I caught me some good stories that way. I'd run my palms along those hounds' long lanky sides while they lay dead asleep, whining and twitching from hunting in their dreams. Those dangly ears so soft I had to keep touching em to believe it.

I'd stay under there all day, leaning my back against the cool stones holding Phoebe's cabin off the ground, with my elbows

wrapped around my knobby knees, running my fingertips along
the smooth edges of my two big front teeth as they came in,
darting my tongue in what empty spaces I had left. Sometimes,
I'd just sit there with both my hands wrapped around one of the
biggest stones. Those smooth round river stones stayed cool even
when it got real hot. I'd sit there with my palms wrapped round
that rock till I could hear the river roaring around me.

It was like my hands were thirsty and touching things was
drinking. I'd get caught up in looking at something with my
hands, then I'd start to feel folks' eyes on me, watching me. Usually
women. Most slapped at my hands, muttering and murmuring
to themselves about me being touched like it was a bad thing,
bringing us nothing but trouble.

But there was a few I'd catch watching me like they just remembered a dream they had. Those few stayed sweet to me, giving
me soft or shiny scraps they knew I'd like, and somehow I knew
to keep it to myself. After a while, I didn't hardly look at nothing
with my hands unless I took it under the porch with me.

Almost everything that happened when I was little, I can still see
it. A group of us sitting between the two rows of cabins. Everybody in from work. Resting, visiting, cooking. And us sitting
small between the grownups' feet with everybody talking and
teasing. Then quiet falls over us, smooth as the shadow of a cloud.
Somebody white standing on the edge of our circle.

I never knew what the man said, but looking back on it, I
can see he usually came to tell us what else to do with time we
didn't have. Or else he came to tell us about a sale coming up. But
everybody looked at the ground so all that white man saw was the
tops of peoples' heads and the smooth curves of downcast eyes.

Everybody except me. I was too busy watching him to notice nobody else was. I was running my eyes over him, trying to sniff him out. Who was he? How did he know all those words? And what did he have his hands clenched around in his pockets?

I remember thinking I was doing good because I was sitting so still. I had quit running right up to all kinds of people like I used to, quit trying to touch their raggedy cuffs or the velvet edges of their jackets. Phoebe said that might have been cute once, and white folks did stop to pet me, but then she popped me and told me not to do it no more. Said I was making everybody nervous as a cat walking past dogs.

I learned to sit quiet and I traveled with my eyes instead. But it turns out, I was supposed to quit even that. And sure enough, that white man caught me looking at him one day. I was eating him right up. The way his collar was buttoned tight but worn to shiny, and the way his top lip pressed down hard on his bottom one till I couldn't see either one.

He looked at me like he'd never seen me before and Phoebe jerked me close, stuffing my head into her armpit, then Joe says to him yes, yessir, trying to pull the man's eyes away from me.

After he was gone, they start yelling at me, telling me I best learn to keep my eyes to myself instead of letting them wander all over East Jesus, putting us in hot water. I remember asking Phoebe how much can my eyes weigh anyway, can't be that much, and Phoebe saying plenty, honey, they can weigh plenty.

I do know whenever something really bad happened, like a tornado coming or a mad dog on a rampage, whatever makes everybody grab their people right quick and get inside or underground,

I'd be the last one left standing there. Nobody grabbed me except on second thought. I remember that feeling real well. Kind of like standing after the music stops and no place left to sit down. Just a big empty quiet rattling all around me.

Most everybody else had people. Phoebe took me under her wing but she had a bunch of her own to see about first. Grands and great grands. When second thought came to her, she'd scuttle over and grab me from the yard to pull me inside her cabin, or else tell one of her bigger boys to run quick and fetch me.

In those skinny minutes, I knew Phoebe felt bad because it was the only time she wouldn't let me look in her eyes. Phoebe and I could talk without talking and that's when I knew she was saying child, please just hang on and let somebody else help you because right now, I ain't got enough to go around. It killed Phoebe to get to her end point. It didn't happen too often but it did happen and it scared me as much as it scared her. That was when I could feel how I wasn't hooked to nobody. Felt like I was falling even though I was standing on the ground.

A part of me wanted to say, go ahead and storm, white man, whatever the hell you are, danger, you go ahead and sweep me up. Maybe you'll carry me to where I can find my own place because I'm sick and tired of being second thought. I wanted to be right smack in the middle of everything for once, with somebody reaching out for me first.

Well, Lord let me tell you, you best be careful what you ask for because sure enough you will get it.

Phoebe tried to tell me and she tried to tell me but I had to catch those eyes. Make em see the light moving on my pretty skin. Make em see my good hair falling all the way down my back.

Make em see the spirit moving in me. Like if they didn't see it and reach out for it, then it wasn't there. I had to hook those eyes, make em ask who is that girl so I could say I am.

I had no idea how quick who is that girl turns into I want me some of that girl. But I sure did learn.

When Drummond first came for me, I climbed up in his wagon thinking to myself, now here's something that's finally about me. Drummond said no, he hadn't bought me but I'd be staying over at his place for a while, looking after his family. Miller had told Drummond to come get me before I started my monthlies and he'd fetch me home once I'd gotten bent down some and broken round the edges. Settled was what he called it. I could see I troubled Miller, just my being there troubled him. Too much white in me. And as I grew on up, I guess it got worse.

Turned out looking after Drummond's family meant breaking in his three boys coming into grown. Drummond said he didn't want his sons getting on any of his people. He'd had em so long and everybody was related to everybody and all. Didn't want things getting messed up is what he kept saying.

All his people knew exactly what I was over there for and ain't none of em reached out a hand to me. Not once. They kept their eyes to the ground because they knew damn well how it would go without me there. I was their angel, their lamb, and boy, did they lay me on the altar. Laid me right out and that's when I learned to fly.

All that wandering I did when I was little stayed with me. I went straight back to Miller's place in my mind. Through those fields, down to that creek, right back inside that bull pen. I spent a long time under Phoebe's porch with those hounds. Laying that soft swatch of dangly hound dog ear across my palm so I could keep touching that warm sleekness.

I didn't see everything right away. I was young enough at first to think that eldest son had picked me. I thought he reached for me because he liked the way the sun fell on my skin as much as I did. I thought he came to see me. To visit with me. There is not enough room in this world for all I did not know.

Phoebe had told us and told us about boys and men and how they do, especially white ones. But nothing too much like that had been going on at Miller's place, not that I could see, and I was too deep in my own world to think she was talking about me. I was different and I called myself smart enough to know it. Turns out some things you learn for yourself.

Drummond gave me a cabin all to myself set off a ways and there I was, thinking I was special. Kept on thinking it too, even after that eldest son stepped through my door, ducking his curly head so as not to knock it on the jamb, with the dust hardly settled from the wagon carrying me into that place. I even thought it for the few minutes it took for him to get from sitting on the stool across the room to right up close, with his hands pulling me to him, gentle at the very first, with him only a little bit less ignorant than me.

Those first few moments, it felt good, the strangeness of somebody's hands touching me but not to set me back or to scrub me clean. As his fingers trailed down my neck and across my throat, with his other arm wrapped around the small of my back, I felt a flush that was new and like the sun shining on me but better.

But way too soon, it was way too much and when I tried to turn away, I couldn't. It was too much, rising up around me like a flood, and me having nowhere to go and nowhere to put it all, and him wanting to grab me and rub on me and put his mouth on my mouth and his tongue in my mouth.

I saw that youngest brother come in the door behind him and I thought about Phoebe. I felt my bones in the big brother's hands like a bird fluttering and I could almost hear em snapping. Nowhere to get away and no me there, just a body grabbed and held in his two hands. My body. That was the last I saw of it for a while.

I went into some kind of sleep I only woke from every now and then. Opening my eyes to look around and then shutting them again so I could go back into the land of my mind. People brought me food but they kept their eyes on the ground. Sometimes I couldn't eat because the food tasted like dirt. Other times, my mouth closing around that piece of cornbread sopped in pot likker was the only thing I could stand to feel.

When I was able to step outside, the sun didn't warm me like it did before. Everything felt too bright and I kept wanting to go back inside my cabin and lie down. I was lonely, but if I tried to stand amongst the rest of everybody, I'd feel that quiet dropping over em, just exactly the way it used to do at Miller's when somebody white walked up. Except this time it was me. It was me bringing that quiet hush. Wouldn't none of em look at me anyhow, so I learned to stay to myself.

I woke up every now and then. Sometimes it was the oldest one grabbing and grunting and pounding, and I'm thinking about a rag doll Phoebe made me once, and then him done and gone. Sometimes it was the youngest one, trying to be a big man but still soft and squeamish, the way boys are with women until they cross that threshold and sometimes even after.

He'd try to get up on me but there was nothing in his pants and he groped blind like a baby. In some way back dim corner of my mind, something said I could wrap my arm around him and let him nuzzle into my shoulder like the child he was, but the thought always died out before it ever reached my hand. When he'd go to leave, bossing me and shoving me and telling me not to tell, I was glad I had not hugged him to me. The thought of me telling anything to anybody at that point made me laugh. He thought I was laughing at him so he'd try to hit me one more time before he'd slam the door shut behind him.

That middle brother was some different than the other two and had been from the beginning, but I was too far gone to make it back by the time he came along on his own. I had got so whenever one of them would come through the door, I'd reach to untie the string holding my raggedy shift to save myself from them trying to yank it off me. But when it was that middle brother, my shift would fall around my feet and I would feel just a little bit different. I'd seen him in the barn with the animals when he didn't know I was there, talking soft instead of bossing to make them mind.

Sometimes, when it was him and when my shift fell from me, I felt air on me. I felt dim light coming through the chinks of that cabin and his eyes moving across me. In that time before he touched me, all my little hairs stood up from my skin and I knew right then I was still alive.

That feeling lasted until he laid his hands on me. Soon as he touched me, I felt myself get real still. I felt myself leaving, even though I saw him trying to touch me real soft and careful instead of grabbing me. I saw him waiting for me to reach for him but all I could do was look at him from far away.

By this time, there was nothing tying me to him or nobody else. Or if there was, the rope was way too long and I was out of sight. I couldn't find the strength to pull myself towards anything. Lord knows I wanted to. I was so lonely I'd have taken whatever came my way at that point. Even this white boy who thought he loved whatever he thought I was.

He tried to be sweet but I laid there like I was dead. I knew I was still breathing because I saw my chest moving but my body was this big empty room I was wandering around in. I saw his hands drawing soft patterns on my chest and belly. I could tell from how light he was touching me how good my skin felt to his fingertips, but the closest I came to feeling any of it for myself was watching the look in his eyes. I couldn't lift my hand if I tried. I'd look down at that hand of mine, telling it to lift itself to the smoothness of his shoulder, but it just lay there.

He was a good man but not good enough. As gentle as he was with me at first, it always got up on him sooner or later. He'd wait for me for as long as he could, but there wasn't that much time in the world, so he'd go ahead. What surprised me was that I'd feel something new break inside me each time he went ahead without me. After all that time of me thinking there's nothing left in there to break.

I don't remember much else. I must have tried to go out to the barn to be around the animals. Before I knew it, they'd taken to tying my ankle with a good strong cord to a ring they bolted to the corner of my cabin. Needed to know where I was, they said. Needed me to be where they could get at me is more like it.

Wasn't like I was going nowhere. Even I knew I was too lost to run off. I didn't see how come they couldn't tell that. So I came into womanhood the same way I came into childhood, tied to the corner of a cabin.

Lots of times, I felt like I was drifting way off and the only thing that kept me in the world of the living was that damn cord. I chewed through it several times just for something to do but even then, I didn't go nowhere.

One time they found me, I had tied the two chewed parts together again. Guess I was afraid I'd float right off. Course they got a good laugh out of that one. Wondering what God had put inside my head instead of a brain. I wondered that too sometimes.

The medicine was what saved me. Learning the medicine gave me something to hold on to that was not a person trying to take a piece of me. It gave me a place to stand.

Phoebe taught it to me. I used to pester her about it when I was coming up, wanting something of my own, but she'd shake her head and cut her shoulder in to hide what she was doing. She kept saying no, she was not going to show me the medicine or the rootwork either. Said thin skinned as I was, I'd likely fall into it and go too far.

It was right then when Drummond drove up and I climbed straight in his wagon without even waving to Phoebe since I was still mad at her. She'd heard some talk about Drummond but didn't know for sure so she didn't say nothing to me about it except I'd be fine.

But when she saw me coming home after those three years over at the Drummond place, she sagged down just from looking at me. She grabbed me and held me as I stepped from his wagon, saying how she should have warned me, how she should have given me something to carry with me.

I remember watching the ground over her shoulder, running my eyes over the grass like a rake, feeling myself floating above the body she was hugging and kissing. I felt so old and so far gone, if I'd a felt this way when I was littler, I'd a thought I was dead.

They didn't need to tie me up anymore. I'd sit by the door to my cabin, staring at the pattern on the boards, waiting for folks to come. But nobody came. Miller told me I'd have to do something besides lie on my back. They tried to give me some work to do but they kept finding me staring at the wall or the floor, whichever was closer. My hands slack in my lap and my work scattered on the floor at my feet.

They tried everything. Holding back food, yelling at me, knocking me around. But Miller never did whip me. Said I was giving him the spooks, just staring right through him. Phoebe kept telling him give me some time.

It was late summer before Phoebe found a chance to come for me in the middle of a full moon night. She led me down to the far S bend in the creek where it pooled up good and deep. Where the bank flattened a little and had some clay in it. Wet grass on my bare feet and then cool sand. She lifted my dress over my head. The night air breathed on me and her palm rested warm on the back of my hip. She laid me out at the edge of the water. I heard the creek running quiet and close by my ear and I saw moonlight falling bright on me.

Phoebe knelt by my waist with her hands moving over me real slow but not ever touching me. Told me to close my eyes but I felt the heat of her palms when they passed over my face. Her hands moved up and down my body with her talking real soft. I couldn't understand her but I could tell what she was asking. Calling up some healing so she could put it on me. Trying to see with her hands what exactly needed fixing.

After a long time, she reached across me to scoop clay from the edge of the water. She worked it between her palms until it was soft. I didn't know till later she was adding some powdered colors she'd brought. Ground up roots.

I felt the summer air warm around me and I felt myself coming back. I heard the clay squishing and slurping between Phoebe's strong fingers, with her bony knuckles cracking and her voice rising and falling as familiar as if we'd already done this plenty of times before. I felt drops of water falling on me from the clay she was working.

Then she smeared the cool clay onto the tops of my feet. She drew a thin line, running up the front of my shin to circle around my knee and coming on up, crossing over the front of my hip bone before ending at my navel. Then she did my other leg. I felt myself laying there and I tried to keep breathing.

Stay, is what I kept saying to myself. Stay here.

She lifted my arms and laid em out straight over my head, palms up, and said look here. I turned my head to see. She had the reddest clay cupped in both palms. I looked back at the sky and closed my eyes. She used that reddest clay for my palms, rising up on her knees to reach, rubbing and rubbing like she was rubbing it in, not just coating it like she had done my feet. I felt the grit in the clay harsh on my palms, scratching some kind of itch, and the ground pressing up underneath.

She brought that red down in two thin lines, running from each palm across the insides of my wrists and my elbows. She was careful to draw both lines at the same time, coming along my arms all the way to a point right behind each ear, then back down the sides of my neck and across my chest to meet at my navel. All her lines met at my very middle.

Where you came from, she kept saying. In the beginding.

I felt her hovering over me in the moonbright dark, asking and asking. Then she used the last of the reddest clay for the soles of my feet. Leaned across me to rinse her hands then scooped some different clay, holding it close for me to see it glowing white. Used that white for my lips and drew a line down from the middle of my bottom lip over my chin and along my throat to the hollow place between my collarbones at the base of my throat. She filled that hollow with white.

Like a pool, she kept saying. Like a pool.

She went on down my front, making short bars of white, one below the next, down the bony middle of my chest, then dabbing a scoop into my navel where all the lines came together, saying there's you another pool, and then keeping on with the bars of white until she made it to the end of my low belly. She used the last of the white to graze each tit.

She greased my face with some oil, real slow and careful not to mess the white on my mouth. Then she took two sandstone rocks and she held them just above my face, between me and the moon, telling me hold your eyes closed now. I heard her grinding those stones together and I felt their fine sand falling onto my skin, soft as breath, catching in my eyelashes and the corners of my mouth. She grunted as she lifted herself to her knees and turned to do the same over my crotch. I listened to those stones rub against each other and felt the sand drifting down, tickling a little, but I kept breathing.

When I lifted my head to look, I saw those white bars she'd drawn leading like steps down my front and I saw those shiny bits of mica glittering in my curls of hair. I laid my head back and tilted my chin up, knowing my face was glittering too in the moonlight. I felt the clay drying and tightening where she'd painted me. And I felt myself floating in the air right close above me, but drawing closer and closer, like my lost and gone feeling might be coming to an end.

Phoebe was still praying over me but then her tone shifted and I knew she was talking to the runaway part of me that kept trying to pull away from this life. Telling it to come on home. Saying this body is how you came into this world and this body is your only door. If you ever want to live for yourself, you best find a way to step back inside it and stay put.

Her harshness softened as she ran her fingers real slow up the lines she'd painted, always starting at the tips and working her way to the middle, like she was attaching my parts to my middle with thread, saying come back here.

And I felt my runaway self floating right above me, all jittery and trapped, like it knew its wandering was ending. Phoebe was hunting me down to the end of my trail. She told me just keep breathing slow and steady. Said we'd stay here as long as it took.

I don't know how much time went by of her stitching me back together and me trying to let her. But all at once, I felt something shift. The jittery feeling settled and I got real calm, like I was filling up with warm water or maybe honey. I let loose of my struggling and I felt myself sinking right down inside me. Dropped right back in like I'd never been gone. And I was home. Just that quick, after all that time.

I was so surprised I caught my breath. Phoebe said mmm hmmm, smoothing my forehead, the soft grit grinding a little under her palm.

After a long while, I opened my eyes. Phoebe's face came over me, looking at me so tender. And I lay there, feeling the smile coming across my mouth cracking the white clay she'd painted it with.

Then it felt like time. Phoebe helped me stand and walked me to the edge of the water. The day had been hot and the water was that kind of warm where you can hardly feel it on you. Phoebe urged me out in it with her hand resting on the small of my back. The sandy bottom scrunched up between my toes feeling good and the warm rose around me. I looked down and saw the clay patterns she painted starting to melt into pale swirls on that smooth shiny mirror.

The water kept moving and broke me into shimmery edges but I saw it was me and all I could do was stare. I ran my own eyes over my own self like I'd seen other people do, but this time, I felt it from the inside and the outside. I saw me standing there, glimmering and shimmering in the swaying moonbright water, and I reached out for more.

Phoebe said lift your head up and back, baby. Up and back now.

When I did like she told me, I saw she was lifting a wooden bowl full of water, fixing to pour it over my head, and I pulled away, saying no, not yet.

"Ain't nothing ending, baby. Ain't nothing ever ending. Now lift your head up and back like I'm telling you."

And so I did. I felt that silky water coming down around me and it felt like I was God breathing. Phoebe bent and scooped and lifted and poured while I stood there with my face tilted to the sky.

I felt the water tugging the tight patches of clay loose from my skin and when I opened my eyes and looked into the water and saw all Phoebe had drawn on me running in swooping streaks, I saw she was right. This new sight was as nice as the last and I was still here. Standing here with myself and not going nowhere.

I lifted my head up and back and said pour some more on me Phoebe, pour me some more.

Phoebe brought me back to this world and I let her. But she had to help me find ways to stay, or else all her work was for nothing because I could leave again just that quick. Once you get your door blown open, just because you find a way to reach out and pull it closed don't mean it won't get blown open again. Seems like it wants to go where it knows the way.

I started learning how to shut my door, and better yet, how to hold it closed in the first place. The medicine helped. Like Phoebe said, it kept folks from trying to crowd me. She told me all about it, talking and talking like she was making up for everything she hadn't told me before.

"Long as you have some knowing in your eyes they need, they'll stay back. This medicine, they leave you alone with it. Never hurts to let people think you can turn it on em. Keep em wondering, that's the best way."

When Phoebe took me under her wing to teach me the work, I went. She kept saying she was about ready to head on out and she wanted to hand her medicine over to me. The more she thought about it, the more she liked the idea. If I hadn't had no babies after three years at Drummond's place, then I'm not having none. And I'd best find some way to make myself useful or else I'd be gone to market with the next load of logs.

I was perfect, she said. I needed the medicine and it needed me. Lord knows my mind was good, remembering everything I ought to forget.

Phoebe told me those called to healing always got some kind of sick, right around the edge of coming into grown. Just like I did.

She said death needs to draw close. Any healer worth anything tends to linger on the threshold between this world and the next, deciding whether to stay or go, just like I did. And it didn't matter that my sickness got put on me instead of coming on its own. Sick is still sick, she said, no matter how it meets you. You've been gone and you've been back so you know what you need to know.

I sat there listening to her. What she was telling me was so big I could only touch the edges of it. Everything that happened to me was what made me ready for this work. Soon as this knowing came over me, everything started to shift.

Phoebe said don't think I'm somebody special. Said healing's heavy work, with people coming to you for every little thing and plenty of big ones too. And they stay yours, even after they leave.

I thought about the life most folks want. A cabin and a husband giving me children when God knows what will become of any of us. That picture felt so far from me I couldn't ever reach it, not even in my mind's eye, and I was glad.

I saw myself living in a cabin I had the right to lock up on account of my medicines. I saw myself traveling from place to place, gathering and tending, then coming home. And once I got home, leaving again whenever I needed to.

I sat there smiling and Phoebe said all right then, come here to me and let me show you.

So I walked and I looked. All through the rest of that summer and into the fall. The more I looked, the more I saw. Pale mushrooms glowing white in the shaded hollows of fallen logs. Light falling on the bright green hairs of thick moss growing on the scaly gray bark of that tree. The sound of our feet moving through the loose winter leaves, crunchy and loud higher up the hillside, but limp and tender and dark in the low places.

When Phoebe stopped, I did too. Never knew for sure what Phoebe was looking for at first, but I found myself things to see. Trees growing into each other's arms like sisters, trunks arching in curves, overlapping against the sky. Thick dark knots of squirrels' nests scattered through the stitchwork of bare branches. It was winter turning to spring by the time I started to really see where I was. Branches still naked against the pale sky, just starting to hint at budding out, but still small and brown and tucked into themselves.

Phoebe kept telling me, now's the time to pay attention. Now's the time when you can read the world. With the leaves still down. You see that little hill humping up over there?

I nodded yes.

"You see how the top of it lines up with that notch in the ridgeline behind it? That's how you know you headed right. See how the ground sinks down between? Creek runs through the bottom. That's where we find a lot of what we need."

As spring wore on, Phoebe started taking me down to the creek. Then through it and a little way up the far bank. One day, she stopped at a stand of plants growing thigh high. She stood close, fanning her hand back and forth through the leaves, saying look at this, do you see?

I crouched with green filling my mind. All those leaves close to my face, bending for Phoebe's hand combing through em and then springing back.

"You know how you used to look at things so hard we'd slap you for it? Look at these plants right here just like that. Drink it up."

I stared into that green until I started to see how they grew together in a stand. Like a group of people. Each with one main smooth stem rising straight from the ground, then arching like somebody bowing at you. And big leaves coming off that straight stem, starting halfway up then unwrapping broad and flat, with lines like little valleys, running side by side, coming together at its tip. And right where each leaf unwraps, a creamy white flower hanging underneath.

Phoebe called me back to her.

"Look where you been and where you headed. Sun rising behind you means you facing west. Hear your feet squishing in the low ground? See those spindly trees thinning out and feel these bigger trees looming over you? See that second hill humping up over there where you headed?"

I looked and I saw and I felt my map fall in place inside me.

"See these plants all growing in a patch, just like a bunch of people standing here? In the summer, look for dark blue berries."

I watched Phoebe's hands moving through the stand of plants, showing me. After a while, I nodded and she bent to take hold of a few by the base of their stems, pulling em up real careful, then tucking their tops under her waistband with dirt from the roots falling down her skirt.

"Well, good then. Let's take some. Folks stay wanting Solomon's Seal. Supposed to make men manly. Don't know what we need with more of that mess, but at least trading for it will keep food in your belly. It's the root you want but take you one with the whole plant so you can remember how it looks."

That was how I remembered things. When I knelt in front of a plant, looking to see was it the one I wanted, I'd go back in my mind to when Phoebe first showed it to me. Waiting to hear her voice and see her hands moving through the cool green of those broad leaves arching out from that main stem. If I couldn't see Phoebe's hands moving through the leaves, I didn't take it.

Phoebe had two whole years of showing me before she died. Each of the seasons and then again. She told me not to cry for her and whatever I did, don't go stand by her grave. She kept saying I'm here with you. Right here with you when you come out in these woods is where I stay.

I loved gathering. I'd been trying to wander the world all my life and Phoebe gave me the key. A reason. My feet and my hands finally free to follow my eyes and my mind. I wasn't tied up no more and I wasn't afraid neither. In the woods, I could usually hear trouble in plenty of time to get out of the way, and Miller let me wear a knife. Said that was just him looking after his investment.

I went off most days collecting and I always came back home. I knew what he'd do to the rest if I didn't. My heading out would mean a whipping for them and that lever worked both ways. Their staying in the fields was what let me wander, so when they came to me for fixing, I put my whole heart into it. I used to worry I'd kill somebody by accident, but the more parts I learned, the more they grew together till I was living inside a real house of knowing. And I just got better and better at it.

Miller watched people stepping onto my porch and then leaving healed up. Saw he could earn some real money off me. He even decided to let me learn to read and write. Didn't want me poisoning anybody by accident, getting him in trouble.

Said he'd found him a new Phoebe, he sure did, and without even having to look. He was so pleased, he gave me a horse.

∞

I almost rode right up on top of Wash next time I saw him. It was at that same southwest facing slope, wrapped round by the river, where he'd sent me to find the goldenseal.

And there he was. Kneeling in the middle of that patch. Doing something with his hands. Whatever it was, he quit before I could see good. Laid one palm flat down, then he laid his other palm over the first.

I remember seeing those hands, blunt and thick. Nothing tapered about him. Veins running across the backs of his hands like roots.

He stood up from that patch of goldenseal so smooth and tall. Looking at me, keeping his face flat. Asking what did I want without saying nothing. And I didn't say what I wanted since I didn't know. We stared at each other like that for a little while. I let my horse graze so I could keep on looking.

I had been wondering about him. How was he feeling since I healed him? Had Richardson already put him back at it?

But the answers to my questions floated right to the top where I could see em clear so there was no need to ask. I knew he was feeling good because he was looking good. His eyes shone dark and clear against their whites and the inkiness had come back to his skin. I could tell by the way he stood up so smooth, he wasn't hurting no more.

I knew Richardson well enough to know the rest, and besides, I'd heard about it every which way I turned. Where Wash had been, what he had done at each place, and how he felt about it. All from people who had no way of knowing anything about him.

I had to wait for my other questions to rise up. Not that I'd ask him those either. Funny how some people stay begging for a chance to explain themselves and others, you can spend all day working up the nerve to ask about the weather. Wash was that second kind.

Except for much later when I was lying against him afterwards, in that quiet close time that don't last long. Inside that little slip of time, he'd answer almost anything. But then, when we were dressed again, separate and apart, crossing paths on the road or in the barnyard, that wide open place inside him felt so far away it was like something I'd dreamed.

He couldn't talk about it very well but he finally found the right words. Made me think of Phoebe when he said just cause it's in there, don't mean you got to be touching it all the time. No need to wear it out. But you know that, he'd say. You know that.

As for what he was doing with his hands that first day when I rode up on him after I'd healed him, turns out he was visiting his mamma's grave. Leaving offerings. Wouldn't let me see and didn't tell me till later, but said she'd like us crossing paths again right there. In that very spot.

Wash

I guess the thing Pallas knew was how to be with a body without having to grab hold of you. Having everything yanked from you can teach you. Some people, it makes em need a stranglehold but Pallas was not like that.

Pallas let me come and go. When she needed to grab on to something, she had something besides me. It was way down inside her and sometimes she'd drop me to catch hold of herself. You couldn't expect Pallas to carry you too far. She already did enough fetching and toting is what she would say. But that was all right with me. I wasn't going nowhere.

We inched up on it, Pallas and me. We kept slowing down and slowing down. Seemed like the shorter our steps, the more ground we covered.

Took me a while to get to where I could sit there by her without thinking about getting up on her. She'd stop by to see me on her way back to Miller's and we'd sit there, facing each other across my big hayloft window, looking over the road leading out of here winding through the fields just like a snake. Her saying mmm hmmm real soft but I'm not saying anything.

I felt my wanting reach through that soft night air between us but I was always glad when that feeling faded. I'd learned a little bit about how she was by then. I knew exactly how my reaching for her was the best way to be sure she'd slip through my fingers.

Long as I left her alone, she'd come closer. Took her forever to come across that empty space between us. Said she was in no hurry. Said she'd forgotten all about wanting to get next to somebody and she liked that feeling, a thread pulling up through her middle, twanging in her belly.

And my hands want to pull her to me but she's just smiling. Saying you best keep it to yourself because I sure won't be sitting here when all that wanting makes its way to me. You start that grabbing and I'm gone.

Made me mad at first but it was like she said. There was a whole other place on the far side of wanting and it was right peaceful. All quiet and still, like I'm stretched out inside myself, fields as far as my eye can see, and I'm feeling the night breeze coming through those fields, making me wonder is there a road snaking through me too, and where is the barn in me and how do I get to it?

Once I started seeing what Pallas was showing me, she liked to come sit by me and lean her head on me, with us falling in and out of sleep. Then one time, I woke up in the flat middle of the night with us curled together in the straw. I fell asleep on my back with my arm flung out to the side and her nestled in my armpit with one long thin hand laying on my chest. But I rolled towards her while I was swimming in sleep and my leg started wrapping over and round her like it can't help it.

Before I was even awake, I felt her leaving. She was still laying next to me but she started feeling real heavy and thick, like wood, and I was pulling something dead towards me. All her clear water pouring grace left just that quick and I got a feeling in the pit of my stomach, like sinking.

When I open my eyes, her face tips towards me but she's looking over my shoulder like she's seeing a ghost and ain't even scared. She drags her eyes off the wall behind me, trying to pull herself back to now, but I can see she's looking at me from down a long rope and I know that feeling myself. What I don't like is knowing I'm the one who sent her there.

I roll onto my back, letting my hands fall slack open, praying to turn back into a man she can sit next to. She curls into a ball facing away from me but at least she's still pressed close against my side. We sleep like that till first light then she sneaks out of the barn in time to make it home, with some people seeing her leaving and thinking they know everything about everything, but I'm just shaking my head.

Pallas

Ain't nobody using me for nothing is all I can say. I ain't no boot scraper to get the mud off. I'm not no road and that's what I told him. You will not get wherever you're headed by rubbing up on me. I know that much for a fact. I've been down that way and back. I'm not even thinking about turning my head to look over there. Not in this tiny sliver of my life that's mine.

Even if I was foolish enough to think it might be different this time, my body knows better and she ain't having it. You can't see her stubborn like a mule but I know. She's not going through that stream. Y'all can stand out there all day if you want, but she ain't stepping in that water.

I'm saying this to Wash but he knows it already. And I know he does, but still, it feels good to hear my own mouth saying my own words. Setting em out there like that, all in a row, one after the next, in the warm falling deep blue of a late summer night.

And he nods his head, saying yes ma'am, you better tell it to me so I know where to tip and not to tip. Come on now, you best tell it all to me. And I know he's just liking the sound of my voice pouring over him, same way I like his voice on me. And he's hearing me too, saying lemme see that mule some more. How do she look exactly?

And him asking like that makes me laugh about it a little. He's finally catching hold of it, thank the Lord. I guess I've left him enough times, he knows I mean it. It can't feel good being left like that, after the sweet of sitting next to the only somebody you really want to be by.

And I did want to stay most times. I did want to stay and I thought about Phoebe praying over me that night, telling me my body was my door into this world, and what a shame for me to come all this way and then leave again without ever being able to walk in and out of my own house whenever I felt like it. Have company over if I want.

She said it would be a damn shame if I let those Drummonds take that from me too. Said we all got our Jordan to cross in this lifetime and it looked like this was mine, so I needed to find me a way.

It was Phoebe I was hearing that one night when I turned towards Wash from where I was sitting right there by him. It was only when he managed to leave me alone for a minute that I had a chance to reach for him. Wrapped in the silvery curve of that blown down tulip poplar. Sitting side by side, leaning against the trunk. Watching the moon on the water.

I put my hand out to him, laying it palm up in his lap. He looked down into my hand and then over at me for a long time. I dipped my chin, yes, all slow like molasses, so he carried his palm to meet mine. I felt the air thick between our hands before they touched. Then I felt the solid weight of his hand in mine. My belly turned over but I stayed.

I lifted his palm so I could lay it on my throat where he could feel me breathing. It was heavy and warm resting there. I laid my other palm on my low belly, saying to myself, just stay. Using my own hand on my own belly to pull myself back inside myself when that runaway part kept trying to skitter away.

I turned to face his side and wrapped my legs around his hips. I scooched my front up against him and it felt good. Like when I'm bareback. I lifted his arm, wrapped it around my shoulders. I scooched closer against him, saying pull me to you, and his hip felt good and hard against my crotch. I laid my head on his shoulder, tucked in under his chin, and felt his arm wrapped around the top of my back nice and tight, like a vine up a tree.

Just checking him, or maybe it was panic from thinking about those bird bones fluttering, I flinched back, pulling against that tight vine holding me and yes, he was seeing me and hearing me because it gave, gave as sudden and light as it had been heavy before. His arm lifting off me like that was what made me able to come close again. I felt him smiling over me as I burrowed in there.

He looked out at the night for a long while then he turned to me, tipping me back a little with his hands on my shoulders so he can see into my face, then dropping a hand down to each of my hips and dipping his chin to look at me with a question. I leaned forward as my answer and he cupped his hands around my behind to lift me into his lap before wrapping his arms back around me.

I tipped into panic but did not lurch. He got me settled good with my front up against his front and my cheek against his throat. His chin resting on the top of my head and my feet hooked together behind him. We'd sit belly to belly like that and everything was fine.

Sometimes I'd sit behind him with my legs wrapped around, my feet in his lap, and I'd rub his back. Tracing each tight knot down its long muscle to the root, telling it come on out of there now. He'd grunt and I'd get tickled.

Other times, I'd feel something else welling in me. A hand reaching up from inside the middle of me, wanting to grab on to something without knowing what it was. Hot flooding my belly, making my arms and legs feel full, with steam rising through my chest and I'm wanting to press against him or else bite down on something.

It was nice but it was new and I was tipping too close to those Drummond boys and I couldn't see how to walk right past that hellhole without it reaching out and grabbing me.

I remembered how long it took for Phoebe to lift me from that pit. But now Phoebe's gone and I wondered who can pull me out this time. Wash didn't know enough yet, no matter how sweet he was being. And it wouldn't be me, since I'd be laying there in pieces on the floor.

I did feel the wanting well up in me and carry me over to him. But I was stoking the same fire that had burnt me already. So I'd start out and then I'd stop, snatching myself back to myself. I'd reach to pull him close but soon as I'd feel him coming back at me, I'd freeze, with my hand turning into something not my own like it used to do at Drummond's, and I'm gone.

I couldn't talk about it much but I tried. He'd say see can you tell me. And I'd say it's a rising up, like a storm. It'll toss me and break me apart till I'll be all in pieces. Broken open. I'm saying it so soft and into such dark, I'm not even sure I'm saying it out loud till I feel him hearing me. And he's saying it's a storm but it's just trying to carry you some place new.

I'm looking at him.

"You know how clean and smooth and wide open it gets after a big storm? The sun shining new on all the colors, making em double what they was before, with everything quiet and still, like God trying to catch some breath after all that?"

I'm nodding yes.

"That's what broken open feels like."

I'm hearing him and I'm wanting to believe him but I'm climbing a long hill just to find some level ground. Sometimes, I'm glad we only get some chances here and there to be together. Each visit holds so much, seems like I need that whole time between just for me to take it all in.

One night he says he has an idea. He figures what I need is to be around it without it being scary to me. Says he had to do this same kind of thing with Queenie's filly, after the side panel fell off the hay wagon right behind where he had her tied to the barn. Said she must have thought that wagon was reaching out to grab her and eat her up. She panicked so hard she broke her halter, trying to get away.

Said it took him days of walking that filly back and forth past the spot so she could see everything clear, and it was another few months before she could handle catching sight of that wagon. But she made it. Said all it took was time.

Next moonlit night, I'm laying beside him on the dry grass next to our tulip poplar by the pond. He's stretched flat on his back and I'm snugged in close on my side, running my fingers across his chest under his shirt, and I'm feeling it well up in him, making him breathe out real slow and start to turn towards me like he does, making me want to pull away like I do, and that right there is where we go past talking for the first time.

He asks me do I feel it coming up in him and I nod, yes I do. My hand is frozen, laying on his chest and I'm hearing him say that's from my being right here by you. But you know what? You ain't got to do a damn thing about it. You just sit tight right here by me. You ain't got to do nothing.

He lays one hand over mine, pressing it tight to his chest, saying feel my heart. He's holding my hand against his chest then running his other hand down his belly. Opening his pants to wrap a hand around himself and talking to me real soft till I can feel his talking in his chest almost as loud as I can hear it with my ears. And he's moving his hand while he's saying I'm just wanting to get closer and closer to you. Best feeling place I know.

See, here it is, coming up on me like waves. You never seen the ocean. I need to tell you about the ocean and it's something to see, but this right here is pretty close.

And he has set up a steady moving all in and through him. Not a big moving but steady, with his heart beating hard as a hammer through it all and speeding up. He's asking me do I feel it and I'm nodding, yes I do, and he's saying ain't nothing you got to do about it except let it come close.

He's moving more now and my head can't rest on his shoulder, so I sit up but stay real close, with my hand still flat on his chest, held tight under his hand. And he says look at me, and I can see his chest and his low belly moving to different music but going together somehow, and his hand is moving, with his face staying so calm, right next to all that moving, and he turns a little so he's looking at me.

Then, right while I'm sitting there, feeling his heart hammering under my palm and looking in his eyes, I'm watching it moving over him. I see his face so calm, even as the pale comes across his rising and falling belly, with him still looking at me from wherever he's off drifting and floating, and I can see he's in pieces. But then, after a little while, here they are, all coming back together again.

He's saying falling into pieces is part of it, and I'm saying well, I guess it depends. But my hand feels nailed to his chest like I'm never taking it off and I can't help feeling like a child busting with pride. After a time, his heart slows down and he says I can look after myself. You ain't got to see about me. And I say well, that's a load off my mind and we fall out laughing without really knowing why.

Sure enough, with this new answer for the feelings I bring up in him, I manage to let more and more of that moving come closer to me. I reach out for him and I climb right up him, just like that vine, then I sit back and watch. And before too long, I'm starting to want me some of that moving. Each time, I'm headed farther and farther down that same road myself and he's just holding me, watching me and seeing me. He showed me what to do and he left me to myself.

Bit by bit, I got closer and closer, till one night I was going so smooth and steady and fast, covering so much ground, I felt like a bird flying down a road. I could see my story hovering off to the side, out of the corner of my eye. All the trouble I could get snagged on. Me standing in that cabin. That middle brother even. But I just kept turning my mind away from those pictures I did not want. I kept looking straight on down my own road, trying to see where I was going instead of where I'd been.

Then all the sudden, it was like the road started curling around, coming back towards me, and I'm blooming open inside to a place I didn't even know was there and then I'm drifting so soft and nice with Wash wrapping himself around me and saying see, baby, you see that? And I'm nodding yes, I do.

He gave me some time and I felt myself drifting, just the same way I'd seen him drifting, and after I don't know how long, I felt all my pieces settling back in place inside me with his arms around me and I'm home without even trying. I felt his voice thundering inside his chest, even as low as he was talking, asking me did I like that and was it all right with me, and I said yes, it was.

Not such a bad place is it? And I'm saying no, it's not so bad at all.

You think you might like to go back there again some time? I'm nodding yes, I might could do that, and he's pulling me close, looking out over me into the night, and I'm feeling us so peaceful with my heart picking up a little bit from thinking, well, may be. May just be.

Not that it was all easy and sweetness and light with Wash and me. He came into this world full of edges, and his life brought em on out, so we fought.

It's hard for a man to be sweet all the time, even when it's only part of the time, and I had to back him off me every now and then. I told him just because I let you close don't mean you can take hold of me whenever you want. But it was hard for Wash to think about asking, seeing as his work didn't have much to do with asking.

Some days, just as sudden as he came in, he'd leave, trying to get clear of me before he started breaking things. And he'd go long stretches without coming by. I'd meet him at our pond and he'd sit way down the other end of the log from me, picking up sticks and breaking em. And I'd be thinking fine, break all the sticks you want.

One day he stopped in at my cabin needing to see me. It was a Monday after he'd been gone. But he hadn't taken the time or trouble to shrug the trip off him before he came ducking through my door. I was in a hurry, pulling my medicine together, trying to go see about some folks waiting on me, when he grabbed my wrist and pulled me to him, like I was just something he saw and wanted for himself.

If I had not sat next to this very same man out by that pond and heard what he had to say to me, I'd have gone after him right that minute. As it was, I yanked my arm from his grip and turned on him.

"What the hell's the matter with you? You want to spend your whole damn life tied up in somebody's barn? Don't you want to carve out at least one corner that's yours?"

He's backing away but I keep after him.

"Don't you come to me till you pull yourself together. I'm working hard to hang on to my little patch of clear and I will not let you track all kinds of mud in here."

I'm yelling at him but low and steady like a whisper.

"It's the grabbing that brings a whole bunch of nothing right back at you. And then you stand there empty handed, shaking your head and acting like you're no different from the rest, even when you and me both know better."

He stands there looking at me but he's not seeing me.

I tell him, I can draw some of that mess out of you. If you want. Give me the hand you stay itching to hit me with. And I step closer to lay his palm on my belly.

I'm looking at him, asking him, you want this grabbing feeling to come off you or not? You need to want it gone for it to go. Now do you?

He jerks his hand from me, sweeping it wide enough to knock my medicines off my table onto the floor, saying goddammit, take me as I am.

I got real quiet and I said let me tell you what. You ain't gonna grab me and you ain't gonna hit me. Not you and not nobody else. Those two things ain't never happening to me no more. Ever. I'll put a bigger hole in you than Nero had.

I see him right quick remembering how I wear a knife, and he's backing up because he knows I'll use it.

"There's another way to be, and if you want to stand next to me, then you best find it. Now get the hell out of my place."

After that, he knew not to come see me when he was in one of those moods.

Part Five

Early October, 1823

Richardson rides once again through the last of the woods toward his place. Mary and Quinn hadn't wanted him to take this trip to Nashville so soon after judging the murder case. It's only been three weeks since the trial and Charlotte still haunts them all. Sitting up late sharpening her pastry cutter then killing the husband and wife both, leaving a flurry of fear in her wake. Richardson told Mary and Quinn they both needed to steady their minds because there was no way out of this trip. He had to meet the commissioners himself to make sure they chose Memphis for the county seat.

At least they've had some rain since then. After these last two thunderstorms, golden leaves lie shredded and torn on the cool moist ground, silencing his horse's footfalls. He's glad he chose this young bay gelding Bolivar for the trip to Nashville. Omega would have been dragging by now. Two full days on the trail and both of them up most of last night. A panther kept screaming to establish his terrritory, first from one side of the valley and then the other, until Bolivar needed to stand close to Richardson's fire and look right into his eyes to keep from bolting.

Tired and dirty as he is, Richardson feels less and less ready to get home. Soon as he rides through his gate, they'll all be pulling on him and he won't have a good answer for any of them. He finds himself making a detour to the spring they had used when he first came out here. It should be running after this rain and he can wash up.

He guides Bolivar onto the deer path leading down behind the ridge where they had built their very first fort. As he rides past the spot where his brother David was ambushed and killed, the young gelding snorts and blows. Richardson nods his head in understanding. It has always felt spooky to him too.

As they reach the spring, he dismounts and loops his reins on a branch low enough so the gelding can graze. He steps around to where the ground drops off, remembering how pleased they had been to have created a kind of spigot so the springwater poured out from waist level and they could wash like civilized people. Not having to kneel at the water's edge like Indians.

He rolls up his sleeves and stretches his hands toward the shining stream of water. The cool of fall has gained a cutting edge. He stands in a patch of sun but cannot feel its warmth. He starts in on the caked mud and blood from last night's rabbit but ends up just standing there, holding his hands under the water and losing track of time. Watching his hands curl and curve into each other as if seeking refuge without finding it. Thinking about those first few of them, so young and ambitious, having made it through the Revolution and headed West all those years ago. Determined to get away from slavery but then running right into the Indians.

So many of his early companions are dead and gone now. The corner of his thin lipped mouth twitches in a wry smile as he realizes he only misses some of them. The ones he saw die in front of him are the ones he misses the most. And his brother David. Despite the relentless womanizing, Richardson misses having someone who shared his story. At least parts of it.

Get there first was what their father told them on that first Christmas dinner after Independence. Don't go empty handed.

And they hadn't. Richardson and his brother had received those first land grants fair and square. Their brand new government, flat out of cash, paid its soldiers with grants to western land it did not yet own. Their father had lent them money to gather more. They bought some grants from soldiers who didn't want to move west, some from those too broken to know what they had and then simply took the rest from those who never turned up to claim theirs.

All this would have been obvious to any quick thinking man so Richardson convinced himself that he'd earned it, if not with the fighting and sitting in chains, then by coming all the way out here and taking it. Making it his. Pushing back the Indians and writing up statehood. He had even laid out his first small town like his father taught him. Got the road and the county seat both that time.

He set his sights on Memphis next, no matter how deep Chickasaw Bluffs sat inside Indian Territory. Once he secured the federal commission to draw the boundary line, he and his partners acquired the title soon enough. It was a substantial investment but promised to yield a good return. They drew up a map and marked out lots in preparation for the upcoming sale. Lobbied the commissioners hard to make sure they made Memphis the county seat.

But now they've just denied him. After all that money spent and liquor sent, he's ridden all the way to Nashville to be told that the commissioners want some dusty spot in the middle of nowhere for the county seat instead. They insisted the other town was more central than Memphis but Richardson suspects they did it mainly to thwart him.

Act like you know was what his father always said to do, but this time it didn't work.

Seventy years old and Richardson dreads having to write his father about losing the county seat. He can already hear him saying opportunity lies all around, you have only to bend it to your hand. The old man is nearly ninety himself but keeps writing that he wants to visit. Even take a tour of Memphis. Richardson can only imagine what he'll have to say when he sees the second family store sitting in its sea of mud, next to the old fort tilting like a crooked tooth at the top of the steep slick embankment that is still the only way up from the river.

Memphis will grow but not as fast as he'd hoped. Not as fast as he needs it to, with all the lots he has to sell and the sale right around the corner. Not much time to recover from this blow. Maybe he does need another traveling negro and soon. Just not another Nero. It's either that or find a way to wring more money out of Wash.

His hands chill from being held for so long under the mountain coolness of the water but he does not move them. He turns his mind toward the ache that comes from the cold, hoping the pain can tell him something. At least this pain is located. Specific. Unlike that other ache which coils around him like smoke and is difficult to understand.

He comes to by realizing he's damp all down his front. Some of the drops glancing off his hands have been falling onto the moss but almost as many have been falling on his breeches and his boots are soaked from the splashing. It strikes him once again how tired he is. Cold, wet and dirty, too.

He flings the water from his hands then wipes them dry on his dirty britches. Bolivar snaps his head up, knowing home is just over the next ridge. Wads of rich green grass with clods of dirt still attached swing from his mouth. Richardson tears the clods loose as he gathers the reins tight to keep the gelding from walking away while he mounts. He lifts his left foot to the stirrup and buries one hand in the horse's thick black mane so he has a good grip. As he swings his leg over the horse's back, sure enough, Bolivar starts off before Richardson gets settled in the saddle. Irritation rises sharp and hard, twining around the pain shooting from his hip through his ribcage that seems to be here to stay. He steers his horse toward home.

When he rides through his own gate, a motley little cluster of white people stands waiting for him. They're on him as soon as his feet hit the ground. The taller of the two women steps forward saying they have papers for him to sign.

Papers for him to read first and then sign, he corrects her. He doesn't yet know who these people are, or which case this is regarding, but he does know his hands need to be cleaner than this if they plan to file these documents at the statehouse.

He does not have to read very far down the paper the woman holds out to him before his eye catches on the name Charlotte. Damn that case. He has already sent the family of the murdered couple a check from the state, reimbursing them for the value of the woman, but apparently they're already fighting over it. Needing it legitimized and in a hurry. He steps back, aggravated. They'd have all the time in the world if it was them owing him but with this state restitution money, they hover close.

Thank goodness for Emmaline. He sees her walking to the table under his biggest elm, carrrying a second basin of warm water with a clean white towel over her shoulder. He waves the group off with one small motion. They step back and fall quiet as he walks over to Emmaline's two steaming basins.

The soap and the nailbrush lie right where they should and he feels her standing beside him as he lowers his hands in the warm water to scrub dirt so ground in he has to use the brush on his palms and knuckles too. He lifts his gritty hands from the now gray water, letting them drip well before lowering them into the next basin. Traces of soap scum spread across its clear surface. He bends to splash some of this cleaner water onto his face.

Straightening up, he lays his wet hands palm down on the towel Emmaline holds out for him. As much as this closeness to Richardson has cost Emmaline over the years, it has helped her protect her three grandsons so she intends to hold on to it. She folds the towel over the back of his hands and rubs them between the two layers. Not looking up at him once. Rubs between his fingers good and halfway up to his elbows then hands him the clean backside of the towel as if to say dry your own face.

Soon as he's done, she takes the towel from him. He nods thank you but she has turned away. When he heads toward the group to deal with their business, he can hear the tearing sound of Emmaline pouring her basins of dirty water at the foot of the old elm.

No sooner does he get that paperwork sorted out than he finds himself walking in on the tail end of his wife's Bible study. The ladies seem particularly flustered on this Wednesday because somehow they found themselves deep in the Song of Solomon. Their buzzing hums like bees and then falls quiet as a blanket when Richardson steps into the front hall where they stand gathering their things. His wife shoos them out quickly but the obvious discomfort some of the women show upon his arrival piques his interest. He steps close to ask Mary about it in a low voice with a small smile but all she says is I will not be baited.

Richardson makes it through dinner without mentioning the bad news about Memphis. He lets Mary carry the conversation as he counts his drinks and bides his time until he can go upstairs. These days, it is not until he retreats to his study with its window facing the big barn that he can start to know his own mind. He thinks if he can just get in there with the door shut behind him and a drink in his hand, he will be able to see more clearly. But he doesn't know what he's hunting and holing up like this puts him at the mercy of a past he'd just as soon keep buried.

The urge to be down in that dark barn talking to Wash tugs at his sleeve. But the last time he went, he'd felt eyes on him as soon as he rounded the corner. He paused to look up and saw Pallas sitting with Wash in the shadowed opening of the loft window. The pale soles of their bare feet hung from the ledge. They had looked down on him with faces so impassive Richardson could not bring himself to hold their gaze. He continued his circuit, acting like he was checking on things, even as all three of them knew better.

Once he came upon them so quietly that he heard them before they heard him. He couldn't quite make out their words, just a rising and falling murmur scattered with pauses. Every now and again soft laughter. Some back and forth but then long stretches of one telling the other a story.

He had stood there, one hand resting on the side of the barn, just before rounding the corner, embarrassed to find himself eavesdropping but nevertheless straining to hear, wondering what in the hell they could keep talking about for so damn long. He considered trying to get closer then realized the nickering of the horses would give him away before his foot reached the second step.

That memory keeps Richardson in his study tonight. Probably just as well. As he flips through his letterbooks full of his own careful looping track, each page numbered, each letterbook dated and segregated by category, containing copies of all his correspondence, he can call everything right back to him. All the details he has attended to and all the managing he has done.

He savors that remembered feeling of competency. Each time he sat down to write one of these many letters, the task had felt doable. Even now, he can feel the effort he has put in, almost literally, like a physical substance, a layer of intention that lies over and above the layer of ink under his fingers.

He never has understood those businessmen who do not keep copies of their correspondence. Their complacency has always irritated him. It makes trustworthiness regarding prices per pound and interest rates uncertain, even among old friends. He knows he cannot remember those numbers in enough detail, not in the different markets, and he doubts they can. It occurs to him tonight for the first time that maybe they've been relying on him all along to keep track of everything for them and this irritates him even more.

Going through his carefully ordered papers used to make Richardson feel calm and more sure of his world. Like a channel boat pilot going over and over his maps of the river bottom until he can steer through the maze on a moonless night. It used to give him confidence but the more he has lived through, the less sure he has become.

Now, when he sits in the quiet middle of the night, flipping through his letterbooks, seeking the comfort of overview, it feels like so much spilling. All that time and effort and management, pouring across the page and running off the edges. Rereading his letters from this distance, he can see now that this recipient or that one had never truly understood the issue, neither its urgency nor its complexity. And sometimes, more often than he ever suspected, neither had he.

It is galling enough to be reminded of the relatively few marketplace miscalculations he has made over the years, selling cotton and tobacco too soon or in the wrong market, but the worst are his letters to all those military men and government officials, practically begging for an official inquiry into his conduct which would clear his name. He'd had no luck but he had kept at it nevertheless. For years.

Some of the letters he wrote during that time are unbearable to read, the cravenness so humbling, that Richardson finds himself reaching for his knife as he opens that one letterbook until its covers touch in the back and its pages splay open. He holds the covers together by their edges with one hand and uses the other hand to press his blade flush against the inner binding. This way, he can out the offending letter without leaving enough margin to tip off any future readers to what he has done. Unless they are reading so closely as to notice gaps in the page numbers, which Richardson now regrets having inked in.

The house has fallen quiet by the time he pulls out Wash's book and the small packet of current bills and notes not yet deposited. He unfolds the notes and smooths the bills flat. He always spends some time counting and recounting before he sends the notes off, either south to New Orleans for more merchandise from his store or west to pay for Memphis.

Then he turns to the book. There are four letters lying un-folded inside its front cover. Letters from men requesting Wash's services with several dates suggested. As soon as Richardson logs the details, he responds with a short confirmation but keeps his wording vague so that his letter will remain almost meaningless to anyone besides the recipient. After sealing and addressing his replies, he burns each request. Exactly as expected. Theirs is an open secret but they figure there's no need to borrow trouble.

Even though the last of his work is completed, Richardson cannot bring himself to stand up from his desk. Going to bed feels like giving in. When it gets late like this, so late that there's nothing left to do but lay his head down on his pillow next to his wife, once and again the same thing as it has been for the past thirty years, it feels like defeat.

He can tell himself over and over why he married Mary but all he can think about is sliding under the covers next to Susannah. It's been nearly fifty years but he's standing in one of the many rooms they took, looking at Susannah curled on the far side of the bed with her dark red gold hair spread across the pillow. He sets his papers down and watches her sleep as he unbuttons himself. Hangs his clothes loosely over the back of the chair and then steps quickly, tall and thin and pale, across the pool of lamplight. Bends to lift the heavy white cotton coverlet by its corner to slide in next to her, loops his arm gently around her hips and pulls her against him.

He buries his face in the nape of her neck as she murmurs in her sleep. As she relaxes into him, he reaches to turn down the lamp. The two of them lie there entwined, skin to skin, breathing into one another, so easy and relaxed and endless, the next thing he knows the rising sun beams through the window, bright and creamy in the cold morning grayness.

In his twenties, he'd been the best recruiter between Baltimore and Philadelphia, signing up men to fight his Revolution, and the work gave him more chances to see Susannah. She would slip away from home and ride to meet him dressed as a man. Wherever he was. And it had not mattered to her when he was taken prisoner in one of Washington's bungled retreats and was sitting filthy and chained to Thompson on that stinking boat instead of soldiering through at Valley Forge like his brother David.

She'd come to see him anyway. Bursting with the news of their pregnancy. Wanting to make plans. Pick out names. But he had not known what it was she'd come to tell him so he'd had the guards turn her around. Hadn't wanted Susannah to see him like that. Not until he could ride up to her parents' house on his horse in his colors and carry her off.

She'd come because she had tried to contact him several times through his parents but his father made sure to let her letters fall by the wayside. Said he never had thought much of her people. When Richardson had first told his father about Susannah, the old man had cut him off, saying yes, but what will she bring you? His father had his own small empire outside Baltimore by then and wanted a more advantageous match for his eldest son. By the time his father finally wrote him to say she'd been by several times asking after him, their baby boy had already come and gone, dragging Susannah away with him.

Maybe they both would have made it if she'd had the right care but there was no knowing that now. Richardson had not even found out until a full year later when he was released and headed to her parents' place first thing. But they didn't let him step across their threshold. All they did was send him out in the country to the same maiden aunt they'd sent their daughter to for her confinement. So no one would know.

When the aunt finally came to the door, she didn't invite him in either. She just handed him back the tied bundle of letters he'd sent Susannah from that prison ship. His letters full of his plans for their life together. But he'd been thinking only of himself and he hadn't even known it. The last third of the letters hadn't been opened.

He'd stood there in front of that maiden aunt's house for a long time after she'd shut the door in his face, trying to let the truth of Susannah's death sink in, but it never would. And it still hasn't. Here he is, nearly fifty years later, drinking through the belly of the night so he won't have to go to his own bed and discover once again that she is not in it.

He picks up the Bible that Mary keeps digging out from under piles of paper on his desk to set in plain view. He flips back and forth, hunting. The thin pages shudder and cling to his fingers. Candlelight falls across them and their red edges look stained. Eventually, he has to go to the table of contents to find the passage.

There it is.

Let him kiss me with the kisses of his mouth: for thy love is better than wine.

He draws in a ragged breath, touches his glass and reads on.

Because of the savour of thy good ointments thy name is as ointment poured forth, therefore do the virgins love thee.

This is what he hates about the Bible. Just as soon as you find a line that rings good and true, you bump right up against a knot. He continues skimming, prepared to be disappointed, and sure enough, there is the usual talk of kings and the upright. His eye catches on *I am black, but comely* but he forges ahead. Soon bored by the recitations of amounts of jewels, he's about to give up. But he keeps reading one more line, just one more line. Then he falls into it as into Susannah's long smooth back.

A bundle of myrrh is my well-beloved unto me . . .

The passage strikes him so strongly he goes back over it several times. He does not realize he's reading aloud until he hears himself say *our bed is green.* As he feels his voice move through his chest, his eyes swim and he is shaken. He closes the book and, for the first time in a long while, gives thanks. If not to God, then to something.

A yowling snarl rises close to the house, then another joins in, drawing him downstairs. By the time he and Emmaline and Mary gather outside the back door in the deep middle of the night, the two raccoons that trapped the big orange tomcat in the basement have made short work of him.

Richardson notices his wife staring at him, her broad face suddenly pleased above her long hair hanging still dark and young down the front of her nightgown. He glances down at himself, wondering what she sees, and realizes he still holds the Bible in his hand, with his index finger buried in its pages up to the last knuckle, holding his place in the Song of Solomon. He slides his finger out from between the pages, letting it take its place alongside his other three fingers, clasping the book shut against his thumb as he clears his throat to speak.

"Emmaline, shut that basement door. Nothing left to bury. Have Ben set some screen over the grate and put traps out tomorrow. Now let's get back inside."

He heads for his study knowing Mary won't ask him in front of everybody when he's coming to bed but he does wonder how he will react if she starts quoting scripture to him again.

Richardson

My wife ran my house exceedingly well but I knew better than to try turning her face to the storm. All she'd do was try to turn mine towards the Word. Her habits of faith always differed from mine but I thought I'd convinced her it should be possible for us to leave one another alone about those matters.

Once she began meeting regularly with a new minister, his influence on her grew steadily. When it became apparent he also had designs on me, I made it clear to both of them that the children were the only ones in need of religious instruction.

One Saturday morning, as I sat in my study catching up on my accounts, Mary was teaching our Lucius some bars on the piano we kept in the ballroom. I'd left my door open so their conversation came and went. I don't know how they made it to the troublesome topic of slavery. Must have been all that time my boy spent tagging along behind Wash.

I can still hear Mary patiently explaining, in response to Lucius's questioning, that the negroes had become our slaves as the result of a curse. For having been the sons of Ham. But when Lucius asked her what this Ham had done to bring this curse upon himself and his descendants for so long, all the way up to now, Mary started to hem. I didn't have much use for the Bible but I certainly relished its way of placing its many adherents in occasional discomfort. I set down my pen to hear how she was going to tell our boy what had actually happened.

The story goes that Noah, overjoyed to have dry ground under his feet, had taken himself on a tear, embarrassing both himself and his family through too much wine, and when Ham lifted the veil of his father's tent, instead of looking away to preserve their father's pride like his brothers did, Ham had held the veil up and he had looked. Ham stood there staring upon his father's drunken sprawling nakedness. And for his refusing to look away like his brothers did, Ham was cursed. Him and his. Forever.

Nice story for a child. I'd always told Mary to watch out for that Bible. I'd warned her that using it the way she did would land her in hot water. And sure enough, she simply told my son that young Ham had been headstrong, disobedient and disrespectful towards his father. All I heard Lucius say was oh.

After Mary versed them in Bible stories, I spent endless mornings with my boys, going over my duties as land surveyor and tax collector, using some of my own records as examples. There was much I didn't tell them and more I didn't show. I was waiting for the right time, even as I was beginning to doubt it would ever come.

Cassius took to it like a fish to water but he had limited vision and was rapacious enough to make me miss William, despite all his ideals. Lucius had to keep dragging his considerable mind back to the numbers. He was so like William, interested only in finding his own frontier and never very good at concealing his intentions.

Too bad Livia was born a woman. She'd have left her brothers in the dust. She and Augusta both. But Adele, Diana and Caroline made a trio. I saw early on that they'd just want nice things. And Mary Patton would always need tending, long after Mary and I lay dead and buried. So maybe it was best for all of us that Cassius kept his hungry eye on the bottom line.

And I tried to do what my father taught me. I did. I was determined to build my city on a hill. Got myself so deeply invested in Memphis, it had to prosper or we were sunk. But we faced suddenly steeper odds, once the county seat was denied me.

I can see now that I must have known it from the start. This location on the route west, along with its river connection to the New Orleans market, would make the trading of negroes a booming business, whether I wanted any part of it or not. I do remember hoping to avoid it. But looking back from this distance, I think I must have suspected it all along. Some piece of this trade might prove to be our salvation.

But diversity on this matter raged at the time, even within my own family. William was becoming more open about his abolitionist sentiments, no matter how often I cautioned him against it. Ever since he was a child, William had tried my patience with his pursuit of integrity, honoring the bonds forged with his pickaninny playmates well beyond what was appropriate. I thought it was merely a case of youthful idealism, but this dangerous trait of his wore on into adulthood with the persistence of a lingering cough.

And when Celeste came along, I had hoped he'd leave her down in New Orleans, but if he had to keep her with him in Memphis, I told him repeatedly, he certainly didn't need to marry her. William kept insisting that Celeste was different, reminding me that she spoke French and could talk politics with any man. Not that those attributes could count for much when she was colored. Maybe they counted in New Orleans but not out here. In fact, in Memphis, they only made matters worse.

I'd heard the rumors about his drinking but I decided they were just that. People find all kinds of things to say about those who try to stand outside the status quo. And once William decided to let his negroes earn their purchase price, so as to remove himself and Celeste from the whole business altogether, the gossip rose to a loud buzzing.

He and Celeste were such likable people, most folks tried to forgive them their mixed marriage. Even their abolitionism. But the whole landscape had already started to change after Denmark Vesey scared all the whites in Charleston half to death, despite his rebellion never getting off the ground. Just the simple fact of his standing up had shifted the balance. I tried to warn William but he remained sure he'd be exempt.

Meanwhile, Cassius worked steadily with Quinn to increase our reliance on negroes. My second son insisted on their profitability and continually denied the endless difficulties associated with them. He maintained that the road to success in this field lay in proper management. He kept telling me it was simple, saying you'll see.

I tried to listen but I remained astonished by the blindness of youth. It had begun to dawn on me that you cannot do very much for your children after all. What I could do for mine was try to reduce debt and create income, leaving them with as little burden and as much opportunity as possible. After that, it would be up to them.

So when that tall redheaded Scottish woman named Miss Isobel Bryce swept into my foyer talking about her plans for a farm, a kind of utopia which would allow us to rid ourselves of what she called the stain of negro slavery, I knew immediately we were all in trouble, and William and Celeste particularly so.

Her plan was to buy two thousand acres near Memphis in order to set up this utopia. And she had backers. Certainly LaFayette and Jackson. Maybe even Monroe. So many slaveholders had assured her they wanted out badly enough to donate their negroes to her cause, she felt sure she'd have plenty. Plenty of the halt and the lame, I wanted to say. But I bit my tongue as she talked on.

While all those donated negroes worked on her farm to earn their freedom, she would teach classes to ensure they'd be civilized enough to handle their liberation responsibly when it came. Freeing both owned and owner in one fell swoop, she said. As soon as everybody saw how simple it was, she told me that night in all seriousness, replicas of her utopia would spring up everywhere and we'd soon be rid of slavery once and for all.

Miss Bryce was charming that night at dinner but she was relentless. She aimed her gaze at me as brightly as a child while she hammered away with questions whose answers she thought she held in her own uncallused palm.

Did I know that our Founding Fathers, as we now called the men I'd fought under, had been deeply vexed by the problem of slavery? Did I know that many had predicted trouble but that others refused to listen? That Jefferson had even twisted himself into the indefensible and illogical position of blaming the King of England for our dilemma?

Did I know?! I remember a feeling of great hollow emptiness inside. Words surged up like waves but they were useless in the face of such innocence. I saw Mr. Jefferson standing there, holding our snarling wolf by the tail, looking ridiculous.

All I could bring myself to tell Miss Isobel Bryce that night at my dinner table was that slavery was something to be endured for the sake of our brand new and extremely fragile Union, which we'd all agreed upon as the higher priority by far. And yes, I was well aware we'd tried to get ourselves out of it and failed dismally. Hell, I'd tried to get myself out of it and failed. Dismally. Moved nearly a thousand miles west to get away from the messiness of it, only to find it right on my heels.

It tried my nerves to entertain people who knew so little about the world yet remained hell bent on educating others. But I'd long since recognized this subject for the quicksand it was, so I let her talk herself out. It was hard to listen to her plans for her experiment, knowing as well as I did what the outcome would be. I just hoped she wouldn't drag William and Celeste down with her. All they had done thus far was befriend her but I suspected even that might be too much.

Sure enough, not nearly so many men actually donated their negroes to her as had promised. There's only so much generosity you can afford. Once the first theft occurred within her compound, she found herself having to give the stripes to two of her pitiful crew and her utopia began to unravel. Soon she and her farm were an utter wreck. She took off for wherever she came from to recover, leaving us to clean up the mess she left behind.

Yet it remains difficult for me to watch the young lose their innocence, no matter how dangerous that innocence might be. Miss Bryce was glorious in her earlier days, reminding me of both William and Lucius. The way their idealism shone while they so earnestly insisted upon all my compromises having been unnecessary, when they had absolutely no idea about any of it.

Somehow, this idealism enlivened me as much as it aggravated me. I found myself curiously hoping against the inevitable destruction of such shining optimism. Watching the excitement and determination on their faces made me want to say aloud, if I cannot have my innocence, then you at least should have yours.

∞

Wash pushes the girl's mouth from his crotch as Eaton yells at her to get back at him and Richardson flinches but doesn't look away.

She stands up, trapped between Wash about to knock her back and Eaton getting after her. Then all Wash can see is that girl's mother's face when he watched them ride in on Eaton's wagon. Nervous. Wary. Looking around. One hand clutching the side of the wagon and the other on her girl's shoulder. Always wondering what's next. What the hell will be the next damn thing. That picture of this girl's mother, looking around all worn down, rises up in Wash's mind and freezes his hand in midair.

It is a Sunday in mid-October, crisp and bright outside the closed barn doors. Late rains have brought forth one last blast of color before winter strips the leaves from the trees for good. Richardson has made an exception to his usual rule and decided to let his old friend Eaton put two of his girls with Wash. Here on his own place, in the big barn. Eaton has had no luck since he left Charleston. One of the two men he bought there turned out to be sick from the start then died before they had even crossed the Tennessee line, taking the second one with him not too long after.

But Richardson's relieved their stopover coincides with this particular Sunday when most of his people are gone for the afternoon to a prayer service over at Miller's. He's surprised by the difficulty Wash seems to be having and he starts to regret his decision. This was a favor and they never work out. Makes him glad he's been sending Quinn to watch after Wash these days instead of going to see for himself. But Quinn has today off too. He'd disapprove of this exception and he'd be right.

Wash drops his hitting hand as the girl bites off her scream and they all stand there for a minute, hearing each other breathing. Eaton's horses are stamping and snorting with impatience at being left harnessed after having come at a good clip all morning. They jerk at their bits, wanting to stretch their necks down so they can

scratch the sides of their itchy faces along their bony knees. The
dust they have kicked up spins in the light.

As slow as an old man, Wash settles on the end of the bench
they've dragged in and lies back. He clamps his eyes on his loft
and lets his arms hang off the sides of the bench to the floor. His
hands rest in the dust, palms up and open. The girl moves back
over to him, soft and quiet as leaves falling, to kneel between his
legs. Something drops even Richardson's eyes to the floor as Eaton
turns on his heel to fetch the second of his girls.

And way up in the hayloft, Lucius pulls back from where he's
been looking down over that high edge, watching Wash with the
girl. With his father and his father's friend and the horses. After
meeting Wash's eye for an instant, he turns away to curl up in the
blankets. His stomach heaves, even as his first sexual flush rises
through him, but he works to stay quiet. He buries his face in the
blankets to smother his crying, smelling horse and smelling Wash.

It is the next Saturday afternoon when everything rises up in
Lucius all at once. His family comes home from a neighbor's
wedding, bringing two boy cousins for a visit. It is just as they
climb down off their horses and out of the back of the wagon. It
is when Emmaline steps forward to take his knapsack. It is when
she reaches out to pull him to her, teasing and playing a little like
always, but now it is in front of his whole family and his cousins
as well, and now, today, it is all wrong.

Hatred rises so fast he can taste it. Like dusty bricks. He hates
Emmaline for all she is and all she is not. He hates her for being
his mamma and for not being his mamma. For being her baby
but not anymore. He hates her for tending him as steady as a
low flame and for not being able to save him or herself or Wash.

He slaps her away from him, stomping toward her and yelling at her. He calls her all the nasty dirty names he has heard the older boys use. And he does it in front of as many people, black and white, as he can. Then he stands there, feeling her hands fall slack and away from him and seeing her mouth make a small o as the warmth drains from her face.

Richardson doesn't see it happen. He's busy giving Ben careful instructions on how to tend one horse who has come up lame on the trip home. Lucius runs off with his cousins come to spend the night. Without Emmaline to make them change, they head out into the woods in their good clothes, hunting something small to kill. All through the rest of the afternoon, they feel flush with power and togetherness, giddy with belonging.

But Lucius's running carries him away from the other boys until he finds himself lost. He runs on through the woods yelling. Then he is screaming and crying, then gagging and coughing, cutting both his pants and his legs on thickets of hawthorne and blackberry. Running and running until the tearing in his chest matches the tearing in his heart and he trips and falls to lie there with his face in the dirt. Grabbing fistfuls of fallen leaves and dirt and rocks and pounding the ground with them until the sound of his own rattling breath has died down.

After what feels like a long time, Lucius sits up. Everything is quiet and everything is different now. This same forest that has always felt like his own leafy insides whenever he'd wandered through it with Wash now stands with its face turned away from him.

He realizes one of the sounds he's hearing is the river so he knows which way to go. He stands up stiff and already sore. As he walks slowly back to the house, even the last few bright golden leaves seem to curl away from him, as if refusing to feather his passage like they used to, and Emmaline's face keeps appearing before him, her eyes stunned flat and the small o of her mouth refusing to close and smile and act like nothing happened.

That night, just like many more still to come, he has to see her and be tended by her, eat what she fixes him and step into baths she has drawn for him. But she acts so dry and careful, it's like the somebody he knew has died and left him but still stands there looking at him. He stays cross and rough with her to keep this ghost from coming too close. He hopes she will reach out for him as much as he hopes she won't. He hits a lot of things after that, especially animals and especially when they are least expecting it.

Wash

Oh, it's a lure all right. I can see doing how they do. Even that boy.

Makes it too easy, having everything laid out in front of you. Seems like the mean comes up in you whenever weakness lays in front of you. Like you got to stamp it out before it gets on you.

I felt it come up in me sometimes. Certain ones they put me with. All that wriggling and screaming did was make those pecker-woods feel us helpless all the more, so sometimes I did knock her back. Put us all out of her misery.

I knocked CeCe back and I broke her tooth. And I know I put fuel to their fire that see, we're all just animals, and so it's fine to do us this way.

But what I did was, I got it over with. It was CeCe trying to hang on to herself that made them want to take it. That's the part she won't see. It's that tight grip that's sure to get broken. Draws their eye right to it, and then they need to do something about it.

There's ways to hang on to yourself. You just learn em, that's all. But CeCe wouldn't see, and her carrying on was taking up room we didn't have, so I knocked her back and I got it over with.

Her mamma knew though. She's old enough and seen enough to know how things go. Nothing works like you think it should. Everything's backwards if it's even in that much order.

Her mamma did not turn away from me. Even when she held her girl's head in her lap, sopping up that trickle of blood and smoothing her forehead, she didn't turn away from me. She looked up at me where I stood in the doorway leaving, and she just looked at me. Knowing why I did what I did.

She'll pull her girl through and not by putting it all on me. She'll tell her it's more like the weather than one somebody. More like a windstorm passing through, tearing things up and breaking em like sticks. Never meant to. Weather never means to, it just comes through.

That's what I felt like sometimes. That's what it all felt like sometimes.

Pallas

I'd sit in my chair, or I'd stand looking out my window, and I'd feel my fingertips running across my lips real light. Thinking about the way Wash does that. Running his fingers over my face like he's blind. Touching my mouth after I say something, like he's tracing the words to their source.

And I saw what he did to that girl's mouth. I fixed up CeCe with my own hands and all the while, she's cutting her eyes at me since she's heard I talk to him. And I want to say shut your mouth. I want to say I put him back together just like I'm doing you and don't think you can even start knowing one thing about me. But I don't.

And I can see his arm raised and his hand coming down through the air towards her face. I can see it all when I look inside her mouth with that jagged broken off tooth.

I put some poultice in there to mend the inside of her cheek where it keeps cutting open against that tooth. I tell her mamma, let's put some wax on there for the time being, with her mamma nodding. And then that same night, I sat there by him in that hayloft window, holding the hand he hit her with.

So I kept an eye out and I stayed ready to roll out of the way, or else I steered clear altogether. He'd never mean it, but I'd leave this world before I'd take another knock and he knew it. But people didn't mean half the things they did and sometimes, slack was all we had to give each other.

∞

Pallas is one of the few who has decided not to dull her sight or look away. She tells herself things cannot stay like this. Somehow, some way, this world of theirs will shift and slide into some new shape. All of this will tilt and fade and crumble in the long run. The only question is just how long is the long run and can they hang on long enough to make it? And if not them, then theirs.

She makes an odd hard peace with Wash's situation which she has to make over and over again. When she can manage it, she takes comfort in finding his features and his manner in more and more of the youngsters she sees on her rounds through the neighboring places. She pictures herself working to bring enough of these children of his into this world to make sure some part of Wash will last long enough to stand in the free and clear.

In a strange way, these waves of his children please her. They are like one of those slow but steady rising tides he has told her about in an ocean she has never seen. And in a quiet, central part of herself, in the part that can be about more than just herself and what she wants, she is proud of him. But the two parts of her wrestle over it, with sometimes one winning and sometimes the other.

She has to work to be kind to that woman over on Grange's place. Molly has made her four girls a family. Insists on calling them Richardsons regardless of how Grange lists them on his ledger. And she waits for Wash in her cabin, refusing to be one of those closed faced women in Grange's barn. Soon as Molly gets word of Wash coming, she cleans up all her girls so they can stand around him in a neat quiet ring, mesmerized by seeing their own features in his face. She wants to be sure they know he is their father, no matter what people say.

Just last year, Molly lost the fifth girl at three weeks. Pallas was one county over when it happened but she tells herself she would have tried just as hard as with anybody else. And she knows better than to say one single word about it to Wash. If he wants to tell her about walking all the way over there for the funeral then deciding at the last minute to watch from well back in the woods, that's up to him.

But Pallas can be hard for Wash because her first instinct is too often a turning inward to a place where he cannot follow. When she gets gone from him, he tries to tolerate it by reminding himself he has that inside place too. Mena had made sure of it. He used to know how to find it on his own but that was so long ago he's almost forgotten. Until Pallas came along.

Just in time to call his remembering up in him before it disappeared completely, buried under all that has happened to him since. Even that first week, watching her moving around that hot sticky cabin tending him then sitting down for a minute with herself, his own remembering had started to come back to him. Like hearing an echo.

All those endless days on the island. How he used to walk way out into the soft still water of the sound before curling into a ball so he could sink to the bottom and lie there, lightly bumping against the sandy floor, tugged by the drift and pull of the water but barely. Held for those few long moments, balancing between his body's relentless desire to rise and breathe the air of this world and his spirit's hungry hunting for a dimly familiar grace and ease.

So he understands Pallas. He does. The only difference is that Pallas does not need the sound or even a pond, and she can stay longer than anyone he's ever known. And it's easier to envy her this gift than to remember how he'd once had it himself. Feeling her slip through his fingers opens a wanting door he needs kept shut. When he starts to feel left behind, he panics and a blind rage can well up in him.

He tries to turn and walk away. Climb down the steep bluff to the river running deep and wide under the overlook. Slip into the water just between dusk and dark when nobody can be sure exactly what they see. Water's cooling fast and the current is too strong for him to drift quiet and still on the bottom like he used to but he has found ways to make it do.

He strokes out into the middle then turns to lie flat on his back with his toes pointing downstream, tipping his head until his ears go under. Breathing shallow, keeping just enough air to hold himself up. Even though he's being carried downstream, if he closes his eyes to the branches passing by overhead, he can recapture that old familiar stillness of water all around him and the drifty float of disappearing.

He never knows how long he's been gone until the swim back upstream but usually, it's long enough so the strained pulling feeling of Pallas slipping through his fingers starts to ease. Long enough so the tingling in his hands of wanting to grab her and pull her to him, of needing to jerk her out of that trance of herself, of wanting to slap her if only to shatter that world to which he has no access, long enough so all that starts to fade away.

Somewhere in midfloat, Wash comes back to himself by realizing he's been gone. After letting a few more sycamore branches pass by overhead, glowing pale against the dark sky, he turns over, slick and lithe as an otter, to swim upstream against the same current that has carried him down. His hands take hold of the water, his feet kick hard and strong and regular. Moving steadily against the current soothes him, making him glad to be in this body in this world. Working, pulling, breathing, getting somewhere. Then he picks his way up the faint path through the dark, brimming with the pleasure of knowing he has once again pulled himself back from the brink.

For a good long while, Wash manages himself pretty well, hanging on to what Mena taught him and letting Pallas remind him. He makes small altars in hard to find places and leaves offerings whenever he can. Always careful to make it look like an accident. Just some junk.

He buries most of his gifts to make sure they won't be found. Buried this last one right in back of the barn where it's close by and he can call on it. Once the weeds grow tall enough, he'll leave offerings on that nondescript patch of ground. But never anything that would be seen as such. Always something that could have landed there anyway. A curved paring of horse hoof taken from the pile left after the last trimming.

As Wash sets that dull gray arc nipped from Bolivar's hoof among the tall weeds, he gives thanks for having made it this far. Then he asks for help in holding himself together as he covers the miles ahead. Maybe even with some of that horse's ease and grace in the doing. And that piece of hoof lies there undisturbed, letting the weeds grow around it, calling no attention to itself because it could just as easily have been carried there by one of the dogs seeking a quiet place to gnaw.

And Wash makes talismans and wears them like Mena told him. Collect up treasures to strengthen you and speed you on your way. Say your prayers over them and wrap them tight. Keep them with you. Take care of them and they will take care of you.

This last one he made, he included a small swatch of dark glossy hair from the young bay gelding's tail because he wants to remember to carry himself like that horse does. High and light but easy with some spring and a long swinging stride. Wash likes the way Bolivar switches his tail in pleasure whereas most horses switch theirs only when irritated, so he takes a few strands of Bolivar's black tail and tucks them in the small leather pouch along with everything else before he sews it up tight, says his prayers over it and pushes it deep into his pocket.

But it only takes that one time when his pocket has worn a hole without his knowing it yet. He's at Grange's barn and done for the day. As he steps back into his clothes, his talisman falls down the leg of his pants. Lands right there next to his foot on the dusty floor of Grange's barn.

Wash is still moving slow and before he can grab it, Quinn kicks it out of his reach. Shakes out his dirty handkerchief and bends to pick it up. Rolls it onto the square of cloth with a stick and then collects up the corners. Even Quinn knows not to touch someone else's talisman.

Neither one says a word. All Quinn does is cut Wash one sharp look before he turns toward the house for the banknote so they can head home. As Quinn passes by the fire circle in Grange's quarters, he tosses his dirty handkerchief with Wash's talisman tucked inside under Anna's big bellied cook pot. The smell of burning hair slams into the smell of her soup and she cries out, digging amongst the logs with her big poker, but the fire's too hot. Wash's piece is already gone.

That piece of himself he'd put together so carefully, choosing each element for its symbolic correspondence to qualities he knew he needed, weaving his prayers and his breath and his spirit throughout the mixture, then wrapping it up tight in leather and keeping it with him. Feeding it and being fed by it in turn. That piece had been not just a part of him but it had also been him. Himself. The thought of it being manhandled by Quinn, even through a cloth, is almost worse than its being burnt up in Anna's fire.

Wash swears he'll never make another one. No matter what his mother said. After that day, he uses stones. Smooth ones. Picks them up from places he's been. Rubs them between his fingers when things get bad, sets them down once he can breathe easy again.

And when the wagon carries him across the next bridge, he sits up to toss the pale gray stone ringed with dark circles that he'd picked up on his last trip to see Pallas over the rail. He listens to it fall, then settles back down into the flour sacks lining the wagon bed, just like that stone settles down into the riverbed to lie shoulder to shoulder with all the rest. This way, he can think about that stone when he needs to and nobody can take it from him.

Wash

It was pitch dark on that new moon right before All Souls'. I'm sitting up in my loft after another fight with Pallas and I knew I was forgetting. All the now kept coming at me so hard and fast. Sneaking up on my bad side, just like that hammer. Threatening to knock my story right out of my hands.

I sat there trying to remember what I knew about how to keep things straight between this world here and the one inside me. I heard Rufus talking about his grandfather and then I saw him clear as day in all that dark. Standing so close he's looming over me, tipping that staff till his forged bird on top nearly touches my temple, telling me over and over, what you need to do is.

I knew if I could stay inside my mind's eye long enough, I'd see my mamma too, picking and choosing all careful just like Pallas does, and I'd be able to remember what I'm supposed to do so I'll always have someplace to go. Someplace peaceful and green. Full of thick woods where old man Thompson leaves us to ourselves and the deep sand on the narrow path stays cool under my bare feet.

Long as I can manage to hang on to my own story. Steer my mind away from all the mess people talk about me. Follow those turtle tracks across the mud flats to meet Pallas at the pond. Keep my touch on her so light she can't quite tell if it's my breath or my mouth. Look into all the faces of these children of mine coming up all around. Picture them grown up strong and walking around in the new world they will make.

I knew what to do to make it through in one piece. But enough nights having to listen to Richardson talking at me in this barn, enough days having to head out in his damn wagon, and I stayed a threat to lose my grip. Right about now, on this one night, all I could see was my mamma dragging her African like some heavy logs and letting go was starting to make more and more sense to me.

But then Pallas's face flashed into my mind. She's standing there all drawn up inside herself, with her bottles and packets lying broken and scattered on the floor, and she's as far from me as if we'd never met. Then I hear Rufus telling me how Juba stayed too hard till he broke. I can see the jagged edges of that broken file trying to kiss across the gap and I'm sitting in that small hot shop watching Rufus come apart all over again.

That's when it came to me. This is what Rufus did. He let go of making sure his mind stayed a place. So I dove back inside my story. Trying to hang on to everything I knew was true for sure. Working to keep my mind a place. That house of remembering I keep having to make and remake to give myself somewhere to stand and see out from.

But no matter how many sweet spots my story holds, it carries me right towards the mouth of the devil and more than once. I may go back hunting peace, but once it's loosed, my story starts rolling through me with its full force whether I want it all or not. Don't matter why I started in on the telling, it just wants to move.

Happens to all of us. Pallas and Richardson too. You either tell your stories or else they tell you and it's hard to know the difference sometimes.

Richardson

I sat up in my study on that same All Soul's night, but I never intended to seek solace in my past. Solace should lie in all I had accomplished and accumulated. The past was merely an arena in which I'd either triumphed or been thwarted.

I had just finished logging a slew of new dates in Wash's book and I was burning the last letter of request when my Lucius came through the study door I'd forgotten to close. As he stepped across my threshold, I was so startled I nearly spilt my drink. He looked so much like my younger self that watching him walk towards me through the last of the rising smoke gave me vertigo.

I slid Wash's book underneath my blotter as Lucius held an old lesson notebook out to me, asking what's this? I took the battered notebook from him and lay it open without asking why he was still up. I didn't yet know about his rift with Emmaline and was surprised he was coming to me instead of going forever after Wash.

When he stepped in closer, I remember being struck by a strong urge to put my arm around his narrow waist. Pull him close. I managed to resist the urge but found myself grateful when he laid one hand on the back of my chair and the other on the near corner of my desk, then bent to look over my shoulder so I sat almost within the circle of his arms.

I turned my attention to the notebook and recognized William's younger handwriting immediately. When William was Lucius's age, he'd spent hours carefully copying his own distilled versions of Plutarch's stories into his notebooks and then drawing all the scenes with maps marking where they took place. This notebook was mostly drawings. Hardly any writing.

"These are the pictures William drew when he should have been doing his lessons."

I heard myself sounding snappish and tried to soften my tone as the drawings swam in front of me. Lucius flushed pink from feeling rebuked, which I regretted instantly, but he soon turned back to the drawings, full of questions.

"Who's this boy and what is this shiny city supposed to be?"

"That's Theseus and the city is Athens."

"What about this scary man? Why's he standing beside that bed?"

"That's Procrustes, blocking the way."

Lucius stood waiting for more but I couldn't bring myself to tell him. Not yet. Maybe not ever. All those nights when William was as young as Lucius and even much younger. How he'd come to me just like this. Except he'd climbed right into my lap without even checking first. Somehow, he was the only one I'd ever hugged.

I flipped through the fading pages of my firstborn's old notebook. And there they were. All those damn crutches William was forever drawing. Bunches of crutches along with cut off feet, lying scattered and bleeding all along the margins. William had latched on to the story of Procrustes and would not let it go. He'd been obsessed with this monster who blocked the road to Athens, forcing travelers to climb onto his rack where he either stretched them to fit or else cut off their feet.

Theseus finally slew Procrustes but William had fretted so about the feet. Said that was too high a price to pay for entrance to Athens, no matter how shiny the city seemed. At the time, I always told him he would feel differently when he was older. But by now, I had begun to see his point.

I felt my Lucius standing so close that night, needing my answers, not just about Theseus and Athens, but about all of us. Who we were. What had happened to us. I felt our stories fluttering inside me, all at the same time, but I could not find where to start or how to proceed from there. Rivers of words and I can't fit any of them through my mouth.

But I see it all. Thompson's pale blue eyes water from the stench of our prison boat as he laughs with relief from finally realizing he wants out of this business. Mena's sharp eyes hook me out of that auction crowd as surely as a fish on a line. Heddy's wildest girl Charlotte stares at me from the stand, refusing to defend herself, and the skulls of my two scalped scouts glow pale against the dirtied snow. Mary's fingers wrap around her Bible so worn it's starting to look grimy while Susannah's face hovers above mine from within the circle of her hair hanging down, making a redgold room to hold us both.

And this was just the beginning of what I wanted to tell. But I remained convinced there was not enough room for my whole story to fit inside me, along with everything else I needed to believe. Something would have to give and there was no telling what it might be, so I simply screwed the lid down tighter, hoping it would hold.

Lucius waited as long as he could, but then grew restless and turned to go. His heels thudding across the floor snapped me out of my reverie. I called out as he left.

"Shut the door behind you."

"Yessir."

Maybe it was Lucius standing there looking so hungry, maybe it was the rivers of words dammed up behind my mouth, maybe it was just that there was no moon. I have no idea. But pretty soon, I'm headed for the barn. I don't need a candle.

As I stop to speak to the hounds so they won't bark, I start to wonder whether I've worn a trail. I know I should stop. But I can't.

Wash

I do mess with Richardson and some nights, I enjoy it. He comes to me and when he does, he's got that gleam in his eye. He looks down to try and hide it but it stays, that gleam he gets from fingering this edge. Everybody knows he ain't supposed to be coming down here and talking at me like this. Everybody and the devil too. So I will grant him that.

And he's finally starting to creep up on some truth. Getting his words on out. Words a man like him wouldn't be caught dead holding in his hand. Trouble with Richardson is, he wants me to listen to him and not hear him. Both at the same time. He wants me to lift him right up off that hook, but at the same time, he wants me to catch him redhanded.

It don't make things any easier for me, walking around carrying his stories along with mine, but I'm listening mostly to hear the sound of some truth being spoken, even as I'm hunting to find what part can I use to hit him with. This man who thinks he can speak so freely.

What I say is if we're gonna speak freely then lets us speak.

Most times, he knows if he can get me hard and in there, then that's it. Don't matter much what she has to say about it, she's still soft and wrapped round me. If I'm lucky, that soft being soft on me will clear out the rest so none of it can get to me.

And Richardson makes sure about those girls. Said he wasn't going to drag me all the way over to somebody else's place and then have me not make it. Awkward was what he called it. One place, it's Binah's two granddaughters. The younger one coming into curves and the older one flush in love with a new husband.

But everybody needs that dollar and soft will do the trick. When I can manage to unlatch my mind. Just unhitch my mind and let it swing loose. I can't be hanging on to how I don't want this. All that'll do is get me sold down the river or maybe even the islands. Then I'm looking at five more years tops, from what I hear, and cutting cane all the way.

If I can make it far enough down this road, push everything else away, I can stop having to work. The floor of me starts to rise and I'm in my own world spinning and it feels good. It feels good and it's out of my hands. I'm lost to her and she's lost to me and most times, I need it like that.

Sometimes I come up out of it with somebody jerking to stop me cause I'm hurting her. Stopping me right then, before I get the job done, throwing all we just went through right in the trash. Shoulda put grease on her in the first place. If I started worrying on things like that, we'd never get nowhere with it.

Some of em I don't hardly touch. I know better. They're spitting glass and I just try to get through it sooner rather than later. You got to be careful who you put your hands on in this life.

But there will be some few with some sweetness left. What little they can stand. And they look at you and they know you don't mean it. They know you backed in a corner you can't get out from and so they help you both through it. They come carrying all they been holding pent up for theirs long gone, and they hold you, hoping somebody's holding theirs somewhere, somehow.

With these few, I pull em right up against me instead of pressing down. But I try to angle it so peckerwood won't ever know. No reason they need to see my mouth on the side of her neck.

We all got our nature. Don't matter who I am to her so long as I hold her right.

But those others, the ones spitting glass, I just want it over with. Get the job done and get out. Sometimes I make it and sometimes I don't. But I can't afford too many misses and neither can she. She keeps coming up empty, she'll end up sold and gone, and the last thing she wants is leaving her mamma behind and those that raised her.

People paying for this, Quinn keeps reminding me.

People paying is right is what I say to myself.

They expect to get their money's worth or they won't be back, he tells me. And the word will spread and then where will you be? That's what he says to me.

Some few, even I steer clear from. They'll cut me soon as look at me. When I see Quinn coming with one of those, I fix on him like he's clean out of his mind. We'll stand there awhile, me and him, but if I stand there long enough, he'll hitch his head over to the side, just like somebody jerked it, saying get her out of here. But I can't play that card too much or it won't never work. Costs me a lot to put my foot down so I best be sure.

It's when he brings one to me and I see that looking down on me look, that's what I can't take. Thinking she knows about me. Like I'm some kind of animal and she's not like me. She's too fine for this world. Makes me want to say for this time right here, I am this world, so you can't be too good for me. That kind of look raises my hand sooner than anything. They hear this about me so most of em learn how to step out of the way. Step out of the way into the way, I guess.

It was Vesta pulling away from me that made me need to grab her. I caught hold of her just as she was heading for the door. Can't have her bringing Quinn in on it, so I took hold of her arm. Felt her bones under her skin, all small and delicate just like a rabbit. Eyes panicked just like that too. Same shallow breathing. Backed her up against the wall, shoved her tight, just to hold her still.

I can feel her breathing under me and I can see her heart beat in her throat. I'm trying to get her slowed down, calmed down, looking at me, listening to me, seeing me. But sometimes, the more she struggles, the harder I get. The harder I get and the harder I go after her till I'm not remembering her at all. I'm a hammer and I'm coming down and that's all there is.

We carry everything inside. Everything in the whole world is lying full and complete, inside each and every one of us. This life will bring out the deepest thing that's in you and you just can't say how you would do.

Best thing is to find you some time and somebody where it don't work to force it. Like I found Pallas. Even when she gets gone, I still have the thought of her, spreading quiet on my mind.

Richardson

I won't let Quinn give mine the stripes. I don't want them torn up. Even a fool knows whipping is best avoided. Makes them harder to sell. But if it needs to be done, I do it myself. Even my negroes will run over a man they think too squeamish to do the job.

I take care of mine myself. I have to. But it's different than with the horses. With horses, the whip is not for hitting them. Lay into them and they'll just tear around, walleyed and goosey. No horse, no matter how fine, shows his quality when he's tearing around like a rabbit.

You crack the whip but just behind them. It's the whir of the whip through the air and the sound of the crack at the end that keeps them moving forward but you can't ever hit them. Not if you're after what I'm after. That easiness like water flowing grace in a horse that will carry you to town and back all the way on a loose rein.

But with negroes, it's different. Crack the whip and don't strike a lick, all you'll do is make them mad. The only thing that truly turns their mind away from trouble is that whip cutting into some skin.

The feeling is totally different. With the horses, it's all in the wrist. But giving the stripes is more in the shoulder. You must put your weight behind it or it won't cut. And if it doesn't cut, then there's not much point. You're right back where you started, with them thinking they can push you around.

Best way not to have to is be sure they don't want you to. You must lay into it. Sometimes, I can feel it the next day in the muscles running down my right side. I'll raise my arm to take hold of my stirrup and yesterday will come rushing right back at me when that tight soreness catches me along my ribcage.

With the way I keep mine, it usually only takes one stripe, but sometimes it needs more. If I have to go past one, if I get to three, then I'll find myself hard, pretty much without fail. Sometimes

I won't even realize it until I feel the cloth of my britches pulling tight against me. That's the only time I ever feel like taking one of mine for myself. They know it too and they scatter, which is fine with me because there are some lines I try not to cross.

Wash

There are times when I know he gets like that. Any fool can see it come over him when his arm rises and falls. You can see his britches and read his mind.

You make somebody do something and he'll find a way to like it, no matter what it is. Almost like God put that in our natures to test us. Makes choosing matter more.

It'd be too easy if it was only the good things felt good. How else would God know you meant what you said?

Richardson

It's finding the balance between the threat and the execution that keeps things stable. Threats don't work unless one is carried out every now and then. The only threat that has never worked on my place is altering. They know I won't do it.

Sometimes I will with the horses, if one of my studs has become too much trouble and is not worth repeating. But I don't get much satisfaction from it. Seems almost like breaking something just so you can keep the pieces. What good will the pieces do you?

If you have room for separate paddocks and good strong stalls, there's no reason to alter. It's like stealing from yourself. If you don't want him, then get rid of him whole.

Better to sell trouble off than to try to alter it. That's the beauty of selling. That threat works better than any other with mine. It's so simple and it lets you get through without having to whip too many.

Make your place tolerable enough and most will want to stay. Thompson taught me that and he has stayed right all the way to now. Mine are no fools. God knows where they might end up. Goes from good to bad to worse, even right around here, and I make sure mine know it.

That is one of the reasons I'm so free with them. They can grow their own vegetables even if they do use it for barter to get God knows what. I'm relatively liberal with my passes and I hold two big feast days for them a year instead of the usual one. In honor of old man Thompson and everything he taught me.

Mine know to count their blessings. There are those few who can't reason this out, or who know it clear as day but simply cannot keep themselves in hand. I don't want those here anyway.

Unless they are fine. There's an exception to every rule and you're usually all right if you keep your exceptions to a minimum. This is why I put up with Wash.

Wash is worth keeping and Pallas is the same way for Miller. Even though she's barren and spooks plenty of whites due to how quiet she stays, Miller keeps her because she makes him good money with her doctoring. But he agrees with me it might be risky using her on your own family. With Pallas, you can look right into those pale gray eyes and never quite know what you see.

But she makes Miller a pocketful of money bringing in these little ones. Crops go up and down but these keep coming year round. And we don't have to worry about her going clean out of her head like Grange's old granny, helping some of those women to take the life from their babies just as soon as they get here.

Pallas knows how to stop babies from coming but so long as she doesn't interfere with Wash's get, we let her go ahead because those others are usually mixed and we know that they will grow up to cause nothing but trouble, running around all these places looking like nobody so much as their fathers.

Wash

As different as we can be, we're no different in some regards. His daddy taught him, just like the next man. You take what your daddy teaches you and you only got two choices. You either go with it or you go against it.

His daddy taught him he knew best and to stay in charge so he did. His daddy gave him the right and he took it. He went on and gathered up the reins. Never looked back. Looking back is a waste of time was what his daddy said.

Course that daddy of his never did tell him how heavy that weight he took up was and how quick it can wear you out.

Part Six

Thanksgiving, 1823

This Thanksgiving, Richardson's table centers around a platter holding one of Emmaline's hams, smoked to perfection then sliced thin and laid out in overlapping arcs of lustrous pink edged with strips of pale white fat and black salty pepper.

Richardson hopes William will make it back in time to join them, mainly because he's bringing news of the recent sale of Memphis lots, but there's no sign of him yet and it has started to snow. Cassius has taken William's seat next to their father and grows sullen as Richardson's attention catches on even the smallest movement outside the window.

The conversation becomes heated as it often does whenever their abolitionist neighbors join them. Anson Carpenter has become staunchly antislavery in his old age. Round, blond and firmly convinced of man's potential goodness, he has founded a chapter of the Manumission Society to help those who want to start freeing their negroes. Richardson founded his own chapter of the Colonization Society just as fast, working to send these recently freed negroes back to Africa as soon as possible, then writing a law requiring any stragglers to leave the state within the year.

He and Carpenter can joke about their differences, with Richardson saying, "All right, Anson, if you insist on freeing yours to clean your slate, then I'll have to get them gone. The more freedmen running around, the harder you make it on the rest of us. I'm sure this Liberia is just as nice a place as your backyard or mine. And there's no such thing as a truly free negro. Not yet and you know it. Mine are much safer owned and they will stay that way."

Both men have decided not to shield their children from this debate but today their banter feels more pointed because a traveling journalist named Dexter sits with them, listening a little too closely. He's from New York and has been riding around the South, gathering opinions for a piece he's writing on the slavery question. Mary invited him for a two week stay, wanting to serve as a good example and making sure he met the minister. Richardson distrusted Dexter's earnestness from the start and doesn't want to turn up in any book he's writing. The fact that Diana and Caroline have fallen for the young man's ginger curls doesn't help.

Dexter has already worn out his welcome and tonight he seems determined to push Richardson and Carpenter further than they intended to go.

"I hear Atkinson lost his temper and beat one of his men so badly that he died the next day for lack of proper treatment."

Richardson has a ready answer. "That case led us to legislate a twenty four hour waiting period before inflicting punishment. Gives everybody time to cool down."

"But how do you enforce it?"

Before Richardson can answer, Carpenter leans in with a different story for Dexter. "It's the situation at Hargrove's that haunts me. His old man Moses died of natural causes, so it wasn't the death. And it wasn't Hargrove's wanting to bury his Moses in the family cemetery, right beside his own plot. It was his insisting on doing it by himself and then getting so drunk that he lost all sense of proportion."

Dexter interrupts, having heard parts of this story already. He savors these details because he knows they will make good copy.

"From what I heard, he dug the grave too shallow and too short both. Ended up climbing on top of Moses then jumping and stomping, trying to make him fit."

"Hargrove's not much for doing his own work," Carpenter says. "But the worst part is that Moses's two boys saw the whole thing. Lying belly down under the magnolias. Said Hargrove was muttering nonstop, crying then yelling. Cursing Moses too, but they knew better than to try to stop him. Hargrove carries a pistol with him always and he was well past drunk enough to use it that night."

Cassius cuts in, more irritated than sympathetic. "But Hargrove's gun didn't stop Moses's boys from carrying their story straight down the road to the next batch and the next until we've had a rash of nightwalking, cut up cows and broken tools."

"They are trying to make you rein Hargrove in and doing a hell of a job of it too," Carpenter says, almost proudly.

Cassius looks to his father, expecting him to step in. Puzzled by Richardson's surprising reticence, Cassius tries to speak for him. "A fine does need to be imposed on Hargrove, but we can't let it seem like the negroes have forced our hand."

Richardson is determined not to give Dexter any help in fleshing out this story so he doesn't tell them that Moses's eldest boy came to him, asking for help. Richardson has already been to see Hargrove, who was embarrassed enough to let him negotiate Moses's reburial as quietly and quickly as possible.

All he says is, "These negroes will take a hell of a lot without flinching, but when it comes to the burying of their dead, any misstep serves as a match to tinder."

"That's the beauty of your cooling off period," Cassius says. "Letting our neighbors get carried away only makes matters worse for the rest of us since we are all bound together whether we like it or not."

Richardson hears his second son sounding more sure than he himself has ever felt. He thinks about William riding from Memphis, still believing he can spread abolition as easily as grass seed. His two eldest sons are utterly opposed. One wants into the system and one wants out. But from where Richardson sits, both viewpoints seem a luxury. Cassius has no idea what he's in for and William would hardly be the mayor, managing his own store, unless Richardson had made sure he was well set up. It would be a different story if either one had to start from scratch.

On William's last visit home, Richardson had come down the stairs into a fight between his two eldest boys, with Cassius lecturing William on the dangers of abolition and Miss Isobel Bryce while William let his mother's bland smile play across his lips, saying all he'd done was lend Miss Bryce his reputation. Cassius had raged at William then, insisting it wasn't his to lend. Both sons fell quiet as soon as they saw their father but Richardson has heard the gossip. People in Memphis have started to question William's stability and competency. Whether it's the alcohol or the abolitionism, it almost doesn't matter.

Tonight Richardson watches Lucius look from Cassius to Carpenter and back, with those dark brows hovering high under his widow's peak. He's glad to see Lucius show some interest in his own family now that he's finally quit shadowing Wash and Emmaline. But it's hard to watch the boy trying to decide which side to take when Richardson suspects there's not any real choice. Not yet.

Lucius idolizes his eldest brother and it didn't help that Emmaline pumped him full of talk about William being her hero. The boy has even started to ask about going to live out in Memphis with William and Celeste. He's still too young but that excuse won't last much longer.

Voices rise and fall then rise again as opinions begin to shoulder each other roughly aside across the long dinner table littered with now empty plates and serving bowls. Only the wine glasses are still in use. Richardson snaps at Emmaline each time she tries to clear.

"Just leave it. We'll ring for you."

Mary sits opposite her husband, growing first anxious then annoyed, both with Dexter for his lack of manners and with her husband for letting it go this far. She uses the side of her hand to groom the crumbs from her end of the tablecloth into her opposite palm then drops the small pile onto the edge of her plate.

When Dexter starts trying to get Cassius to open up about whether or not he or his friends ever go to the quarters, Richardson snaps. He sets his wine glass down carefully and then, quick and fierce as a squall, his hand slams down, rattling the china.

"Now wait just a damn minute."

A sudden clear quiet catches Dexter midsentence.

"I have had enough. I've worked for over two full weeks to put up with you. Anson and I are lifelong friends, yet you think you can set us against each other, as if you were at your own personal cockfight, and then sit back to watch so you can write it up, thinking you have discovered something important.

"Let me tell you something. You know nothing of us. Nothing. Whatever you've seen that you think so awful is merely a dim shadow of what truly lives here. Not everything can be put into words."

Dexter's open mouth gradually closes of its own accord.

"It's a wonder how you traveling writers survive, carrying as little common sense as you do. The cities you come from must be easy, sterile places indeed, where a man's true nature never shows itself.

"I prefer this place, even with its chaos and confusion. Terrible things happen here. And many of us respond from our baser selves.

But unlike you, we do not suffer from the illusion that we are not human, not subject to pitfalls and glories in equal measure. We are susceptible, fallible, far from perfect. The difference between you and us is that we live a life which forces us to accept this central fact about ourselves.

"I would always choose this situation of mine over the aimless, stateless life you lead. Wandering this land, thinking you are seeing it, when all you are doing is forever misunderstanding it by comparing it to some figment you carry in your mind of your own home. Whatever image you carry of a place where men stand only in their higher good, never bending to put their foot on another man's neck, that place is merely a dream because it does not exist."

Mary can endure it no longer. She stands to start clearing the table herself, if for no other reason than to escape the room, but her husband's voice freezes her hand as it reaches for Livia's plate.

"I'm not finished."

She sits back down, drawing her hands into her lap and scanning the room, looking for what needs fixing. Listing tasks helps her quell the old panic that rises whenever chaos threatens. She makes a note to herself to take the curtains outside to clean them as Richardson turns back to Dexter.

"What you refuse to understand is that we are not the same. Different stories walking hand in hand with different times have shaped us each differently. You cannot see me clearly from where you stand. It is circumstance which will bring out the deepest part lying hidden within you. Until you are prepared to accept that, I'm afraid there's no longer a place for you at my table.

"Excuse me for my candor, but I feel it is the least I owe you. I have some paperwork to attend to now. Emmaline will see to your needs as she has for the past fifteen evenings. I trust you will sleep well and thereby be rested for your next adventure. I will let Ben know to have your horse fed, groomed and saddled so you can get an early start."

Richardson pushes back his chair and stands. Everyone else sits perched like birds on their nests, looking across at one another with quick sharp glances, until Livia falls into her wide open laugh, full of the pleasure that rises in her whenever the truth gets told. She is joined by everybody at the table except for Dexter who remains perfectly quiet for once.

In the hush that falls over the table, they hear William stomping the snow off his boots on the porch. As soon as he's inside the door, they are up and hugging him. But Livia lingers in the empty dining room, leaning across the table to smile down at Dexter, still sitting at his place.

"Well, you can't say I didn't warn you. I guess you didn't see his bottom line until you'd already ridden right across it."

She turns away, still laughing a little and looking very much like her father. Dexter stands beside his chair, watching the Richardson family gather around William in the front hall without realizing he's blocking Emmaline. She stands behind him with her arms full of dishes, waiting for him to move so she can get past him to the kitchen.

Before William even makes his way out of the front hall, Richardson is onto him for news about the sale of Memphis lots. Energized from having said his piece, or some small part of it at least, he feels potent, full of life. He's certain they've made money, especially considering all the whiskey he sent out there to stimulate the bidding after they lost the county seat.

"So, tell me. How did it go?"

William smiles and holds his hand up to say wait a minute because he's still greeting everybody. He has to extract himself from Lucius's bear hug before he can pour himself first one drink then another. Richardson works to be patient while everyone talks to William at once. He paces the hall, unable to stand still, giving only a nod to Carpenter, who hovers in the doorway leaving.

After a few times up and down the hall, Richardson realizes that William avoiding his eye must mean he has bad news. He picks up his son's knapsack, knowing the letters from his Memphis customers lie bundled in the outside pocket.

"Even today?" Mary calls after him but her words are drowned out by his feet on the stairs.

Sure enough, the letters bring only complaints and requests. Just as Richardson feared, the drunken boatmen and rowdy squatters already well settled in Chickasaw Bluffs have scared off most new settlers. Brawling and eye gouging remain much more common than prospective buyers would ever guess from the ads he and his main partner Sullivan ran. Word must have gotten out about the roughnecks and the county seat both.

But you would think more men would have recognized the potential. Even the Indians knew the bluffs were the only logical place to cross the river for a hundred miles in either direction. Why are the whites so blind to this fact? Yes, there is uncertainty, with the river continually changing course and disease in the swampy areas, but how can they not see that the future is headed right this way?

William lingers downstairs. He dreads having to describe the failed sale to his father. Too much cheap liquor served too early, the broadsheets torn and crumpled into the mud, the silence stretching long and empty whenever that fancy auctioneer from

Cincinnati paused for breath. Pockets of quiet so deep the man talked himself into laryngitis and few serious bids.

It was embarrassing more than anything else, was what Sullivan had kept saying, but William understands the problem. Many of the potential bidders are his customers at the Richardson store. Fond as they are of him, he knows they have trouble with his trappings. More his rich backers than his colored wife, but his abolitionism makes them increasingly uneasy. He also knows that the roughened settlers who have lived in this muddy little frontier outpost for years are offended that three investors they barely know can buy the Bluffs, then meet with a judge to draw up papers allowing them to sell off the lot next door plus those down the street.

William climbs his father's stairs thinking maybe his grandfather's town building scheme works best when practiced on more virgin land. He remains confident that Memphis will grow and even flourish, but he has already realized this growth will happen on a much longer timetable than the one his father has in mind.

Before William even steps into the room, Richardson has decided he does not want whatever news William brings about the sale. Not now. He's mad at himself for his outburst and spent by it as well. He looks over his shoulder at his firstborn standing in the doorway and cuts him off before he can open his mouth.

"You must be tired. Go take a nap. Memphis will take time."

As William, relieved, pulls the door shut behind him, Richardson turns back to his figures, thankful they fill his mind. Writing and rewriting them into ever straighter columns, adding then checking and rechecking soothes him, brings a sense of order to his world. But pretty soon he runs out of calculations and there is nothing left to do. He doesn't have the heart to go over the map of Memphis they had commissioned, with its four squares and a promenade along the river.

As the afternoon light starts to lengthen, Richardson looks through the tangle of bare branches to the lay of the land beyond. He remembers being able to cast his eye across those hills and valleys just like a net, seeing immediately the best way to divide them into desirable parcels. Riding across those virgin acres with his surveying tools, carving up this frontier as easily as a hunk of meat, then selling it off to his newly arrived neighbors.

Now when he looks out across that land, it won't bend to his hand, not even in his mind. It sprawls there, impassive and vast. He is surprised to feel himself finally starting to turn against the way he was taught. It has taken all the way until now because the lesson was drilled in so deep. Gather, increase and pass it on. At all costs.

But as he watches the people his children have become, he sees how having and being given changes you. Blinds you to certain necessities and leads you to take too much for granted. Mainly, it weakens you. Robs you of your own decisions.

Even as he has worked so hard to build his temple to leave to his boys, he has also begun to want to tear it down. Take it with him when he goes. Give them the chance to make their own way. It is turning out to be harder than he expected to give a gift to those who refuse to see how it has been made.

He unfolds Gamma's pedigree, drinking and planning which stud will be the best choice for her last few seasons. As each of her grown foals fills his mind, he can feel the animal under him, the length of its stride, both down a wooded trail and across the meadow. The house is quiet, the sky blues toward purple as the snowstorm clears and the liquor begins to shroud all he has tried to put out of his mind. Soon his cheek rests on his elbow and he's asleep.

Emmaline hardly ever lies in her loft, looking out this west facing window, watching the sunset. She's usually too busy. But on this Thanksgiving, when all the Richardsons have eaten a large late lunch and then disappeared to nap it off, she has time to finish cleaning up, with a minute left over to climb into this loft Richardson built for her. Tucked between the kitchen ceiling and the floor of his drinking smoking room. This place of hers that does not give her room enough to sit up without knocking her head on the enormous beams supporting the house's second floor.

Today she has time to let the trapdoor at the top of the steps from the kitchen fall closed behind her. Time to crawl stiffly across this low loft on her hands and knees to her pallet then lay herself down. Time to pull her Bible from the worn front pocket of her apron and set it on the windowsill. Time to feel the wonderful stillness of finally not having to move anymore seep through her as she watches the tatters of the day go by.

She lies there on her back with her shoulders propped up against some sacks of meal. She lifts one hand to graze the ceiling of this den of hers with her fingertips and looks out the small rectangular window Richardson had insisted on putting in for her, saying everybody needs to see out, Emmaline. She remembers how she had responded to his comment inside her head.

"Well, I don't know about you but I might rather stand up than look out, seeing as how that world out there goes on mighty well without me. But you go on and you do what you think best, Mr. Man, since that's exactly what you'll do anyway."

She thinks about how Richardson put her right smack in the middle of things, folded into the heart of his house, like a raisin into batter. Telling her about how he wants her where he can get at her and how he hates the look of all those little outbuildings scattered around, making everything look raggedy.

She remembers letting his talk swirl around her as she decided to make having to be his anchor work for her. She thinks about her three grandsons, most likely sitting around somebody's fire down in the quarters, or maybe even gone off courting on this holiday, and she's glad to be buying them some room to maneuver.

She pictures all that her boys might be doing out there in the wider world as this loft of hers, well warmed from the kitchen below, falls into darkness and the redgold tongues of this particular winter sunset stretch across her upraised arm like honeyed amber candlelight. Pure molten gold pours from a bright crack in the deep indigo of the passing winter thunderclouds. All of it framed by the jigjaggedy black arms of the bare tree branches. Makes her glad of the window, even though this is the first time in longer than she can remember when she has seen anything out of it besides flat blueblack dark.

Next thing she knows, it's dark as the inside of somebody's mouth and Richardson's banging on the kitchen ceiling underneath her. Hard and sure, three times, with the tip of his walking stick while she swims up from the bottom of her dream as he calls out for her, saying it's time to lay out some supper and asking where has she been.

All right, all right, she's saying. It's all right there and I'm coming.

Still groggy from his own unintended nap, Richardson had stepped stiffly into the gloaming of his darkening kitchen, empty for once of Emmaline. So quiet it made him feel naked and old. Laid bare. He wants to walk into his kitchen and have Emmaline moving around in there. Cooking, making, tending, keeping, fixing. Doing all the work that adds up to his life.

Emmaline feels almost like his heartbeat, so when she climbs up in that hutch of hers to lie down for a minute, when she finally stops moving, Richardson finds himself overcome by that skittery panicky feeling that hits just as he falls into a deep sleep or wakes up out of one. Whenever he has been lying so still for so long that his heart has truly slowed down. That feeling of being caught and pulled under until the only way out of it is to move a little to make his heart gallop, trying to catch up with him.

It is in that instant, when he realizes how slow his heart can beat, how close to stopping it can come, that he sees how all the activity he had thought was his own life is really just a fluttering against the deep quiet that his heart stays forever wanting to fall into.

Richardson does not like it when Emmaline slows down. As if she could slip under and pull him down with her by stopping like that. So he keeps her hopping. Makes sure of it.

∞

Richardson

By some miracle, my father rallied in his nineties, giving my younger brother Henry the chance to grant him one of his last wishes. He wanted to see what he kept calling my empire. None of my other brothers had done quite so well, he was fond of telling me, and what he wanted was a trip to see my world before he left this one. Henry told him he could die out here, if not on the way. But my father said it would be about damn time, so Henry loaded him up and he arrived on my doorstep in early March looking tired and perhaps a bit thinner but exhilarated.

He found what he called "the whole thing" heartening and I was moved by the pride he took in my accomplishments. He was far more interested in the house and the barn and the mill and the gin and the nail factory than he was in any of my children. He glanced at each one as I introduced them but his gaze soon skimmed over their shoulders to take stock of my fields and my furnishings. He constantly interrupted their stories at dinner to go back over and over the specifics of my development of this place.

He did seem to see Cassius out of all of them. Perhaps because my second son made sure of it. Or maybe because we were up to our ears in another one of his improvements. Determined to drag us into the future, Cassius had insisted that I expand both the kitchen and our adjoining smokehouse, saying we'd outgrown my original design.

I didn't like the idea of so much change, nor did Emmaline, but we'd let ourselves be overruled. Before we knew it, there was a great hole in the wall. Predictably, the work spilled over into my father's visit but there was nothing to be done about it.

My father insisted on hearing about Memphis and wanted to go there but thankfully, a trip was out of the question after the latest road repair washed out again. I told him only that our plans were coming along and then tried to distract him with some mechanical or technical matter. But he was like a dog with a bone, hewing avidly to the exact issues I would have preferred to avoid. Lot sales, the road and the county seat.

Because aging requires so much energy, my father was unable to appear even remotely interested in anything beyond his few core obsessions. He kept after me about Memphis and I dodged the truth for as long as I could. Then I simply turned to face his disappointment. It was almost a relief to tell him about the failed sale. To admit that Memphis was still staggering, almost willfully refusing to prosper. As soon as he had broken me down, he started sweeping up the pieces, telling me not to worry, that everything would work out fine.

My Lucius used his considerable charm and their shared interest in Memphis to get the old man to tell stories even I'd never heard. But my father could only sit still for so long. He insisted on going and doing, dragging Lucius with him everywhere he went, even through a sudden snow that made a lie out of our early spring. And so no one was surprised when he showed signs of a flu before his third week was out. He went downhill fast.

Doctors were no use. I sent for Pallas and she came.

Perhaps we all have moments in our lives to which we can trace awakenings. Usually they are few and hard to hold on to. Sitting there with Pallas, seeing my father out of this world, was the day my vision started to clear.

As often as my father insisted he was ready to go, he wasn't at all. We sat there in that shrouded room with his words pouring over us like water. He'd get on a jag and couldn't be turned from it. Staring at the ceiling, reciting endless lists of transactions, and repeating his dictums over and over.

"Brick by sodding brick. That's how you lift yourself from the gutter."

"Men without property are not thought much of."

"Opportunity lies all around, you have only to bend it to your hand."

The hammering from Cassius's renovation echoed beneath us, syncopating its rhythm into my father's ranting. I felt sandwiched between the generations and I remember wincing as I finally heard something of the way I must have sounded in all I said to Wash. Just like my father. And Pallas just sat there, resting her smoky gray eyes on me and refusing to look away. She was watching me start to see and we both knew it.

There were revelations. I knew he'd crossed from England alone when he was about the same age as my Lucius. But I never knew until his very last day on earth that my father had been orphaned at seven years old. As for those next seven years, wandering the streets after his parents died and before he made it onto that boat, he never spoke about that time. Not even in delirium.

All he said was, "They died. One then the other. And I was alone."

But I could see the fear in his eyes. He looked at me and didn't see me. He was that small starving boy once again, that boy he'd spent a lifetime banishing. Building cities, towns, an empire. Overeating his whole life. Trying to outrun this terrified boy who dogged his tracks all the way through and then caught up with him in the end.

It was in that moment when I caught my first glimpse of my own lifelong push. I was shocked to discover I'd been driven all my life by my father's ancient and frenzied fear of the gutter. I shouldn't have been able to hear his grasping desperation from where I stood, but that was the day when I saw it had haunted me throughout. Perhaps even fueled me.

The moment did not last long. Then it was gone and my father was breathing his death rattle. Pallas stood to lift his shoulders so his head could fall back. She was trying to help him breathe, acting like we wanted him to live and our wanting could make it so. I reached out to touch her arm where she had it looped around behind his neck then shook my head no and sat back in my chair. She looked at me hard and I nodded. She pulled her arm away and laid him back onto the bed.

She and I sat there together, one on either side of him. We did not look at each other anymore. Instead, we sat watching my father die. We were the gates he was passing through and we let him go. I'd hoped he would come naturally out of his delirium for a moment before he passed. I hated the thought of him going through this one last door still terrified, still scrambling, still thinking he was nothing. But that is exactly what happened.

Pallas stood up to lay two fingers against his neck, feeling for a pulse. After a long pause, she did not even look over at me. She just went about her business. Crossing his hands on his chest, pulling the sheet over his head and opening the curtains, whether to let the light in or the spirit out, I had no idea.

She fetched her basin of water and set clean rags on the table by his bed. Then she stood there looking at me. Waiting for me to go so she could get started. Waiting as if to say go on, go tell everybody. Go on and stand around with each other, putting your mouth around whatever words you all use at times like these.

In the face of her calm capability, tinged as it was with impatience, I felt as helpless as I'd ever been. Almost translucent. For an instant, I wanted to take the cloth from her hands, dip it in the water then wring it out as I bathed my father's body myself. But it seemed somehow impossible.

Pallas was ready and she was able. I bowed in the face of my failure and left the room. I shut the door behind me and went to my study to pour myself a drink using hands that felt like they belonged to somebody else.

After I don't know how long, Cassius knocked. I thought he'd come to offer his condolences but I doubt he even knew about his grandfather yet. As he charged across my threshold, I turned to pour him a drink but he shook his head.

"Not now. You need to take a look at this."

He was carrying something in his hand, a stout and twisted stick, coated in a chalky white dust that was still falling across the floor and down between the boards. Cassius brandished this twisted stick at me as if it were somehow my fault but I'd never seen it before it my life.

"What is it?"

"It's mojo, goddammit, and it's everywhere. I've told you and Quinn has never stopped telling you, but you won't listen. Wait till he sees this. No wonder he made sure to build his own cottage himself."

As my second son badgered me while my father lay dead in the next room, I stared at that stick. It was almost as long as my arm and only half as thick but gnarled and knobby. It was two sticks really, each twisted around the other, like two snakes mating, making a kind of braid, with sinewy humps lumping up wherever they overlapped.

Two different kinds of wood woven into one but not by human hands. They'd grown around each other on their own. I'd seen that kind of thing in the woods myself sometimes but never thought much of it. Now that I was looking more closely, I could see that it carried an undeniable charge.

"But I don't understand. Where did you find this?"

"It was plastered into the wall of your kitchen all along. From the very beginning. And you never even knew."

By this time, Emmaline was hovering behind him, careful not to step in the dust lying scattered in an arc on the floor. She had her lips clamped down hard and Cassius kept jerking the head of the stick over his shoulder towards her, saying she had to have known. She had to have.

Emmaline kept trying to hand him a cloth, saying hold it with this, even as she had to duck back so he wouldn't hit her with it. Eventually he stopped thrashing and stood there. Emmaline's eyes met mine over his shoulder and she watched the thought come into my mind. Virgil and Albert. My first two men. Those first two men I bought in Charleston. I could see them. Tall and quiet and solid. Small eyes set deep in impassive faces.

Thompson had warned me not to buy saltwater negroes, but they were so dark I didn't even see those thin laddered scars climbing their cheeks until I was miles from Charleston. By then it was too late to turn back. Both men had already been here for years before I bought them and they turned out to be such good workers that I soon quit worrying about their country marks.

It must have been them. They had built that kitchen wall while I bricked the front one. They had worked alongside me, looked me right in the eye, then plastered their mojo into the walls of my house.

No wonder they never would step across my threshold. Always stood outside, waiting for me under my big elm. I thought they were being respectful. Polite. Made me wonder what else they did and who else had laid curses on us over the years.

No wonder Emmaline wore that Bible like a shield. I guess she'd had plenty of curses sent her way as well for having the key to my smokehouse. I knew she couldn't read but she always said it made her feel better just to touch the words. I never suspected she was using it as her talisman. Mary would have had a fit had she known but it made perfect sense to me.

I sent Cassius off to burn the stick and turned my mind to burying my father. Cassius went straight to Quinn, who came after me right away, ranting about how he had kept on telling me and telling me but I couldn't hear him. I sent him after Cassius so I wouldn't have to listen.

Thank God Emmaline had her grandson build them a separate fire down by the quarters. They were about to throw that twisted stick in her kitchen fire but she wouldn't hear of it. She stood there all afternoon, making sure. Not that it mattered much since the damage was already done, but as Emmaline always said, there's no reason to spit at the devil.

William made it back from Memphis in time for my father's funeral and by then, even I had to admit the drinking was beginning to show. His broad face remained as smooth as ever but his hands had started to shake. Soon after he returned to Memphis from his Thanksgiving visit, he'd written that he and Celeste had been banned from the city limits on account of their support of Miss Bryce. Her disastrous fall had tarred them too. But he'd closed the letter by telling me not to worry.

William, God love him, never did accept a thing about human nature. It's not that he didn't understand it because he did. He fought my last war by my side and was held prisoner with me in that dungeon of Beauport long enough to know the depths to which men can sink. He simply refused to accept the truth of it, insisting anyone could be lifted up. And I mean anyone. He always swore there must be a better way.

As much as I admired my firstborn son, the trajectory of his life was painful for me to witness. I remained staunch in my support of him in the face of increasing criticism. I can see now that it was because he carried some part of my younger self I'd long since abandoned. But William's determined optimism is what destroyed him.

It was the gap between the ideal and the real that finally broke him. Not so much the gap as his drinking to bridge it. The alcohol abraded his capacity to react, dulling his instincts until the people out there couldn't rely on him anymore. They stopped listening to him and started telling him what to do instead. There was not much I could do for him except watch him go downhill which is a difficult thing to do for someone you love.

Just like William, my Lucius worked hard to find his way. He left Emmaline and Wash behind as he tried to grow up, but I couldn't tell him the stories he needed to hear and my father hadn't left him enough room to find his own. And as much as my boy wanted to move to Memphis, he could see that William was in no shape to guide him, even before Celeste wrote to say it was impossible.

I think it was hearing William gone slurry at my father's funeral that made Lucius mad. He left the room before William even sat down. Headed out in his good clothes. Mary wanted me to send someone after him but I thought what he needed was time. The rain caught him at his farthest point, waking the flu we didn't even know he'd been fighting.

His cheeks always flushed so rosy, we hadn't noticed anything and he never said. On that day, I'd just assumed it was his temper flaring. Thought he was upset about his grandfather and William. I may have even told him he needed to try feeling less strongly. Rein in his emotions. Don't take everything so much to heart.

He fell sick just as my apple trees flowered. One month before he was to turn fifteen. Doctors came and went but there was nothing to be done. At least Wash would've known to keep him out of the rain.

Once again, Pallas tended him with me. I continually sent my wife away as if the boy had been mine alone. Pallas and I sat there with him as he disappeared over the edge. I was determined to bathe him myself but I'd only wet the cloth to wipe his forehead before Pallas stepped up and took it from me.

I don't know how long I'd been standing there, smoothing those dark brows against his pale forehead. Just like mine. But this time, I stayed in the room and I watched her until she was through. I built his coffin myself that afternoon.

∞

Richardson takes his best bourbon to Wash in the barn. For once he has nothing to say. Not one word. Grateful he has caught Wash alone, he sits down next to him. On the same step. Closer than ever before but Wash doesn't move away.

Wash knows Lucius has died because Pallas stopped to tell him on her way home. But he blocks the boy from his heart, just like he has most of his own children. All those growing up boys, sassing him in front of Binah and everybody else. Even those girls of Molly's. Not to mention the ones he doesn't know. Just thinking about it is too much most of the time, so he rebricks the wall he's built between himself and all of them.

Richardson hands Wash the bottle then takes it back. Richardson likes drinking after Wash. Bringing the hard round smoothness of the bottle's mouth, still wet, from Wash's mouth to his own. Feeling the liquor's clear fiery nothingness at first. Then a burning warm down his throat from out of that cool glass mouth. Feeling that heat moving through him and knowing Wash has just a moment ago felt exactly what he feels now. The liquor's warm tug.

Moonlight falls into the big barn through high up knotholes. Richardson tips back until the edge of the next higher step digs into his low back. Wash leans away, against the side wall. Their two pairs of long thighs jut out in front of them, side by side. Wash's thick under the worn cloth of his coveralls and Richardson's narrow under the corded twill of his breeches straining across the points of his bony knees.

Wash knows without looking that the older man is tilting his head back to look at him from under those hooded lids. Feels those eyes lying heavy on him. Wonders what's next. What is the next damn thing?

Wash feels his hands being drawn towards Richardson. He imagines one hand hooking under Richardson's jawbone, sinking into the softness of his neck while the other wraps around the bend of Richardson's temple. That old thirsty pull. But he tells himself no. No matter how satisfying it would be.

He hears Richardson say without saying, come closer. Tell me. Let me know. Wash looks down at his hands where they rest on his thighs. Trying to keep them still, he tightens his fingers around that ticklish place just above his knee. He hears Diamond tell his story.

"Beat the tar out of this nigger."

Wash sets his face against the coming grin and he can feel Richardson wondering what he is thinking about. Let him wonder, dammit. Let him stew.

Next thing Wash knows, his hands are wrapped around Richardson's face so tight he can feel the skin slide between palm and bone. Somehow Richardson has been dragged across Wash's lap.

He lies there staring up at Wash from inside the frame of Wash's squared off fingers. What little light there is gleams off the wetness of his eyes and Wash feels Richardson's want without having any answer for it.

Wash could kill him right here and now and they both know it. One quick wrench of his head from his neck and that would be that. But then there he'd be. No way out. Nobody else could have done it but him. Folks around here act like they don't see Richardson steady coming to Wash in this barn but they do. They know. All of them. It would take less than a day for it to come out.

Wash watches Richardson's eyes gleam wetter and wonders. Is it Nero? Does he want the same rush that flooded him when he stabbed Nero? Is he trying to make Wash push him back to where he had a life he was willing to kill for? But he's not reaching for his knife. Both hands lie open, palms up, in his lap.

Wash feels his grip tighten until he starts to sense some give and then he gets it. What Richardson wants is his story. He wants to know how does it feel. To be trapped. To have your grip knocked loose over and over but keep going. How to find a way out of no way. Richardson wants to own him and his story both but there's no way.

This understanding pours through Wash like relief, loosening his grip until Richardson starts to roll off his lap. Wash jerks one knee up, pushing Richardson the rest of the way, sloughing off his bony drunken weight with an involuntary shudder. Then he looks down, watching Richardson throw his hands out, trying to break his fall. One palm slides along the edge of the first step, catching an enormous splinter in the web between his thumb and forefinger, as his other palm hits the floor where his long pale fingers starfish in the dirt.

Wash sits there, watching Richardson scrambling for purchase, and shakes his head, almost laughing as he does every single time he realizes he would choose his own lot over this other. No question. Lord have mercy.

As this knowing pours over him, running down his sides like foamy waves, Wash feels Mena, pleased and glowing. She's so close he cannot see her but he knows her top lip is drawn tight to shiny across that crooked front tooth from the small downward arc of her grin. Her arms are wrapped around herself and Wash knows exactly how her palms cup her opposite elbows as he stands up, turns to climb the stairs and then the ladder, leaving Richardson good and behind him.

That next morning, Wash runs Richardson's northern line of traps. He steps down from the crest of the bluff toward its edge. Each step loud in the crisp cold quiet. He passes the sooty circle of ash where he and Lucius used to build their fire and feels the boy hovering close. As he scans the ridges of the surrounding hills, Mena and Rufus draw even closer.

First they linger on the edge of visibility, like the pale green hazing through the bare winter branches. Then they fill his mind's eye. He can see them both watching him marching off to meet his maker back at that big Thompson place, so cocksure and not listening to a damn word they said. The helplessness they must have felt then courses through him now and, although they are both long dead and gone, their sudden closeness catches him hard like a shiver.

Rabbit running over your grave, Mena says, rubbing his shoulder.

Wash shifts his weight, shaking his head at how her knowing keeps unfolding long after the point when he can look her in the eyes and tell her yes, he does see and yes, he does know. And she feels this turning in him as he comes to understand all she'd worked so hard to give him. He likes knowing she feels all this now, right along with him, just like she did last night in the barn when he decided not to kill Richardson and to live instead, and she is pleased.

As he turns for home, he notices two deer cresting a distant ridge and wonders how any of those runaways ever make it to the county line with the leaves down. He tries to imagine leaving but wonders whether he will still be able to feel Mena so close if he goes. He knows she's inside him and with him always, but staying here in this same landscape where they had lived together makes her much easier to hold on to. Each time he passes under the huge elms arching together over the road, he hears her saying how there's nowhere for your eye to travel round here. Each time he steps over the pale tangled roots of that biggest beech, he sees her trailing her palm across its smoothness.

Soon other pictures flood his mind. Pallas's slender shoulders disappearing down the path ahead of him into the heart of the swamp. The pale bone colored turtle shell she found for him to hide in the leaves covering Mena's grave. All these children, growing up looking just like him whether they like it or not. Wash knows he could carry these pictures with him in his mind wherever he goes, like Mena had to, but he wants to be able to lay his hands on all of it for as long as he can, come what may.

That same afternoon, Richardson watches Wash coming back. He's standing beside Lucius's grave. A mound of impossibly fresh soft dirt spills under the skirt of the hemlock that hides Richardson from Wash's view.

His body feels as if it's hardening and there are sharp pains whenever he moves. All the forward momentum that had once seemed effortless has disappeared. It feels as if the strong supple body he always thought of as his has run away and left his spirit trapped in this box that cannot and will not do what he asks of it. This spreading stiffness must be what ice feels like when it is forming in water and it enrages him.

Liquor loosens him and lets his mind wander. With enough of it, he finds that slice of time when he can float back to how things used to feel. Regain the sense he'd once had as a young man of being on the brink, full of certainty that the understanding he's been chasing for so long will soon be within his grasp. Just a little more, always just a little farther, and then he'll be able to see everything clearly.

But that same mist he remembers stepping through earlier in his life, hunting clarity, all it does is continue. He is no closer now than when he started. There seems to be no end to it and that can't be right. All the elements that should hold worlds within them, his plans, his city, his sons, his books, his own heart, all of which had always seemed so deep and endless, have become shallow bowls. He is not sure how this has happened and there is no one to ask. No words either.

He can see Gamma and all her foals through the years. The horses they became. He can see his family spread out everywhere and growing. His empire taking shape, his status accumulating. His second son planning to pick up where he left off, expanding his reach. Richardson can throw his mind like a net across everything he had intended but when he draws that net in, it is empty. There is nothing in his hand.

Richardson

I remember thinking my own life was the only one I had. Once it had ended, it would be over. I was convinced we were as clamped inside time as a stone set in a ring. It took being broken open to lift me to some higher ground.

My raising had rendered me unable to see that my story might be a live thing. A creature with intentions of its own. Thompson had tried to warn me, and more than once, but I couldn't hear him. Whenever he tried to suggest that my story could be using me as much as I was using it, I brushed him off. Told him that sounded like mojo to me.

Accomplishments were what mattered. Failures were gaps to paper over. Being good was being right. Being wrong was due to some secret hidden brokenness. Evidence to be buried. And suffering was to be avoided at all costs.

Each era is knit together by its own logic and we certainly had ours. Most forgeries are discovered only by succeeding generations. The slight gaps and giveaways don't show up until later because all those living inside the same time as the forger share the same eye and can be more easily fooled.

What interested me was when someone cropped up in his own time with a differing eye. Like my William. And Lucius. They were proof that some few of us can see outside of the logic we are given.

But I knew that seeing alone can't build enough of a bridge to carry you across. Usually all that seeing does is break you instead so I feared for my boys and rightly so. I may have even urged them to blind themselves a bit, so as to make their journey through a world not of their making slightly smoother.

I had decided early on that all the paths across time and between eras were gone. No one in any time to come would ever be able to see us clearly, so why even hope? What surprised me most was how powerfully I wanted things to be otherwise.

As I aged, I was haunted by dreams of standing deep in tall grass, down close by the edge of a broad shiny river. Even as I remained convinced I would be unable to cross, I remember feeling that strong swift wetness surging up over my shoulders. Pouring around my mouth. Sometimes my whole face. I kept stepping out into that current over and over, even as I was sure I would drown, so I must have known something about the landscape of eternity after all.

Wash

Just cause it's over, don't never mean it's finished.

And no matter how different he was taught, Richardson's stories stick just as close to him as mine to me. No matter how hard he worked to bury the ones he didn't want, just like his daddy told him to, they keep pushing up through the dirt like hardy weeds. His dead brother lying scalped, right in the middle of the trail. Those hogs rooting at the men he left behind. Even old Hargrove, still stomping on Moses. But Richardson never did learn to tell his stories to himself, so he left this barn empty handed every time.

What I see now is, our pictures hover close, no matter whether we hold them tight or push em away. Took me all the way till now to see just how far you can fall inside your story and how fast. And every time you try to tell it, that story starts moving, making you find your way through it all over again.

One thing I do know, whichever path you decide to take through that story, it's up to you to steer your mind one way or let it go another. Every minute of every day. All the way from then to now and beyond.

I remember my mamma telling me to watch out for the pull of that first path. She said once that very first creature makes its way through the tall grass, the rest of us tend to fall right into that same trail, whether it's the way we meant to go or not. Force of habit cuts a groove and that groove has a pull to it. And every single time I felt myself dragged towards one white man then the next, I saw the truth in what she said. Long enough of that and you start to learn.

But I fought my knowing just as hard as Richardson here. Even when I knew better, I fought it just as hard as I fought everything else. Lucky for me, my stories wore me down till I had to take the truth in my teeth and bite it. Chew it up and swallow it down.

Come to find out, we stay swimming through time whether we like it or not. Everything is now. Already and always.

All those stories you don't find some way to tell will wrap round your legs, just as sure and sharp as saw grass. You'll walk through this life and the next, bumping into your memories just as real as Emmaline's hams dangling in the dark of Richardson's smokehouse, coated gritty gray with salt and gone dusty with bluegreen mold.

Knock into one of those and you're wearing it, no matter how hard you try to say otherwise.

Pallas

When I watch Wash falling back into the grip of his story, him and Richardson both, I can hear Phoebe telling me, remembering is more than just falling right back in there. Remembering is more than that. She told me if you don't watch out, those stories of yours will come right up in your yard and worse. Dropping crumbs on your floor and won't go nowhere.

"Those stories piled up on your doorstep, they need to learn to let you be. They don't own you. Let's see can you travel lighter. Make you a box and lay those stories in there, then close it up good. That way, they'll be there when you need em and they won't have to hound you every minute of every day."

And I can remember sitting there, staring over Phoebe's shoulder, trying to hear her, trying to picture what it would feel like to be that free, and I felt myself floating right up off the ground.

But not everybody hears Phoebe inside, and you can see their story twining up around them. They stand there, trying to grow tall like a tree, but there's poison ivy vines climbing hairy and thick, wrapping around that trunk to choke it, no matter how strong. Makes you wonder who'll win out.

But Phoebe kept after me. Saying those damn stories so greedy and shortsighted. You can't give em everything they want, they'll swallow you whole. Then where will they be, with you gone?

See those stories for clear, was what she told me. Some are children and don't want to grow up so you got to do the tending.

Then she asks me, how come you think it is I'm still here, standing in front of you, babygirl? How do you think that is? And she's hugging me to her, and I'm hearing her telling me yes ma'am, we all got a right to the tree of life, and I'm feeling my knowing start to come alive and move.

When I watch these two men get caught up all over again in everything that has happened, I try to remember that feeling of my knowing unfolding inside me, wet as new wings. But I keep my mouth shut because if there is one thing I know by now, it's that some things you need to come to on your own.

Part Seven

Early summer, 1824

S ummer comes early after a wet spring. Richardson is up late again and restless. He wanders outside into that small pocket of quiet after the cicadas have stopped and before the birds start. The heavy dew soaks his boots after a few steps.

Between the house and the barn, there is a dip where the ground sinks and gets marshy, by the pond where cattails and cane grow thick and tall in the low ground. Richardson had made sure to swing his road out wide behind the house before cutting across to the barns to stay clear of this dip that sprawls here. But tonight he has had too much to drink and thinks he should be able to go straight at a thing, damn the consequences.

Wash wakes to Richardson's thrashing and muttered curses. When he steps across the loft to peer down through a high knot-hole, the moon is still bright enough for him to see the trail Richardson has blazed. The tops of the cane rustle and cussing drifts out like smoke.

Wash shakes his head, almost smiling. Notices he's not even mad. That's when he realizes he's become a new man. He climbs down the ladders and stairs, slips through the small side door, then walks across the dewy grass to the closest edge of the thick patch of cane. Waits for a break in the thrashing, then coughs once into the silence. Claps his hands softly a couple of times.

After Wash gets Richardson pointed in the right direction, the cane give way and he breaks through in a couple of steps. He's a mess. Neither man speaks. Richardson gestures loosely back at the thicket as if trying to explain. Although Wash keeps his face smooth and blank as a stone, he nods then turns and Richardson follows him back to the barn. The horses rustle and blow but don't call out.

Once through the small side door, the two men walk together down the aisle to the foot of the first set of stairs. They climb side by side, in step with one another. Richardson pauses to check Gamma's last foal before settling himself on the fourth step, just high enough to see over the side of the stall.

Wash leans against the far wall of the aisle, expecting Richardson to start in on the foal. Its dam, its sire and what he had wanted from this particular combination. But Richardson stays quiet. They sit there for what feels like an hour, watching the new bay foal nurse. He shoulders in next to the old gray mare's flank, snaking his head under her stifle, butting her in his earnestness then settling in for long sure sucks, his short tail twitching with pleasure.

Richardson sits bolt upright but when Wash sneaks a look at him, he sees his eyes have dropped to half closed and sometimes farther. Seems kind of crazy to come all the way down here just to get some sleep but Wash finds himself grateful for the quiet. Once Richardson slumps against the wall with his mouth dropped open and snoring a little, Wash makes his way back up to his blankets and falls straight to sleep.

Both men hear the morning bell cutting through the misty predawn. Richardson wraps his dream around the sound of the bell ringing until it eventually tears his sleep from him. He jerks awake there on the fourth step, his mouth dry as dirt and sour, his clothes sodden and striped by the cane, sharp tips of grass caught in the cloth. The foal sleeps in the straw, his nose tucked behind his folded front feet, while Gamma stands over him, idly sniffing, with a piece of straw hanging from her forelock.

Parts of the night come back to Richardson. Wrestling to walk with the damp cane slapping him in the face, cutting him. Why hadn't he come by the road? What had he wanted? What had he said and what had Wash said in return? His mind hunts for answers but keeps coming up empty. He thinks about getting back to the house and changed before Emmaline is up and knows it will not happen. The new day settles down on him like a lid on a pot as he pulls himself to standing.

It is on one of these trips to the barn when Richardson takes the book to Wash. He just wants to show it to him. Thinks Wash should know. Thinks Wash would want to know. Richardson even thinks Wash will be grateful for his having kept such careful track.

Somehow, he pictures them sitting there, side by side, turning the broad pages together. He's already told Wash about it, more than once, but he doesn't remember having done so. Liquor makes everything seem possible but then sweeps it all clean, like a broom drawn over the dust of a yard. No more tracks. No more record of anything. Just an uneasy feeling.

Richardson sits heavily on the second step, sets his bottle down, then pulls the book carefully from the canvas bag slung over his shoulder. He lays it across his lap, smoothing its broad brick red surface with his hands as if to clean the dust and chaff off of it.

He sits there looking from the book in his lap to Wash standing in front of him at the foot of the stairs and then back at his hands moving slower and slower. He waits for Wash to come sit next to him but Wash stands there, saying nothing. The worn leather feels so soft under Richardson's hands. He keeps on smoothing it, over and over, until he has lost track of what he intended and forgets Wash is even there. Before too long, Richardson is asleep. Just like last time. Right there where he sits leaning against the wall.

Wash stands so still for so long the first birds are beginning to sing before he bends to take hold of the front corners of the book and draw it carefully toward him, pulling it slowly from under Richardson's hands which are spread upon it. Richardson does not even stir.

Wash stands there another good while after that. Holding the book close against his chest with both arms crossed over it and his fingers wrapped around its edges. Eventually, he climbs carefully past Richardson and into his loft. He curls around his book and sleeps. He never even opens it. By the time he wakes, the sun flashes bright as the horses pour in from the pasture for breakfast and Richardson is long gone.

Pallas warns Wash to be careful with that book, the worst would be for somebody to catch him with it, but he tells her not to worry. He'll bury it deep in his sack, under plenty of bloody skins from his traps, until he can hide it good. As for Richardson, he doesn't remember taking the book to Wash. He does not even realize it's missing until he goes to make his next entry a few weeks later. By this time, it's tucked deep inside a silvery gray hollowed stump in the middle of the swamp where Wash and Pallas spend much of their time looking at it together.

Wash sits on one stepped ledge of the creek bank with his feet dangling in the water. Pallas sits close behind him on the next higher ledge, leaning her front against his back, with her legs wrapped around his hips and her ankles crossed in his lap. She rests her chin on his shoulder, watching him trace with his finger all the names and all the lines connecting them. Page after page after page.

Wash had not realized it had been so many. Whenever his finger slows to a pause under one of the names, Pallas says the name aloud. Wash feels the vibration pass from the front of her chest into his back. Right between his shoulder blades. The shape of the sound of each name enters him at the back of his heart.

Each name, poised at the tip of his forefinger, conjures up a world. When Pallas says Vesta, Wash sees her. That gawky gangly girl at Miller's place who tried to stay dirty and skinny and out of the way but failed. Wash sits there by the creek on this warming up Sunday, feeling Pallas's legs wrapped snug around him, as he watches Vesta grow up.

She stands taller and more serious each time she flashes into his mind's eye. As the years pass, their three boys stairstep their way up her lean sides, staring hard at him from under his own wide brows before turning their broadening shoulders away, kicking at sticks as they head for the fields. That husband she finally took hovers pale as a sycamore in the shadowy woods surrounding Miller's quarters, watching Wash go.

Wash traces the lines connecting Vesta's name to those of each of their boys, pausing under each one long enough for Pallas to say the name. Edward, Sunday and then Wash. Each name followed by a series of numbers. Their dates of birth.

He shakes his head. All that life shrunk down into these marks on a page. His life. Their lives. He works to breathe, trying to expand his chest against this steady weight of written words wanting to press him into a smaller space than he can fit. Trying to shrink him. Him and his. All of them.

Words are not enough. There is not room in any one name for all the life it holds. Makes him glad he never learned to read.

Never learned to squeeze his world down into these spidery little shapes that can't hold nothing.

He does not realize he has spoken this last thought aloud until he feels Pallas's hand close around the talisman he has finally allowed himself to remake. Tucked so deep in the pocket of his coveralls that the small lump of it rides halfway down the outside of his thigh. Pallas's fingertips are light and warm around its edges as she presses its small dense weight against his leg.

"That's all right, you don't need his book. You made yours already."

He keeps this last talisman buried out here in this silvery stump where it is safe from Quinn and everybody else, whether white or black. Feels good to put it in his pocket, even if just for this short time they get to spend out here.

Wash can feel it resting in his palm always, whether it's nestled deep inside denim and cotton or sitting in the dark heart of that pale stump. He uses his mind's eye to look at everything he had collected and laid inside this small circle of leather, each item standing for whole worlds without shrinking any of them.

The last of the dirt from old man Thompson's island, reminding him that life had once been otherwise and so could be again. A thin scrap of pale green cotton covered with his mother's careful looping stitch, reminding him to keep his mind in mind. He can see her dark fingers against the pale cloth, each stitch echoing her spare words. You got to intend. By this time, Wash knew to add a few strands of gray from Gamma's tail to the glossy black strands taken from Bolivar's because he needs her steady endurance as much as he needs her shiny bay colt's alert lifting stride.

He feels gladness rise up in him. He has finally managed to find the willingness to return to everything Mena taught him.

How to choose what to use, how to shroud each element with prayers, how to breathe his spirit into them before wrapping the leather tight and stitching it closed with bright red string. How to lead this last talisman into understanding itself as a piece of him. How to soak it with spirits sprayed with his own breath from his own warm mouth, energizing it enough to watch over him. All that knowing lies tucked into this small dark bundle, pushed down deep inside his pocket then cupped in Pallas's palm pressing against his thigh to remind him. His own book.

He closes the pale pages of Richardson's book, leaving its dull brick red covers to sit heavy in Pallas's hands so he can stand and stretch. The wind passes through the trees as he unhooks his coveralls to let them drop then steps out of them and into the water. Pallas watches the water climb his legs and then his broad back. She knows how a long swim helps him calm down. Helps him put everything back where it belongs.

While he is gone, Pallas pores over each broad page full of women and children. Going in close for the details then trying to stand back to see the whole picture clear enough to hold it. Yes, yes, yes. Just like she had thought. Dempsey is Wash's. And Willis and Solomon. Charity's last two boys and Miranda's first three girls.

Each grouping stretches across the years as fragile and inevitable as a spiderweb. Pallas knows pieces of this story but the pages of this book fill in the rest. Looking stings some but it lets her be sure. Her chest fills with thankfulness that Miller had let her learn to read.

She is surprised to feel herself thankful, in some deeper harder way, even for that time she spent over on Drummond's place. If only because it had scooped her empty enough, left her lonely and hungry enough, to take hold of what Phoebe had to give. And Wash too. She knows it's not always that way. Too often, people stay too tied up to take what they are given.

And yes, the writing does shrink it all down, but how in the world could everything fit otherwise? As long as you keep your mind's eye good and strong, you can use the words to open a thing back out to how it really was. Just like tracks. A cluster of pads, tipped with claw points, can summon up the whole wolf.

Pallas works to open her mind wide enough to hold it all. Someone has to. She knows Wash won't carry it. He can't. He's had to turn his face away from so much of it. When his hand comes down, when his chest threatens to crack open, when his life gets too big to lift, he looks away. And Richardson won't carry it either. Pallas knows that he, like lots of white folks, writes things down so he can forget them. She knows it's up to her.

∞

Now it is full summer. Late afternoon. Pallas turns to lead Wash off the trail. After a while, the woods open out into the edges of the marsh where clumps of swamp grass stud the mud flats, growing thick like hair. As they move deeper into the marsh, the flats get wider and wider until they start to join together. By the time Wash and Pallas reach the first water, the mud makes a beach.

She pauses for Wash to read the swooping pattern of tracks crossing the mud from the water to the cover of the grass and back. A heron stalking the waterline, hunting frogs. A fox tipping along, stopping here to sniff at this empty crab shell or there at that old fish bone before continuing on. A turtle lumbering in the straightest line possible.

Pallas finds a shallow channel cutting through the flats and she leads them up its very middle, placing one bare foot right in front of the next so the slight but steady current will wash away their footprints. The shallow water laps soft on their bare feet and the mud feels smooth between their toes. They turn again, stepping out of the water onto a spreading island.

Before they leave the water's edge, she bends down, reaching under an overhanging clump of swamp grass to scoop a handful of soft gray mud. She turns to Wash, saying take off your shirt and nodding toward a branch to hang it on. He does what she tells him and faces her, lifting his arms a little.

Slowly and carefully, she smears a thin layer of mud down his sides. It's cool as she reaches around to coat his low back, through his armpits, and back down the insides of his arms. Then lightly up the outsides of his arms, around his neck and under his ears. She drops to a crouch to do his legs, saying these skeeters love them some ankles. Before she has finished the tops of his feet, Wash feels the mud beginning to tighten on his neck as it dries.

She straightens, motioning for him to put his hands out, palms up, so she can transfer the remaining mud onto them. She had already taken off her dress and rolled it tight in her pack. It is the pale glow of her loose underslip Wash has been following. After rinsing her hands, she unbuttons the front of her shift and steps out of it, reaching to hang it next to his shirt, then turns to face him, waiting.

He stands there looking at her for a long minute until she wraps her still muddy fingers lightly around his wrists, drawing both his hands, palms facing her, toward her body. He aims for her breasts but she steers his hands just above so they land higher on her chest.

"Let's see can we leave them clean. Just so long as you daub around my neck good, and my belly and my back. Skeeters love my low back."

Wash bends over her careful and slow. After a little while, she says come on you, twisting away from him to dip for one last handful to dab on the backs of her knees. She rinses her hands then slings the water off. After tucking his shirt into the waistband of his pants, she turns up a game trail toward the center of the island with the mud drying on her back and her shift hanging from her hand, swinging a little as she walks.

As they move deeper inland, the ground turns from clay and mud into sand. Thick trees around the waterline open into small glades and she leads him to her favorite one where a thin vein of creek water cuts toward the middle of the island and a cluster of young maples provides some cover. They squat side by side on the high bank, looking out across the slough. The bare trunk of a long dead tree arches smooth and pale out of the water and then back in. By the time they get to this spot of hers, the low light reflecting off the water throws bright patches against the underside of that curving trunk.

She takes his shirt from where it's tucked in his waistband and she spreads it on the ground. He takes his pants off and hands them to her. She lays them out below where she has put his shirt. He lies down inside the shape of him she has made. She sets down her pack, takes her dress out and spreads it on the ground next to where he lies. Then she hooks her shift on a branch, steps across her dress and lays herself on top of him.

Pallas

Sometimes I'm over him and other times he's over me, holding himself up over me so he can see into my face. He knows how I am about looking over somebody's shoulder. Somebody up on me and I'm just having to look over his shoulder until it's over with. He knows about that part because I told him and he's careful about it now.

He's over me, looking down at me, holding his eyes on my face and arcing towards me, and I'm rising to meet him, feeling my body finally knowing itself and its place, and I'm finally having the sense to just follow it, following it up and to him, and up and with him, and we are making our own net and I can feel myself coming together again, all my parts coming back together and then falling open and apart, back into pieces, but it's all right this time. This time it's happening inside this place we made between us and there's a net. A net woven from our looking and strewn all through with our seeing and our stories and he is looking at me and seeing me and holding me with his eyes.

And yes, the other stays always there, like a shadow and tugging at me, but more and more, I can hear something saying, this is not that. I hear my body saying to myself, this is not that, and his face is rising back up through all those other faces and his hands are not those other hands, and this is giving not taking, and I am staying and staying and staying until I fall open and pieces of me drift down, falling across me and him and the ground as soft and light as petals.

A long while later, once they are separate again, lying side by side on their backs, each inside the shape of their own clothes, they look up through the canopy of bright green. The thin layer of mud on their bodies has caked and flaked and mostly been rubbed off. The light bouncing off the water has moved from the smooth underbelly of that curving trunk to dance against these young maple leaves arching overhead, making their new green flutter into brightness and then back.

Wash falls right to sleep but Pallas sits up to look out over the water, hearing Phoebe telling her if you can find some quiet sitting, looking close at something God has made, seems like life can't get on you so hard. Some of the women talk about praying and Pallas isn't so sure about that. But a little while of sitting still and looking close, lost to time passing, carries her back to the sweetness of being small.

She casts her eye across the pale tan floor of the creekbed. Starts to see how it's covered by an endless web of shadows cast by the light falling through the trees, all twined one into the next by overlapping branches, some arched like an eyebrow and some crooked like a finger, but all of them coming together to make this bigger pattern. A web as full and complete as any creature.

She studies it and thinks, here it is. This is how we all connect. All kinds of different people who don't have one word to say to each other, but we're all lying tangled together on the muddy floor of this life. Making new shapes that don't look like any of us on our own. It's the light that lays us down together like this.

She lies back and watches the constant fluttering play of brightness on the leaves overhead. The water stays always moving like breathing, lapping against edges as countless creatures slip in and out of it. Fish surface then disappear. The tweedy thrum of crickets swells and fades. Pallas thinks to herself, well, they got their church with their light falling red and purple and blue through their Jesus in the stained glass, but this is chapel enough for me.

The raucous cry of a heron cuts through the steady hum and wakes Wash. They sit up to watch the bird take off from another dead tree. He moves so slowly at first it seems he might fall right out of the sky. By the time he crosses overhead, he has gained some height but they can still hear the slow screak of air moving against his wings. They step down into the water, scrubbing the last of the dried mud off each other.

"We best go. Moon's coming up full tonight."

Once they are dressed, she leads the way out of the swamp to the road, asking him over her shoulder does he think he can find that place again and he nods even though she isn't looking back to see him. They part ways before the end of the path but only after stopping to listen good. They each slip out onto the road, heading in opposite directions, and they both make it to wherever it is that they're supposed to be well before dawn. Plenty of time to slip onto a pallet and wake up like they spent the night there.

Pallas

All at once, it came to me. Sitting there next to Wash, looking close till I saw that great big web laying across the creekbed leading out to the slough, that's when I knew. This right here is how they'll see us later.

All those people who'll come along later, trying to see us, trying to make some sense of our lives. First, they'll only see the bigger pattern laying on the bottom, the one made by our shadows knocked down on top of each other, just from the way the light falls across us, with most our details gone. We'll be all blurry and twined together in that net, laying under the water like ghosts.

I just hope some few folks will have sense enough to turn their heads to look around and see. There are all different kinds of trees, some closer and some farther away, each one standing in its own patch of ground with its own stance, all coming together to make this one web of shadows. And yes, it does make a picture but it's only one out of all of em. There's always more. You can be looking at the exact same thing and get different pictures just from changing the way you look.

But what I didn't know yet was, we'd still be here this whole time, watching you look. Seeing if you see. That's what death does, it lifts you up. You can see everything from here, much more than you ever saw from inside your own life, but you can't get your hands on none of it. And sometimes, you just want back inside something you can touch.

Soon as you get gone, you start wanting to come back. Both at the same time. And it stays like that all the way through. Turns out the veil between the worlds is real real thin and we tend to pass back and forth for a long time before we get anywhere close to done.

∞

They have high water late that summer as if to make up for last year's drought. That's how Simpson's new man Booker comes canoeing up the branch hunting turtles and sees Wash sitting on his stump, holding the book open on his lap. Sees him well before Wash knows he is there.

Before Booker even has the chance to holler at him, Wash is up and walking into the deep shade. He knows it will take Booker longer to paddle back to Simpson's place than for him to reach his loft. As he stuffs the book inside his pack, he tips his head to Mena, asking her to clear his path, and then flattens his face just like Rufus taught him to, and sure enough, those few folks he does pass on the way home take one look and step aside. Wash hides the book behind the wall under the far eaves of his high loft before he can breathe easy.

Caught him redhanded is what Booker keeps saying over and over to Simpson, determined to get his reward, whether it be a dollar, a bottle or a day off. Simpson rides up to Richardson's door that next morning, demanding Wash be whipped for reading. Richardson keeps insisting Wash can't read but Simpson won't let that fact matter.

"My man Booker swears he saw Wash holding a book out there in the marsh, a big fine book, holding it wide open in the broad daylight. That is good for three stripes or else a fine and you know it. Somebody's got to do something. You said it yourself."

Richardson assures Simpson he'll take care of it just to get the man off his doorstep. As he turns, shutting the door behind him and climbing the stairs, it comes together in his mind. Of course. That's where the book has been. With Wash.

Even as relief pours through him, he feels that familiar panic pressing at the very top of his chest near his throat, a panic that comes over him whenever the extent of his drinking is made clear to him by some slip, some mistake, some lost time. A shudder runs through him and he actually has to gasp to get some air as his hand tightens on the banister. At least he knows where the book is now.

Rumor swirls so fast that Wash hears about his whipping before Richardson has even decided what to do and certainly before he says anything to Wash or even to Quinn. But tonight is the second of the two big celebrations Richardson holds for his people each year. The whipping will have to wait.

Flames jump golden into the falling dusk. Emmaline's two oldest grandsons turn a pig roasting in a deep pit at the edge of the side yard between the house and the quarters. As the fat starts to crisp, every mouth waters. Small groups wind their way over to this feast, singing as they come. Their burning pine knots glow hot yellow against an indigo sky.

Richardson stays away for most of the evening. He knows how his presence alters everything. He doesn't want to watch the show his people inevitably put on for him nor does he want to watch them drink till they start to cut the buck. He'll only have to crack down. He has decided the less he sees the better. Cassius has assured his father he can manage so Richardson has decided to try and let him. For tonight, at least.

Wash stays away too. Waits until the tail end of the evening. By this time, most folks are so drunk on the liquor and the singing and the licking orange flames they don't take much notice. They let him step into the circle so long as he stays on the edge.

Richardson eventually drifts across the lawn toward this circle long after the rest of his family has headed to bed. All that is left is more singing. Standing around in the dark, passing the bottle, letting the harmony reverberate through them.

Richardson pauses near Wash but still half a step back. The pale of his face shows in the firelight only when a log pops and shifts. Even as he wonders whether Wash knows he's close, Wash catches his scent. That particular mixture of hard soap blurred by bourbon. Wash doesn't turn to look at Richardson. He knows he won't dare start with the whipping business. Not here, not tonight. But still.

When the bottle makes its way around to Wash, he takes a long swallow then holds its round golden smoothness out toward Richardson at an angle where the rest won't see. Nobody notices Richardson drinking after Wash before handing the bottle back.

They start in on the psalm about the rivers of Babylon. Richardson's favorite. They go round and round with the psalm until

Richardson can feel the water pouring over him too. He feels his heart drop open during one particular harmony and even more so at the long moment of perfect silence that follows it. He turns to leave. No topping that.

As he walks through the dark with the psalm ringing in his chest, he remembers Plutarch's warning:

> . . . *how dangerous a thing it is to incur the hostility of a city that is mistress of eloquence and song.*

He sees Cassius brandishing that chalky twisted stick. The white powder fallen dusty across his floorboards. Virgil and Albert's mojo, buried there from the beginning. Then he hears Quinn saying over and over, I told you but you couldn't hear me.

Another psalm circles the fire, passed from one throat to the next just as surely as that bottle but with endless variations and harmonies. A city that is mistress of eloquence and song. Whatever else they may be, he thinks to himself, his negroes are certainly that.

Unable to bear going upstairs to bed, Richardson sits on his dark porch listening to song after song. When the level in his bottle has sunk considerably and the last of the singers has drifted off to bed, Richardson remembers that Wash's book is down there in the barn. He must go find it.

Wash has been into his own bottle too, so this is the one time Richardson has ever been able to sneak up on him. Richardson surprises even himself with his sudden strength and sureness as he climbs carefully, very carefully, all the way up to where Wash sits in the window of the highest hayloft, holding the book open on his lap, running his fingers across all the names. There's plenty of moonlight but Wash sits next to a candle in a tin can. He hears Pallas telling him be careful with this book, keep it hidden good, but he figures everybody is too drunk to take much notice tonight.

Richardson moves so quietly Wash has not yet noticed him. He stands next to the top of the ladder, not thirty feet away, watching Wash turn the broad creaking pages to touch the names. He feels relief running through him. He even has time to wonder whether Wash can in fact read and he just never knew it.

Feeling somebody staring at the back of his head, Wash turns with a start and scrambles to his feet. He tips so violently in the big open window Richardson thinks for a moment he will fall out but Wash catches his balance and straightens up, holding the book by one corner so it falls open as it dangles from his hand.

Richardson sees where blood from trapped skins has darkened in splotches on its pages and tells himself, yes, he knew it. Of course, the book would be here. With Wash. Before he has finished thinking this thought, Wash steps closer to his candle, bending just enough to touch the corner of one splayed open page to the tip of his flame.

Richardson stands there stunned. Verses from the hymn still ring in his brain as he watches the flames jump from the corner of the first page to the next and the next until the book hanging open from Wash's hand blossoms fully into orange.

Richardson remembers having seen a pile of old horse blankets just to the side of the last ladder he climbed. They are right here by him. All he has to do is reach over, pick one up, then hold it outspread so he can tackle Wash and the fire he has started. Stop him, smother it.

But the dark mouth of the big loft window yawns behind Wash and the book and the flames. Tackling him means they would both fall and Wash knows it so he just stands there, watching Richardson watching him. No longer needing to say this is my story. My book. Mine.

He lets the burning book fall toward the flattened straw. Richardson stands unable to move, mesmerized by seeing the impossible happen. By the time he manages to take even one step, it's too late. The flames are already climbing the nearest walls, speeding along the broad tracks of dustladen spiderwebs straight on up to the roof.

All Richardson does after seeing Wash set his barn on fire is turn to climb carefully back down the ladders and stairs then walk down the aisle, unlatching stall doors to let his horses out. Wash follows him and they stand together, watching the horses scatter across the barnyard and through the quarters as the roar of the fire builds overhead.

Several horses refuse to leave their stalls. The hay in the loft is blazing above them and they are disoriented. Gamma will not come, even after Wash wraps his arms around her foal's chest and haunches and carries him outside. With no one to hold him, the terrified foal runs back inside the stall where his mother screams and spins in circles, tossing her head.

Wash gets a rope around Gamma's neck and pulls on her while Richardson beats her across the rump with a whip he grabs off the wall. Wash pulls so hard that her head and neck stretch completely flat and Richardson's blows rain down until he has raised welts across the gray of her crouched rump but she won't go.

Wash gestures Richardson to come to him then spins him around to grab his shirt collar at the back of his neck, yanking the shirt from his shoulders so he can wrap it around Gamma's head to blind her. She lunges forward so hard her shoulder cracks the post by the door of her stall but she is moving and, between the two of them, they beat her on out of the barn with her baby skittering behind them.

The big barn burns all night but it takes less than five minutes for the whole place to erupt like an anthill kicked into swarming. People burst from every door, pulling on clothes and sobering up fast because fire can lead to debt which can lead to auction just that fast.

The barn burns almost backward, starting at the top and working its way down, so there's time to save all the horses, most of the tack and even the wagon. Nobody knows Richardson had been in there with Wash before it started. They just figure he was quick on the draw like always. Right in the thick of things, telling everybody what to do, the only one besides Wash still wearing pants from last night.

But the sight of his bare torso is shocking. Glowing a pale bluish white underneath the dark smudges of ash. Bony ribs and collarbones mapped by dark veins. Nobody can remember seeing him under his clothes before but they will certainly never forget it. Gamma trots back and forth in the near paddock, tossing her head trying to rid herself of Richardson's torn white shirt still tied around her brow like a crown, calling and calling as if she has no idea her foal runs right behind her, wheeling with each turn.

After that first rush to save what they can, everybody stands bunched together, hypnotized by the red hot mouth of the barn. Richardson steps out of the light and kneels by a bucket to wash the embers from his hair. The heat holds the rest of them back in a loose semicircle and their nightclothes glow orange until Ben picks up bossing where Richardson left off, putting half on bucket brigade and the other half to digging.

All they can do is wet the grass and dig a trench between the barn and the quarters so the fire won't spread but this work takes until almost dawn. The birds have already started before the last of the stragglers trail back to the quarters carrying a whole new story.

Richardson stands there alone watching the day come. The smoke rises into the low pink light like breath in the cold. The stone walls of the foundation trace a pale footprint through the ash underneath the charred overhang of the big elm. He finds himself almost dizzy, it is so disorienting to be able to see straight through where the barn had stood to his fields falling away beyond.

That beautiful barn, built by his first two negroes. Virgil and Albert had hewed those broad beams from the first enormous water oaks Richardson had worked alongside them to fell. He had designed it but they had built it. There was not one nail in the whole thing. Pegs held together all four stories of the big dark evercool barn which had become his refuge.

God knows what kind of mojo those two had woven into this one place where he had finally managed to tell his story to Wash. Was that why? Were Virgil and Albert pulling his stories up out of him from where they lay buried under the ground? But now all those stories and the truth he had finally started to forge from them, all of it is gone without this container to hold it. Just ashes and smoke rising. The ground underneath everything that happened in that barn lies steaming as if breathing. Newly freed. Watching him. Asking him, where will you put everything now?

Richardson did not want to build on that same spot but Cassius insisted and he let himself be overruled. Time to let his second son take the reins, for better or worse.

A brand new barn soon covers the pale footprint the old one left but Richardson doesn't like it much. Too new, too square, too plumb. Made with new wood so orange it looks cut and bleeding against the bright green grass. He'll be dead and under the ground before that wood starts to silver but there's nothing to be done about it.

Even as he wonders whether Wash will set up camp in this new loft or take up somewhere else, he understands he'll never know for sure because his trips to the barn are over.

Wash

I don't remember knowing what I wanted exactly. All I knew was, I didn't want him having me in his hand like that. Written down in that damn book where he could get at me. Not him and not nobody else either. Pallas had us all laid out clear in her mind's eye and everybody knew to go to her. That way, she can decide who to tell and when.

I didn't set out to burn that book. When my hand held it to the candle, it was something inside me, running deeper than my mind. I remember feeling all peaceful and settled inside, even with flames roaring and horses thundering round calling.

All I did was go to that pile of tack and grab some lead ropes. Caught the horses one by one and led em to the lower pasture. Each time I walked away from that barn, I felt better. Once I got all the horses down there with the gate good and latched, I laid on the ground watching the clouds glow.

Wasn't too long after the fire when I got word of Rufus. Took him ten years to catch hold of himself but when he did, he got those Thompson boys good. What I heard was, he masterminded a rebellion. Made skeleton keys for every single shackle he forged. Got nineteen people good and gone, then he trailed behind to give em enough cover to make it through the swamp.

He headed West instead of North, knowing he'd made those boys mad enough to lose sight of the big picture, and sure enough, they followed him instead of the rest. Just like he planned. He drew those boys right to killing him, just like I'd tried to do, except he didn't draw back. He ran right for it and that's what made sure the others got all the way away.

I was real glad to hear that story. It was Diamond who told me. Under our maple tree by the side of the road. When I saw him looking at me hard after he was done talking, that's when I realized I was fingering my brand. Rubbing that spot where the leg of my R kicks up and feeling Rufus real close.

It was pretty soon after that day when my time came for me. I guess living full on like I did wore me out. I'd learned not to let my anger light me up so bad, and Pallas stayed steady helping me smooth my edges. But still, my day came much sooner than I thought it might.

I was sitting under the willow like I always do, except on this day, I have Pallas with me. Leaning against the back side of Richardson's brand new barn. Soaking up some sun on a late winter day. Storing up. Waiting on whatever the hell might be next.

It came right on me out of the clear blue sky. Didn't have no time to fight it. Felt myself lift up out of myself, like I'd felt plenty of times before, but I could tell this time was something different. I could tell this time I wasn't coming back, so I turned my eyes to Pallas.

Pallas

We were sitting there together. Not saying much. I was waiting on my water to boil for some tending I was doing over there. His hand was resting warm and heavy on my thigh.

Then I felt him get real still. I turned to him and saw him looking at me. His grip tightened on my leg but his face stayed just as peaceful, drinking me like water. He had his head resting back against that barn but turned so he could see me.

I reached to lay my first two fingers in against his neck just under his jaw and I heard it all. The slow pounding speeding up and then stopping. Then more pounding and stopping. I knew from the starting and stopping that I was losing him and there wasn't nothing I could do, so I gave him what he wanted which was my eyes to look into.

They filled up and spilled over but I looked right at him and I nodded real slow, saying yes, he could go on and go if he needed to. I sat there with him, seeing him on his way and feeling myself tear in two with wanting to pull him back towards me and trying to let him go on ahead.

I held his eyes in mine until I knew he had stepped out of them and I watched this world close up behind him. Then I turned to look down this long road I'd have to travel without him, knowing I'd go on ahead.

After sitting there so still and quiet for I don't know how long, I lifted his hand from where it was resting on my leg and set it down on his. Then I stood and walked away. Wanted to hold on to my last picture of him looking into my face.

I went around the corner of the barn. Soon as I saw Ellen's two boys play fighting, I told em to fetch me those two sawhorses, put em in that empty stall at the far end of the barn and then lay that

old door across. Don't ask me why, just do it, and they did. They
helped me lay him out on that door, then I sent em on a faraway
errand so I could climb up there and lay right close against him
for that last little minute while he was still warm.

Seemed like a long time later when I headed up to the house
to let Richardson know but he was out seeing about something.
I was just as glad to let Emmaline tell him. I didn't want to have
to lead him by the hand through this too. Some things that old
man needs to learn to do for himself.

Then I went on back to sit with Wash so nobody could mess
with him once word started getting around. I already knew where
he wanted me to put him. He always told me he didn't want any
part of that cemetery Richardson kept for his people. Said don't
shoehorn him in between all these folks who stayed steady turning
their backs on him while he was alive.

What he told me was he wanted to end up right where he
started. Next to his mamma on that southwest facing slope where
the river bends. Right there where he was kneeling at her grave
when I rode up on him that day when I was hunting me some
goldenseal. That was where he wanted to be.

Said I would know just how to carry his last wish to Richardson. If anybody could persuade the old man, it was me. And if
the place fell on the far side of his line, and Wash figured it might
well, then just tell him to act like it didn't.

You take him there, Wash told me. He'll go. He's been wanting to
know where I buried my mamma all this time. You take him and show
him. He'll find a way. If you help him. So that's exactly what I did.

It was almost dark by the time Richardson stepped inside the stall
where I had Wash laid out. He didn't see me sitting against the

front wall. He didn't even step close. Just stood there drinking and watching all those stories he'd told Wash pouring away from him as fast as he could swallow.

I couldn't bear him looking at Wash like that for too long so I stood up. When he turned to face me, he was all closed up inside himself. Took his words a long time to reach me.

"What happened?"

All I did was lift one shoulder to say I don't know exactly. Then I touched my right forefinger to my heart. I stood there looking at him, knowing he wouldn't have nothing to say about it and he didn't. He moved right on.

"Did he say where he wants to be?"

"It'll take some doing."

"I figured as much. Where is it?"

When I told him about the place, I saw right away he knew the spot. I watched him realize it was across his line, then I saw him decide Miller never needed to know. I didn't have to say one word.

He brushed past me leaving the stall. Said he'd be back at full dark to help me take Wash out there. He'd ride Bolivar and use Omega to drag Wash behind him on some kind of sledge. Just like an Indian, he said.

But I'd need to ride astride to keep Omega steady. Once he had us situated, with the hole mostly dug, he'd leave me to it and then I'd ride Omega home when I was done. He talked about how Omega knew the way, like he forgot I did too.

Moon rose real late, like it knew we needed that time to slip past everybody. So many folks stayed crossways with Wash, we had to put him someplace where nobody else could ever find him. Nobody besides us.

Richardson

Even as I laid him down in the hole I'd dug, I had trouble believing Wash was gone. Losing my barn was one thing but losing Wash was another.

All I knew was, I couldn't even look at him. Pallas had wrapped him in red and I was in a mighty hurry to cover him up, but as soon as I took my shovel to start laying the dirt back in, Pallas stopped me. Told me go home. Said she'd handle the rest.

I snatched up my reins and left but the whole ride home, all I wanted was to turn around and go back. Wash was holding my whole life, even as he lay under the ground, and I never knew it until now.

I'd always thought he was just like my own story. Both of them put here to serve me. Do what I told them to do. But they never ever did. Neither one of them.

I was so determined to believe what I'd been taught, that I had dominion. I never suspected it's a dance. Of course Mena knew this part. And Emmaline. And Wash. They'd been taught too. But theirs was a very different story. And why in the world should they tell it to me? I wouldn't have been able to hear them either.

I hovered in the shady shallows of my story for years, insisting on my own version, thinking I could arm myself with words. But as I sat in my darkening barn, drinking and telling Wash everything I had intended for my life, I could not stop the flow of pictures rising up from underneath. I finally started telling him the truth but never when I was sober enough to remember it. I'd made Wash carry it all and now he was gone, dragging my story with him.

I never dreamed the truth was what I needed. That my failures and my mistakes might be the very gifts I had to give, whether my descendants ever choose to accept them or not. And I never dreamed I'd be caught here till my truth was told. That we'd all be caught here together until this story finds itself finished with us. All of us. As unbelievable as that may seem.

∞

It is full winter again and again until Richardson is finally old and in bed, fed up with the doctors and deeply irritated by his death taking so long. He opens his eyes to Pallas bending over him. He can't move much but he runs his eyes down her long thin neck to her bony collarbones. The dip between them where the skin thins enough for him see her pulse surging slow and steady underneath.

She looms between him and the bright windows then she sits by his bed, her face thrown into deep shadow. The darkness blurs her features so he can talk to her as if she is not there, just a silhouette. Nobody but a listener. He has been missing that since Wash passed.

Too much chittering goes on around here. Too much talking back. Having raised his children to have strong opinions has worn him out. He needs some peace and quiet so he can hear himself think.

Most times he lies there looking out the window. But sometimes he'll start in on some question he can't seem to find the answer for, hunting clarification even as he suspects there's none to be found. What Memphis should have done. What all he had intended. Wanting his position to be understood. By Pallas if no one else. But most of the time, he just watches his life drift through his mind, floating like skeins of thread in dye water, with no idea where to start untangling.

Richardson tells Pallas not to worry. He has made provisions. He's bought her from Miller and written her into his will. She cannot be sold off. He has made both Cassius and Quinn promise him. He only hopes they are good for their word. And he has put her in the cabin at the foot of his driveway for good. That way she'll be easy to get to for those who need tending.

The dispatch in his tone catches her breath in her throat but once she takes a minute to think about this new situation, she calms herself. You never know what will happen, might as well let yourself be glad when what comes along turns out to be something you can manage.

She settles back in her chair as he starts explaining why he is not freeing her, or any of his for that matter, on his deathbed. Not only does he not believe in it, he can't afford it. He doubts his boys would carry out his wishes anyway. He tells her that freeing negroes is more complicated than it seems. Even Washington had tried but he'd caused nothing but trouble.

Pallas can only shake her head each time she witnesses the true craziness of some white folks. With Richardson, if his mouth does not form the words and tell them to somebody, then the thought itself never crossed his mind. No wonder white folks think if something never gets told, then it didn't happen. No wonder they keep filling up this world with every single thing they ever thought about, just like God doesn't know it all already.

Still, sitting there listening is not too bad for her in some kind of way. Despite the fact there are plenty of other folks she could be helping, people who are still living instead of lying here trying to die, Pallas reminds herself that shepherding somebody out of this world, even this man, is doing something too. Besides, Richardson seems so lost he makes her feel found and she likes thinking about the past. She misses it and the people in it. As exasperating as he can be, this old man is one of the last ones around who remember most of what she remembers. He even knew Phoebe.

It makes her smile to think about Wash having to put up with him. And back when he was worse. Much worse. Lord have mercy. She can see Wash sitting there in that barn, leaning his back against the wall, twirling his piece of straw, sitting just as still as he was lying in his grave, with Richardson's words pouring over him, rising up around him till he has to swim through them, making him feel lucky that Mena taught him how. Richardson talked so much, Wash said seemed like he could float in it. Just like those waves.

Sometimes Richardson will get to talking about his lines. Horses. Hounds. Negroes. All the lines he has made. Their fineness. Their lasting quality.

Pallas listens closely to this part because she was only able to look at that book for a little while before Wash burnt it up. All of it gone before she'd had time to get everything nailed down good in her mind's eye. She is glad of the chance to sit there by Richardson's bed, dipping her washcloth and wringing it out to lay it on his forehead, listening to him shape his mouth around all those words, all those names of all those women she knew, all those names of all those babies she had pulled into this world, with all of it leading back to Wash, coming together in Wash, passing through Wash as through the eye of a needle and then opening back out again on the far side of him into a giant shimmering net, linking him to all those who had come before him and who would come after him. His mamma and his daddy and their mammas and their daddies and cousins and uncles and grands and great grands, with her being the only one living and breathing and walking in this particular world who knows about all of them for sure.

Just like Wash said, if you've got any kind of thin skin, you can feel all these spirits hovering all around you. Everybody who has been here and gone. But it is harder to get the details without somebody to tell you. And you need the details. Who's who. What they had looked like, how they had talked and walked and laughed.

With Wash's people, she'd never seen any of them with her own eyes except for Mena, and neither had Wash, but he laid them into her mind as clear as a picture, just like his mamma had laid them in his. That auntie of his daddy's with the big front teeth, a rawboned lanky woman with a kind of a donkey laugh, her head thrown back and her hand slapping down. Those pictures have been laid well enough in Pallas's mind till she can recognize people she's never even met and she has the sense to thank God for that.

Same with Richardson. She had sat there with him while his daddy died, and then his son too, and now she sits here next to him as he gets ready to go. She knows he does not want to go like his daddy did. Struggling and afraid. An orphan all over again. She can see it starting to dawn on him that he has already spent too much of his life that way and this should be different. He wants to go calm.

When the flu comes back, this time Richardson knows it's going to take him and he's glad. He lies there in his bed by the window, resting his eyes on Pallas and she lets him. Sitting there in the rocker right by his knee, looking out the same window but at a different angle. Their fields of vision overlap. Nothing left to say. Feels like days pass that way but it's really only two. So peaceful and quiet between the coughing.

Richardson has her call Emmaline's youngest grandson. Nelson is just a little older than Lucius was when he died and almost as good a draftsman as William had been at that age. Nelson brings a pad of paper because Richardson has had him draw designs out for him before. Says he has a good eye.

He tells the boy pine. A pine box is what he wants and this is how he wants it. Simple and plain. And the headstone plain too. No epitaph. Just the dates, under his name. Under the trees. Near his brother David and next to Lucius, leaving room for his wife and the rest of them.

Nelson draws it all out for him. The coffin, the headstone, even the trees. Richardson nods, pleased, and falls back asleep. He wakes to cough and then sleeps again. Pallas dozes in her chair and Nelson snores softly where he sits on an old trunk, leaning asleep against the wall.

In the bustle of activity surrounding Richardson's last bout of coughing early that next morning, there is confusion. Mary rushes in, finally able to take over from Pallas now that Richardson can no longer intervene. As she jerks on a choking Richardson, trying to lift him so he can breathe, she sends Nelson out of the room in a rush. The small notepad full of his drawings falls behind the trunk where he'd been sitting when he fell asleep the night before.

Pallas knows from the way Richardson pulls against Mary's arm and looks over toward her that he wants Pallas to make Mary lay him back down on the bed and let him go, like they did his father. But Mary won't have it. Pallas stands back by the wall holding his gaze until it's over because that is what she can do.

Death always comes as a surprise. So much happens so fast and yet each single day stretches endlessly. Cassius sits with his mother, writing out an inventory of the estate so debts can be paid, credits collected and taxes determined. Together they parcel out what goes to whom. Land and lots, furniture, books, animals, farm equipment, negroes. What and who will be given to which family member, who will be sold, and who will be hired out to provide income for the rest, especially Mary Patton. Then they have the big fancy funeral Richardson no longer wanted.

Cassius runs the place with Quinn at his right hand. After one mojo incident too many, they decide to dig up what they had always assumed was just trash piled up under those first cabins Richardson built. They send everybody to the fields for the day and wonder why they linger.

Before the sun has even started down from noon, Cassius and Quinn find stones, bones and shells. Even knives and one old gun. Everybody denies knowing anything, but here's the proof Quinn never could find for Richardson, lying right underfoot all this time, buried safe as a secret where he had never thought to look.

Cassius starts that same day, burning down the old to rebuild his way. One cabin at a time. Each raised off the ground on its own four blocks. He tells each family to sleep in the barn for the week, then keep that new cabin clean. Says if he can't see daylight under the stairs, he'll burn it down again, no matter who's inside.

He tells the swelling ranks of abolitionists to come and see for themselves. Conditions are much improved. After having seen what ambivalence had done to both his father and his brother William, Cassius will have none of it. The young slaveholders of his generation do not remember the window that opened during and after the Revolution. They know nothing about some Founding Fathers' ill fated attempts to stamp out the trade and they care even less. After faltering for years, slavery takes the bit in its teeth and runs.

It will be the buying and selling of negroes that finally energizes the town of Memphis. The growth in cotton production will drive the prices for negroes so high that Nathan Bedford Forrest will become a Memphis millionaire before he ever signs up to fight in the Civil War. While Richardson died thinking his dream of a city high on the bluffs of the broad Mississippi River was a dismal failure, William will live long enough to wish it had been.

∞

As the years pass, Pallas looks for Wash coming up in his children and she finds them around her wherever she goes. The ones who can listen, she tells them all about him. So some of those children grown into old people will have a dim remembrance of this pale thin woman laying her cool hands on them and telling them about their daddy.

"Thick and heavy as wood and burning just as clear as that fire right there."

The two boys sitting there in her cabin look at her and then at each other, still suspicious because they have different mammas. But something about the look coming across her face while she's telling them, like she's barely in the room, like she's still looking this man in the face she's telling them about, something about the way she's seeing him so clear convinces them she's telling the truth. And somehow they know to take that truth, awkward as it is, and tuck it away deep inside. And they know not to ask their mammas about it, or their daddies, whom they look nothing like.

She takes the hand of the taller quiet one named Horace, turning it over and then back again, gently splaying the fingers out then touching her palm to his palm.

"Yep, you got his hands with those long squared off fingers."

And the younger one named Daniel starts asking what did I get, what did I get? She takes his chin in her hand, turning his earnest little face to hers and looking into it hard, then smiling to say you got his eyes with those thick brows so broad across your forehead like wings, and those dark dark eyes that let you fall right inside. And those lashes curled back and tangled, she murmurs to herself as she turns away, like it hurts a little.

Some of his children choose not to believe her. They go running back to their mammas, one of whom comes storming into Pallas's yard, jerking at her skirt and twitching mad about how come Pallas don't know how to leave well enough alone. And Pallas looks right at her, saying now come on, Harriet, you know as well as I do, anything can happen on any day and we got a lot we need to put inside those little minds. No harm in starting early and you know it.

"You want to go on lying when they already know they ain't their daddy's sons, shooting up past their sisters and brothers and dark like that, you go ahead. Why the hell you think they came to me in the first place? It's their own sisters and brothers shutting em out, calling em names, and all the while wondering if you are a whore.

"No need to tell the whole story, but I sure as hell won't watch his children wander this earth without giving em nothing. Not even one thing to hold on to. I'm giving em whatever they want, just as soon as they start asking for it. And I'm going to keep on giving it, as long as they keep asking, and as long as there is breath in me. Now get out of my yard."

One day she comes upon young Earnest in Miller's barn, staring up at one old gelding hanging his long lean face over the stall door. She tells the boy all about how his daddy was good with horses, the ease he had with them, and the way they came to him and stood so close. She sees Earnest's face shine with the wonder of learning about his daddy as he scratches an itchy spot on the gelding's throat until his big bay head hangs almost down to the dirt. Earnest loves hearing this secret said out loud and Pallas loves watching him being his daddy without even trying.

They all carry some trace of Wash, no matter who they came from. Sometimes Mena, but mostly Wash. Some little hint in the shape of a face or a look in the eye. Maybe just the mannerisms. That dead on, straight ahead way he had. Wade right on through the water to get to the other side. No looking for a boat or some other way across because that's just a waste of time. Besides, he was always strong enough.

When Pallas tells her stories about Wash to his children, she gets to be with him herself. She describes how mean he acted when she first met him, how he liked to have bit her head off when she took him that first supper.

Then she tells them how sick he was and how she held the hand of this big strong mean man. Pulled him back from where he was staring straight into death's door and how he turned out to be a real sweet and tenderhearted man underneath it all. And how he had returned the favor by bringing her back into the world of the living.

They asked her were you sick too? And she said not exactly baby, not exactly, but I was a little lost and he came and found me.

It would be easier for her if Wash hadn't burnt the book but she understands why he did it. And maybe it's better this way.

Who knows? There's no telling. But at least she had seen it all written down. She had run her eyes and her hands over and over those names as she sat there snugged between Wash's legs wrapped around her, holding the book open in her lap and leaning her back up against his chest, his chin resting on her shoulder as he looked at it with her. She had felt him crying too, jerking with sobbing but quiet, and holding on to her as tight as if he were being pulled hard downstream.

They are lucky to have you, is what she kept saying to him.

"They are lucky. Just look at em, coming up so strong and beautiful. They got you and they got your mamma and your daddy and your careful uncle and your sweet granddaddy. And the scary one too.

"They got all y'all, and it was me who pulled em into this world. They'll be all right. They'll be more than all right. They will shine. They are coming up all over and they will shine. Don't you worry, I will tell them. The ones who can hear me, I'll tell them, and even if I can't get through, they'll find a way to know. You'll see, they will know."

It is winter again and the trees around Pallas's little house are bare. Leafy bunches of squirrels' nests catch her eye where they make knots high among the latticework of bare branches. Richardson has been dead ten years and Wash nearly twelve but Pallas somehow looks the same. She didn't get sold and she still lives in this cabin because Richardson wrote it in his will, just like he told her he would.

A flock of blackbirds arrives in a cloud like music then settles in the treetops, falling quiet and disappearing into the stillness of its roost, but only for a moment before some internal disagreement, or maybe a hawk, sends them on again. All those small single bickering birds pour from their separate roosts, woven by movement back into one living breathing thing.

In that moment of seeing them fall in and out of moving together, Pallas knows, as sure and clear as a footprint, how things are and have always been. She sees that all of them, her and Wash, his mamma and Rufus and Phoebe, and even all those white folks, good and bad, here and gone, all of them are and have always been part of this one living breathing thing, moving through a time and a space bigger than any of them ever knew.

And yes, there are moments when they fall out of moving together into the stillness of their separate roosts, moments when all you can hear is their aloneness and their apartness and their bickering, but at the same time as all of that, and just as true, is their capacity to pour out of their separateness back into this swooping graceful oneness where each of them knows somehow when to glide and when to bank.

Pallas has felt this knowing before and then lost it because it comes and goes. It never seems to stay. She has had glimmers before, sitting beside the water sometimes, but it has taken her until she is old and stiff and alone to see it clear.

As this clarity presses then burns across her forehead and at the base of her throat with what Phoebe used to call the annointing, she can see Binah placing Wash's outstretched palm just there at the base of her own throat until he feels the heat pulsing under his fingertips. Pallas touches the same spot, just below the small hollow Phoebe had filled with white clay.

Never mind that Pallas was not there on that day to see what Binah did with her own eyes because now she knows this feeling for herself. She can finish the story Wash started for her, just like Wash learned to finish the stories Mena started for him, saying to himself, oh, now I see, this is what she must have meant, all full of that feeling of the world falling back into place.

Pallas remembers how easily she used to move into this knowing, most often by herself as she walked through the woods, disappearing into the green walls of snaking leaves, but also sometimes with Wash, walking out into the soft dark water of their summer pond, feeling its rise on her skin.

She can feel both his stories and hers, everything they told one another, playing and pulling around her like the current in the river running below the bluff where her little cabin sits, even now. She sees the faces of so many of his children who came to her because she alone chose to stand inside her knowing and let it anchor her.

And she remembers falling out of it too. Days when the interlocking patterns connecting everything seem to have faded into gone, leaving this world drained empty of all the meaning it had once held.

What Pallas understands now, finally, is that this knowing leaves in order to grant you the chance to call it back. To take hold of it again. It falls away to give you the joy of its return. Sometimes this knowing is given but most times it is made.

The side of the porch presses hard and steady against her back as she sits watching. She feels her heart swell and contract right along with that flock breathing in the sky and she knows, just as sure as the shape of her own hands, we are all of us one thing. All here, all connected, all the time, regardless.

Acknowledgments

Special thanks to Corinna Barsan, Elisabeth Schmitz, Deb Seager, Morgan Entrekin, Zachary Pace and the whole Grove/Atlantic team, Marly Rusoff, Mihai Radulescu, Beverly Swerling, Stuart Horwitz, Karen McBryde, Rob Spillman, and Elise Cannon.

Thanks also to my hometown of Birmingham, Alabama, for being such a thorough teacher; to my parents for protecting my imagination by getting rid of the television and for making sure that I got outside of the South enough to see it clearly, even as they taught me to value my heritage; to Ida Mae Lawson and her descendants for helping me learn to hear more of the notes; to Tot Goodwin for sharing his graceful connection to the natural world; to my former students in both Birmingham and the West Bank for modeling bravery and integrity; to Lonnie Holley, Jimmie Lee Sudduth and all the visionary Alabama artists who inspire me; to Patricia, Jeannie, Maple, Helen, Karen, and Chris for guiding my understanding of the bigger picture; to Flight of the Mind, Hedgebrook, and Mesa Refuge for giving me space and time; to the Tennessee State Library and Archives, the Southern Collection at the Birmingham Public Library, and all the curators and archivists at historic sites throughout the South for the various ways they seek to address the thorny issue of interpreting our collective past.

This story has carried me down a long road and brought me a great deal of help along the way. I am so grateful to the many generous spirits who resonated with this story and helped carry it to this particular destination, to those who saved a place for me when this work took me away from them, and to those who taught me what I needed to know.

Finally, I want to thank all the ancestors who haunted me into unearthing these stories and weaving them together into one.

Wash

Margaret Wrinkle

ABOUT THIS GUIDE

We hope that these discussion questions will enhance your reading group's exploration of Magaret Wrinkle's *Wash*. They are meant to stimulate discussion, offer new viewpoints, and enrich your enjoyment of the book.

More reading group guides and additional information, including summaries, author tours, and author sites for other fine Atlantic Monthly Press titles, may be found on our Web site, www.groveatlantic.com.

QUESTIONS FOR DISCUSSION

1. Wrinkle has a hypnotic way of enfolding the reader into backstories as characters recall their histories. How does her use of multiple narrators and overlapping chronologies fit the concerns and themes of her novel? How do the present and the past relate to one another, both in each character's story and in the novel itself?

2. Nigerian poet and novelist Ben Okri's *The Famished Road* provides the epigraph for *Wash*, which closes with the startling statement about living as a spirit: "We feared the heartlessness of human beings, all of whom are born blind, few of whom learn to see." Consider what Okri might mean about learning to see, and how the characters in *Wash* both resist and embrace learning to see. What moments of both moral and interpersonal blindness stand out? What surprising insights, connections, and generosities sometimes occur? On the other hand, discuss how looking and seeing can be dangerous in a slave society.

3. Storytelling becomes an active art and mystery, within both the enslaved and slaveholding communities. Think about the characters' use of storytelling to fill young minds with the fundamental tools to find their way in life. Consider the differences between what Wash is taught by his mother and what Richardson is taught by his father. What kinds of legacies are passed down and how are they accepted or rejected?

4. How does Wash's childhood on the island provide a foundation for his sense of self and help prepare him for trials he will face later in life? What do Mena and Rufus teach Wash

about how to use his mind's eye? Discuss how the mind's eye relates to the development of Wash's inner place and helps him survive.

5. What do you glean from the novel about the function of altars, talismans, and rituals in the lives of the enslaved African characters? Consider what Mena means when she tells Wash, "Take your journeys in the spirit world first" (67). Why does Thompson call her teachings "mojo"?

6. How does the novel address the role of initiation in traditional African life, for both boys and girls? Mena knows that "death must draw close . . . but how close . . . and how do you meet it so it will pass on by?" (108). What is Rufus's relationship to this ritual, both before and after his enslavement? How do Wash's teenage trials serve as a kind of initiation? Consider whether any of the slaveholding characters face similar initiatory trials.

7. The natural world plays an important role in the lives of all the novel's main characters in differing ways. Why might some turn to it for solace and healing while others tend to see it as a challenge to dominate and subdue? How might the power dynamics of slavery drive these different ways of relating to the natural world?

8. What role does secrecy play in the book? More specifically, how is it attached to the ideas of power and freedom? Think about secrets kept and secrets told. Mena and Wash hide their altars and talismans, Wash hides Mena's grave just as Pallas and Richardson work together to hide his, and Richardson and Wash both hide the logbook. What are the historical

ramifications of all these secrets? Why does Pallas ultimately decide to tell Wash's children about him?

9. Wrinkle chose to tell this story using both first- and third-person narration. Why might it be important for a novel about American slavery be told from differing and often contradictory points of view? Consider how each character views the role and function of storytelling differently.

10. How are conflicting views on slavery presented in the novel? Were you surprised that slavery was a controversial issue even in Revolutionary times, or that slaveholders and abolitionists could be friends? Consider what Richardson means when he tells the combative Isobel Bryce about the dilemma faced by the Founding Fathers: "slavery was something to be endured for the sake of our brand new and extremely fragile Union" (304). How does William's abolitionism affect his slaveholding family?

11. Are similarly conflicting views on spirituality and religion portrayed in the novel? Compare Mary's use of the Bible as a justification for slavery with Emmaline's use of the Bible as a talisman, or Virgil's and Albert's use of the twisted stick as a form of conjure. What does Richardson mean when he says, "I was so determined to believe what I'd been taught, that I had dominion" (393)? Think of all the reasons these characters need and practice religion of any kind. What expressions of spirituality seem specifically African in origin?

12. Richardson stabs Nero to avoid being strangled. How does this violent incident reverberate through both the slaveholding and enslaved communities? Why is Richardson so

conflicted, both about this event and his struggle to write it down? Discuss how Wash makes sense of the incident.

13. When Wash gets hit in the head with a hammer, how does Mena help him? What meaning does he choose to make from the incident, and does he come to this understanding at the time, or later?

14. How is the encounter between Wash and the chestnut stud (212) a turning point for Wash? What is his revelation about slack and breaking point? How does the insight help him understand himself and reenvision the arc of his life?

15. Sexual exploitation is inherent to the institution of slavery. Why does Richardson decide to use Wash as his "traveling negro"? How does Wash see the advantages and disadvantages of this work as compared to the other options available to him? Consider how this work both isolates and endangers him.

16. What do you make of the incident in which Wash knocks out CeCe? How does he deal with the tendency toward violence that is brought out in him both by his past experiences and by his ongoing challenges? How do CeCe's mother and Pallas view the incident? Discuss whether Richardson, Thompson, and Eli face similar dilemmas in their ongoing struggles to control the enslaved people they own.

17. How might the legacy of violence required and engendered by slavery continue to affect us now? Consider what other patterns laid down during slavery might still be shaping our contemporary society. Do you see any parallels between

Wash's struggles and the challenges faced by young black men today?

18. Wash and Richardson, while often utterly opposed, share certain qualities and circumstances. Each gains and abuses power, and both are isolated and disempowered in differing ways. How are Wash's and Richardson's respective struggles for self-mastery parallel and how are they divergent? How does each man change throughout the novel?

19. Thompson is an important bridge figure. Think about what he teaches Richardson, what the Ibos teach him, what he learns from the loss of his third son, and what he manages to give Wash. How are these lessons linked? What kind of suffering do Richardson and Thompson undergo? Why is Richardson able to tell his story to Wash but not to his own son, Lucius?

20. Consider the relationship between empathy, compassion, and perspective. What does Wash mean when he says, "Same current pulls on white folks too. Sometimes I think maybe it's worse for them. So much more pulling on em and so much less to hold on to. What little they got must feel like reeds" (48). What is this current? By what calculus might whites have "more pulling on em" and "less to hold on to" than enslaved people bereft of physical freedom and material wealth?

21. Wash says of his relationship with Pallas: "Me and Pallas, our minds are alike. Two night birds, right on each other's tail, swooping then banking" (34). Discuss what is unusual or special in the relationship between Pallas and Wash.

22. Like Wash, Pallas also undergoes a traumatic sexual ordeal. Why does Drummond decide to lease Pallas from Miller and why does Miller agree to it? Why might it be important for Pallas to tell the story of both her trauma and her healing? Discuss how Wash and Pallas's shared history of sexual abuse both unites and divides them. What are some of the ways in which Pallas and Wash help one another to heal?

23. Wrinkle sensitively depicts the aftereffects not just of enslavement but of specifically sexual violence as well. What does the narrative suggest about the possibilities for healing these wounds? Can any scenes be said to have healing power for readers and characters alike?

24. Martin Luther King Jr. contended that unearned suffering can be redemptive, while James Baldwin has said that if you cannot face your suffering, you can never grow up. What does this novel suggest about the potential function of trauma and suffering?

25. Consider how the enslaved characters achieve some measure of autonomy. Pallas muses, "It's like Phoebe told me, everything's fine so long as you find a way to manage it" (1). What are some of the ways Pallas and Wash "manage" the brutal predicament of slavery? Conversely, what hampers the autonomy of the white slaveholding characters?

26. Signs, symbols and writing are important in this novel. How do Wash, Richardson, and Pallas view writing and reading differently, and what might slavery have to do with these differences? Many of the enslaved characters come from an oral culture, are denied literacy, and are controlled through

the use of written documents. How do differing kinds of literacy—textual, spiritual, emotional—come into play in this story? How and when do these various ways of reading become a matter of life and death?

27. Wash reflects on the place of written documentation and its absence in the lives of the white and black communities: "They'll write down who they are and what they did . . . Put it all in a book, then close it up and put it on the shelf. Just to know it's there so they can sleep at night. . . . But there ain't no writing this down. No book to put this in. Some of us shut our eyes at night and wake up in the morning, not written down nowhere. And still don't disappear" (6–7). What, according to this passage, is the implied role and consequence of record keeping and the writing of history? Consider the writing of the novel *Wash* in respect to this issue.

28. Discuss the novel's title *Wash* in light of all the water imagery it contains. For instance, Thompson's narration (57–65) recalls Wash's initiation into the sea even while still in the womb. Richardson, too, is eased by the Rivers of Babylon psalm when he "can feel the water pouring over him" (383). At what other times—and in what other ways—are Wash, Pallas, and others redeemed, restored, and interconnected by water? Does the title *Wash* have multiple meanings?

29. In a traditional African paradigm, everything is interconnected and animate. The dead and the living are intended to coexist in a reciprocal arrangement, each helping the other. How does the novel speak to this potential

interconnectedness? Consider the consequences of such a worldview, both for those who hold it and for those who don't. What might the dedication mean when it refers to "all those in Deads' Town"?

30. Which encounters between enslaved and slaveholding characters stood out? Discuss where collisions of personality, imbalances of power, and failures of understanding lead to conflict. Is there a difference between prejudice and mistrust, and did you ever feel that prejudice was every truly eroded and trust was truly built? Is this kind of cross-racial understanding possible in a slave society? What about in contemporary society?

SUGGESTIONS FOR FURTHER READING:

Beloved by Toni Morrison; *Jonah's Gourd Vine* by Zora Neale Hurston; *The Blood of Heaven* by Kent Wascom; *Gilead* by Marilynne Robinson; *A Girl Made of Dust* by Nathalie Abi-Ezzi; *Things Fall Apart* by Chinua Achebe; *Dominion* by Calvin Baker; *July's People* by Nadine Gordimer; *Lost Nation* by Jeffrey Lent; *Master Harold and the Boys* by Athol Fugard; *The Bone People* by Keri Hulme; *The Sound and the Fury* and *Absalom, Absalom!* by William Faulkner; *Go Tell It on the Mountain* by James Baldwin; *Incidents in the Life of a Slave Girl* by Harriet Jacobs; *Narrative of the Life of Frederick Douglass* by Frederick Douglass; *Kindred* by Octavia Butler; *The Icarus Girl* by Helen Oyemi; *Slaves in the Family* by Edward Ball.